Marina Vantara

Mission HOMO LIBERATUS:
The Beginning

To all the peaceful victims
of wars, terrorism, and coercion on planet Earth

Table of Contents

Prologue

Cowardice is one of the most terrifying human vices.
I dare to disagree. Cowardice is the most terrifying human vice.
— Mikhail Bulgakov, *The Master and Margarita*

Evening, March 22, 1943. Belorussia*. Less than an hour has passed since the 118th Schutzmannschaft Battalion, having completed its grim task, left Khatyn. In the chilling silence of twilight, amidst the whiteness of bare birch trees and wet snow, a dark stain of ash looms on the ground ominously — this is what the executioners had turned the village into. The charred remains of peasant homes are blazing, sending tendrils of acrid smoke into the air. Over one of the ruins hangs a persistent stench of burnt human flesh. It lingers in the windless forest. The only sound on the street, which was bustling with life just the day before, is the crackling of smouldering wooden beams, breaking the unbearable silence.

Leading away from *that* barn are several trails of human footprints. At the end of each trail lies a corpse sprawled in the snow, arms outstretched, backs riddled with bloody bullet holes.

Suddenly two figures materialise out of thin air — a young man and woman, short and well built, immaculate, as if they just stepped out of a fragrant bath. They are barefoot and dressed in light green Greek-style tunics. Their finely sculpted silhouettes look as though someone has cut them out of paper and cynically tossed them in ashes. The strangers bear no resemblance to the fair-haired locals or the blond Aryans. Instead they are dark-skinned and black-eyed, like Gypsies. Yet their faces, unlike the restless, troubled expressions of Gypsies, radiate an unearthly calm against the charred, bloody carnage that lies before their eyes.

For several minutes, hand in hand, they survey the scene of devastation. Then the girl's thoughts ring out like a scream.

“Such inhuman cruelty! Could we really not have stopped this?”

“This is precisely human cruelty, my dear. It cannot be stopped. At least not yet,” the man answers. His boundless sorrow washes over his companion. “Let’s focus on finding *him.* I’m starting to fear he didn’t survive.”

“I believe he did! He’s your son, after all!”

The man casts her a grateful look. “He’s so little… If only I had known this would happen today, I would have taken him with me when I left for the Unity! But I felt sorry for Polina and wanted them to have as much time together as possible. Foresight isn’t my strong suit… I just hope this hasn’t cost Yasik his life.”

They approach *that* barn. The smell of burnt flesh is overwhelming. The charred bodies lay naked, with only a few shreds of melted clothing clinging to their remains. Among these blackened corpses, twisted in their final expressions of terror, it seems impossible to recognise the beautiful Polina, the village herbalist.

“Look, Simon, some of the women are lying face-down. We need to turn them over.”

“Why? Haven’t you seen enough?” the man replies with disgust.

“Just do it!”

Without moving, he stretches out his hand toward one of the female bodies and slowly turns his palm upward. The corpse rolls onto its back, revealing beneath it an almost unburned infant, suffocated to death.

“Now do you see?” the girl insists. “The mother tried to save his life. Come on, we must hope! Look over there!”

She points where the barn door once stood. A charred female body is petrified in a grotesque pose as if she died on all fours. Simon moves closer and extends his hand beneath her torso, finding what first appears to be empty space. Yet at once he feels the warmth of his child.

“Yasik! Don’t be afraid, it’s Papa!”

An invisible bundle morphs into a three-year-old boy. His dark, tangled hair and piercing black Gypsy eyes peek out from under Polina’s corpse. The child appears more surprised than frightened but makes no sound and doesn’t even reach out to his rescuers. Simon frees the small body and holds the boy against his chest. Casting one last mournful glance at what remains of the woman he loved, he turns away.

Meanwhile, his companion flips over all the other face-down bodies and finds one more barely alive child. She vanishes into thin air with the baby, only to return moments later empty-handed. Approaching Simon, who still clutches his miraculously surviving son, the three of them dissolve into the damp air of the March night.

---

* The names and spellings of geographical objects (regions, cities and streets) are used as they were during the periods in which the events described are set (M.V.)

Chapter 1. The Return

My first independent interplanetary teleportation nearly killed me. I made a desperate effort not to disintegrate into atoms, not to dissolve in the overwhelming whirl of barely familiar sounds and scents buried in my childhood memories. Then, suddenly, I saw a pair of wide, astonished eyes. They were the colour of a stormy sea, and they anchored my astral body to my physical, manly essence. After that, I hit my head and plunged into darkness.

I woke up lying on a narrow cot in a spacious, smelly room with plank walls and a low ceiling. In the centre stood an iron monster of a car the color of a pleasant blue sky. On the back of the machine, right at my eye level, was the inscription *Zhiguli*. The oily petroleum stench emanating from the car intensified my dizziness, making it hard to focus. During astral journeys, we are devoid of the sense of smell, but now, with my physical body back on Earth, this stench, rising from the labyrinths of forgotten childhood nightmares, left a bitter taste in my mouth and made me ill. It was almost impossible to catch the pleasant herbal aroma barely wafting from the opposite corner of the room. I struggled to lift my head to look and saw a fair-haired teenage girl standing with her back to me next to a flat glowing red disk on three legs — an electric stove.

Preparing to return to the homeland of my ancestors — the most important event of my life — I had made numerous astral forays to various corners of Earth. But full interplanetary teleportation required special mastery. It had taken more than forty years to acquire it, and even after endless training, I had ended up much farther south than planned and nowhere near water, which explained this persistent nausea.

"I need to get acclimated," I thought, trying to move my fingers and toes. *"Nothing seems broken. Now try to move something else,"* ordered I to myself.

High on a shelf protruding from the wall, near the girl — who had presumably dragged me here — stood a harmless-looking cylindrical container. I simply wanted to move the object down but failed my first attempt at telekinesis under Earth's gravity. The can, performing an awkward pirouette in the air, crashed to the floor. Its loosely sealed metal lid flew off, and a liquid substance reeking of ammonia erupted in an emerald fountain, drenching my rescuer. She let out a short squeal and spun to face me. *"What a way to say thank you!"* flashed through my mind.

The girl stood frozen, almost entirely green and paralyzed with shock. After a few seconds, she whispered, "What will I tell Mom? And Dad? Oh God, how will I go home?"

The shock miraculously brought me back to life. With some effort, I levitated the empty metal cylinder smoothly off the floor and returned it to its original place. The girl still hadn't moved, watching in disbelief as the paint can floated back.

"I'll fix this," I tried to reassure her, "don't move," and began returning the green substance to the can.

Yes, Earth's gravity was indeed stronger than that on New Lemuria. That too was impossible to feel during astral journeys. Big and small droplets, the colour of spring leaves, lifted off the girl's dress and hair, weaving themselves into thin threads as they floated back into the metal container. My accidental victim, pale as a cloud, barely stood upright, leaning against an old cabinet filled with some iron parts. *"She's strong!"* I thought. *"Anyone else would have fainted by now."*

Meanwhile, she was thinking, *"I see this, but it can't be real! Am I dreaming?"* She pinched her arm. *"Apparently not. Then how? Like magic... Ugh, what magic?"* She imagined kids at school pointing and whispering about her — many considered my new acquaintance strange already. *"Well congratulations! You've officially lost your mind."*

I hurried to help:

"No, no, Polina. You're perfectly sane. Your name is Polina, right?"

"Y-yes," she nodded, eyeing me suspiciously. "How do you know?"

"Let me clean this up first. Hold on." My voice and a hint of suggestion seemed to calm her.

When I returned every drop of green paint to the can and restored her dress to its original sky-blue colour, Polina raised a finger and pointed at the air.

"The lid…"

"Ah, of course!" I agreed, securing the metal cap more tightly than before.

"Who are you?" Polina demanded. "And just so you know, I don't believe in wizards or aliens."

"You should," I smirked.

It was time to explain — after all, she couldn't hear my thoughts! But I was on the verge of exhaustion. The landing on solid ground instead of water, the head injury, the strength of Earth's gravity, and worst of all, the unbearable stench of ammonia and gasoline had taken their toll.

"It's a long story…" I mumbled with a grimace. "I'll tell you once I get some fresh air. I've never had such a headache! Is there a lake or river nearby?"

"Of course!" she replied, puzzled by the question. "About a kilometre away… But can you make it? You've got a cut on your head and might have a concussion. You should go to the hospital. But I don't know what to tell the doctors…" She hesitated.

"… so they don't think you're crazy? No, your hospital is definitely out of the question."

"I'll make you a compress. Here, apply this." Polina handed me a towel soaked with a herbal infusion. "Too bad it's warm…" I pressed it to my forehead as she returned with a metal mug filled with the same infusion. "Drink this. It should help with the pain."

"Thank you, dear." I took a sip and felt my strength return. My heart suddenly raced at the memory of another Polina — my mother — who used to prepare the same remedy. "I won't have to walk," I explained. "Here's what we'll do: you head to the lake, and I'll rest with the compress. I'll meet you there. I know you're dying of curiosity."

Without further questions, Polina grabbed her jacket and left the garage, locking it behind her. But a minute later, I heard the lock turn again, and her long braids appeared in the doorway.

"You can't go out in those rags!" She rummaged through a pile of her father's old clothes, found a decent pair of trousers, a checkered shirt, and a dark-green sweater, and handed them to me. "Here! Wear these!'

She added a pair of slightly oversized brown shoes and finally left for the lake. I too was eager to escape the company of the stinking monster called "Zhiguli," which did nothing to improve my condition. And besides, I felt drawn to this girl. Even with little knowledge of the area, I no longer feared getting lost. The bond that had formed between us at my landing felt so strong. It felt as if I couldn't possibly lose Polina, whether at the farthest corner of Earth or the most uncharted point of the Universe. I had already figured it out: falling here, right at her feet, was no accident, for kindred souls are drawn to each other like magnets and guide one another like a compass. I felt as if I hadn't landed on an alien planet but rather somewhere I already considered home.

The teleportation to the lake went surprisingly smoothly — aside from the fact that I had to muster my last reserves of strength to do so. Tuning into Polina's thoughts — she thought quite loudly — I materialised out of thin air within arm's reach of her.

Sitting on a narrow wooden bench by a small round pond, the girl squirmed impatiently, then let out a soft squeal upon my "magical" arrival, even though it was already the second time she had witnessed it. A few fishermen on the opposite bank were so absorbed in their evening catch and private musings that they paid no attention to the teleportation that had occurred practically right under their noses. However, when I waded into the water, they immediately noticed and began pointing at the "lunatic who decided to go swimming in mid-April." The water was indeed rather cold, but it revived me better than the tropical sun-warmed waters I was more accustomed to. Within a few minutes, I was already sitting on the shore, drying my soggy, over-sized clothes without undressing by raising my body temperature, while Polina watched in amazement as white steam rose from me.

Finally, everything dried, and I stretched out on the soft grass, enjoying the sight of sparse, fluffy clouds tinged with a pinkish grey in the twilight sky. Polina slid down from the bench and sat next to me on the ground, hugging her knees. The lakeshore was densely lined with bushes and beautiful white-barked trees. Their slender drooping branches were covered with swollen brown buds and, in some places, sticky newborn leaves. Tiny midges, recently awakened, buzzed around, while fuzzy bumblebees striped yellow and black hovered clumsily around clusters of flowers resembling sea foam. My mind and body quickly began to recover, soaking up the energy of the life swarming all around. Now I could get a better look at Polina.

At home, I had often heard about the attractiveness of Earth women. My mother, who oddly enough shared the same name as this young girl, was the only homo-sapien woman I had known until that day. Memories of my mother were always tinged with sadness and bitterness, blurred by time and space. Only by looking at my new acquaintance did I begin to understand my fellow Lemurians, who kept returning to the abandoned Earth despite the inconveniences and destruction caused by humanity .. The feminine energy of this teenage girl drew me in, though it was unconscious and untamed as if it was born from the springtime rabblement surrounding us. From the moment I landed, I was enchanted and saved by her eyes, the colour of a stormy sea, equally dangerous and mesmerizing, but now, fully recovered, I finally realised I was in love. It was impossible to explain or stop. My gaze, much like my thoughts, kept returning to her.

Despite the girl's a little awkward teenage figure, she was on her way to becoming a beauty. Her clear skin and rosy cheeks spoke of frequent time spent in Nature. The forest's energy practically overflowed from Polina — that must have been how she'd managed to drag me to the garage all on her own. She was slightly plump which only emphasised her transformation from girl to woman. Her soft, stretchy dress clung to her growing breasts more tightly than it should have, and her parents probably hadn't noticed this yet to suggest some looser clothing. If only I could, as naturally as back home, reach out and caress that budding breast to send a sweet shiver through her body. Then, let my hand glide along her rounded shoulder, brushing against her neck under the two heavy braids which were the colour of dried grass and fell past her shoulders. Pull her close and kiss her — kiss her endlessly…

Polina couldn't read my thoughts and had no idea what storm of desires she had stirred in the alien who had fallen at her feet. And I had no idea how to talk about feelings… I'd never done anything like that before! Moreover, both my knowledge of homo sapiens and my instincts told me that love on Earth was far more complicated than on New Lemuria. So, I made the required effort and took control of my hormones. I brought my body under my will and restored clarity to my thoughts — for a long time.

At fourteen, Polina was already taller than me, and her plumpness didn't spoil her appearance. However, I noted that people of her size no longer existed among my kind. We don't eat the flesh of living beings, nor do we extract sugar from plants or produce anything artificial. Instead, we exchange energy with Nature rather than storing it as fat in our bodies.

In moments of tension, the girl had an adorable habit of biting her full lips. A faint vertical wrinkle had already appeared between her eyebrows — likely from frequent attempts to make sense of the world inside and around her. Her light-green eyes, rimmed with grey and framed by dark brows that often shot up in disbelief, revealed a teenager's curiosity and a stubborn desire to believe in miracles. She was convinced there was more to the world than the human eye could see, even with the most powerful telescopes and microscopes. Questions had been crowding in this young head for a long time, and today, there came even more.

"My name is Yan," I began. "I was born in 1940, by Earth's reckoning, in the village of Khatyn."

"Wait, so that means..." Polina stared into space, mentally calculating. "You must be forty-five years old!" She peered at my face. "So you're... older than my parents? They were both born after the war. That's impossible!"

Her surprise was understandable — she had grown up among homo sapiens, who have no idea of true harmony and, therefore, age quickly. To her, I looked like the new art teacher, no older than twenty-five, and very much unlike her parents and their beer-bellied friends. Reflecting on the mental image Polina had of her teacher, Bagdasar Arushanovich — an Armenian with dark, deep, smoky eyes — I did resemble him somewhat in age, height, and features. After all, ancient Lemuria was in the Indian Ocean, and we had inherited traits from modern Asians.

"Let's leave my appearance alone for now. You'll understand more soon."

Polina twisted her mouth sceptically. "But wasn't Khatyn burned by the Germans?"

"You know about that?"

"Everyone knows," she shrugged. "So, you survived?"

"Thanks to my parents. My mother hid me from the fire with her body and died from her burns. My father arrived too late to save her. He found me in the ruins after the chasteners left," I said calmly, though these memories once haunted me. Polina, however, was more intrigued by another detail.

"Arrived? From where?"

"New Lemuria. My father, Simon, is a Lemurian."

"New Lemuria? Where's that?"

"A couple of light-years away. That's the planet's name now," I said tensely, realising I'd need to explain more, including the truth about our existence on Earth.

She stared at me, searching for alien features.

"She's part of my world," I reassured myself. *"She carries a drop of homo liberatus blood. It's better if she knows the source of her awakening power before she learns to use it."* My attraction to her left me no choice. Only the truth could keep Polina in my life — the truth about me and herself.

"All right, listen..." I said.

Chapter 2. Homo Liberatus

“A million years ago, there was an island called Lemuria in the Indian Ocean with a blessed climate and abundant, generous Nature,” I began. “Its inhabitants advanced much further along the evolutionary ladder than the rest of Earth's creatures. They learned to use the full potential of their brains and gradually lost fear at the genetic level.”

“People without fear?” Polina exclaimed. “That's impossible! Didn't they have anything to be afraid of? Predators, for example?”

“Dangers, of course, existed, and still exist, but fear is merely an emotion, the survival response of a biological creature unable or unsure of its ability to deal with a threat. But when survival resources are more than sufficient, that reaction gradually disappears. Naturally, the Lemurians did not overcome fear immediately but through a process of self-development.”

“Oh, sure! If someone attacks you, you can just teleport away!” the girl guessed.

“That's just one example. Although first, my ancestors learned to influence the behaviour of other living beings, thereby eliminating the threat of being eaten.”

“They hypnotised tigers?” Polina laughed.

“Something like that,” I smiled.

“Then why didn't other people on Earth learn to do the same?”

“Unfortunately, I can't pinpoint the exact reason,” I sighed, realising Polina didn't believe me. “I think most ancient homo sapiens lived difficult lives, while my ancestors achieved a higher level of development largely thanks to their isolation in a paradise called Lemuria. The islanders hadn't travelled farther than they could swim, until they mastered teleportation. Only having met the species who considered themselves the kings of Nature, Lemurians realised how different they were from homo sapiens and called themselves *homo liberatus*, that is *free humans*. Free from fear."

"How did it happen that they didn't travel at all before teleportation?" Polina exclaimed with a note of pity. "Didn't they make boats on Lemuria?"

"Why would they?" I asked.

"Why?" The girl was surprised. "To fish in the sea, for example, or discover new lands."

Now it was my turn to laugh. "Why search for better when you already have the best? Isn't that what you say? My ancestors were happy on their island."

"And they weren't curious about what lay beyond the ocean?"

"Of course they were, but you see, you're reasoning as a product of human civilization," I teased. "Wanting to overcome difficulties at any cost, you immediately invent tools. You draw resources from the outside rather than from within yourself."

"And that's a bad thing?" Polina said, offended by my attempt to lower what humans prided themselves on most. "Just look at what humanity has achieved with its inventions! »

"What has it achieved?"

"What do you mean? Airplanes, telephones, various electrical devices, harvesters... A lot of things! And all these inventions help us move through space, communicate over distances, even fly into space!"

"And when you say 'us,' who exactly do you mean? Yourself?"

"Well, not me personally..." she said, faltering. "Humans in general!"

I extended my left palm. A barely noticeable seed was stuck to my finger. I dropped the seed to the ground and directed a beam of transparent white light onto the tiny object. Right before the girl's eyes, the seed turned into a small green bush with carved leaves within seconds, and within another minute, it was covered in white flowers with yellow cores in the middle. Polina squealed with delight.

"Oh! Daisies! How did you do that?"

"The way all Lemurians do," I replied, enjoying the effect. "By controlling energy."

"What? Just like that? With your hand?"

I shrugged. "Every adult homo liberatus can do this. My ancestors aspired to swim like fish, fly like birds, smell like animals — and understand everything said with words and without, making no tools and relying only on their Nature. Eventually, they learned to control energy. The downside of your inventions is that they aren't a part of you. Devices, machines, and tools must always be carried with you, meaning you must own them. And if the most necessary tool is lost, broken, or taken by someone else, you return to a state of helplessness. You can't fly anywhere without a plane or talk to someone at a distance without a phone, whereas we… Well, you've seen it yourself," I gestured, avoiding demonstrating gravity-defying skills in front of people who were meditating with fishing rods on the other side of the lake. My companion stared at me, stunned by the obvious problem that "kings of Nature" prefer to forget. The problem people don't teach their children to think about. "On the other hand, homo sapiens haven't changed or evolved over hundreds of thousands of years. Doesn't that seem strange to you?"

Evolution was only briefly touched on in school, but the girl immediately blurted out, "How have we not evolved? Humans came from apes, right? Isn't that a huge step forward?"

"I can't be sure where humans came from," I admitted, meeting the girl's wild-eyed gaze.

"What do you mean? Any first-grader knows that!" Polina laughed. "They say, 'The ape picked up a stick — and became human.' The work created humans!" She rattled off truths she had memorised but hardly comprehended. Something needed to be done. My goal was to show Polina a world beyond the homo sapiens matrix.

Taking a deep breath, I countered her statements. "What people say doesn't make it true! First, how do they know? And second, don't confuse tools with work. Work is merely transforming one type of energy into another, like food. Horses, oxen, donkeys, and other livestock have worked for humans for centuries in exchange for food and care. But has their intelligence sharpened because of it? Quite the opposite if they so blindly allowed themselves to be enslaved! Wild animals also work, constantly searching for food-rich territories, yet they only undergo physiological changes to adapt to natural conditions. So why didn't they become intelligent while apes supposedly rose above their instincts and developed intellection?"

"Why?" my young companion asked. Her confusion was so endearing that I couldn't hide my goofy smile of love, hardly appropriate for such a deep discussion.

"Symbolically, a stick is a tool that helps one expend less effort," I explained. "You use it to knock fruits off a tree without climbing it or to harness the energy of horses by driving them… So, it turns out that humans evolved from apes by working less."

Polina was totally confused, trying to piece everything I said into a coherent picture.

"I guess so…" she murmured.

"Darwin was, in principle, right, but he didn't know the most important thing: evolution can be both horizontal and vertical."

"What does that mean?"

"Horizontal evolution is a biological phenomenon — it concerns only physical matter. Vertical evolution happens in the realm of the subtle body: the mind, soul, and emotions…"

"What kind of body?" The Soviet schoolgirl had never heard of subtle matters.

"The system of energy centres that every living being has," I explained without delving too deeply into details. "They are also called chakras."

"They didn't tell us about this in school…"

"Of course not." I wasn't surprised by homo sapiens' refusal to teach children the most fundamental laws of Nature. Legends circulated in Lemuria about how carefully they hid the knowledge that could make each person independent of others. "Most people are taught not to believe in the existence of anything they can't touch. But disbelief doesn't negate the phenomenon itself. Do you agree?"

"I think so…"

"So, homo sapiens have seven such centres, most mammals have three, and monkeys have four. The more centres, the more complex the system, the higher the intelligence and the better the ability to control energy. That's why monkeys advanced more than other animal — they began to redistribute their energy. So, they probably are our closest relatives — but not because of labour."

"Are you saying that physical work makes us dumber?" the girl, steeped in materialist ideology, exclaimed as if I had crossed some forbidden boundary.

"You study instead of working, don't you?" I asked instead of answering. "And you find cleaning duties — both at home and school — the most boring chore in the world?"

The girl blushed and nodded.

"Interesting. Why?" Without giving her time to respond, I continued. "But when you walk in the forest, you love looking at different plants, touching and smelling them. Sometimes you even dig roots out of the ground to study them. You pose questions, explore, and find answers."

"How do you know all this about me?" Her dark eyebrows shot up in surprise. She had indeed been fascinated by plants for a long time but was embarrassed by this passion of hers which no one at school knew about. Her family didn't even support it because Polina's habit of bringing home random weeds created a mess in their small apartment.

"I can hear your thoughts — haven't you realised that yet?" I laughed and the girl let out an embarrassed huff. She probably needed time to get used to this.

"Let's continue. Your curiosity is what helps you develop — and you've already learned how to make a strengthening herbal decoction that works!"

Hearing praise for her secret craft for the first time, Polina blushed like the morning dawn.

I felt an urge to end the lecture, grab her in my arms, and shower her with kisses. But it wasn't the time. Not yet. I gathered my will and went on.

"Knowledge and skills are resources that are the hardest to take away. Now imagine that instead of studying and observing, you had to do physical labour for eight or ten hours a day — say, growing the same plants or taking care of the same animals. Would you want that? Be honest."

Polina shook her head no. For some reason, she looked embarrassed.

"Now tell me — why not?"

"Well… a lot of people live that way," the girl said, objecting to the question instead of answering it. She truly found cleaning unbearable and did it only grudgingly. At the same time, children were constantly shamed both at home and school for avoiding physical chores.

"To be honest, it would be a bit boring…" she said.

"And what makes repetitive work boring?"

"What do you mean?" Polina laughed. "The repetition itself!"

"Exactly! So, what helps you develop more — acquiring new knowledge or performing the same action over and over?"

"Taking care of animals and plants requires learning too!" Polina pouted.

The school constantly emphasised that all work deserved respect, although she had often thought that the teachers seemed insincere, as it was hard to imagine them sweeping streets or cleaning floors.

"Of course. You need to learn everything," I agreed. "But not everything takes equally as long to master. Simple actions are easy to learn — and then there's a dead end."

"Someone has to grow food!"

"In the homo sapiens world, yes. But in reality, growing food isn't so necessary. Nature provides enough food for everyone. In Lemuria, we've never cultivated anything — and we live happily. For hundreds of thousands of years, we've fed on wild fruits and haven't wasted precious, irreversible moments of our lives on the hard work of farming."

Polina imagined me in an animal hide climbing a palm tree for a banana and burst out laughing. "So, you still live in a primitive community?"

"Yes — if you can call a community of beings who've learned to defy gravity, heal all diseases, and possess telepathy, telekinesis, and teleportation primitive!" I snapped.

The girl froze. How deeply she was stuck in the swamp of basic human ideas!

However, I wasn't ready to give up.

"Humans invented theories about social structures to justify their chosen way of collective survival. My ancestors in Lemuria never suffered from hunger and learned to understand Nature from the very first day of their lives, so they didn't depend on others as much. We believe humans were created by curiosity, which drove homo sapiens to seek new experiences and make discoveries. How else could they have figured out that grains grow from seeds?" I winked at her. "Thanks to curiosity, humans developed new chakras and redistributed their energy centres, which made them human. Discoveries led to creativity — and that's where our paths diverged. While homo sapiens focused on inventing tools — essentially improving the stick — homo liberatus focused on their inner abilities and developed an eighth chakra."

Polina was struggling to squeeze everything I had said into her school-taught worldview. She wasn't having much success, and her brain was about to explode from cognitive dissonance. It turned out that humans were not the kings of Nature, and fairy tales were just as real as the alien who had teleported right before her eyes and was now lying casually on the fresh grass. She needed time, so I remained silent.

Finally, Polina spoke hesitantly. "So, let's start from the beginning. A monkey became human because it learned to make tools, right?"

"Let's say so. I won't argue," I replied with a sympathetic smile.

"Then why do you say that homo sapiens stopped evolving after inventing tools?"

"Good question. The key word here is 'learned.' At an early stage, using tools did improve the brain of ancient humans — but later, it also slowed down their development."

"But how?"

"There are only a few inventors among homo sapiens — the rest think it's better to save mental energy than to spend it. They just take devices invented by someone else and use them."

"That's true!" the girl giggled. The refrigerator, vacuum cleaner, and washing machine were her family's best friends.

"And it all comes down to the fact that most people no longer invent anything. You've entrusted your survival to devices created by the most talented among you — in other words, you've made yourselves dependent on various versions of that stick. And now it's the stick, not your species, that continues to evolve in what you call technological progress. As a result, tools are improving, but the vast majority of homo sapiens are not. Quite the opposite. By using inventions, you strain your bodies less — and become physically weaker. And your minds, after mastering a hundred or so operations, get bogged down in routine and often even degrade."

"Yeah..." Polina said. "Any fool can press buttons... even a monkey!"

"Button-operated machines are quite a logical phenomenon. The culture of homo sapiens has revolved around helper tools since time immemorial. Even the heroes of your fairy tales need devices to perform magic — that is, to control energy: a magic wand, — which is, in essence, the same apes' stick! — some kind of ring, or various talismans and artifacts..."

Polina began recalling the fairy tales she had read as a child.

"Oh, you're right!" she exclaimed, and giggled again, adding, "By the way, I always thought carrying around a magic wand was kind of inconvenient! It's so easy to lose it!"

"Correct!" I laughed. "Using artifacts for magic in fairy tales is a projection of human weakness, while the prototypes of wizards from your stories — my fellow homo liberatus — don't need any tools at all."

"Wow," the girl said. "That explains a lot..."

"For your species, having a good stick — a wand — has become an obsession, almost the meaning of life, and the key word here is 'having.' Left empty-handed, homo sapiens feel weak and helpless, and experience a fear of death that enslaves them. In such a state, freedom is fundamentally impossible. So, it turns out that humanity sacrificed its freedom to the very stick that created it."

"And you're different?" Polina finally thought to ask. She was listening to me with her mouth open.

"Exactly!" I was delighted, sensing that we had finally made progress. "The inhabitants of Lemuria always followed their curiosity, which was based on the same survival instinct as yours, but their motto was 'can' rather than 'have.' Since our ancestors never started farming the land, they always had free time, which…"

"Oh, I get it! Instead of working in the fields, they developed superpowers!"

"Well, not all at once, but basically, yes!" I replied, feeling relieved. I had never had to put so much effort into explaining something before. "Although almost everything we can do is also inherent in humans. Modern homo sapiens use, at best, one-fifth of their brain. The rest is hopelessly suppressed, conserved, and almost atrophied, just like the Lemurians' ability to feel fear."

Polina finally grasped the connection between acquiring superpowers and losing the sense of fear. "If you can do everything you can, there's nothing to be afraid of!"

"Exactly," I confirmed. "We believe that our evolution was precisely what led to the loss of the fear gene, although, of course, it took us millennia to unlock the full potential of our brains. Homo sapiens and homo liberatus chose different focal points for their efforts."

Suppressing a brief sigh of envy, Polina asked, "I wonder how it all began?"

"Oh, we know that very well!" I replied, encouraged by her curiosity. "At first, our ancestors reached an awareness of symbiosis — the interaction and interdependence of all living things — about a million years ago. They saw themselves as just a small part of a vast, unified world in which everything existed to sustain one another rather than to destroy. Back then, the islanders didn't even know about the existence of other homo sapiens or any other paths."

"Did not you go hunting?"

"We haven't hunted for many thousands of years. At the dawn of their existence, homo liberatus were meat-eaters, but having discovered their deep symbiosis with animals, they understood that eating meat was like sawing off the branch they were sitting on. For example, hunting birds meant destroying the forest's caretakers, which would upset the balance in our own home. To be fair, replacing meat on Lemuria wasn't difficult, as food grew abundantly all around us. And giving up eating corpses had another wonderful side effect: the heavy energy of death gradually left the bodies of homo liberatus. That's when it became clear that our abilities extended far beyond hypnosis and telepathy."

Talking about food suddenly made me realise that we were both starving.

"Are you hungry?" Of course, the question was rhetorical, as I could easily sense her biological state. Polina, who had been ignoring the rumbling in her stomach for quite some time, nodded enthusiastically. "What edible things grow around here?" I asked.

"Now?" The girl looked surprised and spread her arms. "Nothing! It's spring now. There are different berries in summer, and, in autumn, there are mushrooms, forest nuts, and tiny wild apples. You could even live in the forest then..." she added dreamily. "You can also catch fish." Polina pointed at the men with fishing rods and giggled at the look of disgust on my face. "Oh right, you don't eat corpses!"

"A continental climate is very inconvenient. No wonder people are afraid of running out of supplies. And on Lemuria, you can live in the jungle all year round without worrying about food."

"I should run home and bring something, but..." Polina hesitated. "It's getting dark soon, and my mom probably won't let me out of the house until tomorrow!"

"There's no need to go anywhere. We'll sort this out right now," I promised. "Close your eyes and imagine your home."

Intrigued, Polina lowered her eyelashes obediently and concentrated on picturing the apartment where she lived with her parents, waiting for what would happen. Entering her imagination, I saw a box-like room inside an even larger box, a building made of artificial, rectangular stones — bricks. The floor was covered with a narrow carpet runner, and above the bed in the corner hung a thick, intricately patterned rug which housed a thriving microscopic ecosystem. Across from the bed stood a large old wardrobe, and by the window was a desk where Polina usually did her homework. The wall above the desk was lined with shelves stacked with human information carriers — books.

Naturally, I wanted to examine everything more closely, but hunger was a big distraction. On the desk, I spotted a large plate with nuts, fresh and dried fruits, and something wrapped in damp paper that smelled delicious. *"This will be more than enough,"* I thought. With effort, I materialised the treat on the grass before us.

Polina clapped her hands. "Cool! My mom always leaves this for my afternoon snack," she said, mimicking her mother's teacher tone. "So I 'don't forget to eat my vitamins.' Although I already skipped afternoon teatime. Dig in!"

I began picking up the shelled, oily nuts that looked like tiny human brains. Chewing, I pointed at the delicious-smelling soft white mass wrapped in thin paper. "What's this?"

"It's a sweet cheese bar. Cottage cheese."

"What's it made of?"

„Um… milk. And I think sugar and vanilla. Try it."

Eager to sample my first human-made food in years, I curiously peeled back the wrapper, pinched off a piece of the bar, and put it in my mouth. The taste of cottage cheese was familiar from early childhood, but the mixture I now tasted was so disgusting that I immediately spat it out.

"Ugh, gross! It's so sweet!"

Polina broke off a piece, tasted it, and shrugged in confusion.

"It's just a regular sweet cheese bar. Not even that sweet."

After such a shocking taste experience, I completely lost my appetite. *"I'll figure something out later,"* I decided, and while my companion was finishing her vitamins, I continued my story.

"So, gradually, the Lemurians mastered what you call superpowers. After achieving awareness of symbiosis with other species, telepathy followed. My ancestors easily learned to communicate without words — first over short distances, then over long ones. This turned out to be a useful skill since most homo liberatus are loners by nature. Each of us is capable of surviving without the others' help, and many do just that. Almost simultaneous with our discovery of telepathy, we learned to hypnotise animals and make ourselves invisible to them..."

"Can you be invisible to people too?" the girl asked with her mouth full.

"That's even easier than with animals! After all, animals can also recognise us by scent, whereas people — rarely." I glanced toward the fishermen. Then, I vanished from my new acquaintance's sight for a couple of seconds and reappeared in the same position.

"Wow! What about hypnotising people?" Polina exclaimed, then, recalling something she'd seen on TV, immediately added, "Though that's a silly question. Even some humans can do that."

"Yes, it's fairly easy with people because they have a vivid imagination that can be used during hypnosis."

"What about with each other? With another Lemurian?"

"Depends on what you mean by hypnosis," I answered vaguely. "It's impossible to impose someone else's will on a Lemurian, unless they decide to follow a leader voluntarily. Some humans can't be hypnotised. You might be one of them." I began preparing the ground.

"Really?!" Polina exclaimed, unaware of the responsibility her potential abilities — and origin — might entail.

"We'll see," I answered, and hurried to change the subject. "When my ancestors learned to concentrate and direct energy, their quality of life improved dramatically. After all, it directly depends on energy. Every homo liberatus can cook food without fire and heal themselves or others without any tools or medicine.

We don't get sick and we live an average of five hundred years. Though I might only live three hundred..."

"That's so sad," Polina responded very seriously. "Why not five hundred?"

Her naive disappointment made me laugh.

"Because my mother was a homo sapien. But don't forget, that's still far beyond the lifespan of an ordinary human! By Earth's standards, I'm now forty-five, but proportionally, I'm even a bit younger than you, and that is based on only three hundred years!"

Polina grabbed a stick and began drawing calculations in the dirt. Then she burst out laughing. "So, we're almost the same age? Can we go on a first-name basis?"

"Well, in a sense... And sure, we can."

Of course, at forty-five, I had long since left adolescence behind in every sense. I simply had more time to enjoy life, learn, and accomplish something important — like my mission. In Polina's case, it meant that our age difference, which was significant by human standards, was negligible by Lemurian ones. So, I was both pleased and a little surprised at how easily she had rethought our hierarchy. Humans are often considered conservative creatures. Though of course, this girl wasn't entirely a homo sapien...

"You've already seen teleportation, and so far, that's the highest achievement of our kind, though we mastered it even before the rise of ancient Egyptian civilization."

Polina suddenly recalled the most important question. "Wait, how did you end up on another planet?"

"That happened quite recently, just before I was born. The discovery and use of radio waves by humans threatened the secrecy of our existence. Airplanes began flying over the ocean, and more and more ships entered the energy-protected zone of our island. If humans had discovered the existence of homo liberatus, they would have done everything to turn our free people into tools for achieving their so-called great goals, which are driven by fear, aggression, and the thirst for power."

"How could you be forced to flee? Aren't you much stronger than humans?"

"That's true when talking about humans as a biological species, but technological progress, if it hasn't already caught up with us, eventually will. Besides, there are only a few thousand of us. More importantly, we never use our abilities for murder or domination, whereas nearly half of human inventions are created for precisely those purposes. So, our spirituality could have become our weakness. The oracles of Lemuria unanimously predicted our imminent enslavement and urged us to flee."

I decided not to tell the teenage girl that humanity's insatiable drive to exploit Nature and one another for profit was not only the reason my race left Earth but also the reason I had returned.

Instead, I simply said, "There was no point in looking for another place on Earth, because very soon human technologies will be everywhere. By astral traveling through the Universe, my people found a similar planet within about ten years. They called it New Lemuria and settled in a climate zone suitable for our way of life. It's a relatively young planet, and we hope to turn it into a more harmonious version of Earth."

"New Lemuria," Polina echoed. "What's it like?"

I looked at the girl and winked conspiratorially. "It's better to see something once than to hear about it seven times — isn't that what you say?" Polina's eyes widened, and I raised my hand in a comically defensive gesture. "Easy, easy! I'm not promising anything! A lot will depend on whether you're willing to learn some of our skills — and that will take a lot of effort. A whole lot!"

"Wait, you mean this can be learned?!" the girl exclaimed, unable to believe her ears.

"I told you, all abilities are embedded in homo sapiens," I replied without going into detail about her distant kinship with my race. Until the first part of the mission was complete, I couldn't promise anything to anyone. "First, I need to visit our colony."

"On Lemuria?" Polina asked cautiously.

I couldn't resist teasing her. "You don't know geography at all, do you?"

"I do!" the girl objected, offended. Geography was her favourite school subject, and she dreamed of seeing the whole world. "I do know! That's why I'm asking. I don't remember any such island!"

"Okay, okay, don't get upset," I said, squeezing her cool fingers. Polina instinctively pulled her hand away, and suppressing a sigh, I continued. "Two hundred thousand years ago, when an undersea earthquake began, the ancient island of Lemuria sank. It's not on any maps because it no longer exists."

"Oh!" The girl exhaled, feeling both relieved and annoyed at how easily I had tricked her. "So where have you been living all this time?"

"Thanks to their deep connection with Nature, my ancestors foresaw Lemuria's destruction and found a new home in advance. By then, they had already learned to teleport over great distances, and the first signs of catastrophe — underground tremors — made the Lemurians consider relocating from the Indian Ocean to the Atlantic. The homo liberatus settled on one of the islands in the Bermuda Triangle, which my people have managed to keep hidden from homo sapiens to this day."

"So, the mystery of the Bermuda Triangle…"

"Is us. Until the start of World War I, that island was our home. After we relocated to another planet, a small colony remained there. The Lemurians could never completely part with Earth."

"But what happened to the people who disappeared in the Bermuda Triangle?"

I sighed. It was a painful topic.

"Bitterly enough, the homo liberatus became unwilling jailers for unlucky travellers who couldn't be released. Believe me, no one is happy about it, but exposing our colony would mean its destruction."

It was almost completely dark and very cold by then. Polina looked around as if waking from a dream.

"I really need to get home now, or my mom will worry!" At the thought of her mother, the girl suddenly grew anxious, her pulse nearly doubling. That struck me as a little strange, and she quickly stood. "What are you going to do? You can stay in our garage overnight. My dad's away, and Mom never goes in there."

"Oh no! Not the garage!" I snorted at the thought of being surrounded by smelly old cars. "I'll sleep outside."

"In the cold?"

"I won't be cold, don't worry. I'll use my abilities," I said with a wink at Polina. "Let me just teleport you straight to your room. You're too worried, and now I know where it is."

"Will it hurt?"

"I don't think so. Give me your hand!"

The girl offered her pink palm but quickly pulled it back and asked a question that had somehow not occurred to her until now.

"Why did you come to Earth now?"

"Well… first of all, I always wanted to visit Khatyn, where I was born… but I only recently learned interplanetary teleportation, and I came here right away."

"And second?" Polina pressed.

"And second, I have a very important mission on Earth."

"I wonder what that is," the girl thought, but was too shy to ask.

"Better if you don't know," I smiled. *"Too heavy a burden for a young mind."*

Polina pouted in irritation, thinking she might get more information out of me tomorrow. I answered her thoughts again.

"No, you won't. We'll meet again, but not tomorrow. Some time will pass, and I can't say exactly how long."

Polina let out a frustrated sigh. "Stop eavesdropping on my thoughts!" She reached her hand out to me again and hesitantly asked, "Do you promise we'll see each other again?" with such desperate hope that it made my heart ache with tenderness.

"Of course, dear! I need some time, but I promise I'll come back to you." As I made this promise, I stroked her hand — and this time, she gave me a questioning feminine look. Polina couldn't read my thoughts and didn't know how enchanted I was by her eyes, how they had awakened in me that eternal love so many legends spoke of. A love most beings of both races could only dream of…

A minute later, the girl, stunned by her first — but far from her last — teleportation experience, was sitting at the desk in her room, staring at the empty plate she had brought from the lakeside. Another minute later, the doorknob turned — I barely managed to disappear in time — and Polina's mother walked in. Her eyes widened.

"Oh my god, you're home?!"

"Yes, Mummy, thanks for the snack!" Polina chirped, licking her lips and showing the empty plate with a dazzling smile. *"What luck!"* she thought. *"Good thing Mum didn't walk in while we were teleporting!"*

"I was sure you weren't back yet!" her mother began to grumble. "I've been sitting in the kitchen worrying. When did you get here?"

"About half an hour ago, Mummy. I didn't want to disturb you," Polina lied smoothly. "I already finished my vitamins. Thanks! I ate everything just now and don't even want dinner. I'll take the plate to the kitchen."

After kissing her mother on the cheek, Polina led her out of the room, giving me the chance to leave.

“Don’t ever do that again!” the woman scolded, slightly exaggerating her concern. “You’re getting out of hand while your father’s away on work trips…”

***

Sleeping in a Belorussian forest, where the spring night indeed promised to be chilly, was the last thing I wanted. Yet venturing to the Bermuda colony without coming to terms with my wildly pounding heart seemed equally unwise.

Of course, the Lemurians always support those facing a difficult choice, since making such choices is the only path to wisdom and harmony, especially during the first century of our lives. However, in my current state of mind, appearing before Bermuda colonists whom I barely knew felt almost improper. My turmoil and doubt would be evident to everyone due to telepathy. They were waiting there, believing in me, and I…

It had been foretold that I would be able to free the planet of our ancestors from the vampires — homo sapiens, who, like parasites, feed on the energy of their kind and Nature in general. For the Lemurians, my return marked the beginning of what was perhaps the most important mission in humanity’s history — and by humanity, we meant both our species.

When I departed for Earth, I had believed I was ready to act, but this unexpected love for a teenage girl caught the new messiah off guard, paralysing the hero within me. Before I could begin saving Earth's Nature, I first needed to rescue my troubled mind. More than ever, I longed for solitude. Only solitude allows us to restore order in our primary home — the soul. In the end, everyone must decide whether to turn to the wisdom of their brethren or to seek answers by merging with Nature in meditation.

For solitude, I headed to one of the islands in Halong Bay, far to the east of the Asian mainland. Its warm, humid climate and abundance of plant food reminded me of the corner of New

Lemuria where I grew up. Simon, my father, loved visiting Halong Bay even more than Bermuda, and many of our kind enjoyed it there, both before and after relocating to a distant planet.

Only the omnipresence of the ever-multiplying locals — and later, with each passing decade, the influx of tourists — prevented us from moving our colony to this blessed corner of Earth.

My father and I had visited here many times astrally, so I knew exactly where to look for the nest-like structure in the trees, specially built by our kind for solitary retreats. The hut was hidden in the impenetrable tangle of tropical leaves and was almost always vacant, concealed for decades from humans and animals by an energy dome. Now, having reached it in the physical world, I shed the bothersome human clothes and savoured the moist warmth of the air, saturated with the sea. I relished the taste of unfamiliar local fruits, several of which I quickly gathered nearby. After eating, I finally fell into a deep sleep at the bottom of the nest, lined with a soft bed of dried grass. I slept despite the midday sun. The events of what had seemed like an endless day had exhausted me so much that I kept sleeping for almost an entire day.

Only the next morning did I truly appreciate the beauty of this place.

The nest was built on a tall tree that grew on a hill, so I could see almost the entire island from that spot. The dense jungles below me resembled a verdant sea, shimmering with hundreds of shades of lush, vibrant green. Beyond the island's borders, the true ocean reigned, and from its capricious turquoise ripples, limestone island spires emerged, like a herd of clumsy giant reptiles resting. How sad it must have been for my people to leave this magnificence, abandoning their wondrous homeland to reckless brothers far less deserving of Earth's generous beauty! The Nature of the planet New Lemuria was also bountiful, but it was still more modest than Earth's tropical exuberance. Or perhaps it was just my human soul longing for its rightful place…

I am homo liberatus only halfway, although I have grown used to thinking of New Lemuria as my home. The love between a Lemurian and a human is not uncommon, yet mixed children are born rarely and only when a Lemurian consciously desires it.

Such children usually remain among humans. They are unable to share our way of life because they have the most dominant gene of homo sapiens, which blocks the full range of abilities inherited from our species. Consciously or not, the primal fear forces any living being to direct nearly all its energy toward ensuring safety.

I was born without the gene of fear, and over the past two millennia, I was the only one the Lemurians took with them — after the boy named Jesus. My arrival to Earth had been foretold by several prophetesses, and Simon, like Gabriel once did, wandered the Earth for nearly a hundred years in search of a woman who carried the blood of both homo sapiens and homo liberatus. Only then could Lemurians hope that a child would be born without fear yet still retain the ability to feel like humans.

During his travels, my father studied homo sapiens well and learned what treacheries they were capable of when driven by fearpro and what they almost never dared to do because of it. Simon met several women distantly connected to the Lemurians by blood, but he could not promise them what earthly women seek: protection and a strong family. To take by force or deceive with lies was as repugnant to us as it was to Nature itself. Such an act would have made my father an outcast.

At last, Simon saw Polina. He stopped in a grove of white-barked trees fragrant with wild strawberries to replenish his strength right when my future mother, a village herbalist, was gathering medicinal herbs there. She was a stately, fair-haired beauty, and even despite her mature age, Polina miraculously retained the aura colour that revealed her kinship with homo liberatus. She was a wonderful combination of feminine passion, boundless kindness, and bold calm, so unusual for a person practicing "unscientific" healing in such intolerant times. It seems that was what captivated my father.

Simon and Polina bonded in rare harmony, one that needed no words even among humans. Their love flared up like sun-scorched grass and swirled in a hot whirlwind, leaving them unable to part.

The thirty-six-year-old childless widow neither worried about her future nor cared what the villagers might say about her mysterious dark-eyed lover. The neighbours assumed Simon had strayed from a wandering tribe and, laughing, gossiped behind their backs that the witch had bewitched a Gypsy and that they were two of a kind. In truth, these rumours weren't far from reality, as Roman Gypsies are the closest relatives of homo liberatus. They even resemble us in appearance.

And fair-haired Polina? From her distant Lemurian ancestor, she had inherited heightened intuition and the ability to "hear" plants. By day, she worked on the collective farm, and in her free time, she healed with spells and herbs, often more effectively than the paramedic in the larger neighbouring village. The paramedic despised her and called her a charlatan, but Polina never charged for helping locals or visitors, so the authorities had no reason to bother the single woman, especially since no one could calm the animals on the farm better than she could.

Shortly after my birth, the war began. My father, of course, took no part in it and sided with no one. For homo liberatus, killing is a crime against Nature that cannot be justified. He stayed with us in Khatyn, clouding both "our" and "their" minds with hypnosis. He went on a short leave from the village only three times a year.

My mother's death had been foretold. Hiding the inevitable from her, Simon cherished every moment with his beloved, secretly hoping to outwit destiny. I don't blame him for coming just a few hours late as he couldn't have known exactly when or how it would happen, but I do blame him for refusing to help me forget…

Every day of my life, I remembered the weight of my mother's body falling onto my back, already beginning to grow cold amid the smouldering logs of *that* barn. I remembered it as vividly as if it had happened yesterday. I relive the last day of my home village and the person dearest to me over and over again. This pain does not fade. It only grows stronger with time. It prevents me from finding the inner balance so natural to homo liberatus.

"Use your hypnotic power!" I begged my father. "You taught me everything I know, and you can do so much more…"

His response was always the same sad look that pulled my thoughts into such an abyss that fragments of my childhood memories of the tragedy began to seem like mere wisps of clouds above that chasm of sorrow.

"Forgive me, son, but you'll have to heal this wound in a more complex way. That's the decision of the Unity. This pain makes you capable of fulfilling your mission," Simon reminded me. "I believe in you and will always be there for you." Though he secretly thought that to heal me, he would have to make me forget *her*. My father himself could never trade his longing for the lost love for the blank slate of oblivion. It would be like amputating a piece of his soul. And that shared loss bonded us so deeply that he could hear my thoughts even across the interplanetary space.

Like all Lemurians, Simon could not lie. I knew early on that I was destined to return to Earth, and that only my pain and anger — rare emotions for homo liberatus — would ensure the success of a mission meant to usher in a new era on Earth. He prepared me for that first journey himself.

So, saving worlds seemed possible only through sacrifice and suffering… Jesus suffered in body, and I was doomed to suffer in soul. Was I willing to accept this? In my youth, while years still separated me from my mission, I even took childish pride in such a purpose. Until my return to Earth, I saw no other path, but now I stood at a crossroad. And so, I fled to these Vietnamese islands instead of beginning the mission immediately.

Breathing in the warm, humid scents of the jungle, wandering along the white sand beaches that shifted underfoot, and moving between the most deserted corners of the islands, I was stalling for time because I felt that my soul had somehow softened. My anger had turned into a dull ache, like a splinter you forget about when something more urgent arises. The green-eyed miracle, the first being I encountered on Earth, had dimmed the fiery determination with which I had arrived. My feelings for the teenage girl, as pure as the shimmering lakes of New Lemuria, almost neutralised the burning desire to face my mother's murderer — the desire that had tormented me all these years.

When you find the rare gift of love, the greatest blessing that can befall a living being, you want to rejoice and bring joy, not seek vengeance. My mission began to seem foolish, no longer such an important or necessary endeavour. After all, it didn't directly concern my people since homo liberatus had relocated to another planet long before I was born, and freeing Nature from vampires was primarily needed by humans, who were the ones destroying that very Nature.

On the other hand, I longed to be near Polina and dreamed of teaching her to use the abilities inherited from our shared ancestors, the powers she didn't yet realise she possessed. And my beloved lived on this planet… My motives were becoming increasingly entangled.

I even undertook an astral journey back to New Lemuria to seek my father's advice. He merely shook his head and said, *"Unfinished business poisons the soul."* It is impossible to force a homo liberatus to do anything; our sense of duty is inseparable from free will. Moreover, I could not ignore my father's doubts.

His bitterness toward the mission awaiting me was no secret, thanks to the Unity. The Lemurians shared Simon's feelings as best they could, although most of my kin only knew such emotions through our shared experience.

Perhaps that was my last Unity.

Since the days of Old Lemuria, three times a year, all adult homo liberatus gather for a collective meditation, as if the streams of our people's souls merge into one great river. They intertwine, exchange currents, and then pour back into the vast ocean of life. During this time, a Unified Consciousness arises — a state where the thoughts, feelings and knowledge of one become the possession of all.

Our young mature quickly by gaining direct access to the wisdom of the elders. This is how our people make decisions without undermining minorities. In Unity, we sense each others' needs and contradictions as our own, thinking and feeling as one being who naturally desires happiness. That is why none of us seeks to impose our will on others. Lemurians freely share everything with those in need and are always given whatever they themselves need. We are not afraid of losing by giving. We are not afraid, period.

In our world, no one needs to prove their righteousness. For the Unified Consciousness, a conflict of interests is the same as an internal conflict within a single person. To resolve a problem, all pros and cons are weighed. Unity leads to harmony, not compromise. We achieve this harmony because we all desire it equally.

The commandment "love your neighbour as yourself" came to humanity from us, but this is not a metaphor for the homo liberatus — it is a reality where each person temporarily becomes the other and sees the world through their neighbours' eyes. When an entire race thinks and feels as one, no one's pain or joy goes unnoticed, and no one's needs are pushed aside, unless a

Lemurian is willing to make a sacrifice. As Jesus did. And as I was foretold to do.

The Unified meditation lasts not just hours, but days and even weeks. Yet the journey through the labyrinths of our people's souls spares us the need to write laws. The Unified Consciousness makes decisions, and then each person lives their life and does what needs to be done. That's all.

Being a part of this wonderful whole is the highest bliss, both spiritual and physical, but it is also our most vulnerable ability. Homo liberatus do not join the Unity until they have achieved a deep understanding of themselves and the world, mastering the art of living in harmony.

Balance is a law of Nature, not of humans, and Nature is not a machine. It is like music, both a system and improvisation, infinite variations of ever-transforming reality. Only those who can tune in to its rhythms and follow its subtlest signs achieve harmony with Nature. That is what the Lemurians teach their children. And near the age of thirty — though each in their own time — the young, having reached harmony, begin to discern what is good and what is evil for Nature. Then they hear the call of Unity and become a part of it.

Once they enter the Unified Consciousness, the harmony they have gained becomes as vital as air. If they disrupt Nature's balance, they lose both harmony and the ability to hear the call. They become outcasts, irreversibly, forever. Millennia of experience suggest that, fortunately, thoughts never alter anything and only actions that disrupt balance make one an outcast. Perhaps this is why, despite my anger and thirst for revenge, I was still part of this beautiful whole…

Homo liberatus do not judge or punish — they completely trust Nature. It is Nature that strips a balance violator of their ability to merge with the Unified Consciousness. Falling out of Unity is an extremely rare event for us. In my relatively short memory, there has not been a single case, but our elders say it is a misfortune worse than the most painful punishment. An outcast stops hearing the call. And even the kindest, purest Lemurians cannot love a fellow whose soul has become unknown to them, the way they love themselves.

The outcast's existence, devoid of blessed harmony and eternally confined to their own mind, becomes bitter. They eventually grow like homo sapiens and leave to join their new kind.

The search for the man who ordered the destruction of Khatyn, the murderer of my mother and fellow villagers, was supposed to be the first step in ridding Earth of energy vampires. Being only half-Lemurian, I wasn't sure I could spare the monster, vampire or not, who gave the order to burn *that* barn.

And after dealing with my offender, how would I handle others like him? Energy vampires were the main violators of Earth's natural balance, but no one knew whether Nature would forgive the physical destruction of even one of these creatures.

The homo liberatus believe that killing out of revenge disrupts harmony as much as killing for any other reason. No one knew if I could ever rejoin my people's Unity after fulfilling the prophecy. The chance of becoming an outcast during my mission was so high that in New Lemuria, they already pitied me, although they tried to support and encourage me in every way.

So, before shifting to Earth, I farewelled Unity in my mind.

Chapter 3. The Silence of Graves

I was stalling for time. The image of young Polina kept appearing before my mind's eye as she waited for my return every day — I could hear it even from the opposite end of the Asian continent. Yet I couldn't, or perhaps wouldn't, detach myself from her thoughts. Love stood between me and my mission — or was it the mission that stood between Polina and me?

I didn't know how long the search for the vampire I was hunting would last. I didn't know either the face or name of this monster who had commanded the punishers of Khatyn — but it was certainly someone who had managed to avoid the punishment determined for such a crime in the homo sapiens' world. In other words, the scoundrel was still alive. But not for long, if the prophecy was correct. I understood that as soon as I faced the torturer of my village, I would most likely commit murder. The consequences were impossible to predict, as no Lemurian had taken a single life for centuries. Becoming an outcast would mean living on Earth. Then Polina and I could be together forever…

But would she love a man with blood on his hands? Would it not be better for her to remember our fleeting encounter as nothing more than an incredible adventure, like one of her childhood fantasies? What good is there in awakening hope within such a young girl only to shatter it later? I could not allow that. So, my resolve to postpone our next meeting until my situation became clearer only strengthened.

I had to act.

***

And so, I found myself exactly where the village healer had brought me into this world. Now, stone reigned here.

In the morning silence, a solitary metallic chime echoed across the field, resonating with a cold shiver in my shoulders and forming a burning lump in my throat. I remembered trudging barefoot along the dusty village street as a three-year-old, holding the hand of my beautiful mother. I remembered the living hedges, the warm log houses, and the endless fences where neighbours hung their blankets to air out… On *that* day, the wooden houses and hedges burned to the ground, leaving only brick chimneys standing above the ashes, as if the outstretched arms of peaceful villagers had frozen while reaching from beneath the earth in desperate prayer.

For twenty-six years, the chimneys had remained untouched. Then an architect replaced them with twenty-six slender granite columns topped with small bells. These columns rose above twenty-six stone-paved rectangles symbolising the twenty-six burned houses. Black plaques on the columns listed the names of the residents who were driven from their homes *that* day and burned alive in *that* barn. Every five minutes, the mournful sound of a single bell tolled, spreading a chilling echo through the silent, wooded surroundings… To ensure the tragedy was never forgotten, people had built a memorial complex on the site of the vampire-destroyed Khatyn.

At the outskirts of the village, where our house, the twenty-seventh one, used to stand, now there was only fresh green grass. It was blissfully unaware of the insatiable fire that had raged forty years ago. I recognised the birch tree that once grew right by our gate. The silver birch was the same age as my mother would have been now. The white-barked beauty had miraculously survived. It still stood there alone, sad and aged, guarding the secret of the village healer's existence. Simon and his girlfriend Mina had carefully erased memories of my mother and me from the mental space of earthlings, so in place of our burned house, there was neither polished granite nor a bell.

Prior to landing on Earth, I had visited Khatyn astrally a couple of times. Back then, I imagined that this silver birch contained my mother's soul, so, in my mind, I called this tree

Polina. During such journeys, we are unable to hear sounds or feel touch, but now I could finally run my hand over the tender white bark and feel the warm roughness of its black veins! Press my cheek against it, as I once did against *her* shoulder in my childhood… Of course, I knew all too well that this birch tree had not become a vessel for the village healer's soul: on Earth, the remains of the dead are placed in boxes and buried deep underground. Why? It is the result of humanity's twisted perception of life beyond death. Or perhaps it's their way of coping with the fear of mortality — hiding their dead from sight, pressing them down with cruelly hewn and therefore equally lifeless stones, as if for certainty. Sending the human souls straight into oblivion. Perhaps Earth is weakening so rapidly because even the birth of ever more young homo sapiens cannot compensate for the vanished wisdom of ancestors…

On Lemuria, the bodies of tribe members who have completed their biological existence are burned, and a young tree is planted in the soil mixed with their ashes, thus creating a new home for the astral body. We know there is no death, only another form of life. That's why our cemetery is a garden where all the trees have names and whisper with the voices of those who have left us. And here, in the village burned down by vampires, there aren't even individual graves. All those who perished in *that* barn were placed in a mass grave, under one huge smooth slab. So, herbalist Polina disappeared without a trace, along with the others.

Groups started arriving. I followed one, then another. What was I hoping to hear? There were many blanks in my memory about the story of Khatyn. All I could recall was the flood of deafening, heart-wrenching cries, the stench of burning flesh and smoke, and the overwhelming waves of terror emanating from the people inside *that* barn surging toward the chasteners. Those waves were so strong that they knocked me down. For a small child born without fear and barely understanding what was happening, it all seemed senseless. I was merely curious and followed the others. When my mother crouched over me, her voice fading as she rasped, "Stay quiet!" I was surprised again but obeyed, as always. Those were her last words, though I didn't understand that then.

Later, on New Lemuria, when I finally realised I had lost her forever, grief consumed my little heart for a while. Only a couple of biological years later did I start asking questions. Simon came from a world without fear — and therefore without greed, hatred, ideologies, or wars. His explanation was simple. "Your mother was killed by vampires." And from a physical perspective, that was true. But in the human world, vampires hide behind thousands of masks! I knew little about their cunning and cruelty — certainly not enough for even a meaningful first step, let alone a successful mission. So I decided to seize the moment. Listening to different museum guides, I heard the story of Khatyn's destruction presented to me from a human perspective for the first time.

"On the evening of March 22, the Nazis burst into Khatyn, drove the elderly, women, and children into the streets with rifle butts, and herded them into a collective farm barn, which they then locked, surrounded with straw, and set on fire. The barn was wooden and immediately caught fire..."

"...The terrified people inside, packed so tightly they couldn't move, screamed, while the children suffocated in the smoke and cried..."

"...The barn doors collapsed under the pressure of the bodies, and the people rushed outside. But there, they were met by Germans with machine guns, who were ordered to leave no survivors. The Germans shot everyone who managed to escape the flames."

"...This stone roof is located exactly where *that* barn stood..."

"Where my mother died!" I thought.

"...And next to it, you can see the mass grave of the villagers."

Grief pressed heavily on my heart like this granite slab. Right here, among dozens of other human bodies, the remains of herbalist Polina rotted and decayed, and her soul died forever, crushed by stone just like the souls of all our kind neighbours. I had never cried before in my life, but now salty liquid flowed from my eyes, releasing years of pent-up sorrow. Along with the sorrow, my energy drained aimlessly into the atmosphere of the sunny morning — and I didn't care. Despite the pain stirred up by the flood of memories, I wanted to hear more. And I listened.

"...A total of 149 people died in Khatyn..."

"One hundred and fifty," I mentally corrected with childish resentment. *"No one remembers my mother!"*

"Seventy-five of them were children. Only five children and one adult survived," continued the guide Olga. "The village blacksmith, Joseph Kaminsky, lost consciousness from wounds and burns. He woke up only after the Germans left and found his son Adam gravely wounded. The boy's stomach had been pierced by machine-gun fire, with his intestines spilling out."

At these words, some of the more imaginative teenagers immediately envisioned a man, barely able to walk, carrying a mutilated boy through the smouldering ruins. Although these teenagers had never seen war, never lost loved ones to vampires, and never heard gunshots or explosions, their mental pictures of the Khatyn tragedy were eerily accurate and resembled my memories. That struck me most of all! Some students even felt aches in their stomachs, and their imagined fear seeped out in cold waves, so real were their impressions of horrors that occurred over forty years ago!

"The child died in his father's arms." And here the guide abruptly fell silent.

Like an actress deeply immersed in her role, Olga paused to bring her audience to the peak of empathy. The story of Joseph

Kaminsky always deeply affected visitors to the memorial, whether they were schoolchildren from nearby villages or tourists from Europe. However, for Olga, her work was more than performance — she held Khatyn in her soul, inspired by her grandfather's stories of partisan resistance against the tormentors of their homeland. A recent history graduate, she knew she was doing the right thing by keeping the grief of her people alive so it would not be forgotten. So it would not be repeated.

No one following her dared to utter a word, and the group's silence blended with the frozen stillness of the dead village, broken only by the faint, carefree chirping of birds from the forest. Another toll of the bell atop the post above us tore through the air, making everyone, including the guide, flinch and instinctively lower their heads. Olga pointed toward the towering statue of a gaunt old man in rags, holding a lifeless child with limp arms.

"This six-meter-tall sculpture in the centre of our memorial complex is called *The Unconquered Man*," Olga stated. "Although it represents a collective image of the village's residents, the story of Joseph Kaminsky inspired its creation. Joseph Kaminsky died in 1973. Until his death, he lived nearby, in the village of Kozyri. They say he continued visiting Khatyn until his final days."

As soon as she fell silent, the wind carried the words of the guide from another group to my ears.

"Khatyn is just one of six hundred Belorussian villages destroyed by the fascists during the Great Patriotic War. The residents of one hundred and eighty-six of them were burned alive, just like the people of Khatyn, and these villages, completely wiped off the face of the earth, never recovered after the war..."

I hadn't known such details before. That's because Simon, the only expert on Belorussia in both Lemurias, deliberately avoided going into these details. After living in Khatyn for four years, he knew each of the farmers who died in *that* barn by face and by name. The anger inevitably stirred by thoughts of the vampires' brutal slaughter of all those people would have prevented my father from raising me as a true Lemurian, teaching me everything that frees homo liberatus from the need to feel fear. Simon rightly considered this his main task, his personal mission, and forbade himself from thinking about *that* day…

But wait! One hundred and fifty perished Khatyn residents multiplied by one hundred and eighty-six Belorussian villages… It turns out that a handful of vampires killed more people than the entirety of the homo liberatus race! Or were there not so few vampires there after all? And what if we count all the people who died in wars on this planet, at least over the last hundred years?!

What I heard sobered me up, and the love that softened my heart has finally taken its rightful place in my life — the second after the mission. Now I was truly ready. If there was even the slightest hope of freeing humanity from monsters like those murderers of Khatyn before it was too late, then becoming an outcast wasn't such a high price to pay for trying. In fact, even dying was worth it if it meant the tragedy of Khatyn, neither the first nor the last in homo sapiens' history, would stop repeating itself, growing worse with each new turn!

The residents of our Bermuda colony report at every Unity that more and more homo sapiens prefer accumulating various kinds of energy rather than exchanging it — in other words, they behave like vampires. Imagining such a global violation of Nature's primary law is simply unthinkable for someone who grew up in a world of harmony.

Only here did I truly realise the seriousness of the problem, and once I understood it, I knew that even the most experienced homo liberatus — which, at forty-five, I certainly was not — couldn't handle all the vampires on Earth alone.

Sadly, I couldn't count on help from my fellow Lemurians either. Although they pitied homo sapiens, valuing all the beautiful things humans have created that are worthy of preservation, they didn't want to get involved in human quarrels and just moved to another planet.

Until now, a race evolutionarily ahead of those who called themselves kings of Nature didn't believe in the need to interfere in "royal" matters. That was the leitmotif of practically every Unity. My brethren thought it was a waste of their precious lives to fight a battle that humans needed far more than they did. This mission was assigned to me and no one else precisely because no Lemurian, living in harmony, could feel the same burning desire to deal with the vampires that I now felt. I was born fearless yet still human.

Now, it turned out that I couldn't do without helpers among homo sapiens, which seemed like a difficult task since I knew very little about people. I agreed with Simon: I should choose only those who consciously remained faithful to Nature — that is, as they say, to "the laws of good." This meant I would have to examine the minds of many to select a few worthy ones. And so, I began observing the homo sapiens specimens available among the tour groups.

"Beyond *The Unconquered Man*, you can see the cemetery of villages," the guide continued. "During the construction of the memorial, our volunteers visited the sites of burned settlements, collected urns of soil from each, and placed them beside the names engraved on black granite slabs. Therefore, this cemetery is only symbolic. It was created so that we would remember the cruelty shown by the German invaders on our land. The remains of the deceased residents are in mass graves scattered throughout Belorussia."

The guides Nina, Yulia, and Olga were local and knew firsthand that there wasn't a single family in the area that hadn't lost relatives in the villages destroyed by the fascists. They had no doubts about the importance of their work, but they hadn't seen the war itself, compared to which the worries of these young women should have seemed insignificant. Yet even minor concerns troubled them with an intensity that was far from minor.

Thirty-year-old Nina worried about her daughter, who didn't want to go to nursery. *"Maybe the other children are bullying her,"* the mother thought, and her heart began to pound, her fists clenched with resentment and anger. *"I need to talk to the nursery teacher. What if the little one gets sick? Maybe I shouldn't have gone back to work. But then, Misha's salary barely covers our expenses... And what will my mom say? She'll start criticising him again! I'm already afraid to talk to her. What should I do?"* And Nina's heart pounded even harder from her powerless frustration.

"How can one fear their own mother?" I thought, but then remembered Polina's anxiety over coming home late. So, fear penetrated even the closest relationships in homo sapiens!

Single mother Yulia worried about her mischievous ten-year-old son, but in truth, she was scared of the school principal. The strict grey-haired man had held his position since Yulia's school time. He was feared by both adults and children alike. Yet again, I couldn't quite understand why.

Olga, the youngest of the women, had just graduated from the history program at Minsk University, entered post-graduate school, and planned to write her PhD dissertation about the Khatyn tragedy. Interesting... But despite her love for the subject, her thoughts didn't impress me either. *"I hope my supervisor approves my topic! What if I don't get a teaching position in the department? Will I have to survive on a stipend again?"* She also worried about whether the new dress she planned to wear on a date would impress the young man she hoped to marry. *"What if it appears too flashy or too ridiculous to him?"*

For the entire tour, the worry about her boyfriend's opinion on the dress stung Olga's mind like sharp bee stings, causing serious turmoil in her soul. This worry consumed an enormous and utterly disproportionate amount of energy. The future PhD clearly lacked the skill of her energy management!

Hmm… How is it that people, even in the absence of real danger, find reasons to fear almost anything? Perhaps it's an unused gene that forces homo sapiens to seek insecurities, just as the instinct to reproduce drives them to seek mates? Maybe they believe that not fearing must be wrong. And so, they cling to even the smallest hints of threat, just unconsciously, to keep their instincts alive… How much time and energy do homo sapiens waste, consumed by such emotions, so groundless and, often, instilled by someone else! And all this despite the brevity of the lives they have been granted… The pity I suddenly felt for people was akin to pity for blind kittens crawling about aimlessly. Such trembling creatures would not only fail to resist vampires, but they would also prefer not to believe in monsters at all just to avoid being completely paralysed by panic.

The excursionists in the tour groups were Polina's age. These homo-sapien children differed from one another: each experienced what they saw and heard in Khatyn in their own way. Scrawny and pale Vanya, for example, followed the guides, listening to stories of fire, human cruelty, and suffering with eyes wide-open as if these tales were helping something big and important grow in his soul, which resonated like a taut string. The boy imagined how he would have joined the partisans and become a hero, even posthumously. Too bad he was only twelve…

Meanwhile, Seryozha, a freckled red-haired lout with small grey deep-set eyes, lagged behind the group for a completely inappropriate reason. The teacher had to go back for him.

"Komarov!" hissed Anna Pavlovna. "What are you doing here? Aren't you ashamed? Get moving and catch up with everyone, you rascal!"

"All right, Ann Palna," Komarov muttered, reluctantly letting go of a bug with black spots on its orange wings, arrested by the boy for sitting on the mass grave and utterly unaware of the threat posed by the excursion group. Rolling his eyes in exasperation, the boy trudged after the teacher. Evidently, neither the monuments nor Khatyn's horrifying history, nor history in general, made much of an impression on him. The imagination of this young homo sapien extended no further than his own physical body, and his mind shielded itself from anything that did not directly concern him. He saw only what he saw — a pile of granite. So, the boy had become fascinated by something alive and tangible, and, in a vampire's manner, would inevitably have taken the bug apart, limb by limb, absorbing that tiny bit of energy that would have left the dying creature. Without realising it, Anna Pavlovna had saved the poor insect's life. I found Seryozha's ignorant intentions revolting.

The excursion groups were also accompanied by history teachers who I soon realised only pretended to listen attentively to the guides. These adults visited the place every year and knew the lecture about the extermination of Khatyn by heart, so their perception of the tragic story had dulled dramatically. Instead of visualising the horrific events, their minds were preoccupied with daily chores and worries.

A sense of duty in the teachers' mental space was like an unquenchable red light, and their thoughts resembled an incredible cacophony of motifs unbelievably similar from one consciousness to another. Lesson plans for tomorrow, grading assignments, the tutorial hour, extra sessions for struggling students, the history club for upperclassmen, summoning Komarov's parents to discuss his unacceptable behaviour during the excursion, preparing for both a staff meeting presentation and, most meticulously, an observed lesson… These thoughts were accompanied by fears of mistakes, failures, and a shortage of time — or all of those horrors combined! And the teachers' success too often depended on other homo sapiens, the immature teenagers who make you feel like you are sitting on a powder keg. And finally, somewhere in the corner of a pedagogue's mind, shame over their own second-grade son's math test failure pecked away like a woodpecker, and the haunting wraith of an empty fridge commanded them to stop by the store after the Khatyn trip since the fridge could not fill itself.

These experiences drained the teachers' energy as quickly and uselessly as water splashed out of a shallow container carried by a running man, leaving nothing for moments of true thirst. Above all, the chances for energy recovery were so scarce that teachers' mental lives operated in strict resource-saving mode: their decisions followed universal routines, and their overloaded minds could neither absorb nor process anything outside well-worn paths. Almost everything history teachers taught in school came from textbooks and was memorised like the museum guides' speeches, which varied little from tour to tour and labelled Khatyn's chasteners as Germans. Neither the guides nor the teachers saw any point in questioning that narrative. Germans? Fine, Germans. The truth no longer mattered.

Without having been on the battlefield, it's hard to judge the loudness of cannon fire. And who cares about the sound of a shot fired before you were even born? Few homo sapiens live to be a hundred, which is why their truths are so short-lived too.

In the human world, reality turns into stories after about forty years. Since homo sapiens lack the ability to telepathically transmit experience, as soon as most eyewitnesses die, no living soul can vouch for the truth of history. The reality of recent witnesses is too quickly overgrown with speculation. The life of Jesus is a prime example. The long-lived Lemurians, who have secretly coexisted with humanity since its time in the cradle, have observed for far too long the tricks a short memory plays on homo sapiens. It was my ancestors who suggested the idea of Moses wandering in the desert for forty years to help the Israelites forget slavery. The Lemurians cared for the "chosen" people because our prophetesses foretold the birth of Jesus among the Jews, and Jesus could not be raised as a slave.

The most astonishing thing is how, in homo sapiens' stories, heroes and villains easily switch places, depending on the narrator's intent. Heroes become branded as criminals and villains become exalted rather too often. Defenders are renamed into invaders by their own descendants. And new homo sapiens, unaware of prospective wounds and scars, march off to fight evil that was recently considered good. The human world would be much calmer and more balanced if they lived at least two hundred years. But what if, in another forty years, the people of Khatyn, burned alive by vampires, completely disappeared from the memory of their descendants? What if the war that had taken my mother's life was entirely forgotten? And what if people started calling the vampires — the murderers of Khatyn — heroes, and the partisans who attacked the Nazis from the depths of the Belorussian forests tormentors and bandits?

No. It couldn't be. It couldn't.

In my childhood memory, over the cries and screams of tightly pressed, frightened people, the words of one of the doomed still echoed. "Pray to God, because everyone here will die!" And the shrill, hoarse voice of one of the executioners, rough from a spring cold and bloodthirsty excitement, still rasped back with a malicious sneer. "Oh, you trampled icons, you burned icons — now, we will burn you." Was this spoken in a language I understood as a little child, or had my ability to comprehend beyond languages already manifested back then? Here in Khatyn, as well as three hundred kilometres south, where I met Polina, the language sounded similar but not identical. Were there not only Germans? Should I have searched for *my* vampire nearer?

My task might have been easier if I had known the face of that pious fascist, but in the spring of 1943, it simply could not have come into my view — for at three years old, I saw more legs than heads. A whole forest of legs reeking of the cold sweat of terror. I only remembered the voice of the executioner, whom I now suspected was not German. Of course, that vengeful cur was just a pawn, not the leader, but the commander must have spoken the same language as his soldiers, otherwise, how could they understand his commands? What language was it? I had no answer yet. The granite slabs were silent. History teachers and children had nothing to offer, and I stood among Khatyn's graves, pondering, delving into the minds of the homo sapiens who came for the tour. I was disappointed. All I could do was hope that finding assistance wouldn't take another century.

Suddenly I got lucky. A man with completely white hair emerged from the information centre building and hurriedly limped toward the group I had joined. He approached the guide and quietly said, "There's a phone call for you." And he added in a half whisper, "It's okay. You can go, and I'll finish."

The woman nodded and rushed toward the building with a worried expression. The grey-haired man turned to the children.

"Kids, who can tell me where Nina left off?"

Several hands shot up in response. The new guide picked Vanya, who clearly and thoughtfully said, "Six people survived the fire, and only one adult." The boy pointed to the giant statue in the centre of the field. "That is a monument to him and his son, who died in his arms."

"Thank you and well done!" praised the old man. "What's your name, and where are you from, young pioneer?"

"Vanya Yakovlev. Minsk School number 135," the boy replied crisply.

The elderly man smiled, thinking, *"An eagle!"* Then he continued the tour in Nina's place.

"Yes, village blacksmith Joseph Kaminsky was the only adult among the six survivors. A few others were picked up by residents of nearby villages, but they died within the next two days. For example, Kazimir Yetka, covered in fatal burns, followed the executioners and begged them to shoot him, but the fascists just laughed and said, 'We won't waste bullets on you! You'll die anyway, but first, you'll tell the neighbours what awaits them for helping the partisans!' The Germans knew that most civilians supported the partisans and tried to intimidate the people," the new guide said, his voice hardening. He clenched his fists, slightly breathless from his quickened heartbeat. "But the fascists failed. After reaching the next village, Kazimir Yetka died of his burns, and Belorussians continued to support the partisan units. How could they not? Their family members fought there! And this was even though massacres of civilians continued. Two more girls, Maria Fedorovich and Yulia Klimovich, miraculously managed to escape from the burning barn and crawl through the forest to the neighbouring village of Khvorosten. Locals took them in, but soon the fascists burned that village too, and Yulia and Maria died anyway…"

The memorial director fell silent. Before his mind's eye, ghosts of carts rolled slowly between chimney stacks that loomed ominously above the black ruins. Farmers, hunched with grief and horror, came from nearby villages hoping to find surviving relatives but instead took away only charred, unrecognisable remains to bury. All these people travelled, staring straight ahead and not noticing the scout from the partisan unit that retreated the day before. And the soldier, frozen on the side of the dirt road, swallowed tears of guilt and helpless anger…

No one in the group dared to break the heavy silence. After a minute, the old man, shaken out of his memories, shuddered, took a deep breath, and continued.

"The rest of the survivors were children your age or younger. Nine-year-old Sonya Yaskievich hid in her aunt's basement, and her thirteen-year-old brother Volodya escaped to a potato pit. Their younger sister Lenochka was less fortunate. She first hid in the yard and then tried to run into the forest, but the Germans saw her and started shooting. When the fascists realised the bullets hadn't hit the girl, one of them caught up with her and shot her in front of her father, then killed him too." The grey-haired man fell silent again. Even Komarov, whose thick mind had finally begun to picture the tragedy from the old partisan's words, stood frozen with his mouth slightly open.

Another toll of the bell pierced the silence.

"Seven-year-old Vitya Zhelobkovich was shielded by his fatally wounded mother Anna, who was hit by a bullet," the guide said. "The boy was also wounded in the arm but survived."

"That must be the boy Mina saved," I thought. *"She carried him and left him on the porch of a house, knocked, and waited invisibly until people opened the door and took the child in. Why do they say he was found here?"*

"Anton Baranovsky was also wounded and mistaken for dead by the fascists."

"And not just them!" I marvelled. *"Simon and Mina didn't notice either!"*

"Villagers who arrived the next morning picked up both boys and nursed them back to health." After another short pause, the old man concluded, "That's how Khatyn died."

The astral body of our narrator was overflowing with anger and guilt that had not subsided over the years — guilt for something buried too deeply to decipher right away, but this unspoken torment had gnawed at the old partisan throughout all the postwar years.

A clear voice from the group of excursionists rang out again — it was Vanya. "And what happened to them afterward? To those children?"

The museum director smiled, whether at the pioneer's curiosity or the thought of the survivors.

"They stayed with neighbours until the end of the war. Then, they were sent to the Pleshchenitsy orphanage. Four of those five children are still alive today. Sofia Antonovna Yaskievich works as a telegraph operator at the post office in Minsk, and her brother Vladimir works at the Minsk automobile plant. Anton Baranovsky was the only child who survived while being inside *that* barn, but, unfortunately, he could not escape the fate of his fellow villagers. In 1969, he died of suffocation in a fire that broke out at night in a barrack in Orenburg, where he relocated for work."

"And it's unclear what happened there..." the grey-haired man thought to himself. *"I don't believe in such coincidences!"*

"The oldest of the surviving children, Sasha Zhelobkovich, was thirteen. When the chasteners arrived, his parents put him on a horse, and he rode through the forest to a neighbouring village. Sasha's uncle fought in our partisan unit but was captured and tortured by the Gestapo. When the boy grew up, he saw no other path for himself but to become a defender of the Motherland. Lieutenant Colonel Alexander Petrovich Zhelobkovich recently retired and now lives with his family in the city of Grodno. He is a frequent guest in Khatyn and took part in the opening of this memorial."

***

So, among the silent graves, there were still a few living threads leading to the events I needed to unravel. After the tour, I followed the former partisan toward the information centre.

"Matvey Ivanovich!" I called out.

The museum director turned around and looked at me questioningly from under his grey eyebrows. "Do we know each other?"

"No, but I have a few questions."

The old man nodded. "All right, come in," he said, unlocking the office door. "What are you interested in?"

I hesitated, studying the sad human gaze that contrasted so sharply with his formal tone. Since March of 1943, I hadn't met anyone else who had seen violent death — very much of violent death – and carried it out too, even though by necessity.

"From your tour, I gathered that you fought somewhere nearby — in a partisan unit?" I began cautiously.

"Yes, that's true," the museum director confirmed with a nod.

"The thing is, I'm investigating some details about the burning of Khatyn."

His white eyebrows rose. "Oh? You're not the first. What exactly are you looking for?"

I decided to be honest. "I want to find and punish the one who gave the orders to burn and execute people at the crime scene. There's information that the commander of the punitive unit is still alive. It wasn't a German, was it?"

"What organisation do you represent?" the former partisan interrupted, frowning.

"None," I faltered. "I'm a private individual."

"Then I have nothing more to add to what you've already heard during the tour."

"And if I were an official representative? The information from the tour wouldn't be everything, right?"

"Goodbye, comrade," Matvey Ivanovich said irritably, gesturing toward the door.

"Please, understand, this is extremely important!"

"I've said everything I have to say," he replied, staring at me with steely eyes. He pressed his palms firmly against the desk, leaning forward, unconsciously but effectively channelling his energy to push me out the door. He undoubtedly would have succeeded if I were a homo sapien.

But my reflective block absorbed and dissipated the force directed at me by this strong-willed man, and I simply stood there, patiently waiting for him to realise the futility of his efforts.

I didn't want to invade the old soldier's mind — I wanted to win over the first worthy adult homo sapien I had met on Earth. This was a kind of experiment.

My opponent didn't back down, so I resorted to a bold trick. Right before his stubborn eyes, I turned invisible and then reappeared.

The museum director's jaw dropped, and his eyes bulged as he sank into his chair. Then he shook his head, deciding he must have imagined it, but I repeated the trick. Twice.

"Matvey Ivanovich, you're not losing your mind," I finally reassured the stunned man.

"Who… are you?" the old man croaked, wiping sweat from his forehead with a white handkerchief checkered with blue squares, pulled from his pocket with a practiced motion.

Before continuing the conversation, I focused on his circulatory system and stabilised his heart and blood flow within seconds to ensure the veteran wouldn't suffer a heart attack.

When his health was no longer at risk, I teleported from the middle of the room to the visitor's chair opposite the director to convince him once and for all of the reality — and uniqueness — of what was happening.

"It's a long story, but you can trust me."

"Are you from the KGB?" Matvey Ivanovich stammered.

"What's the KGB?"

Thinking, *"Did he fall from the moon?"* the old partisan stared at me in surprise. "I don't understand!"

"Let's just say I'm not exactly human," I explained.

"An alien, then?" The museum director couldn't resist a sarcastic chuckle.

"Yes and no," I replied, avoiding unnecessary details. "I just need information."

I paused, but the director waited silently, staring at me.

"May I continue?" I asked.

Matvey Ivanovich nodded.

"Then answer me this: who really burned Khatyn?"

The old soldier sighed, stood, opened the wooden cabinet door, and took out a long transparent bottle and two glasses. He poured a pungent liquid into both glasses and, after drinking his in one gulp, looked at me questioningly. "Not drinking?"

I shook my head.

"Your loss…"

If only he knew how wrong he was! Alcohol destroys not only the physical body but also the subtle one. Promoting drinking culture is yet another tried-and-true vampire tactic to block superpowers in humankind.

Meanwhile, my companion asked, "So why do you need these details?"

"I need to find the person who gave the orders that day and bring them to justice."

"Well, that's a righteous cause," the old man said thoughtfully. "But I doubt I can help you, because I wasn't in Khatyn during the tragedy."

"Yes, I know that you returned to the village only in the morning," I said, pointing to my forehead in response to his questioning look.

"But… you can do it yourself too…" the old man objected, also tapping his forehead with his finger.

"Yes," I smiled. "Without a doubt, I could break your mind like an old barn lock, but out of respect for you, I don't want to do that. And besides, I feel like you've been wanting to pour out something for a long time — something you seem unwilling to talk about. So at least tell me what you know," I said, hoping that clearer memories might surface during his story.

"Well, all right." Matvey Ivanovich paused for a few moments, deciding where to begin. "Back then, I was fighting in Uncle Vasya's partisan unit." Noticing my confusion, he clarified, "Our leader's name was Vasily Voronyansky. Do you know what guerrilla warfare is?"

I shook my head and made a questioning face, encouraging him to continue. During the tour, I realised already that the old partisan was a good storyteller. He had even worked as a history teacher at school for a while.

"It's fighting the enemy on territory that's occupied by them," Matvey Ivanovich explained. "When the Germans invaded in '41, I had already served in the Army. The Soviet Union wasn't prepared for war, and Belarus was occupied so quickly that few managed to join the front. As a result, many adult men remained in the area and the partisan movement formed almost immediately. At the start of the war, our groups were scattered. Local men simply went into the forest and tried to harm the Germans as much as possible — cutting telephone wires, blowing up railway tracks and bridges, attacking supply convoys, and raiding food and ammunition warehouses. When different partisan groups did this without coordination, it sometimes caused more harm than good... Do you understand?"

"Basically, yes," I replied, patiently waiting for the story to get to the interesting details.

And Matvey Ivanovich continued. "By 1943, the partisans had united and already had headquarters in Moscow, which is why an uncoordinated attack on a German convoy was unlikely, and no one later believed that we didn't know about that attack." The museum director grimaced bitterly and added with despair, "And they still don't believe us!"

"Sorry, I don't understand. What attack?" I deliberately avoided reading his thoughts, wanting to hear the story in order rather than as a chaotic stream of consciousness, but the feeling was so unusual that I was starting to lose patience.

"Ah, yes. They don't mention this during the tour... That morning, when Khatyn was burned, a German convoy was ambushed on the nearby road, and an officer was killed. It turned out he was an Olympic champion from Germany, a world record holder in shot put. We only found out afterward. So, this officer, Velke, was Hitler's favourite — that's probably why he was accompanied by an entire convoy, even though he was just heading to the railway station to go on leave."

The museum director took a deep breath, frustrated. "Everyone thinks the ambush was our doing, but we didn't even know about the attack. We didn't need that convoy!"

"Why not?"

"Because there was no point in attacking it. It wouldn't have caused the Germans much material damage. You see, our main goal was to disrupt their ability to fight, not to kill their Olympic champions. And most importantly, the Nazis' reaction — their vengeance on the local population — was entirely predictable. And why would we want that? Almost all our partisans were from nearby villages, including a couple of people from Khatyn."

"And you too?"

"No, I'm from Kozyri, but I often went to Khatyn. The villagers were always welcoming to partisans. When someone attacked the convoy that morning, we were heading to the village to stock up on food. I was especially looking forward to spending the night in a warm house, something that rarely happened. I can't forgive myself!"

"What can't you forgive?"

"We had just entered the house and then the Germans came. We ran out, fired back for a while, then retreated into the forest through the gardens, taking out a few more Nazis along the way. And by noon, their commanders sent the police to punish the village. It turns out we had exposed those people! Do you understand?"

"Why didn't the villagers leave?"

"They didn't have time. They wouldn't have gotten far — nearly half the population were young children. And the snow was still deep. Where could they have gone in the forest? They hoped it would pass… and they died."

"So you think the village was burned because of you?"

"That's the rumour the Nazis spread. After Khatyn, partisan units were even ordered not to stay overnight in villages. But you can't bring back the dead! And even now, some historians bark that the Germans burned the village because of us." The old man sighed and shrugged. "They don't tell visitors about it because it would tarnish the image of the partisans. The authorities want people to see us as heroes, as examples for children. I even had to quit teaching and take this honorary position," the former history teacher smiled bitterly. "Because I wanted too much to unburden my soul to the young, and I was not allowed to do so."

I was surprised. "Aren't you heroes still?"

"That's not the point," Matvey said with a wave of his hand. "First, heroes are people too, and they make mistakes. And then, we fought because we couldn't just sit and wait to be burned alive in barns. We fought for our lives, do you understand? There's nothing heroic about that. It's just nature's law. You've heard it: one hundred and eighty-six villages wiped out forever, along with their inhabitants."

"Okay, but if Khatyn was burned as revenge for the champion's death, then why were all the other villages destroyed?"

"Is it really so hard to find a reason?" the old partisan sneered. "As the fable says, 'You're guilty simply because I'm hungry.' Hitler promised his soldiers land in Eastern Europe as a reward for fighting. By exterminating entire villages, the Nazis were clearing space for their future farms." He clenched his fists. "Can you imagine?!"

"Then it turns out the killing of the German officer was just a pretext… and Khatyn was doomed, like the other villages, right? Then it's not your fault."

"Yes, I know…" Matvey agreed sadly. "And the villagers understood too. But it doesn't make it any easier for me."

"How strange," I thought. *"A man feels guilty for the death of an entire village, even though he neither gave the order to*

burn people alive nor carried it out. His only fault was giving in to the temptation of a warm night indoors. And those others who shot children with their own hands are now hiding somewhere. And perhaps they are even happy. How different people are!" Before meeting the former partisan, I thought no one's heart could ache more than mine had all those years earlier. But I was wrong.

"Who oversaw them? Who gave the orders when they burned the village? Did you see him?" I wanted to hear what interested me the most.

"I don't know," Matvey responded. "Like I said, we only came close to the Germans occasionally, and we returned to Khatyn the next morning when we found out what they had done..."

The former partisan closed his eyes, unsuccessfully trying to recall any of the enemies' faces. Instead, a memory surfaced, one of an encounter that took place years after the war. The old historian didn't remember the reason for the meeting, nor its contents, nor the exact time. The entire event was shrouded in fog. Only the image of his conversation partner remained, a stern man who might have seemed unremarkable, almost faceless, if not for his strange eyes. Back then, the stranger's gaze sent shivers down the old partisan's spine. The man's eyes were not the same colour: his left eye was yellowish-brown, and the right was so light blue it seemed transparent. Those eyes stared directly at Matvey Ivanovich without blinking and paralysed him in a kind of stupor.

It was this eerie gaze that was seared into his memory for years, locking away something improper like a key turned in a lock... Someone had tampered with the museum director's memory — someone with hypnotic abilities. Someone strong. And it was somehow tied to his recollections of the Nazis.

Commenting on my telepathic observations was pointless as Matvey wouldn't have been able to add anything to what I already understood, so I simply asked, "Who might recognise the face of the Nazi commander?"

"Maybe the kids who survived Khatyn caught a glimpse of him… though I doubt they'd remember anyone clearly."

"Can you help me find them?"

"That won't be difficult," the museum director smiled. "I have their addresses right here in my desk, but they won't tell you much. I've spoken with the survived witnesses many times. They hardly remember anything. They were too scared that day to even remember themselves."

"Well, that's my concern," I replied, far too confidently, as it later turned out, taking the precious list from the old partisan's hands.

"We'll see…" Matvey shrugged doubtfully and, shaking my hand firmly in farewell, added, "My advice is, don't show them your tricks!"

"We'll see about that!"

I stepped outside, pondered for a few minutes, and realised that leaving this fine old man without help would be tantamount to leaving him in the clutches of death.

The next morning, I materialised in the museum director's office again, right in front of his desk.

"You again?!" the old man yelped, clutching his heart in surprise. Although after a couple of seconds, he grumbled good-naturedly, trying unsuccessfully to hide the joy my appearance brought him. "What the hell do you want now?"

His feigned irritation put me in a playful mood. "I just wanted to ask again," I lied, "who ambushed that convoy?"

"I don't know!" the old man said, waving me off in frustration. "If I did, would I let them point the finger at the partisans? When will I finally get rid of you?"

"Don't be in such a hurry to get rid of me, Matvey Ivanovich. The real reason for my visit today is to give you some treatment, as thanks for yesterday's conversation."

“What?” The proposal caught the old partisan off guard, but he quickly recovered. “Thanks, my friend, but we have the best medicine in the world.”

This display of dignity was remarkable, especially considering that Matvey Ivanovich was often ill. The fear of death, which had been stalking him for days, occasionally broke free from its tightly guarded corner in his mind. He even kept a bottle in his cupboard to numb that fear, which was only bringing the end closer.

“Maybe the best in *this* world,” I countered.

“And why didn’t you treat me yesterday?” the director tried to joke.

“Yesterday, you were drinking vodka, and that stuff blocks whatever health your worn-out body still enjoys,” I explained with mock pomposity. “Ideally, we’d wait a couple of days more for it to clear out of your system, but I’m afraid you might not have that long.”

The director’s eyes widened. “Why not?”

“Well, think about it. Your heart is weak, your stomach’s been ruined since the war, and you’ve never spared your liver. And then there’s that old shoulder wound. And most importantly, there are…” I squinted, pinpointing the details. “… three ominous clots in your blood vessels, one of which is lodged in your brain. So, a stroke is waiting for you any day now, no exaggeration.”

Matvey Ivanovich slumped noticeably. Some of what I had said he already knew, but the clot in his brain was news to him.

“So, do you want treatment?”

“What do I have to do?”

“Just relax and leave the rest to me.”

Without further objections, the museum manager ordered through the intercom, “Anya, I’m busy. Don’t let anyone in,” and, for good measure, tossed the phone receiver onto the desk.

“What now?”

I pointed to the worn leather couch in the corner. “Over there, please.”

***

Half an hour later, visibly rejuvenated Matvey Ivanovich was dancing a sailor’s jig in the middle of his office, singing along in a falsetto. The door cracked open, revealing Anya’s pretty, wide-eyed face just as I was pouring the remaining contents of yesterday’s glass bottle down the sink.

“Take care!” I said before hurrying out the door, away from the vocal outbursts of the revitalised old man, whose singing ability was, unfortunately, beyond repair.

Chapter 4. Living Witnesses

"Fed the chickens, washed the dishes, helped my mum, and now I can..." Eight-year-old Sonya Yaskievich entered the well-heated house, puffing as she freed herself from heavy felt boots in the entryway and pulled off the old rabbit-fur coat inherited from her cousin. She was about to head to the corner where her pride and joy awaited. It was a beautiful doll named Jadwiga, the only real doll in the village, as regal as a princess. Sonya's father had brought it from Minsk just before the war, stirring envy among the village girls who came to marvel at the richly dressed dilly with blonde curls, big blue eyes, and coquettish long eyelashes.

When the fascists invaded, her friends had grown up overnight and forgotten about dolls, but Sonya carefully hid Jadwiga under a blanket, not from friends but from greedy policemen. She often placed the doll on the bed and admired beauty. In such moments, her ears would ring with the joyful laughter of her parents, who hugged each other, watching their daughter prance around the room and hug this extraordinary royal gift…

So, on *that* day, after finishing all her household chores, Sonya felt irresistibly drawn to the company of her silent princess, the only thing in the area that kept a happy face.

"Sonya!"

"Yes, Mummy?"

"Come here and rock Tolya! I need to run over to Aunt Stesha."

"Right away! *Oh, I was just about to play..."* Frustrated, Sonya stopped in the middle of the room and then heard a noise outside. "*What is that? Soldiers? Again? So scary..."*

Sofya Antonovna's heart pounded wildly in her chest, just as it had when she was that little girl on the day Khatyn was ruined. Trying to extract something useful from the memories of a surviving witness, I felt the lump of fear rising in her throat and making it hard to breathe. Such a lump is an unshakable companion of war children.

Sonya froze, paralysed by panic, but only for a moment. *"Where's Mum?"* flashed through her mind. Oh, children's faith in their mothers! Sonya believed that her mum would save her from those terrifying men with rifles, who occasionally stormed into the village, stomping like a herd of bulls, grabbing anything they could find in peasant yards, their looting accompanied by crude curses in barely understandable or completely foreign languages.

"Mama-a-a!"

There was Mum, entering with Tolya in one arm while buttoning her blouse with the other. She must have been feeding him.

"What's that noise?"

"Soldiers!"

Both the big one and the little one carefully peeked out from opposite corners of the window, pushing aside the simple chintz curtains without revealing their presence in the house. Huge men in grey coats with rifles at the ready filled the street. Some wore German uniforms, but most were dressed in something else. They moved in a purposeful line, occasionally shouting something. In Sofya Antonovna's memory, the faces of the policemen were blurred, as if someone had smeared them with translucent apple jelly.

"Ah, damn them!" Doubt and confusion showed on the mother's face. "Here's what you do, Sonyushka…"

"Sonyushka? Wow! How tender!" The girl's heart swelled with delight but then immediately tensed. *'She never calls me Sonyushka but instead Sophia, like I am a grown-up."*

"Run to Aunt Stesha, and maybe hide in the forest from there if you can."

"But Maa…"

"Go on, go on, don't argue!"

"Just now I was Sonyushka, and she's so strict again, almost yelling..." The girl slumped but obeyed, starting to pull on the warm rabbit-fur coat. *"Oh well! She must be scared too. Mummy, darling Mummy, you're so warm! And Tolya too, so warm and smelling sweet, baby sweet... And your eyes, big and blue, and the wrinkles around them... I love you, even when you yell!"*

Before leaving, Sonya pressed herself against her mother, and the lump of fear in her throat dissolved and retreated. The mother hugged and kissed her little daughter with such strength and such love, as she had never done so before with any of her children in her arduous peasant life. It was a farewell embrace, but little Sonya interpreted it in her own way. She was heartened and encouraged. *"What could possibly happen if Mum loves me this much?"*

"Go, go!" the woman urged. "Through the gardens. Run! No time to button up!"

"Strange," thought the girl again. *"She always makes me button up to my chin, but now... It's too cold to leave it open, but if I run, it'll be fine."*

She reached Stesha's hut through the gardens.

"Auntie, there are soldiers!"

"I know, I know. Go hide, child."

"Where are all your family?"

"In the village, scattered everywhere."

"Then let's run to the forest! It's so close!"

"It's too late, dear. Just hide. They're probably looking for partisans, but all the guys left this morning after the shoot-out. Maybe it'll be all right..."

Aunt Stesha couldn't lie. She was trembling all over and rushing around the house, which didn't even have many hiding spots.

"Hide, darling! At least in the cellar! I'll lock the door, and maybe they'll think no one's home."

"Don't lock it! You never lock it… They'll break it down anyway."

"You're right…" Stesha froze in confusion in the middle of the kitchen, her hands dropping helplessly. Then she stepped to the door and slid the thick oak bolt into its two iron slots, buying herself two more minutes of life.

"Auntie's cellar steps are so steep! I hope I don't fall and make noise!" The child's heart pounded so hard it echoed painfully in her temples. *"Where should I hide? Maybe in the potatoes? I should fit if there aren't too many in the bin. It's so dark! Should I feel around with my hand? There, okay, I fit. Ugh, the potatoes are dirty and dusty! I hope I don't sneeze!"* At that moment, the pounding of fists and feet hit the door. *"The door's so flimsy. Oh, what a crash… They broke it down! Those bastards!"*

Sitting among the potatoes, Sonya tried to muffle the noise of her heart jumping out of her chest. She must have fainted from the arrhythmia and woken up only when a single gunshot rang out above, followed by a short female scream. Stesha's scream. *"What fell? Did they shoot Aunt Stesha? Mummy, save me! God, save me!"* The girl squeezed her eyes shut, beating back her tears for the kind aunt that emerged unwillingly. Sonya breathed through her mouth to avoid revealing herself with a sob or sniffle. At that moment, she desperately wished she could become invisible.

The wooden cellar lid was thrown open and a flashlight beam pierced the darkness. A man's silhouette, backlit by the light above, looked like a terrifying monster to the girl, but she managed to suppress a cry of fear.

"Anyone here?" a hoarse voice barked.

"What an idiot," the eight-year-old thought. *"Who's going to answer you? Oh no, he's coming down! A soldier. What heavy steps! His boots are brand new, I bet… He's searching… What's he looking for? People or loot? Ugh, he's so scary. Skinny like a*

skeleton. Don't breathe, don't sniff... Please let him leave! Mummy, where are you? God, save me!"

Sofya Antonovna remembered how the policeman dressed in a uniform with dark blue lapels had climbed down into the cellar and muttered something indistinct. In her memory, his face remained obscured by a foggy haze.

The scary man glanced around, and his attention was drawn to the top shelf, where a salami stick rested, spreading a spicy garlic aroma while it awaited a special occasion. He grinned, reached up, and pulled the prize down. Triumphantly waving the sausage in the air like a trophy captured in battle, he reached up again and rummaged around, hoping to find more supplies, but he found only a jar of sunflower oil, and he grabbed it too, then stomped his boots back up the stairs and out of the cellar.

That sausage likely saved Sonya's life. The wind also helped, blowing smoke from Stesha's burning house away and preventing the little niece from suffocating in the cellar.

***

It was a moment I seized to give the telegraph operator a mini session of telepathic hypnosis while the post office was empty, but a whole crowd of people poured in so quickly it was as if they had all been waiting just outside.

"Lady, can you hurry up?" a grumpy woman's voice from the line forced me to break eye contact.

The telegraph operator came to her senses and looked around at the line in surprise.

"Are you feeling unwell?" I asked, leaning slightly over the counter and trying to sound concerned.

The middle-aged operator with dark brown hair streaked with grey fully regained her awareness and flinched.

"No, sorry. I just got lost in thought for a second," she said apologetically, having no idea that she'd been disconnected for a full ten minutes.

Immediately another voice, this time an elderly man's, hissed from the line. "Do you come to work to daydream? Shameful! An old woman acting like some idling young lady!"

"It hasn't happened to me in ages, probably not since that strange doctor visited the orphanage," thought Sofya Antonovna without irritation. She brushed aside the memory of the doctor and ignored the rudeness of the impatient old man. He could have been her father by age, yet the deep wrinkles on her gentle face made the telegraph operator look much older than her fifty years. She was a simple woman who had never expected too much from life, and as a result, she had everything she wished for. Considering it a great fortune just to have survived, the poor woman superstitiously regarded dreams of further blessings as blasphemy.

She could remember neither the faces nor the conversations of the fascists who had destroyed her and mine home village. She was rather glad for it. I suspected that someone had tampered with her mind, just as they had with Matvey's memory. And I envied Sofya Antonovna. It seemed to me that such partial oblivion was what had allowed her soul, scarred by childhood hardships, to go on living in peace with herself and others. Perhaps if Sonya Yaskievich had remembered what the murderers of her family looked like, her soul would have continued to burn with a thirst for revenge throughout her life, just like mine.

Her older brother, Vladimir Yaskievich, remembered even less. When the punishers came, he had hidden in an empty potato pit on the outskirts of the village and, apparently, fainted from terror. Grown-up Vladimir assumed this because he remembered absolutely nothing: from the moment he climbed into the pit, everything was wiped clean.

So, I had found and read the memories of two out of four witnesses to the Khatyn massacre — and I still was nowhere near my goal.

***

Retired Lieutenant Colonel Aleksandr, or Sasha*, Zhelobkovich was my main hope. From the museum manager, I learned that after the destruction of Khatyn, the teenager Sasha stayed with the partisans until the Nazis were driven out of Belorussia, although he was too young to participate in risky operations. Before making direct contact with this witness, I decided to observe him first. I discreetly followed Aleksandr as he briskly walked to the office. I was curious about what the boy, who had escaped death on a village horse in March of '43, was doing now.

A grown man, confident and self-assured, he walked leisurely along a well-trodden path by the river. Every time there was a sunny morning, the retired lieutenant colonel took this detour, just to enjoy the walk and savour life once again. In this, he resembled the telegraph operator Sofya Antonovna. Perhaps no one appreciates the happiness of merely being alive more than those whose lives have once hung by a thread.

The town chosen by the Zhelobkovich family after the head of the household retired was serenely quiet and shone with an abundance of neatly whitewashed, tile-roofed houses. On Lemuria, everyone lives in the open air, without artificial structures. We do not fence ourselves off from Nature, which in turn provides us with both food and shelter without unnecessary hassle. The favourable climate encourages our noninterference in the natural order. Nevertheless, the beauty of architecture created by homo sapiens has always fascinated my kind. Like Sasha Zhelobkovich, I felt that the old white buildings of Grodno exuded unshakable tranquillity, despite their proximity to the national border.

A neat white church with a pyramidal roof was dozing on a cozy green hill covered in rainbow-coloured morning dew. Aleksandr stopped by it. He suddenly turned and looked at the bend of the Neman River, as if trying to absorb the cloudless infinity. Sparkling in the sun with silver highlights, the river, which had seen much terror during the war, flowed quietly toward the horizon, veiled in an emerald spring haze. Sasha Zhelobkovich stood there for a minute, unable to get enough of the peaceful April morning, lifting his face to the sun and the light breeze, and simply admitted to himself, *"I am happy."* The former Khatyn teenager was thinking about his daughter's upcoming wedding to a very good man. He dreamed of a swarm of grandchildren and how he would play with them.

The retired artilleryman was difficult to hypnotize, and his morning thoughts had nothing to do with the last day of his home village, so I could not learn anything simply by observing. The lieutenant colonel was healthy and calm. Despite the tragedy he had experienced as a child, he was not tormented by subconscious fears. On the contrary, Aleksandr was honest with himself and others. He faced difficulties bravely and travelled all over the country. Unlike the museum tour guides, who had been lucky to be born in peacetime yet were full of trivial soul-eating anxieties, he wasn't afraid of life. How does this work with homo sapiens? I needed allies with bright auras, like Aleksandr's, and I dared not violate his mental boundaries without permission, even for this reason. Although, he did look far too content with life to be motivated for a fight.

Reaching a freshly whitewashed two-story building, Zhelobkovich took a key from his pocket and unlocked a narrow door with a sign that read, *Knowledge Society*. It was time for me to show my presence. I approached him from behind.

"You must be tired of journalists by now," I began as a means of introducing myself as yet another reporter.

"That doesn't matter!" Aleksandr replied over his shoulder without a hint of surprise. "I never refuse to give interviews about Khatyn. Not letting people forget about it is my civic duty." And he truly meant what he said.

Zhelobkovich invited me into his office. Now his dark-blue eyes watched me intently. The former military man was always on guard. The recently emerging bald spots made his large forehead, crossed by a single deep horizontal wrinkle, seem even bigger. Smooth cheeks and full lips of fine shape, along with a dimple on his chin — these soft facial features didn't match the image of a professional soldier, nor did his unhurried movements. The bags under his eyes gave him a weary look, though this man was only slightly older than me! Yes, the retired lieutenant colonel had very little energy left…

"Then please tell me about that tragic day."

I prepared to listen attentively, but he asked, "Aren't you going to take notes? Where is your notepad or recorder?"

"Oh… I… I remember everything," I stammered, realising I had forgotten to bring any prompts appropriate for the occasion. "Please, go ahead. Where were you when the punishers arrived?"

My companion closed his eyes. Though he considered it his sacred duty to answer questions about Khatyn, I then realised how difficult it still was for him, despite the many years and the smooth flow of life since then. And these memories felt especially out of place on such a beautiful spring morning, after a stroll filled with pleasant thoughts about his family.

Aleksandr winced slightly but finally, mustering his will, answered firmly. "I was in our yard with my father. He was working on something, and I was enjoying myself on the swings. Dad had put them up shortly before that day. He was always thinking of ways to cheer us up…"

Recalling the scene of the last day of his childhood, stolen by the war, Sasha looked sadly out the window, where a young silver birch flaunted its bright, newborn leaves.

"There were so many of them, they approached in a horseshoe formation, and my father understood they were starting to surround us. Then he ran to the stable and led out our horse. I was thirteen, and I already knew how to ride well. He put me on the horse and ordered me to gallop to Aunt Masha's place in Zamostye."

"And you rode away?"

"Y-yes..." Zhelobkovich's voice sounded hollow, and his face suddenly flushed with shame and anger — anger at himself.

"So, you feel guilty."

Aleksandr stared straight into my eyes. "No one has ever asked me that before. They try to be tactful. You're an unusual journalist."

"That's not a question. It's a fact," I said, deciding to be completely honest with this special homo sapien. "You can't stop thinking that you could have taken one of your brothers or sisters with you — or even two of them — and they'd still be alive today. And you've never forgiven yourself for not doing it, even though you know it was your father, not you, who urged the horse forward, insisting there was no time."

"How do you know that?" My vis-à-vis's surprise grew. "I've never told anyone about my regrets, except my wife."

I kept adding fuel to the fire. "And you joined the military to protect others and atone for the guilt you feel toward your lost family. But deep down, you often think you would have made a good doctor instead. And it's true since you're a kind and intelligent person with a bright energy."

"Bright energy?" Aleksandr asked, puzzled, resting his smooth-shaven chin on his fist. "Interesting! You know more about me than I do. So why do you need this interview?"

His question was tinged with irony, but he immediately guessed the answer:

"You're not a journalist. It's like you're reading my thoughts."

I nodded affirmatively, twice, confirming each of his assumptions.

"Then who are you?" the retired lieutenant colonel asked warily. "KGB?"

Ah, the KGB! Again! I shook my head.

"Then who? The CIA?" he half joked.

"What's the CIA?"

Zhelobkovich stared at me in disbelief, thinking, *"Is he from the moon?"*

"Not from the Moon. From Lemuria."

After a brief, questioning pause, the Soviet Army's lieutenant colonel burst into sardonic laughter. Laughing so hard that he had to wipe tears from his eyes, the man waved a hand near his ear — politely, instead of making the usual finger-twirling gesture by his temple to imply I was crazy.

Finally, catching his breath, Aleksandr said, "An alien, huh? Ha-ha-ha. You must be crazy! How didn't I see it sooner? No notepad, no recorder… Times are changing, and lunatics are coming out of the woodwork again!"

I sighed helplessly as his hand reached for the telephone on the desk. Was I really going to have to put on a show for every homo sapien I decided to tell the truth to? I made sure his heart was stronger than the museum director's and began my demonstration. The folders rose gracefully from the office desk into the air, forming a line and gliding around the room. Having reached the centre, the papers spun in a slow circle without losing a single sheet. Soon, brochures from the bookshelf joined the dance.

Aleksandr's laughter died down. For a couple of minutes, he watched, mouth agape. Then he stepped out from behind the desk and approached the floating items. He tried to grab a brochure as if hoping to snap the invisible thread holding them up. The brochure dodged his hand, gave him a firm tap on the neck, and quickly returned to the lively dance. It was my turn to laugh. I hadn't laughed this hard in a long time!

"Well? Do you believe me now?" I asked, trying to smile as warmly as possible.

He didn't answer. Inside his head, a battle raged between his materialistic worldview and the undeniable facts before him. And as we all know, facts are the most stubborn things in the world.

"You're not going crazy, Aleksandr Petrovich," I reassured him, still sitting in my chair, which was also floating in the middle of the paper whirlwind. "Humans are neither the kings of Nature nor the most advanced beings on Earth, let alone in the Universe. Doesn't that make sense?"

"Y-yes… it does," the chairman of the Grodno branch of the Knowledge Society agreed hesitantly. Slowly, glancing nervously at the floating papers, he returned to his desk. Then, he suddenly remembered to ask, "But why are you interested in Khatyn?"

"I was born there," I replied, gently guiding the documents and brochures back to their places.

"What?"

"Yes. You heard me right. I was three years old. I was in *that* barn during the fire — and I survived, thanks to my mother."

"Impossible!" Aleksandr objected. "You can't be more than twenty!"

"I'm forty-five."

"Let's say you just look young…" He studied my face, searching for signs of age. "Then who were your parents?"

"Polina, the herbalist."

"I don't remember any herbalist… though I knew everyone in the village. Well, let's say I forgot. And your father?"

"My father is a Lemurian, he belongs to a race far more advanced than yours."

"You've got to be kidding me!" Zhelobkovich slammed his hand on the desk.

"You'll remember everything now," I said, grabbing a pencil. "Look here."

As he focused on the pencil, I spoke the code words that no homo sapien could hear by chance. "I'll count to five, and you'll remember. One… two… three… four… five… *Homo liberatus*."

Aleksandr's face tensed for a moment but quickly cleared up.

"I remember the herbalist!" he exclaimed, his eyes widening. "And her… gypsy guy? So, you're the gypsy boy, Yasik? Now it makes sense where your tricks come from! Although…"

"Well, let me be a gypsy boy…" I couldn't help but smile. The fact that we turned out to be from the same village, fellow countrymen, was supposed to help build trust. "Still, tell me… tell me what you know, Sasha."

"What exactly are you after? And why?"

Now it was me being interviewed, which was not part of my plan, so I answered as briefly as possible.

"I was sent to find the vampires who destroyed our families and to free humanity from them, and others as well." It didn't matter that Aleksandr understood the word "vampires" only figuratively. "I don't yet know exactly where to look for them, but I wanted to start by finding the commander who gave the orders, because he was the most powerful there… Anyway, I need you to picture everything you saw that day — and I'll try to read at least some faces from your memory. That's the interview."

"R-read?" the retired lieutenant colonel repeated in surprise. However, the performance I had staged earlier was convincing enough, so he willingly closed his eyes. "All right, go ahead!"

Aleksandr easily focused, as was his habit. Memories flashed in his thoughts: the backyard, a horse's mane… even the sour smell of a sweaty horse. A mad gallop, trees rushing past like a solid wall, a skinny woman pulling a teenager off the huffing animal, the thunderous ticking of a wall clock in the deathly silence of the aunt's kitchen… endless waiting… an unbearably slow journey in his uncle's cart back to Khatyn, and… a charred but already lifelessly cold chimney — the only piece left of the large family home. In place of the blacksmith's shed, there were beams turning to embers. Under the beams, there was a pile of burned corpses.

"You truly didn't see the punishers' faces..." I concluded, pulling away from Sasha's memories. "Who else can help me? I already visited the Yaskievich — and nothing. Only Vitya remains. Is he your brother?"

"Cousin," Alexander said. "But he doesn't remember anyone either, so you might not want to waste your time. No one remembers. I know it seems strange, unnatural. People from other villages burned during the war don't remember the Germans' faces or words either. Like they were bewitched."

"Germans," I noted to myself, then asked, "Tell me, have you ever met someone with different-coloured eyes?"

Aleksandr flinched as if the question had caught him off guard. He shuddered. "Brr... That brings up chills! There was one visiting lecturer when I was in artillery school." And in his memory appeared an auditorium full of cadets. The room was covered in some fog, and in that fog, there was the face I recognised from Matvey's memories. The face with strange eyes, one yellow-brown, the other light blue. "He gave a couple of lectures, I think... but I don't remember what he taught... We were all sitting there, like we were under hypnose."

"I can see that," I said. "And now it's clear: if I can't deprogram the witnesses, I won't find the commander of the punitive squad."

"Deprogram?" my companion laughed. "Do you think we really were hypnotised back then? What nonsense!"

"I don't think — I know," I countered. "For you to remember everything, a code is needed, one only the hypnotist knows. Just like five minutes ago, you remembered about the existence of my parents."

"Are you serious?" Aleksandr Petrovich still didn't believe me.

"Completely serious. And I have one last question for you today."

"Go ahead!"

"Where is the KGB located?"

Aleksandr gave me another wild look but then laughed again, suppressing a chuckle before answering seriously. "The main office is on Bolshaya Lubyanka, in Moscow. Don't think, you naive alien, that they'll just hand you that code on a silver platter."

"No, of course not, but I have my methods…"

"So do they! This isn't like cracking an artilleryman," Sasha smirked, hinting at how easily I had read his thoughts. "And besides, that was in the fifties. If the guy with those eyes was from the KGB, he's probably retired by now. Though, of course, the data should be in the archives. That is, if you manage to access them."

I decided to show him one last trick before leaving: I turned invisible and spoke as if out of thin air, "What about this?"

After a brief pause, I heard, "Well, your chances are better this way, at least. And you absolutely need that guy. With the eyes."

"I know," I said, becoming visible again and raising my hand in a farewell gesture. I was about to leave when Aleksandr stopped me.

"Wait! Close the door…"

I turned back, and he hesitantly said, "You know, I think Khatyn was burned by our people. I mean collaborators… Some have already been jailed or executed, and I attended two trials as a witness. Unfortunately, I could only tell the court facts that were already well known, and I didn't recognise any of the murderers… Still, I can't shake the feeling that there were far more traitors from our side among Khatyn's punishers than actual Germans. And if we, the surviving witnesses, were hypnotised, then maybe… they wanted us to forget precisely that? But why?" The former artilleryman fell into deep thought and, after some time in uninterrupted silence, he added, "My reasoning is just a guess, a logical deduction if you will… Do you understand? And it's not something to talk about publicly."

"It's an interesting guess," I praised Aleksandr before I left the Knowledge Society building.

Chapter 5. Saving Drowning Men Is the Drowning Men's Own Responsibility

My landing was smoother this time. Or rather, it was a splashdown. That is, I teleported into the waters surrounding Bermuda Lemuria. The warm ocean greeted me so gently that I felt a sudden urge to swim to shore like a regular homo sapien. Thankfully I'd had the foresight to take off my shoes back in the woods near Grodno.

Someone called out to me from behind. "Yan! Welcome home!"

I turned and saw the wet, tanned face of a woman not far from me. Her voice was low and velvety, with a slight rasp. She smiled, flashing perfectly straight white teeth, then disappeared beneath the turquoise wave that rolled toward me, only to resurface so close that her nubile bare chest brushed against my inconveniently clothed body for just a moment.

Her dark, sagacious eyes pierced straight through me, instantly recognising how inflamed I was with a passion for an innocent girl, how tense I was from forced abstinence, and how much I longed for a woman's touch. Cassandra — that's her name — pulled back, smiled again, and gave me a playful, inviting glance before nodding toward the shore, beckoning me to follow her.

She swam toward the beach silently, without splashes, as though she were part of the water itself. She kicked her legs wide, teasing me even more. Her powerful energy drew me into a dangerous, unbearably tempting trap, and if I had been naked too, everything might have happened right there in the water.

Cassandra was the younger sister of Mina, my father's girlfriend. She was born on Earth, before the mass migration to New Lemuria, and rarely visited the new planet — only for the Unities. I had never encountered this mysterious woman one-on-one.

Most of the homo liberatus who remained in the Bermuda colony refused to believe in Earth's doom and were in no hurry to leave it. Cassandra would know better, I guess — she was a prophet, after all. She had been given her name in infancy, long before her parents could have guessed that she would grow up to be one of Lemuria's most powerful oracles and one of those who had predicted my mission. Mina had told me all this. She loved talking about her sister.

Even in this place, hidden from so-called civilization, the water reeked of oil and something else utterly incompatible with Nature. It was simply unbearable! One must truly love Earth to stay here…

My pants, shirt, and wool sweater borrowed from Polina's father's closet were heavy with water. When I stepped onto the beach, the clothes clung to me, dripping salty streams into the sand. I stripped them off as quickly as I could.

Cassandra, on the other hand, had gone into the water already nude, deliberately, just to greet me that way. That was how accurately she had foreseen the future!

Homo liberatus generally dislike wearing clothes. Naturally. They only reluctantly cover their nudity when interacting with humans, either donning appropriate human attire for the occasion or opting for light tunics. Two such tunics awaited us on the beach under a palm tree, but my new acquaintance was in no hurry to cover her beautiful body of a flourishing, two-hundred-year-old Lemurian who would appear to be about thirty in the eyes of a homo sapien. Cassandra turned this way and that, ostensibly to dry her smooth, sun-kissed skin, but in truth, this display was blatantly intended for me, a show that delighted both actress and audience alike. Her sculpted figure glistened with droplets of ocean water shimmering in the sunlight. Her prominent, upturned nipples hardened under the gentle breeze, and her flawless long legs parted slightly, beckoning, seducing. It would have been easy to surmise her desire to conceive even if she hadn't revealed this part of her thoughts to me, *"Be brave, my hero!"*

Resisting was impossible as well as unnecessary, and I set aside the questions swarming in my mind for later. After admiring her from a distance for a few minutes, I approached Cassandra and stood close. My hands slid over her, from her long neck to her exquisite breasts, somehow both firm and soft, down to her flat stomach. Finally, my fingers brushed the damp cleft between her smooth thighs. Her body responded to my touch like obedient clay under a sculptor's hands, yielding to my desires. That is the advantage of telepathy when it comes to earthly pleasures. The fact that the seer's thoughts were not accessible to me only teased and ignited my passion further. We did it on the beach, in the waves, and even in the air. I lost track of time, receiving a magnificent welcome to the Bermuda colony.

To repeatedly experience the euphoria of embrace and the bliss of emptiness! To indulge in carnal pleasures and taste the essence of life — this is why Lemurians refuse to transition to purely astral existence! That, indeed, would be mere existence, not *life*! And we rarely deny ourselves this joy, gifted by Nature itself. For homo liberatus, such matters are simple, unlike for humans, at least until the question of having children arises.

At the very beginning of both my mission and life path, I was not ready to become a father, and I especially did not fancy the idea of giving a child to a woman whom I could never fully understand. In turn, Cassandra made it clear that this would happen eventually, although she wasn't in a hurry. That first time, she sought closeness not only out of a desire to conceive from a messiah. Thanks to her gift, the prophetess saw in me a rare hero among Lemurian men and admired me for deeds yet to be accomplished. Her admiration stirred a strange feeling in me, as if I were floating in weightlessness, without any point of support.

I already mentioned that foresight is not my strongest trait. Perhaps it runs in the family, as my father often complains about the same problem. So, I had no choice but to trust the expert, especially one so pleasing to both the eye and touch. Cassandra revealed that she foresaw many trials on my path but was certain I would overcome them. Given this extraordinary woman's proven talent for prophecy, I had good reason to believe in success. Thus, my encounter with her not only entertained but also encouraged me.

Finally done with the pressing matters at hand, we teleported to a plateau used by Lemurians for group meditations. On the island, which my people had called home for thousands of years and upon which I had arrived for the first time, decisions were made in the Minor Unity. Such autonomy was necessary since homo liberatus did not live in Bermuda Lemuria alone, even though they considered themselves its rightful rulers in the sense that here, and only here, they led their lifestyle openly.

The Unity Plateau sat at a commanding height. From there, the entire island was visible. It was surrounded by a natural defence: sharp, bladelike rock fragments jutting out of the ocean as if deliberately placed by Nature to protect my people from unwanted guests. Within this bastion of massive cliffs, sheer drops, and dangerous reefs, Bermuda Lemuria was overgrown with tropical jungles teeming with the lively hum of untamed Nature. Only three tiny strips of pristine sandy beaches were visible from the plateau. On the horizon, far away, only a sharp eye could make out the silhouettes of other distant islands. Yet no one noticed our land, thanks to its camouflaging energy dome. To homo sapiens, Bermuda Lemuria seemed to merge with the ocean.

As soon as our feet touched the warm stones of the plateau, Lemurians in green tunics began appearing from the air. They materialised in singles, in pairs, and occasionally in small groups. About fifty of them arrived in total. As friendly telepathic greetings flowed into my mind like smooth, clear streams, the harmony of the tropical Nature's chorus remained undisturbed.

The island was home to a handful of homo liberatus who fiercely loved Earth and had no desire to leave it. The inhabitants of the Bermuda colony dreamed of restoring *the balance.* They often appeared among humans, inspiring them to preserve and extend life by following Nature. Lemurians sought and often found ways to educate the most capable homo sapiens, believing that only by becoming stronger as a species could humanity free itself from the true threat to its existence, the threat born from fear. Unfortunately, the peaceful path of self-development is slow, while energy parasites — vampires — act swiftly and ruthlessly. They push more and more technologies that weaken homo sapiens, pulling humanity further from Nature and deeper into a cage of fear that turns people into slaves.

That's why they had long awaited my arrival. Despite my preoccupation with the still-unsuccessful search for a vampire, the meeting with the Bermuda Lemurians filled me with hope.

Cassandra raised her hand, demanding attention, and, without opening her lips, addressed her companions. "Friends, we are all well aware of the important and difficult mission foretold for Yan, son of Simon. There are very few of us left on this planet. Why? Why do we refuse the easy path of simply fleeing to New Lemuria, where there are no destructive consequences of the fear-born 'civilization' of homo sapiens? You know the answer: we refuse to abandon our home. We will not leave Earth's Nature to the mercy of vampires. And now, he, our hope for restoring balance on this planet, is finally here, at the beginning of a path none of us has agreed to take until now. And Yan needs our help."

"Depends on what kind of help!" several homo liberatus thought warily. None of them would want to enter any kind of war, even if the enemy were a spawn of hell itself. Cassandra

smirked. “No one can force you to kill. Killing is equivalent to suicide and Nature has never repealed that law for anyone. Yan merely needs information.” With her gaze, she signalled that it was my turn.

“Many of you travel to different parts of the world. Perhaps someone has seen this person,” I said, visualising the portrait of a homo sapien with yellow-hazel and blue eyes, drawn from the memories of the museum director and Aleksandr Zhelobkovich. “Witnesses of Nazi crimes in Belarus, instead of giving me the details I need, recall only this face, which they saw about thirty years ago.”

“Hypnosis,” the Unity guessed in unison.

“Yes,” I confirmed. “Apparently, this man is the key to starting the mission, but I don’t know who he is.”

Unfortunately, I couldn’t find a matching face in the Lemurians' memory, although… Wait! This could be it! Or maybe not? I met the thoughtful black eyes of a homo liberatus named Indo. He smiled in response, shook his impressive mane of straight black hair streaked with grey, and approached me. The others, without any formalities, dissolved into the transparent ocean breeze.

“Why is the memory so faint?” I asked Indo. “And fragmented. Strange… The image is very unclear and I’m not even sure if it’s the one I need.”

“It’s not my memory,” Indo replied, curling his lips. “I glimpsed it accidentally, many years ago.” He sighed. “Come on. You’ll have to meet its owner.” We teleported to the island’s interior, though my companion seemingly lacked enthusiasm for the upcoming encounter.

It wasn’t only homo liberatus that lived on Bermuda Lemuria. Indo and I arrived at a small village nestled in a valley overgrown with dense jungle. It was a real village, consisting of handmade huts. Indo knocked on one of the houses. There was no answer, but we heard a wooden object falling inside. Indo cautiously pressed his ear to the door but then suddenly changed his expression, shouted, “Follow me!” and vanished through the wall.

Inside the hut, we saw a homo sapien hanging by the neck from a rope tied to a crossbeam under the ceiling. His legs twitched convulsively. I was so stunned that I froze, wasting precious seconds, while Indo, more experienced in dealing with humans, quickly grabbed the man's legs and lifted him to relieve the pressure on his throat.

“Cut the rope! What are you waiting for?” my companion roared. This feverish outburst, coming from the quiet, introspective Lemurian who had seen much in over four hundred years, was so unexpected that it startled me even more. Finally regaining my senses and realising it was a matter of life and death, I overcame gravity, reached the ceiling, and began to untie the tight knot with my fingers, human style.

“Knife on the table!” Indo barked again.

By that point, the rope had already given way, and our hapless suicidal friend fell heavily to the floor. Indo began reviving the old man’s breathing, while I approached the table and picked up what was called a “knife.” It was a sharp metal blade set in a wooden handle, evidently made long ago, perhaps during its owner’s time on the continent. I didn’t recall ever seeing such a tool before, at least not during my brief stay on Earth. Of course, if I dug into childhood memories, I would remember my mother using knives for cooking, but I had completely forgotten about this human invention in New Lemuria. Now, I was just dumbfounded at the sight of a living being trying to end its own life voluntarily — an act unthinkable for any creature of Nature except homo sapiens. I was so astonished that I failed to use either the unfamiliar tool or a more practical method — burning the rope with a burst of energy. Instead, I followed my human instinct.

"Simon will have a good laugh at this!" flashed through my mind.

The old man we had saved, meanwhile, regained consciousness. He was sullen, sitting silently on the floor, and blocking our attempts to hear or see what he was thinking — and quite successfully, I may add!

"How is he doing that?" I asked Indo silently. *"He's just a homo sapien!"*

"Oh, that's an interesting story," my companion replied telepathically and then spoke aloud, "You see, a long time ago, the Lemurians decided not to let anyone who accidentally landed on this island during shipwrecks or plane crashes leave, as discovering our last refuge on Earth posed a risk. Unfortunately, we must keep them here against their will." Indo glanced sympathetically at the sullen man staring at the floor. "But we always invite these stranded homo sapiens to become part of our world. We offer them training in everything that makes us fearless and free. Not everyone achieves the same results, but they do improve. These people grow more self-aware and gain confidence. Some even begin to feel a stronger connection to us than to their own kind.

"Anyone who masters teleportation well enough to return to the mainland is free to leave the island. As they say, saving a drowning man is the responsibility of the drowning man himself. In the past, many succeeded. They returned to humanity as enlightened teachers. But in the last hundred years, no homo sapien has managed to leave. Technical progress has made them lazy, replacing their natural abilities and eroding their belief in them.

"Of course, those stuck here do learn some things. Telepathy is fairly easy to master, and blocking access to one's thoughts is even easier. And that," Indo concluded, pointing at the one who just tried to take his own life, "is the only thing this poor man has managed to learn." Then, addressing him reproachfully in the man's native language, Indo asked, "What were you thinking, Jim?"

"I can't take it anymore," the man replied grimly. "I'm sick of you and your enlightened ones. Sick and tired!"

"Why don't you work on it yourself? There is a way back."

"A way for who? Certainly not me. I have only one path, and that is straight to the grave." He hopelessly jabbed a finger into the air. "Maybe, just maybe, I'll see my family there someday..."

"He has a wife and two daughters. He misses them," Indo explained to me, and then said to Jim, "We need your help, Jim."

"Oh really?" the old man snapped angrily. "Since when does a worthless louse like me help the almighty Liberatus?"

It wasn't a promising start, but wise Indo continued in his peaceful tone. "We just need your memories about this man," he said, projecting a transparent image of a military man with strange eyes into the air.

Jim smirked, squinted, and then responded. "Yeah, I met this *comrade* once..."

"Then let us in. And you won't have to explain. We'll just take a look at what interests us," our negotiator encouraged him enthusiastically.

But the homo sapien knew how to bargain better than we did. "No way," he snapped with a hateful glare in his impenetrable eyes, and the defiance of a man with nothing to lose. "I won't give you anything for free!"

His mental defence was like armour. It might have been the only skill Jim had learned on Bermuda Lemuria, but he had mastered it well. What's more, the spark of excitement awakened in the old pilot by this confrontation seemed to strengthen his energy.

"What do you want then?" I asked impatiently. There was an odd irony in the fact that the only barrier between me and my only lead was this frail, bony eighty-year-old homo sapien with a will of steel. I could have tried harder and broken through his defences, but that would have hurt this poor guy whose only crime was resenting the Lemurians for a life spent far from his loved ones. That much was clear even without telepathy. I pitied Jim.

"I want to go home and spend the rest of my days with my family," he said quietly.

"His wife is alive," Indo explained and, torn by doubt, continued telepathically, *"We've never allowed anyone who couldn't teleport on their own to leave the island. What do you think, Yan? Is this hypnotist hunt truly worth making an exception?"*

"Most likely, the outcome will determine whether I ever find that vampire. Whether the mission even starts," I replied gloomily, understanding the dilemma this posed for the Bermuda Lemurians. Indo, as if my despair had become his, felt the weight of possibly losing even this thin thread of a lead.

Without saying goodbye to Jim, we teleported back to the plateau where we had met with homo liberatus of Bermuda Lemuria an hour earlier. They were already gathered.

"You've caused quite a stir!" Cassandra laughed. "I can't remember us ever meeting twice in one day!"

"Ah, youth!" grumbled the oldest Lemurian on Earth, a six-hundred-and-eighty-two-year-old man who had aged remarkably well despite spending nearly all his time on this polluted planet. "We used to meet twice a day all the time when the Europeans discovered America. We kept wondering what to do about them."

"What do you think, Uncle Peresvet?" Cassandra asked, pretending not to know how the meeting would end.

"What can I say, dear?" The old homo liberatus sat on a stone. "To homo sapiens, Jim is as old as I am, and old men just want to go home. That's why I sit here, on Earth, even though teleporting to the Great Unity" — he gestured at the sky — "gets harder every time. And every time I come back, I think the next call will find me buried inside Earth. I want to die at home," Peresvet said, smiling sadly, revealing perfect white teeth. "How can this little man harm us? Let Jim go. It'll be a good deed that will also help our boy."

I was the one he had called "boy," and I did feel as happy as a child, both for myself and for Jim.

We had been gone from Jim's hut for about an hour. "I hope he didn't try to hang himself again!" I worried.

"No way," Indo smiled. "I think he spent the hour living on hope."

We teleported back to Jim and found the old homo sapien sitting motionless at the table, his head resting on his arms. "Well, my friend, rejoice. You're going home!"

Jim slowly raised tear-filled eyes to us. The old man had spent nearly forty years on Bermuda Lemuria and knew that homo liberatus never lied. His chin trembled.

In an instant, his mind opened completely, turning inside out. We were struck by everything this gloomy man had suffered in our earthly paradise, everything he had hidden behind his mental defences out of sheer human pride: the anger of a helpless soul, longing for loved ones, endless loneliness among "wizards" who never became his own. Hope. Hope that had endured for decades, and, finally, despair and meaninglessness that had quietly torn his heart to shreds.

These feelings, painfully familiar to me due to my longing for my mother but alien to the homo liberatus, overwhelmed Indo. He sat beside the old man, placed a hand on his shoulder.

"Forgive us, Jim. I didn't know how much you had suffered all this time… Let us see what we're looking for, and you'll go home to your family."

Forty-five minutes later, Jim stood in a tiny apartment on the outskirts of Jacksonville. His wife, Julia, engrossed in yet another soap opera to keep her fading mind occupied, rose shakily from her large armchair, gasping for air as she stared at her much-aged but resurrected husband.

Chapter 6. Breaking Bad

It turned out our suspected hypnotist had ties to the Soviet state security service. That was the only thing we managed to learn from Jim, and even that, he knew purely by coincidence. Before the crash over Bermuda Lemuria, Jim worked as a pilot on international flights. Once, shortly after World War II, his plane stayed for several days at one of Moscow's airports, and the crew members were housed at the Intourist Hotel, where they were under constant KGB surveillance.

Junior Lieutenant Pavel Pilatov — that's what the ID shown to Jim had said — was one of the low-ranking officers assigned to monitor the Americans. An unremarkable appearance is an advantage for a security officer, but this face was unforgettable because of its eerie eyes: one was yellowish-brown, and the other was pale blue, almost colourless. Under such a piercing gaze, keeping secrets was impossible, but fortunately, a commercial airline pilot had no secrets to keep. Still, when Jim recalled those paralysing eyes, a shiver ran down his spine. It was clear we were indeed talking about our subject.

"What good will knowing his name do you?" Indo asked me with a note of disappointment in his voice. "How do you plan to find this Pilatov?"

I hesitated to answer, but at that moment, Cassandra materialised and interrupted us with the air of someone who had been part of the conversation from the very beginning. "This Pilatov worked in the state security system, and they always keep everything on *pa-per*. We just need to get to where those papers are stored, and we'll easily find out where your python is hiding. Simple!" the seer concluded, putting her delicate hands into the shape of a dish. "And I'm coming with you."

I didn't know whether to be happy or upset about this declaration. Of course, going into unfamiliar territory with someone I trusted was far better than going alone, but

Cassandra… Being near her made me feel uneasy, as I couldn't hear what was going on in her mind.

Oracles are the only homo liberatus who can block their thoughts from others. Their visions must remain hidden. After all, anyone who receives a reliable prediction about the future inevitably alters that future, whether intentionally or not. It's easy to imagine the chaos that would ensue among both the sapiens and the liberatus if everyone could see through the eyes of the oracles. Thus, seers bravely bear the burden of their knowledge alone and share insights about future trials only in rare, truly critical situations. Even their everyday thoughts, unrelated to foresight, are revealed at their discretion. Yet homo liberatus trust oracles like Cassandra without question, convinced that Nature has endowed them with absolute wisdom…

Meanwhile, this enigmatic woman read my confusion easily, amusing herself and teasing me. In the fragmented thoughts she allowed me to glimpse, I could discern nothing but a thirst for adventure. One way or another, nobody else volunteered to join the dodgy cause I had planned, so I had no choice but to rely on the company offered.

***

Finding the right place in Moscow wasn't difficult.

"Well, my hero, where shall we begin?" Cassandra asked cheerfully.

From the corner of the square, we gazed at a massive yellow brick box, its rows of windows gleaming in the sunlight. Even from the outside, it was clear: this building on Lubyanskaya Street could easily house the entire Lemurian race. Moreover, it was divided into hundreds of tiny boxlike rooms.

"And that's just the facade!" my companion commented. "They have a whole city dedicated to state security behind this building. A city born of fear turned into a city that inspires fear. Humans are always like that."

Despite her joking tone, neither of us underestimated the role this stone fortress played in the lives of too many homo sapiens. Naively — as I later realised — I thought, "*Why can't we just ask?*"

"Of course, you can always ask," the seeress replied with a mocking smile. "But who exactly do you plan to ask?"

"Let's go inside and have a look," I suggested.

We entered like ordinary people, through the double doors at the centre of the building's facade. Cassandra, however, insisted that I remain unseen.

We had arrived in Moscow the night before to scout the area and prepare. The Lemurian lady had shamelessly borrowed a business outfit from a foreign currency store and now she wore an incredibly tight black skirt that stopped just above her knees, a perfectly tailored fitted jacket, and a white silk blouse unbuttoned just enough to reveal the faintest hint of cleavage. Her slender legs, wrapped in smooth, dark-beige stockings that matched her tanned skin, ended in black stiletto heels so high and thin that it was hard to believe anyone could stand in them.

In this outfit, with her glossy raven-black hair cascading over her shoulders, my companion looked so stunning that it took my breath away. I couldn't help but wonder how she managed to balance in those shoes. Yet, she moved with surprising confidence, as though she'd spent years striding through human-made plazas and corridors on her toes.

"Beauty demands sacrifice!" Cassandra quipped.

Since arguing was pointless, I agreed that she would have a much easier time talking to the predominantly male occupants of the building without me as her shadow. Invisible, I followed her across the threshold.

Inside the building, right by the entrance, stood a man in a black suit. He monitored the comings and goings. It was his job.

Judging by his demeanour, his thoughts rarely ventured outside the mental box in which they were locked as securely as the documents we were after.

"Good afternoon!" Cassandra greeted him, flashing a disarming smile with ruby-red lips. "We'd like to meet with Pavel Pilatov."

"Who's that?" the guard asked, unable to stop himself from glancing at the parting neckline of her silk blouse.

"He's an employee of the KGB."

The young man's eyes snapped back to Cassandra's face. Blinking in disbelief, he thought, *"Did you just fall off the moon? Pretty but clueless. Do you even realise how many people work here?"*

Still, he tried to remain polite. "You need the personnel department. That's a different building."

Relieved to be rid of the unwanted inquiry, he gave Cassandra an address nearby, and we headed there. I followed her, still invisible.

In the other building, a guard who looked remarkably like the first one — wearing the same black suit and flashing the same sideways glance at the lady's blouse — asked, "What is your inquiry about?"

"It's personal," Cassandra replied with a sweet smile, batting her eyelashes as she gazed into his eyes.

"Miss, we don't provide information on personal matters here," he said. Though he'd also labelled her a pretty fool, he began to suspect some sort of trick. "You need an official request from the organisation you represent."

"I don't represent anyone..." Cassandra replied, feigning disappointment. "So what am I supposed to do now?"

And with deliberate defiance, she strode gracefully past him into the lobby, clearly looking for trouble.

The guard froze for a second, then shouted into his radio, "Intrusion!"

Several men, looking strikingly similar in their black suits, swarmed my companion in a tight circle, from which Cassandra vanished. She teleported to the opposite corner of the lobby next to me. Remaining invisible, the beautiful hooligan let out a loud, exaggerated laugh that echoed through the lobby, leaving the guards glancing nervously around. Then, she showed herself, waved at them with a friendly smile, and disappeared again. The men scattered, searching every corner, but by then, we had already moved upstairs and begun combing the large building's floors for clues.

"You've lost your mind!" I scolded my impulsive friend. "Now they'll double their vigilance, and it'll be harder for us!"

"Let them triple it for all I care! What can those pathetic creatures do to us?" Cassandra retorted defiantly, then added with deep disdain, "Guards! A human occupation born entirely out of fear. Just look at those big guys! How can anyone waste their already short lives standing by a door 'just in case'?"

It was true that the guards' vigilance posed no real obstacle to us. The thought that homo sapiens could spend half their lives guarding doors struck me like a bolt of lightning. It's hard for someone devoid of fear to grasp a system built entirely on fear, and Cassandra only added fuel to the fire.

"If you're going to fight the energy parasites," she said, "you need to understand just how much human behaviour is driven by their need to shield themselves from threats — threats that are more often imagined than real."

She was right, of course, and it seemed only logical to get better acquainted with one of humanity's most powerful security systems on Earth. So, we decided to split up not only to speed up the search but also to give me a chance to look around and draw my own conclusions.

The building's upper floors swallowed me in the tense silence of endless corridors lined with closed doors. Behind each door sat people whose job, in one way or another, was to protect the country's peace. Judging by the number of offices, they had plenty of work. As I moved through the hallways, I caught snatches of conversations and thoughts through the doors.

Changes were brewing in the country. Despite the outward stillness, the kaleidoscope of opinions and energies driving this fortress of security lacked the order every system needs. Instead, it buzzed with a kind of chaos, an agitation born from the long-awaited excitement of bored minds. People's thoughts ricocheted between extremes: from alertness to curiosity, from distrust to hope, from cautious restraint to a readiness to sprint toward a distant, blurry, mirage-like vision of something new, and therefore, seemingly beautiful.

"This is big! It's about time we updated the system!"

"But is it truly a good thing?"

"Andropov had reforms in mind too but he didn't live to see them... Does that mean he saw the need for change?"*

"Democratization is good, in theory. And openness that he *calls "glasnost..." People do want to speak out. Who would know it better than us? But how are we supposed to work with all of that?"*

*"Speeding up technological progress, right? One guy already tried to catch up with and overtake America**, and what was the result? We almost blew ourselves up..."*

"What about foreign policy? Where's he *going to draw the line?"*

No one fully understood the purpose of the changes being broadcast on every screen. Some even suppressed the suspicion that these changes were designed to destabilise the very system they were guarding. Yet, out of fear of being reprimanded for not following orders, they just continued to do their jobs as best they could, for now...

Trying to sneak behind every door would've been pointless and taken forever. Besides, after visiting just a couple of offices, I began to feel how contagious the overall excitement was. It started draining my energy, which immediately fed into the powerful current rushing somewhere beyond the building. Becoming a donor to some unknown force was not part of my plan.

Instead of entering more rooms, I began scanning the labels on the doors, trying to guess where I might find information about our hypnotist. One corridor was blocked by a door labelled *Department of Unexplained and Paranormal Phenomena.*

"This must be the place," I thought, knowing that even something as simple as hypnosis was rare and poorly understood among homo sapiens.

Crossing the threshold, I felt a tingling sensation ripple through my body as a premonition of something significant. Yet I decided not to call Cassandra. Her unpredictability and recklessness threw me off-balance, and I thought she could easily ruin everything. Her earlier stunt in the lobby was already the talk of the entire building. The security officers, wound up by uncertainty, were spinning the wildest theories. The last thing I needed was for her to add more chaos to the mix.

A large man in a military uniform sat in a chair behind a massive, long rectangular desk. Three insignias, resembling pentagrams, adorned the epaulettes of his jacket. After listening to a detailed report about the incident at the entrance to the personnel department, he fixed a look of indignation at a stern, well-groomed man in a black suit, not as baggy as those worn by the guards who had tried to catch Cassandra in the lobby.

"What do you mean she disappeared?" the man with the pentagrams asked in frustration. "You must have let her slip away!"

"No, Comrade Colonel, not at all," the head of security said in an effort to defend himself. "I was there in person. Just happened to walk in by chance. We had her surrounded, ten men in a tight ring — and she simply vanished into thin air! And she was laughing too, loudly, wildly even… She disappeared, but the laughter didn't. It echoed from the far end of the lobby, where she reappeared, but only after the laughter! And then she vanished again. It's like witchcraft!"

"All right," the colonel responded. "Let's assume this wasn't some kind of mass hallucination. What do we have?" He rubbed his clean-shaven chin. "A beautiful young woman, presumably of Asian descent, dressed like a foreign diplomat, asked to see a retired former employee of our department, caused a scene in the lobby, disappeared, reappeared on the opposite side of the same room impossibly fast, and then vanished again."

"Exactly," the man in the suit confirmed.

"So, either she hypnotised all of you, or this woman can both turn invisible and teleport. Either way, this falls under our jurisdiction."

He stood, paced the room, then dropped back into his chair.

"If that's the case, she's probably still somewhere in the building."

"Sabotage?" the security chief suggested nervously, his thoughts spiralling toward panic. It was clear that capturing such a skilled infiltrator was impossible. Worse, she could now roam freely through the most secure areas of the building and access the most classified documents.

"Sabotage?" the colonel echoed, weighing the details of the report. "It's possible... But if she were after classified information, she wouldn't have drawn so much attention to herself."

"Then who is she?" The head of security looked at his superior with confusion and a hint of desperation. "What are your orders?"

The colonel, in a playful tone that didn't match his imposing frame, answered loudly, as if speaking to the air:

"Did she ask for Pavel Pilatov?"

The security chief nodded and began to glance nervously around the room.

"Well then, we've got Pilatov's nephew Andrei working in this department. Let him handle his uncle's mess!" The colonel pressed a button on the phone and barked into the receiver. "Major, is Pilatov in?"

"Yes, sir. Just got back from his assignment," came a crisp voice. "He's working on his report."

"Send him here. Now!" The colonel slammed the receiver down and turned to the head of security. "That's it, Vasya. Dismissed! Report immediately if the lady reappears."

"Yes, sir!" The man in the suit exhaled in relief, grateful that someone else would shoulder this headache, and left the office.

Once alone, the colonel rose and walked to the window. He stood there for a while, staring blankly at the glass, where raindrops from a recent drizzle slid lazily downward. For a moment, his thoughts drifted back twenty years, to the time he had attended advanced training courses and first saw the man with one amber-brown eye and the other a chilling, translucent blue.

Pavel Andreevich Pilatov had taught hypnosis and mental self-defence to the most capable and dedicated KGB agents. Sviridov, only a major back then, had no talent for either, though he had diligently studied the theory. He deeply respected his few colleagues with some aptitude, even holding them in secret awe. Pilatov, however, was a master hypnotist, feared not only for his skills but also for his intolerance of nonsense.

I couldn't extract any more details from Colonel Sviridov's stream of consciousness since the morning's bizarre incident was consuming his thoughts, and his memory of the former hypnosis instructor was fleeting. All I gathered was that the man with the strange eyes no longer worked in these halls.

A knock interrupted the colonel's thought. A tall young officer entered. He bore a striking resemblance to Pavel Pilatov as Sviridov remembered him, except for the eyes. Unlike his uncle's uneven eye colour, Andrei's gaze was evenly grey-blue.

Thankfully, it lacked the unnerving intensity and instead seemed tired, even slightly disenchanted.

The young man's features hinted at refinement: a slightly prominent nose with a bump, high cheekbones, dark, almost black eyebrows contrasting with his light blond hair, and a strong jawline with a dimple in his chin. Andrei Pilatov looked masculine without being brutish.

I thought Cassandra might take an interest in this handsome officer. If she decided to focus on him, perhaps she'd leave me alone for a while. The idea was oddly comforting, so I found myself warming up to the thirty-three-year-old man with a sharp posture and a melancholic gaze.

"Did you call for me, Comrade Colonel?" asked the young man with a soft smile, dimples appearing even on his cheeks.

"Hello, Captain. Come in, take a seat," Sviridov said as he returned to his chair. Once Andrei Pilatov had settled on a chair at the long side of the rectangular table, the colonel gestured downward with his index finger, implying the HR department's lobby, and asked with a chuckle, "Heard about today's incident?"

"Who hasn't?" the captain replied, perking up. "It's not every day we see such brazen enemy sabotage right here in this building… I was sure you'd call for me since the saboteur seemed to be looking for Uncle Pasha… uh, sorry, Colonel Pilatov…"

"Saboteur, you say?" the chief responded. "I'm not so sure… And I'm not even certain whether she or *they* aren't present in this very office right now."

"The old man's starting to lose it," thought the captain. "Here? You're joking, right?"

"Maybe I'm joking, maybe not…" Sviridov replied vaguely. "If I'm not joking, then I'm baiting them with you as the bait. That is, I think they'll come for you first. So, report any contact attempts immediately. I'm assigning this case to you. If there's even a case, of course. You're dismissed for now."

"Yes, Comrade Colonel."

The young officer stood and headed for the door. Just as his hand touched the handle, Sviridov called after him. "Andryusha, don't wave your gun around unless it's absolutely necessary. And call your uncle. Tell him what happened here and warn him to expect visitors."

"Will do, Fyodor Sergeyevich!" snapped Andrei Pilatov, thinking, *"Andropov's departure hit you hard!"*

By the time the nephew of the retired hypnotist left his boss's office, I had already plucked from his thoughts the directions to the KGB dormitory, where the captain kept a small room, the only place he wanted to be after his exhausting and somewhat pointless assignment. Now, he could not escape me. I intended to focus on him closely, but first, I wanted to linger a bit longer with Sviridov. I was curious how the colonel, who lacked heightened sensitivity or even basic telepathic skills, had pieced together such an accurate picture of an incident that was highly improbable from the perspective of the ordinary, stereotype-bound homo sapiens.

This restless man had joined the Secret Service for "real life." He never regretted his choice, despite the dangers he faced, and the occasionally absurd, downright foolish directives handed down from above. Sviridov had a sharp, open, and critical mind. He valued common sense. For someone without access to the consciousness of others, common sense was based solely on personally lived or directly observed experiences. As the Head of the Department for Unexplained and Paranormal Phenomena, Sviridov had grown accustomed to trusting his eyes and facts. Yet, during his tenure, he had seen and learned things that proved the world was far more astonishing and diverse than it appeared to those little figures outside the window lining up patiently for sausage, scurrying to and from work like windup toys, fearing the unknown, and closing their eyes to the inexplicable.

For over twenty years, Fyodor Sergeyevich had tried to turn the inexplicable to the advantage of the Soviet state. He had travelled not the whole world, perhaps, but certainly to its most mysterious corners. Early in his career, shortly after joining the KGB, Sviridov, then a lieutenant, was sent to Tibet. It wasn't an operational assignment; his task was to assess the potential of the spiritual and physical practices, the mastering of which monks dedicated their lives. The leadership's idea was to borrow the monks' knowledge and skills and train the agency's most capable operatives. Sviridov's job was to merely gather information, which was enough to make him realise the limitless potential of the human mind and body. This experience fundamentally shaped his view of common sense, setting it apart from Captain Pilatov's, who worked with ordinary Soviet citizens, the people who got excited over UFO stories but weren't eager to truly believe in miracles. Sviridov, however, knew the world was much more complex and poorly understood. To him, this was indisputable.

So, the colonel did not doubt the reality of the incident in the HR lobby, although he was unsure of whether the troublemaking woman was an alien or an enemy agent. Contact with extraterrestrial civilizations was gradually moving out of the realm of myth, and the colonel sincerely hoped she was an alien. It would leave some hope for a peaceful resolution since signals received from space hadn't caused any catastrophic consequences for Earth so far. On the contrary, the appearance of a foreign spy capable of turning invisible and teleporting certainly boded ill. Unfortunately, the latter theory seemed more realistic. He had no third option — Sviridov lacked the imagination for it.

Finally, having satisfied my curiosity, I left the colonel's office and summoned Cassandra. She teasingly replied, *"Why don't you come to me instead?"*

I obeyed and found myself in the basement of yet another building, the third one that day. The empty room where the thrill-seeker awaited me had cold stone walls, a low vaulted ceiling, and a locked iron door. In the corner stood a small but sturdy wooden table accompanied by two plain, squat chairs.

A half-spherical glass fixture hung overhead without a bulb. Without our ability to see in the dark, we would have had to grope our way around. The room hadn't been opened in at least twenty years, yet there was little dust, for which there was no source except a small ventilation hole near the ceiling.

This basement had once been used for interrogations and executions, often and eagerly. Even after all those years, it was steeped in its victimes' despair and the triumph of well-fed vampires, the sickening vibrations reminiscent of my childhood memories of burning Khatyn. I would never have chosen this room for a rendezvous.

"What's this charming place?" I asked Cassandra, who was sitting on the table, swinging her legs casually.

"You could call it a vampire museum," she replied in a tour guide's tone. "This is where political prisoners were interrogated and sometimes executed. Back in Stalin's time. Naturally, only vampires could handle that job."

"Why are we here?" I asked, shivering involuntarily.

"First, for your general education. Second, for your resistance training against negative energy. And finally, no one will disturb us here."

Cassandra stretched her leg, showing smooth stockings and elegant yet uncomfortable black heels. Unbuttoning her white blouse, she revealed what the guards in their dull black suits had failed to see.

"We're having a boy," the seductive seer purred dreamily. Raising a tiny finger to silence objections, she added, "You owe me. Without my creative approach, you'd still be chasing leads on Pilatov. Now he's in your pocket and sure to help you."

"So, you staged that performance in the foyer on purpose?" I exclaimed, pulling Cassandra close and feeling her quickened breath, heavy with anticipation, against my cheek. Gripping her sculpted shoulders, hidden beneath the smooth silk of her sleeves, I whispered demandingly into her ear, "Then why didn't I hear your thoughts or feel you blocking them?"

"Ahhh…" she purred smugly, her lips brushing against mine. "I can do that too! Some important actions must be spontaneous!"

Cassandra's eyes sparkled in the darkness with a defiant coquetry. She nudged me half a metre away, swept her ever-sea-scented hair over one shoulder, and slowly rolled up her skirt to slip off a delicate stocking. I glimpsed her light lace lingerie, reached out, and brushed my fingers over the soft, smooth fabric that concealed the most enticing part of her, a part that so desperately longed to take me in.

In the basement, thick with the air of human suffering, all I could think about now was the unbearable desire to possess that wild, primal force hidden beneath the alluring shell sculpted by human civilization! Lemurian women, when they deign to dress at all, wear short, light tunics. When the desire is mutual, their bodies are easily accessible, and that's wonderful too, but this ease was something I was used to.

The way Cassandra's "spy" outfit slowly slid off her body as she arched herself seductively on the black table in what used to be the room of death ignited a sharp, unfamiliar, and burning-to-the-limit passion within me. Cassandra knew how to be persuasive. After all, she was a seer. She knew exactly what she was doing. A boy? Let it be a boy…

---

*Yuri Andropov (1914–1984) – Chairman of the Presidium of the Supreme Soviet of the USSR (1983–1984) and Chairman of the KGB of the USSR (1967–1982)

**“Catch up and overrun America” is the famous slogan offered by Nikita Khrushchev to encourage the development of the USSR during the Cold War period.

Chapter 7. The Nephew

The long-awaited evening had finally arrived. In the KGB dormitory room, an old black-and-white television was playing. From the screen, a man with a purple-brown birthmark — like smudged dried ink — on his bald head was persuading the citizens of the largest country on Earth that they had all been living the wrong way for almost seventy years. He argued that they continued to economically lag the West due to rigid governance and the Iron Curtain. He claimed that by accelerating technologies, discussing problems openly, and transferring the service sector to small businesses, Soviet society still had a chance to improve the quality of life and build communism within the foreseeable future.

"Yes, but no," Captain Pilatov thought, resting his large bare feet on the back of an old but sturdy couch. On the floor under his dangling hand stood a half-empty beer bottle, and a paperback book lay nearby. Andrei was trying to relax. His return from the annoying trip that morning was followed by a strange day at Lubyanka. Reading had quickly tired him, but Pilatov struggled to tear himself away from the television, which was consuming his energy slowly but relentlessly. Despite his irritation over yet another poorly played football match, he couldn't help but keep watching. The beer had made him a bit drowsy, but the speech of the new general secretary wouldn't let him fall asleep. The voice from the television gripped his brain like a vise.

"Does anyone still believe this nonsense about building communism? It's hard enough to just hold on to socialism... Is it really about technological progress, or improving the service sector, or a better standard of living? Or even reducing drunkenness? Well, yes, vodka has ruined many good people, and not just in the USSR..."

Captain Pilatov took another sip of beer from the bottle.

"How much longer can we dream about this utopia?" he thought. "*Communism is for perfect people, the honest ones, who love their neighbours as themselves. And what do we have here? Everyone's trying to grab as much as they can, and if they must cheat someone to do it, that's even more fun. It's as if the cheater looks smarter than the deceived and even gets a self-esteem boost as a benefit. What love are we talking about? It's obvious, especially in our line of work. Just last week, we busted a 'healer' who was scamming people, especially the wives of high-ranking officials. This healer... Such a self-content lady with no hint of remorse! She turned out to be a retired actress, a failed one, from some backwater... And that's your small business in the service sector!"*

Lost in thought, Pilatov finally tuned out the insatiable television and began to relax.

"To build communism, people's honesty must be absolute and universal, and there must be no liars or fraudsters anywhere, either on this side of the Berlin Wall or on the other, or across the ocean. Because even if we miraculously manage to follow the moral code and build a perfect communist society here, they'll devour us immediately and tear us apart, since they're not bound by any moral code. They're the sharks of capitalism!

"An honest person can remain honest only among trustworthy people. There is no other way. How does no one see this? And how many people can truly be trusted? Our service is living proof of that. Diplomats smile at each other and shake hands while their countries' spies snoop around, probe for weak spots, and test for radiation, searching forests for nuclear weapons. They spy on us and we spy on them. We deceive each other in the name of security. So, do we deceive out of fear? Even the most honest people break down in this den of self-preservation and start manoeuvring and scheming under the pretence of self-defence. Blaming them for this would just be... dishonest." Andrei snorted in grim amusement.

"Of course, making 'from each according to his ability, to each according to his needs' a reality would be great," he continued. "But first, we need to learn to distinguish needs from 'wants.' A person doesn't need much: a sandwich after work, a beer, and a warm place to sleep — that's about it. Desires, on the other hand, are limitless! As soon as we learn about something good, we want to have it or try it right away. Insatiable human greed is communism's main enemy. And people betray their country because of the same greed... We catch 'moles' every year, but few of them are ideologically driven. Most are recruited because they dream of a rich life. They dig and dig under the system, flawed as it may be, but built with the sweat and blood of honest people. They sell the country off piece by piece, pocketing the rewards. In the end, you can't trust anyone. What kind of communism can there be then?

"So, this new guy — what is he up to? Look at how he twists his mouth. Criticising the system, huh? I'm sure you've licked more than a few backsides to climb your way to power and wealth, haven't you, Mikhail Sergeyevich? The question is why did you need this? Why couldn't you just stay in your Stavropol? Was leading the country some kind of life's calling for you? Or do you think you're better at governing than the ones before you?

"We'll see about that, of course, but something tells me you're going to tear the system to shreds with your so-called truths, and the Soviet people will hardly benefit from it. You twist your mouth because you know perfectly well that the bright future and universal happiness, the declared goals of communism, are unattainable. From the very start, they were a dream, an illusion, and only gullible common folk still take those words literally. That's who you're preaching to, because you're a nobody without them.

"Universal happiness is impossible by the very nature of dialectical materialism, which teaches that contradictions are the basis of development. And if happiness is universal, then

there should not be contradictions, or what?" The young man reached out and picked up a book from the floor, its bookmark showing he'd almost finished it. He glanced at the title, *Sigmund Freud: Selected Works*.

"Marx and Engels wrote The Communist Manifesto *before Freud was even born,"* he thought. *So, the first ideologists of communism couldn't possibly have accounted for the psychology of the unconscious. In turn, all three Russian revolutions happened practically in parallel with Freud's discoveries, which the revolutionaries didn't consider back then, so it seems. They fought for universal equality but somehow turned a blind eye to the fact that universal equality requires universal honesty. And for everyone to be honest you'd need the superego, that is, conscience, to completely and irrevocably triumph in every individual. Then, what happens to the frightened and rule-breaking id, may I ask?*

"Even if there's just one liar who refuses to play by the rules, he'll inevitably exploit the honesty of others and profit at their expense like a virus. An insurmountable contradiction! If only Freud had lived fifty years earlier! He could've been Marx's contemporary. Maybe they'd have met in London and agreed that abolishing private property was impossible without mass lobotomies. Selfishness and aggression that come from fear are inseparable from human nature.

"The thing is, Marxism is compelling. It's convincing. You read it and believe communism would truly bring universal happiness! If only it were possible in a society where deceit is an advantage and honesty is a weakness... We need something else, something in between. Some kind of compromise...

Maybe the revolutionaries loved stardust and adventure more than truth if they refused to see such obvious contradictions. And their attempt to move toward communism through terror? All they did was fill people with more fear than before, and how can you build trust, let alone honesty, out of that? Communism and fear are fundamentally incompatible because you can't force honesty or love, for that matter. These are values that can only be voluntary... So, it turns out, the real obstacle to communism isn't the 'enemies of the people' or the capitalists abroad. It's human nature, on both sides of the border. People cling to their belongings and money, hoarding them for a rainy day by any means necessary. And the more they fear, the more they hoard.

"Sure, the poor shout for equality, but only because they hope to gain more from it than they have in their poverty. And the moment they get money — or power — their dream of equality suddenly vanishes, and all they can think about is how to hold on to what they acquired and make it grow. They're afraid. Afraid of losing it. And it's never enough... Maybe, when life becomes better and safer, people stop fearing as much and feel happier?"

"Maybe, darling, but fear never truly leaves homo sapiens. It's encoded in your genes and activates at the slightest hint of danger, even an imaginary one," Cassandra's voice replied from out of nowhere. She loved catching people off guard.

Instantly wide awake, the KGB captain propped himself up on one elbow and scanned the room with bleary eyes. Then he grabbed his half-empty beer from the floor, holding it up as though the female voice might have come from inside the narrow bottleneck.

"Am I so far gone that I'm hearing voices now?" he wondered in confusion, but still asked aloud, "Who's there?"

At last, Cassandra took pity on the young man and revealed herself to him, appearing in her stunning outfit as she lounged on the sofa's armrest by his feet. That is, if you could call appearing out of thin air, especially in front of a communist materialist, an act of pity. Andrei jumped as if stung and pressed himself into the back of the sofa, wishing he could disappear.

"Wh-Who are you?" he stammered, eyes wide in disbelief.

"Oh, great," Cassandra giggled. "Just when the man starts to relax — boo! Horrors come creeping in, right in his own home!"

She pointed coquettishly at herself with a slender finger. "Come on, stop trembling! I'm not a spy or a terrorist. You've been warned about me a thousand times already! Did you think I only turn invisible and teleport during office hours? We're not alone here, by the way. Yan, darling, don't be shy!"

We had been invisibly present in the room since Captain Pilatov had returned home. Cassandra and I had been carefully listening to the KGB officer's stream of consciousness, trying to get an idea of what kind of homo sapien he was. To keep our charge from feeling cornered, I moved to the wooden stool by the dining table, farther from the couch, before revealing myself to him. I felt a little sorry for the guy, but it turned out that Pilatov had excellent reflexes and composure. He recovered surprisingly fast. We knew this because we could no longer hear his thoughts. His special training had paid off, even though Andrei hadn't advanced beyond the basic thought-blocking technique. At least, not yet. With a steely voice, honed no doubt through years of practice, he repeated his question slowly and clearly:

"Who are you, and what do you want?"

I decided it was my turn to speak. Silently urging my overly dominant companion to keep quiet, I replied seriously:

"We are representatives of the homo liberatus race."

"What now?" the KGB captain asked in a tone of amused disbelief. "That's a new one!"

"Actually, homo liberatus is the oldest human race on Earth," Cassandra interjected scornfully.

I raised a warning hand in her direction and continued diplomatically. "I hope you've heard of the sunken islands Atlantis and Lemuria?"

"Atlantis? Sure. Lemuria? Vaguely. Something about it came up in lectures on mythology… Don't tell me you're from Atlantis!" he finished sarcastically.

Despite his work in the Department of Unexplained Phenomena, or perhaps precisely because of it, his distrust toward such stories was off the charts. The turbulent times in his country were only beginning but Pilatov's worldview was already torn between his solid education in dialectical materialism and his superficial knowledge of mental practices. His sarcasm toward paranormal phenomena had developed after encountering numerous fraudsters, whom his department often had to expose and discipline.

Pilatov didn't doubt the existence of "special abilities," as, after all, the Soviet scientists had documented those and then promptly classified the findings. Moreover, he had spent considerable time with his hypnotist uncle, who had worked in the same department until recently. Still, like most ordinary homo sapiens, Pilatov believed that if miracles existed, they did so far from his own life. Only personal experience could change his mind.

"Atlantis is well-known precisely because its population was wiped out," I explained. "Surely I don't need to tell you that myths are spoken aloud, while truths remain unspoken..."

"Let's assume you're right," the captain conceded reluctantly, unable to deny the evidence of our invisibility and teleportation. "So, the Lemurians survived? If the island's gone, where do you live?"

"Good question."

I proceeded to tell him about New and Bermuda Lemuria.

"Oh, so now there are aliens too?" Pilatov said, his voice dripping with sarcasm again.

Cassandra had been rolling her eyes frequently throughout our conversation and now finally snapped.

"Why are you even bothering with this brat?" she blurted out. "We should've just waited for him to call his uncle as instructed and spared ourselves the trouble of explaining everything. Although..." She gave the young man's athletic build an appraising look. "I could think of something more fun to persuade him than a meeting with that old grouch!"

Pilatov stared at her in shock. Flirting was the last thing on his mind. He had never felt so bewildered in his life.

"So why do you need Uncle Pasha?"

"Let's take it step-by-step," I said, motioning toward Cassandra. "First, she's right: we could have 'spied out' your uncle's location without direct contact with you. I'm explaining all this because I need helpers for my mission. You fit the profile."

"A mission? Seriously?" The captain laughed nervously. "And what if I refuse? Or are you planning to hypnotise me?"

"Hypnosis would take too much energy," I said. "Especially since you've been trained to resist it. Is your uncle to be credited for that?" Pilatov nodded. "Whether or not you decide to help is up to you, but only after you've heard me out."

"Fine, go on," the captain said with feigned resignation, though curiosity burned in his eyes.

"Human existence is still ruled by fear," I began. "That wouldn't be so bad if it weren't for the growing number of energy vampires among you. This survival adaptation could push humanity toward an evolutionary dead end."

Pilatov's eyes widened comically before he burst into laughter.

"Vampires? Seriously? The bloodsucking kind?"

"They don't suck blood!" Cassandra responded irritably. "That's just your fairy tales. Humans need to visualise what they can't see, so you dress up natural forces as human figures. You even imagine God in your own image. You're so busy with your fantasies that you miss what's right in front of you!"

I added in a conciliatory tone, "Cassandra's right, vampires don't feed on blood — they drain energy, which ordinary homo sapiens can't perceive directly. Most people feel it: they are in good moods, full of enthusiasm for life when energy is high. On the contrary, fatigue, apathy, or so-called burnout tells you that energy is low. Does that make sense to you, Andrei?"

"Yeah, it sounds familiar," the captain admitted, sighing as he glanced at his unfinished beer.

"For example, today your energy is very low," I stated. "You spent a lot of it investigating some nonsense. And before we arrived, you were trying to restore your depleted strength as all tired people do, but it didn't go very well..." Andrei sighed again and responded with a sad smile of agreement. "I must inform you that, on the contrary, you've continued to lose energy by listening to yet another vampire's speech and washing it down with alcohol, which also weakens you. And you spent the remainder of your time trying to block us from reading your thoughts, even though we're hardly the ones you need protection from. That blockade is almost down now."

Hearing the truth, Andrei frowned. A flicker of anxiety appeared in his eyes. "So, what should I do? How do I restore my energy?"

"I think you already know the answer, considering you're still functioning with a job like this," I replied with a smile.

"Sleep?"

"Yes, that's the most obvious solution. Meditation, direct contact between your body and the earth, clean water and fresh air, preferably among plants, in a forest, park, or at least on a lawn or flowerbed would also help. There are many ways. Or, like this. May I?"

As I began to rise from my chair, Cassandra, who had long been lounging in the corner of the couch, stopped me with a gesture and, unexpectedly serious, declared, "No, Yan, your energy is too precious. And you've already shared some with me today." She winked at me, hinting at our little adventure in the old interrogation room. The memory of that gloomy place made me shudder. It seemed incomprehensible how easily this woman not only shifted between opposite moods but managed to control all those emotional swings too. "I'll do it!" she insisted.

The seer knelt in front of the young man, who had once again sunk into the back of the couch. She reached out, placing her slender fingers on his temples.

"Relax, dear. Everything's fine," the Lemurian oracle said softly.

She ran her palm over the captain's face, directing her energy flow toward him. Andrei gradually relaxed, breathing deeply and steadily.

"Better?"

He opened his eyes and smiled happily.

"Yes, much better!"

Now, Cassandra looked tired. Approaching the window, she turned to me.

"Well, now he's ready to talk. Good luck!"

Her silhouette faded beautifully against the backdrop of twilight, blending into the encroaching night while I stayed behind to convince the KGB captain to assist me in my mission.

---

*Karl Marx and Friedrich Engels are the authors of *The Communist Manifesto*.

**Sigmund Freud is one of the founders of the psychoanalysis theory.

Chapter 8. Energy Vampires and Where to Find Them

"What an unpredictable woman!" Pilatov remarked as soon as Cassandra disappeared.

"Shh. She might still be here!" I laughed, looking up and pressing a finger to my lips with an expression of comical horror. Of course, I knew that having given and taken everything she deemed necessary, tired Cassandra had retreated to the Bermuda colony at the first opportunity as she desperately needed restorative meditation. To be honest, both the captain and I were relieved by the disappearance of the restless Lemurian lady. Cassandra's energy left no room to manoeuvre: like a swirling, turbulent vortex, it inevitably pulled in anyone, regardless of their species.

I realised this shared sense of relief was a good opportunity for he and I to bond, so I seized the moment. "And... maybe we could switch to a first-name basis?"

Andrei nodded, smiled warmly, showing dimples on his cheeks, and finally relaxed, no longer blocking access to his thoughts. Applying that skill had been a struggle for him.

"Tea?" he asked. After my affirmative nod, the captain put his large feet into worn-out slippers, grabbed the kettle that was sitting lonely on the windowsill, and headed to the communal kitchen. He didn't want the neighbours to know about my presence, which was fine by me.

While he busied himself, I decided to have a closer look at the interior of the brick box that Captain Pilatov currently considered his home. Its walls were covered in old beige wallpaper with a pattern of repeating light-brown flowers. Besides a couch and a television, the room contained a small table by the window, which overlooked the neatly swept courtyard of the dormitory. Two rickety stools hid under the table. Both the table and the stools served their seldom-home owner for solitary evening tea sessions before bed. On rare occasions, he dined here instead of in the KGB cafeteria or jotted down non-work-related notes in the notepad now lying flat atop books on the narrow bookshelf.

That bookshelf was perhaps the most remarkable piece of furniture in the captain's dwelling and seemingly the only one that was cared for. It stood proudly, stretching almost to the ceiling, and was packed with volumes of varying thickness. Some books couldn't even fit on the shelves, and like the notepad, perched on top of tightly packed rows of others instead. The arrangement on most shelves was chaotic: evidently, the owner frequently pulled out books and put them back quite hastily. Few of them had any direct relation to the owner's security service work.

Among the middle shelves, alongside several volumes of Freud, Andrei's recent fascination, a collection of Nietzsche's works stood out, marked with paper bookmarks. An entire shelf was occupied by Dostoevsky, famous among Lemurians for his unique interpretation of Christ's teachings. A black-and-white framed photograph partially obscured the spines of several books. In the photo, a woman, who very much resembled Andrei, was seated in the centre, and my new acquaintance, dressed in his cadet uniform, stood behind her next to the hypnotist I had been seeking for so long. A tattered copy of *A Hero of Our Time* by some Lermontov was squeezed behind the photograph. It was tucked into the far corner of the same shelf as an outcast. Its soft cover was frayed. Multiple bookmarks covered in the tiny scribbles of the young man were sticking out of the book.

I threw myself into examining the bookshelf out of boredom while the captain clattered around in the kitchen. He returned with a mixed expression of hope and worry, thinking I might have vanished. Seeing me still seated at the unstable stool by the table, the young officer exhaled, accepting the fact that his life was about to change dramatically.

Andrei set a steaming kettle on the table, and I pointed toward the corner of the shelf.

"Uncle Pasha and my mum," my host stated the obvious, assuming I was interested in the photograph.

"I figured as much," I said. "But what's wrong with that poor book in the corner?"

"Oh, that?" Andrei twisted his lips into an ironic smile. "I loved Lermontov in my youth. Identified myself with Pechorin, some kind of tormented genius adrift, breaking women's hearts…" He faltered, embarrassed by his fantasies from a decade ago, spread his hands, and muttered, "Nonsense. Foolishness. It turns out, there are more important things in life than ridiculous vanity and egocentrism."

Realising this wasn't a topic worth pursuing, I returned to the main issue.

"So, do you believe us now? Are you ready to listen?"

"What exactly is your mission?" Captain Pilatov asked instead of answering. His tone carried no trace of sarcasm this time. "Energy vampires and…?"

"And saving Earth's Nature from them," I replied. "You defend your borders from Americans, Germans, Japanese, practically from the whole world, but beyond those borders are people just like you."

"In theory," Andrei noted doubtfully. He had never been outside his country.

"And in practice too," I countered. "Vampires are the real enemies, *on both sides of the border*."

The captain, recognising the term that had repeatedly surfaced in his internal monologue, looked at me warily. *"Have you heard my thoughts?"*

Shrugging nonchalantly, I nodded. "Vampires steal and hoard energy instead of exchanging and generating it themselves, as Nature intended. They disrupt the balance. They drain resources meant to be shared equally among all living beings on the planet, not just the selected few. I returned to Earth to find a way to protect humanity and Nature from these parasites."

"Got it," Andrei lied with an expression of deep thought. In truth, he hadn't understood a thing from my rather unsubstantiated explanation. The captain sat at the table, resting his face on his palms, trying his hardest to picture vampire behaviour. Inevitably, Andrei's imagination conjured a scene of someone with a sinister face sucking blood from another person's carotid artery which had been punctured by sharp white fangs.

"What your imagination conjures up are merely characters from folklore," I hurried to explain. "The existence of vampires isn't a secret to homo sapiens, as it's impossible to ignore the sense of moral emptiness and physical exhaustion after interacting with them. However, very few people can perceive the movement of subtle matter, so you need visual representations to make sense of such phenomena. To embrace the concept of energy, people associate it with blood. And frankly, that's not far from the truth, because when energy is lacking, vital functions weaken, blood production and circulation slow down, and there is less of it indeed."

"But there are animals that feed on blood," Andrei objected.

"That's true, but humans aren't among them."

"So, are vampires humans? And aren't they immortal?" The captain's genuine surprise and ignorance amused me.

"Of course they're humans, and they're definitely not immortal!" I replied with a laugh. "We believe energy vampirism starts as a bad habit, but it drives its host down a path that ends in degeneration. Vampires will lead humanity, along with themselves, into an evolutionary dead end unless someone stops them."

"How? Will they drain all the energy?" the captain joked.

"The ones you have around currently couldn't manage that much," I smirked. "The number of vampires on Earth is still relatively small but is growing too fast. At this rate, there soon won't be enough people left to drain energy, or to suck it from, as you put it."

"So how exactly do they take it?" the captain pressed. The portion of energy injected by Cassandra had temporarily dispelled his fatigue, and now his mind, poisoned by materialism yet starved for answers, was buzzing with questions like a disturbed beehive. For me, patience was necessary. I had to satisfy Andrei's curiosity to persuade him to help me. After all, curiosity is what makes a person free!

"There are many ways," I said, "but the most important thing is that a vampire's victims don't notice and don't realise that they're being drained. Otherwise, any average homo sapien can stop the theft by resisting it and even putting up a reflective block."

"Really?!" Andrei sat up straight.

"Of course! You already know how to block access to your thoughts, and creating a reflective block is even easier. It just takes a little imagination and self-control."

The disbelief on the captain's face gave way to excitement.

"Can you teach me?" he asked. The special training in the KGB focused primarily on so-called "useful" skills such as interrogating thoughts for espionage, which he had never quite mastered, or at least preventing others from reading his. Biopsychic vampirism had barely been mentioned there, yet young Pilatov couldn't help but notice how much of his strength had been slipping through his fingers and vanishing into trivial worries, pointless errands, and interactions with random people. He lacked the energy for meaningful achievements, the feats he had dreamed of as a boy but had never managed to accomplish. Instead of heroic exploits in his chosen field, Andrei had retreated into books, even as his short human life crept closer to its midpoint.

"You already know how," I said, cutting off his objections with a gesture. "Any mentally healthy person can do it as soon as they realise that they're being *vampirized*, so to speak. Self-preservation kicks in automatically."

"Where are these mentally healthy people, huh?" Andrei asked bitterly.

"Good point!" I agreed. "Homo sapiens' civilization doesn't exactly encourage inner harmony, which is usually what vampires destroy. The imbalance, in turn, drains people's energy, while parasites feed on it. They benefit from your anxiety and prompt it at every opportunity."

"Are you going to tell me vampires created civilization, too?" the captain challenged.

"I doubt they created it," I replied calmly. "Vampires are parasites and create very little, but they're extremely skilled at making civilization work for them. That is, through the deception and manipulation of your consciousness." I paused, thinking I was doing a decent job explaining vampires, considering my knowledge of them came exclusively from other Lemurians. But I wasn't ready to share the latter truth with Captain Pilatov just yet. "Anyway, a reflective block isn't hard to create. What truly matters is learning to recognise the moment someone forces you to lose or give up biopsychic energy."

Andrei started to get up to move toward the notebook on the shelf but then thought better of it. Taking notes in front of someone who could read minds and teleport between planets seemed pathetic. Instead, he abandoned his half-finished tea, walked to the window, glanced at the dimly lit backyard, and flopped back on the couch.

"Don't worry, you'll remember," I reassured him. "So, people usually lose energy involuntarily when they don't control their negative emotions, such as irritation, anger, anxiety, fear, or pain. However, there's evidence vampires can also feed on joy and attention. Ever noticed how, in your happiest moments, you suddenly feel uneasy and drained?"

"I think I'm starting to get it..." Andrei said. "They try to provoke those feelings to trigger an energy release... That explains a lot!"

"Exactly!" I confirmed.

The captain grunted and scratched the evening stubble on his chin. He didn't have to look far for examples as he'd likely been vampirized earlier that day. The morning encounter with the night watchman, who claimed to have seen a UFO, came to the captain's mind. The old man had kept talking and talking, clinging to the KGB officer's attention like a burr. Everything about him — his voice and his mannerisms — was so unpleasant that Andrei had wanted to turn around and walk away, but both the habit of politeness and the need to file a report kept him rooted in place. The watchman provided no useful information, and after an hour of listening to his ramble, Andrei felt as drained as if he'd spent that time unloading a truck full of watermelons.

I observed his recollection and, in the end, agreed. "Yes, most likely the guy was a vampire. A weak one, of course."

"So, does that mean we need to shield ourselves from emotions? Negative ones or all?" The young man's voice carried a note of disappointment. His inner world was perhaps too colourful for the profession he had chosen. In fact, this often hindered the captain's ability to climb the career ladder successfully.

"Of course not!" I objected. "All of us, both homo sapiens and homo liberatus, constantly experience a whole spectrum of feelings, evoke them in each other, and thus exchange energy. And that's wonderful. Nature has a complex exchange system: you receive from one and give to another. Take Cassandra, for example. As annoying as her behaviour may be, she just voluntarily shared her energy with you, after receiving it from me. Vampires, on the other hand, whether consciously or not, draw others' energy but either don't give it back at all or give back less than they took. Unlike a natural exchange, the energy they hoard doesn't return to circulation, meaning Nature is left with less and less over time as it becomes depleted gradually."

"I understand perfectly well how energy can be drained," said Andrei.

"*No doubt,*" I thought to myself, glancing around his modest living quarters, which spoke loudly of their owner's complete lack of hoarding habits.

"But how can energy be preserved?" he asked.

"Oh, homo sapiens have invented plenty of ways!" I responded. "And vampires are downright obsessed with hoarding any kind of resources that can somehow be transformed into energy. Food supplies, fuel reserves, money…"

"Money?" The captain perked up. "Now that's something I'd like to hear more about!"

"Especially money. Food spoils. Fuel is dangerous. Emotions are unstable and unpredictable. But money… money preserves energy for a long time. It's the deepest trap humanity has ever set for itself. Just think: what is your 'money'?"

"I still remember the definition from my university days!" Andrei laughed, clearly anticipating his favourite pastime — philosophising. "Money is, first, a measure of value, and second, a medium of exchange."

"A measure and exchange of what?"

"Well, everything: goods, services, resources…"

"Exactly. And to create or extract the things for which money is paid requires someone's life energy, doesn't it?"

"Of course," the captain agreed, then paused in thought. "Although the value of money is backed by gold…"

I waved him off. "Oh come on, what gold? It's just metal. You can't eat it or split it for fuel. Sure, gold and silver are pretty and stable, but in essence, their role in energy exchange is no different from that of paper money. Moreover, extracting precious metals requires significant energy costs. We've always been puzzled about why homo sapiens do this. You use both money and metals as intermediaries to evaluate amounts of energy. Both are used as symbols. And you trade in symbols, which in turn grant access to various goods created through the energy investment."

"That sounds complicated!" Andrei laughed.

"It *is* complicated. Your energy exchange system is far too complex. But the real question is, who benefits from all this complexity, and how they do it?"

"Well, how else can you get everything you need to live?" the captain asked, genuinely surprised. "After all, no person can do everything!"

"Can't or won't?" I shrugged. "Or maybe people just want too much. Either way, by paying for something with symbols of energy — money — you compensate for part of the life given up by others to meet your needs and desires. And the person who takes money from you can spend it to meet their own needs. Almost every human need is managed by a separate specialist, who, in turn, needs other specialists. This is where the complexity lies."

Andrei laughed again. "It's as if all we do is go in circles, asking each other to help with our needs!"

"Isn't that exactly what happens?"

"Well, yes," the captain admitted reluctantly. "But when you put it like that, it sounds strange, almost ridiculous..."

"What's ridiculous is that you develop an unacceptably small portion of your natural abilities, and for everything else, you depend on each other and learn very little outside of your so-called profession."

"But isn't the division of labour a form of energy exchange?" Andrei objected. "Learning a profession requires investing energy so that later you can work for the benefit of others throughout your life, giving energy away and receiving it back in the form of money. The more effort someone spends on training the better they perform their job, and the more energy in the form of money they get in return. That's still exchange, right?" I nodded in agreement, and the captain asked, "So where's the catch?"

"The division of labour is indeed a form of energy exchange," I said. "However, to maintain Nature's balance, anyone who gives something for the benefit of others must receive just as much in return, whether from one or several sources. In homo sapiens' terms, your monetary symbols should be able to buy enough resources to replenish the energy and justify the amount of time in your life that you spend working. Otherwise, someone else is pocketing that energy, which, by extension, is the worker's very life. And time, which is life, can't be reclaimed. Humans are constantly vulnerable to this imbalance because you can't measure your real biophysical energy costs and you barely understand them altogether."

"That's called exploitation. That's how capitalism works," Andrei explained with a professorial air, then added with youthful defiance, "And that's why we're building communism!"

"Oh?" I smirked and gave him a reproachful look. "And how's that going? Think back to what you were brooding about here before we arrived. Does the energy invested in work return fully to each of your countrymen?"

Andrei hesitated. Of course, the state provided a lot to its citizens, but was it enough? Although Captain Pilatov, like most Soviet people, had long since ceased to believe in the possibility of a just social order, he, like everyone else, still automatically declared the opposite mantra out loud. When alone, he dared to doubt sometimes, only to bury those doubts in the back of his mind once again.

I paused, then explained. "The exchange of energy is sabotaged by vampires everywhere, *on both sides of the border*. The incomplete refill of biopsychic energy drains human beings. Then, they either find a way to recover at someone else's expense or they don't live very long... And it doesn't matter what the social system is or what you call it."

"Are you saying that low wages for long hours of hard work directly shorten a person's life?" Andrei asked.

"Isn't it obvious?" I replied, and Captain Pilatov nodded in agreement. "Furthermore, the more money employers accumulate, the more potential energy they have at their disposal. Most importantly, money allows them to delay using that energy indefinitely. Money guarantees a one-sided source not only for themselves but also for their descendants."

After a brief pause for thought, Andrei said, "Yeah, that makes sense. What you're saying isn't new. We just aren't used to drawing parallels between stealing someone's life energy and accumulating capital. When you think about it, it's obvious... Whether the capital is private or state-owned, workers never fully get back what they put in."

"Notice how, for homo sapiens, this is a legally sanctioned way of appropriating the lives of their kind. And if you can't prove the money was stolen, no one cares where someone's wealth came from, whether they preserved their own energy or someone else's. It doesn't even matter from the perspective of natural balance, because hoarding energy is a violation in any case. It is a theft from Nature."

"So, what does that mean? Our whole life..."

"Yes, the entire homo sapien civilization, ever since the collapse of tribal society, and maybe even earlier, has been built on violating Nature's laws."

"But why?" Andrei asked, bewildered.

"That's the key question!" I exclaimed, finally getting to the point. "It's all done out of fear that tomorrow won't bring the same resources as today. Fear of hunger and death, essentially."

"But isn't that natural?"

"It's natural to fight a real threat, not an imaginary one. How do you think other species survive? Almost all living things on

Earth feel fear, but aside from humans, very few creatures make large reserves. Bees, perhaps, but even they are exploited by homo sapiens…"

"Yeah… I can't even imagine humanity without stockpiles," Andrei said ironically. His mind was working at an unusual speed, and questions sprouted like mushrooms — I would answer one and two more would pop up. "What if, say, inflation is high in a country and money loses its value? Does that mean energy also devalues?"

I rolled my eyes. I had to explain the obvious again!

"Energy can't devalue, because it's a phenomenon of Nature! Inflation only changes the terms of compensation for a person's energy spending. Do you see?"

Andrei just shook his head in uncertainty.

"Money doesn't lose value on its own, does it?" I said. "Someone triggers that process."

"Essentially, yes," Captain Pilatov agreed hesitantly, oblivious to my irritation.

Homo liberatus had long observed financial phenomena, which had turned into a science shortly before we migrated to New Lemuria. We were concerned, realising that the growing dominance of finance in human civilization meant nothing less than the growing power of vampires on Earth. During Unities, the Lemurians living on Earth often mentioned inflation.

"Inflation is just a trick to separate energy from its symbol and then recreate that connection with a different quantitative value. Essentially it is created to seize naïve savers' efforts and time, that is, life, by deceiving them.

"Imagine you've worked for years, giving your energy and time to your employer, and you had not been spending all your earnings right away because you wanted to save money and buy a house in the future. Then 'suddenly,' inflation strikes, and your dream home turns into just a pair of boots — that's all you can afford now because someone cleverly shifted the relationship between your energy and its symbol. So, where did your energy go, considering that nothing in Nature disappears without a trace?"

"I get it!" the captain exclaimed, his eyes finally lighting up. "If someone loses their savings due to inflation, it means they also irreversibly lose the ability to use the energy they had preserved as their guaranteed bank deposits?"

"The word 'guaranteed' is particularly amusing," I said with a chuckle. "People are led to believe their money disappears forever, while they're simply forced to give up their claim to the natural restoration of their energy in favour of the vampires who cause inflation and profit from it. The scheme is both complex and brilliant. It allows vampires to steal the energy invested in labour by all homo sapiens at once because inflation equally devalues all savings, savings stored in both bank accounts and pickle jars. The genius of vampires is Nature's greatest curse."

"And the worst part is you cannot point to anyone specifically responsible for inflation! It is like they do not exist," Andrei concluded.

"There are always culprits!" I retorted. "Your eternal desire to save energy, which is simply laziness, has created such a cumbersome economic machine that an average homo sapien has long stopped understanding where the system begins and ends, what benefits him, and what works solely to rob and enslave him. You live blindly. And vampires grow bolder the more their schemes go unchallenged. What usually follows a spike in inflation?"

"A war!" the captain, well versed in history, blurted out.

"Exactly. War. That means even more human suffering, and more energy for vampires, whose favourite delicacy is the pain and fear of others. No one else but these parasites provoke and lead all the wars on Earth, especially the prolonged ones, which do not end until the vampires have depleted the resources of all warring parties. And then they just stop the war, pretending to have reached some agreement, only to wait until a new reserve of energy builds up — and drain it again later."

Andrei was suddenly struck with an insight. "So, normal people won't be able to live better or more peacefully as long as vampires rule the Earth?!"

"Do you understand now?" I replied, sighing in relief. The purpose of the conversation had finally been achieved. "It would be best if they not only stopped ruling but also disappeared altogether. To prevent relapses."

"Uh-huh," the captain muttered gloomily. "How?" He pointed at a volume sitting on the top bookshelf: *K. Marx: Selected Works*. "So, all capitalists are vampires because they exploit other people's resources, right? They hoard and accumulate the fruits of others' labour, that is, others' life energy. And they also start wars, for that matter."

"Well, I would not go so far as to say all of them. If the capital is small, the energy, probably, circulates one way or another. Although, yes, capitalism as a system is a creation of vampires. Any form of exploitation of an animal or another human being is the appropriation of vital energy. It is quite self-explanatory."

"In capitalist countries, there are even people who don't work at all and live off dividends from investments..."

"That is, off the energy of those who work for the businesses where the investors' money is placed, right? Whether or not they're vampires depends on how they spend their free time. Your Marx was right about many things, although..." I picked up the book Andrei had been trying to read before Cassandra and I appeared and quickly flipped through it. "... Freud was right too. By the way, both thinkers gave to the world much more than they received in return. One died in poverty and the other got defeated by cancer, which is the most typical reaction of your kind to energy starvation."

"So, are vampires born or do they develop?" Now the captain wanted to get to the root of the problem.

"We're not sure. That's what I need to figure out. Possibly, it's both. We suspect there's a congenital predisposition."

"Like addiction?"

"Something like that, especially considering homo sapiens who gain easy access to substantial amounts of energy. We've long noticed that most people who come to power sooner or later turn into vampires, even if their initial goal in pursuing power was to improve the lives of their peers."

"How true! Yes!" Andrei exclaimed. "So, it turns out no one should have power? Is that even possible?"

"That's exactly how homo liberatus have lived for hundreds of thousands of years!" I laughed. "The most amazing thing is that you all understand perfectly well how it works, and yet you continue to entrust your fates to others, only to fight them later, take power, and become vampires yourselves. There's even a legend about a dragon. I think it is Chinese."

"When a warrior defeated the dragon guarding the gold and became the new dragon?" the captain recalled. Now we were definitely on the same wavelength!

"The dragon in this story is a vampire, a violator of the natural balance, and the cave with gold symbolises unlimited energy. Whoever gets it either does not want to give it up or simply can't."

"Until a new warrior with good intentions comes along…"

"And so on, endlessly."

"It's a vicious circle…"

"Yes."

We fell silent. It was late. The television had been turned off even before Cassandra disappeared, and only the steady ticking of a massive alarm clock on the table broke the silence into seconds relentlessly left behind. Andrei felt like he was losing his already shaky political orientation. He was a Communist Party member, had followed in his uncle's footsteps to work in the KGB, and had always believed he was protecting the interests of the people. *"But the orders we follow aren't given by the people,"* the captain thought. *"They come from those in power... From vampires?"*

To keep him from sinking into despair, I said, "Maybe not everyone who governs human states is a vampire. We have a theory that it's a disease, and its real cause is fear experienced over a long period of time, often in childhood, for example, when a child is constantly deprived of love and attention."

"What does that have to do with anything?" the captain asked, suddenly yawning widely. Sleep was starting to take over.

"Nature has arranged it so that all small children are weak and need an external energy donor, an adult, until the onset of puberty. That's why raising a child is often exhausting. Complete exhaustion leads to death, so a lack of energy is frightening, especially at a young age when there's no experience of compensating one source with another. We believe that vampirism originally began as a childhood coping mechanism, driven by the survival instinct. But if this mechanism is used for too long, it turns into a dependency disorder. Such individuals find it easier to steal energy from others than generate it naturally or join in exchange. This habit doesn't form immediately, but once developed, it's almost impossible to break, like a drug addiction."

"And does it harm the vampires themselves?"

"In the same way as bottle-feeding affects an infant."

"How would I know about infants?" Andrei thought. *"I've never held one!"*

"Neither have I," I replied.

"Stop listening to my thoughts!" the captain protested.

"Sorry, I can't help it. I'm just hearing them," I apologised. "It makes no difference to me whether you think or speak, and blocking out your mind takes effort, which right now seems like a waste of energy. We all think so and never block our minds from each other."

"Okay, you got me!" Andrei laughed. "So, what about infants?"

"That's not the point. Just like with harm from bottle-feeding, the imbalance caused by stealing energy isn't immediately noticeable. People gradually start avoiding someone who triggers unpleasant emotions. Thus, the vampire who is being avoided becomes deprived of energy sources, which only drives him to invent more sophisticated ways of gaining strength."

"So it's another vicious circle?"

"Imagine where walking that circle might lead. Vampires become outcasts of Nature and commit increasingly serious offenses against it."

"Like Hitler?" Andrei guessed.

"Yes, he's the most obvious example. So, my mission is to rid Earth of vampires." I hesitated for a moment, then added, "According to the prophecy, I am the only homo liberatus capable of leading the fight against energy parasites. However, one man can't win a war alone, and I need allies among humans. I need people like you."

"Sure, count me in!" Andrei exclaimed. "And what about your kind? You know... the homo liberatus? Aren't they going to help?"

That evening, I thought it unnecessary to tell the exhausted captain about my race's complete aversion to violence. Yet, a sense of loneliness, unknown to most Lemurians, suddenly gripped my throat.

"I shouldn't count on that," I quietly admitted.

"What do you mean?" Pilatov objected. "Didn't *they* send you on this mission?"

"I wasn't sent. I came on my own. The prophecy said only I had the strength to begin this mission."

"And the one who made this prophecy?" My companion still didn't understand.

"There were several prophetesses," I corrected him. "They only foretold that I *could* do it. The choice was mine."

"Then why won't your people, those up there," he said, pointing upward, "help you?"

"It's quite possible a few vampires could be killed as an outcome of the mission. And one needs either fear or hatred to commit murder. Lemurians possess neither, so they're incapable of killing."

"Then why are *you* capable?"

"Am I? That's not certain either. Even though I'm half homo liberatus and half human." I raised my hand to block the captain's questioning gaze. "I'll explain later, I promise! Like the Lemurians, I can't feel fear, but my mother, who was of your kind, was killed by vampires. The pain of that loss has tormented me since childhood. That's where my hatred for them comes from. Our oracles say my strength lies in that pain." I couldn't hold back a sigh, one as heavy as my burden.

"You feel hatred but no fear? You're like the perfect killing machine!" the captain said with irony, then added sympathetically, "Using your pain as a tool for this mission seems cruel."

"No more than Nature itself. I'd be a killing machine if I *wanted* to kill, but yes, that's the main reason I was chosen. Destroying even some vampires might be unavoidable, and it will likely shatter my inner harmony. The others aren't ready to submit themselves to that. My people will only step in if I find a way to restore vampires to their natural state without killing."

"Cure vampirism like an addiction?" the captain scoffed.

"I wish," I said sadly. "So far, the homo liberatus have done everything to avoid contact with vampires, and they still do, so there's no cure yet. I have much work ahead of me…"

Suddenly I felt cramped in the captain's tiny quarters and almost suffocated. I had been in too many rooms for one day. It was time to return to the trees and birds.

Hoping to end the conversation quickly, I asked Andrei directly, "When will you introduce me to your uncle?"

"Why do you need him?"

Unable to suppress another heavy sigh, I launched into another explanation, hoping it would be the last one for the night.

"The prophecy says that I must find 'my own' vampire to understand the nature of their kind better."

Andrew's eyes widened.

"Wait, are you saying Uncle Pasha is a vampire?!"

"No!" I waved off the idea, annoyed at the necessity to explain everything to this boy while I longed to slip away like Cassandra had. "*My* vampire is the one who ordered the burning of Khatyn, where I was born. The one who killed my mother. Do you get it?"

"And?"

"No one who survived the fire remembers the chasteners' faces. And everyone I've met so far seems to recall only what they were made to remember."

Finally, understanding dawned on Andrei, and he exhaled in relief.

"Oh, I see! You think my uncle hypnotised them?"

"I'm not sure, but I am certain that Pavel Pilatov was involved. I'm hoping for his help…"

"Got it…" confirmed the hypnotist's nephew, covering a yawn with the back of his hand. Now that Andrei was sure his hero wasn't in danger, he gave in to exhaustion and flopped on his side, no longer worried about my presence.

"Tomorrow… we'll go to Uncle Pasha…" He mumbled through the haze of sleep.

"I'll be back in the morning," I replied, and set off for Halong Bay to recover from this crazy day.

Chapter 9. The Uncle

Captain Pilatov slept as soundly as only people with excellent health and a clear conscience can. In the evening, Andrei's mind was so overwhelmed that he had shut down almost involuntarily. My new acquaintance ended up spending the night on the folded sofa bed in an awkward position. Finally, he moved. Wincing from the pain in his stiff neck, he opened his eyes and found himself covered with a blanket — the only thing left from his grandmother, whom he had never met.

In 1942, the Nazi police arrested her and looted her Novgorod apartment under the pretext of searching for weapons and anti-fascist leaflets. The warm and fluffy plaid blanket, brown with thin red and green stripes, escaped the hands of the looters only because the day before the arrest, a downstairs neighbour had borrowed it to wrap her ailing three-year-old child. The partisan courier was tortured to death by the Gestapo, and the neighbour returned the blanket only after the war when Elizaveta, Andrei's future mother, moved back into her parents' old apartment. Later, she gave the family heirloom to her son so that the "poor boy" wouldn't freeze in the dormitory.

The captain had a proper quilt for sleeping, so the grandmother's legacy was usually kept neatly folded on the back of the couch. He used the legendary blanket only for lounging in front of the TV on rare free weekends.

Slowly returning to reality, Andrei thought, *"Who covered me? It couldn't have been the neighbour!"* Suddenly the memories of the previous day burst into Andrei's mind like floodwaters breaking through a dam and jolted him fully wake. He shot up from the unfolded sofa bed, wondering whether his conversation with the visitors could have been a dream inspired by the commotion at work. The thought gave him brief relief, but recalling the details made him doubt it.

"The vampire talk... it was too specific. And that woman... Cassandra, right? Well, they gossiped about her all day at

Lubyanka... But that guy, Yan... how could he appear in my dreams? He seems to be the leader though. My memory's still sharp. I've never met him before..."

"You definitely haven't," I confirmed, seizing the opportunity to appear before the captain. "By the way, I'm the one who covered you with the blanket. You looked pitiful."

The captain's composure was impressive. He didn't even flinch, he just raised his sleepy eyes to me, offering a tense smile.

"So, it wasn't a dream after all..." Andrei muttered with not much enthusiasm, and added jokingly, "That's disappointing!"

"Why disappointing?" I laughed, taking a seat on the stool by the table.

"As if I'm not getting enough excitement in my life!" was the captain's ironic response. In truth, he was only half joking. Having dreamed of heroic spy exploits since childhood, he stood on the verge of disillusionment with his job, which lately consisted mainly of investigating ridiculous tips from attention-seeking citizens. Any oddities reported by the public always turned out to be products of bored imaginations or natural phenomena. In short, he experienced no adventure at all.

"Oh, I'll offer you plenty of excitement!" I spoke. "And I'd like to start right away, with visiting Uncle Pasha... especially since it looks like he's in trouble."

"How do you...?" Andrei began to ask, but caught himself. "Oh, right... telepathy..."

Incidentally, if Captain Pilatov's mind hadn't been crammed full of informational clutter, he might have sensed the vibrations of excruciating pain that had been tormenting his uncle for weeks. He might also have felt the uncle's desperate need for love and support. These vibrations had been reaching from far away and quietly piling up unattended in Andrei's overburdened subconscious, like a queue waiting outside a hopelessly locked door.

"What kind of trouble?" the captain asked seriously.

"Health problems. You called him three times from work yesterday, but he didn't pick up, right?"

Andrei nodded grimly.

"And before that, when did you speak with him last?"

He paused to think. "About five months ago, when we saw him off to retirement. I didn't even notice how much time passed with this damn job!"

Feeling guilty, Pilatov got up from the couch, grabbed a travel bag from the corner, and then froze in the middle of the room, trying to figure out what to pack for the trip. "He must be sick," Pilatov muttered. "I'm such a jerk! Let's have breakfast and go."

"You'll eat there," I said, stopping him with a gesture as he tried to head toward the kitchen.

"But it takes a whole day to get there, by train and then by bus!" the captain protested passionately. Travelling on an empty stomach didn't appeal to him.

"It'll take only five minutes," I said, "and four of those are to give the old man a heads-up."

Andrei stared at me in surprise but dared not ask any more questions. Deciding that "give a heads-up" meant calling his uncle at the dormitory checkpoint, he stepped toward the exit again and said, "What if he doesn't pick up the phone again? Should we go unannounced?"

"Of course he won't pick up!" The captain's pointless stir was starting to irritate me, as I was eager to achieve at least some progress after three weeks of searching for the notorious hypnotist. I pointed to the sofa. "Sit!"

Andrei was entirely bewildered by this point, but he followed the command and flopped down onto the rumpled blanket left there overnight.

"Close your eyes and picture your uncle's house."

"Why —"

"Quiet! Just do it."

I sat on the sofa next to the utterly confused captain, who was still wearing the baggy sweatpants he'd had on since the previous evening. From the chaos swirling in Pilatov's head, I somehow managed to extract the location of his uncle's house and plant the thought of expecting a visitor in the mind of the lonely, dying old man. Then I said to Andrei:

"Now, be so kind as to stand up and hold on to me tightly so Uncle Pasha doesn't have to pick up pieces of you along the road."

Seconds later, we were on the outskirts of Veliky Novgorod, in the overgrown front garden of the Pilatov family estate, where tall grass hadn't been mowed in who knows how long. Andrei had spent many summers in this house, trailing behind his late father's brother.

For some mysterious reason, Pavel Pilatov had always remained single, even though he could have had any girl in the area, especially in the post-war years. He loved his nephew like a son and spent much time with the boy. Despite his busy schedule, Uncle Pasha always welcomed Andrei and was full of surprises. He often devised adventures suitable for a child, whether catching fish as if by command, stumbling upon an abandoned treasure-filled cabin while playing explorers, or discovering a mushroom patch and forgetting all about treasure hunting. In Andrei's mind, the man with the strange eyes didn't seem nearly as frightening as he did to the Belorussians whom the elder Pilatov had "treated." The boy had grown, and so had his admiration for his hypnotist uncle. Over time, he understood the genuine nature of Pilatov's tricks.

Uncle Pasha's log house had a two-story tower featuring arched windows and a roof resembling a flattened pyramid. The front wing was mainly a veranda adorned with beautiful carved wooden tiles that badly needed repainting. At the back of the veranda stood a double-door entrance. The right wing was notable for its large round window, whose wooden frame was covered in cracked orange paint. In short, the beautiful structure in the Russian Art Nouveau style desperately needed restoration. The owner knew this perfectly well but could do nothing about it as his strength was leaving him by the day.

In a monumental leather armchair, Pavel Andreevich Pilatov sat on the veranda. He was a tall old man who had only recently lost his once-luxurious hair and a solid layer of fat, leaving the skin on his cheeks hanging like a loose tunic. He peered at the unexpected guests, whom he somehow knew were coming just minutes before they appeared.

The colonel of the Fourteenth Division had been retired for six months and hadn't answered phone calls in the past ten weeks. Yet the message about his nephew's visit "with a friend" had dropped straight into his consciousness like mail into a box, so Uncle Pasha was expecting something unusual that might entertain him in his final days.

He was dying from a disorder caused by an imbalance in natural energy, a chronic inability to restore vital reserves. The colonel had always foreseen this illness and, therefore, never started a family. He didn't predict the future; he simply knew that when placed in service to a materialistic society, most people with paranormal abilities ended up in the cemetery this way. The elder Pilatov had lived longer than most of them, but now he felt only pain and exhaustion, pushing him closer each day to the black hole of death. Realising that fighting the disease was futile, Pavel Andreevich decided not to burden his sister-in-law and nephew with his suffering but to slip away quietly once he could no longer breathe.

For the past few months, he had survived on liquid food prepared by a woman living in the neighbourhood. The retired spy also paid her for basic chores and errands, and, additionally, to keep silent, strictly forbidding her from informing his family about his state of health. Yet deep down, he longed for warmth from his loved ones at the end of his turbulent life.

Homo sapiens are such strange creatures…

Apart from his neighbour, Pavel Andreevich didn't talk with many of the residents of the suburban village. People were wary of the colonel's piercing gaze. Besides, the Pilatov family's reputation had made the locals avoid them since the time of Andrei Aleksandrovich, a doctor at the local hospital. Pavel's father was a hereditary noble who had miraculously escaped reprisals from those in power. Quietly and without publicity, he practised hypnosis, mainly for therapeutic purposes. Rumour had it in the village that neither the intrusive communist activists during Stalin's rule nor the dim-witted policemen during the German occupation ever dared to touch him, supposedly because they had fallen under some kind of "suggestion."

The doctor's son knew for sure that this was true. He had inherited the ability to influence people's will, too. Moreover, Pavel Andreevich was even more talented than his father: he had reached a new level and mastered telepathy. When Colonel Pilatov was younger, he had even served as a sleeper agent, mentally infiltrating the minds of key politicians from hostile states and extracting information directly from their consciousness.

And now the retired KGB spy was taking painkillers by the handful, which allowed him to occasionally walk — or, more accurately, crawl — around the house. With great effort, he had made it out to the veranda to greet his guests and try to conceal the severity of his condition from us.

Meanwhile, as I had expected, Andrei didn't handle his first teleportation very well. The moment the captain materialised before our host, instead of offering a greeting, he bolted toward the bushes along the picket fence, where he began gasping and retching.

"That's why I didn't let you have breakfast," I commented.

The captain's miserable state allowed me to take a better look at the ailing hypnotist, who was watching us with interest. Pavel

Pilatov didn't seem nearly as intimidating as the witnesses whom I had met had remembered him. Even in illness, the strong-willed old man hadn't lost his sense of humour — I gathered this from the joke that the colonel made to himself about the captain's dash to the bushes, *"Well done, son! Came to help your uncle fertilize the front garden!"*

Our sudden appearance out of thin air intrigued the seasoned intelligence officer, distracting him from his pain. Patiently following his nephew with his eyes, he waited, guessing that no explanations would come until the latter recovered. As for me, I remained standing at a distance, not stepping onto the veranda.

Finally, having caught his breath and wiped his mouth with a crumpled handkerchief he found in the pocket of his sweatpants, Andrei turned toward the house and hurried to Pavel Andreevich.

"Uncle Pasha! Hello! I couldn't reach you yesterday. Are you okay?" he asked, thinking, *"The old man doesn't look so good."*

In response, the colonel moved his lips and pointed weakly at his throat.

"Oh, you've got a cold and lost your voice?" guessed Andrei, feeling relieved. "Well, that'll pass!"

Pavel Andreevich nodded without making a sound and attempted to smile.

"That's what he wants you to think, Andrei," I said. "In reality, he has laryngeal cancer, which has progressed rapidly. It no longer allows his vocal cords to produce sounds loud enough for a phone conversation." I caught the colonel's protesting glance and felt respect for the man. Few homo sapiens could endure pain so stoically and use self-suggestion so skillfully to distract their still-sharp consciousness from the fear of death. Fortunately, I could communicate with the former KGB hypnotist without needing speech.

"By what right? Who are you, anyway?" Uncle Pasha raged, not really expecting an answer. I was even surprised at how much anger could flare up in his barely living body.

"It's a long story," I replied. *"Let's focus on relieving your suffering now."*

The colonel was a little surprised to be heard. He suddenly slumped and even seemed to relax, leaning his head with thinning, unkempt grey hair back. He sighed as deeply as his tumour-stricken throat would allow and, with the composure of a spy, responded, *"Can you?"* Tormented by the pain that bubbled endlessly in his throat like boiling tar, he saw death as the only escape and was preparing for it, convincing himself that he had already accomplished much and that the events of his turbulent sixty-five years could fill several lifetimes. Pavel Andreevich had intended to hasten his end at some point but hadn't yet dared to do so.

"You're still needed here," I replied, and seeing the patient's confusion, I added, *"No, no, you misunderstood me! I'm going to remove your tumour."*

"You can do that?!" With a sharp, piercing beam, hope lit up the old man's aura, clouded by illness, and the bastion of self-hypnosis he had built through sheer willpower instantly crumbled. The colonel wanted to live.

"Undoubtedly," I assured him. *"Just relax."*

Eradicating the sinister tumour that had nearly defeated the seasoned spy required far more energy than what it would take to merely dissolve the blood clots in the museum director's veins. Pavel Pilatov was in the final stage of his illness, and death, which he feared despite all his efforts, had already taken him by the throat, quite literally. When I focused the energy flow on the old man's neck, a white glow formed around it. The colonel's nephew became speechless at the sight of this. He froze on the creaky wooden veranda steps, watching the power of homo liberatus at work.

The deadly cells resisted fiercely, but under my relentless pressure, they gradually dissolved until they were completely gone.

After the procedure, I was so weakened that I couldn't even teleport. "Explain everything yourself. I need to rest," I quickly told Andrei, who was still standing with his mouth agape. Then, I dragged myself to the garden behind the Pilatovs' house. I shook off my torturous shoes and let my bare feet greedily touch the dazzlingly young green growth on the earth, like a starving infant latching onto its mother's breast.

The long-neglected garden had yielded to Nature and was beautiful in its wild simplicity. The fruit trees had spread their heavy, untrimmed branches freely, densely covered with fragrant pinkish-white blossoms. I approached the tallest apple tree, pressed my cold, exhausted palms against it, and closed my eyes.

It turned out to be a place of extraordinary power! The tree responded at once. A stream of Earth's vital energy began flowing from its roots into my weary body, and I blissfully drifted away for a while.

A tickling touch of soft whiskers on my bare foot, made me open my eyes. A curious grey hare was cautiously sniffing my toes. The directed flow of energy I had created for faster recovery must have attracted this inhabitant of the overgrown garden. The long-eared visitor also seemed eager to recharge his batteries during the mating season. I couldn't help but laugh at the little opportunist trying to mooch energy from me. I leaned down and picked the little creature up. The company of the trusting, furry bundle made me smile, which only increased the influx of strength I received. And so, the hare and I recharged together. Then, my new friend cheerfully hopped off to search for a bunny girl, and I returned to the house.

At the round dining table with thick, ornate legs, which stood in the centre of the spacious, old-fashioned dining room, sat the uncle and nephew. They were talking animatedly while devouring breakfast. Since the only food in the fridge before our arrival had been the baby food meant for the patient, Andrei, having changed into his uncle's clothes, had already run to the shop for bread and whatever else he could find, which was mostly canned fish in tomato sauce. The captain was no stranger to rough bachelor food, especially when he was starving like this. Meanwhile, Uncle Pasha was so thrilled about his newly regained ability to eat like a grown-up that he didn't care what he was chewing and swallowing, at least for now. Both Pilatovs were gorging themselves on thick slices of bread topped with brown sprats smeared in sticky reddish-brown sauce and washing it all down with tea from elegant porcelain cups, a retirement gift to the colonel.

Andrei was already wrapping up his story about the race of homo liberatus and the vampires overrunning Earth, although he still hadn't fully come to terms with it. Uncle Pasha kept interrupting with questions, further confusing the already struggling captain.

The nauseating smell coming from the canned fish leftovers and their sauce-covered contents spread across the bread slices prevented me from joining the Pilatovs at the table. I moved to the large window, sat on the wide windowsill, and decided to wait until the officers finished their meal. The stench of fish that had died months ago and been preserved only through some kind of blend of chemicals reached me even there, but at least by the open window, with the occasional breath of fresh air, it wasn't as murderous.

Pavel Andreevich shot me an apologetic look and hurried to finish. *"We'll end your torture now!"* he promised. Rising from the table, he carefully washed his fish-smelling fingers with soap under the tap. Then, as he motioned me toward the living room, he gave an order to his subordinate on the way out. "You're on dish duty, Captain! And rinse those sprat cans too, or our guest might faint from the aromas of our society."

As retired colonel led me out of the fish-scented kitchen, he added, "Let's talk like normal people so *he* can hear us too!"

Uncle Pasha nodded toward the kitchen, where he had just sent his nephew.

The old man enjoyed the sound of his voice, and the joy of his recovery was akin to euphoria — a state uncharacteristic for the senior instructor of the KGB's Fourteenth Division. For almost the first time in his adult life, he allowed himself to experience uninhibited happiness.

Although the Pilatov family hadn't known about Uncle Pasha's terminal illness, his superiors in security services had, so the colonel had been regretfully written off as both an active intelligence officer and a hypnosis instructor. This meant that having unexpectedly recovered, he could finally take full control of his own life, and the constant need to watch his surroundings had vanished. Pavel Andreevich had been reborn, healthy and free.

It turned out that for the colonel, the problem of the world's vampirization was not news. Pavel Pilatov understood the significance of my mission much better than his nephew, and not just because of his miraculous recovery. He knew about energy parasites from personal experience.

"I've encountered many such individuals," said Pavel Andreevich. "On *both sides* of the border."

At that moment, the captain, having just finished washing the dishes, appeared in the living room doorway. Hearing a quote from his own thoughts, he gave his uncle a sharp look and shivered. It felt to Andrei as if the whole world suddenly had access to his mind! The young officer frowned, entered the living room, and sank into a beautiful pale green sofa, casually crossing one leg over the other. Meanwhile, the retired intelligence officer continued, addressing him.

"Only a few can gain power without turning into vampires. So, among the country's top leadership…" He fell silent.

Andrei had not expected such candour from his usually reserved uncle, and most importantly, Uncle Pasha echoed exactly what I had said the day before. After a prolonged pause, during which he finally processed the senior's confession, Andrei slammed his palm against the sofa's wide armrest.

"Then why?!" He was so indignant that he almost choked. "Why did you keep following their orders if you knew?"

"Well, first of all, I didn't realise about the vampires immediately. And even now, I don't know everything," the old man explained, trying to smooth things over. Deep down, he admitted that the young man's anger was partially justified. "Secondly, my conclusions are based solely on personal observations, which are not the ultimate truth, of course." Pavel Andreevich got up from his chair, straightened his back proudly, and raised his voice. "And here is the most important thing. I am a hereditary Russian noble, and I love my country. Unconditionally." Colonel Pilatov began pacing slowly around the living room. "A son does not betray his mother, no matter what she is like. And a mother loves and protects her children, no matter how they behave. Likewise, for a true Russian, serving and protecting the Motherland is an eternal value, regardless of who is in power or how they rule our country." When Pavel Pilatov pronounced the word "Motherland," the capital letter was emphasised. "Any government is comprised of nothing more than people who come and go, and Russia remains. You cannot betray your Motherland simply because, at some point, it was unlucky with its leaders or treated you unfairly. The native land stands above all that, since it is the source of our strength." The colonel gestured toward me with an open palm. "As far as I understand, Yan, you are, in a sense, one of us?"

I nodded, recalling my extraordinary connection with the land in Pilatov's garden. I had never experienced such a powerful surge of energy in New Lemuria. Listening to Uncle Pasha, I realised: it's impossible to uproot yourself and move elsewhere as if nothing happened. That's why homo liberatus are so determined to return to Earth!

"I may have had to cater to the whims of the vampires in power," Pavel Andreevich continued, addressing his nephew. "Nevertheless, no other job compares to working for the KGB when it comes to serving Russia's interests. And my conscience is clear because, in serving my country, I never harmed it, not even once."

The old man kept pacing before us, hammering home his worldview to the indignant and bewildered captain. His low voice carried conviction, and his gestures were unhurried and dignified.

"What's more, I was lucky enough to participate in several secret operations that strengthened our country's position and prevented more than one military conflict, thus saving thousands of lives. That's what most Chekists* do. Our duty is to protect the Motherland. As for the petty scheming of vampire-like, thieving bureaucrats..." The old officer grimaced and dismissively waved his hand toward the window. "That's just one of the occupational hazards."

While Colonel Pilatov delivered his speech like a preacher before his congregation, his renewed golden-orange aura blossomed like a lotus flower. It grew more extensive and vibrant, returning to its pre-illness state. At that moment, I understood how this man could alter the memories of nearly half the population of a large region.

Andrei remained silent. He felt lost. The young man was rather accustomed to observing the tiresome, performative patriotism required for career advancement, so he was struck by his uncle's sincerity. After all, Captain Pilatov had never truly defended his homeland, neither within Russia nor abroad, despite his seven years in the KGB. Spy work, with its dangers of exposing foreign intelligence agents, had never been part of his duties. What Andrei didn't know was that his mother, unwilling to lose her son as she had her husband, had begged her brother-in-law to ensure the "boy" wouldn't be assigned life-threatening missions. Andrei had earned his captain's rank just before being transferred to the Fourteenth Division for arresting and "neutralising" an elusive group of dissidents who had used an illegal printing press to produce so-called "anti-Soviet" poems criticising the system. Andrei hadn't been passionate about that work. In fact, he secretly agreed with some of the dissidents' messages.

"It's not them we should be protecting the country from," he had often thought, *"but those they mock."*

"You love your Motherland too," I said, responding to the captain's thoughts, "though you're ashamed of it for some reason."

"Patriotism isn't trendy anymore!" Uncle Pasha quipped, then, addressing his nephew, he added, "It's a good thing your superiors don't know what you really think, or you'd have been kicked out long ago."

"Maybe I'd like to leave myself," Pilatov Junior retorted without a hint of arrogance. Deep down, he realised that by mandating patriotism, the Communist Party had only stifled true love for their country in his generation, the love that undoubtedly needed fostering, but in some different way. "What kind of work is it carrying out orders from Central Committee rats who care more about their seats and pockets than the cause?"

"And what's stopping you from caring about the cause if that's the real issue?" the colonel shot back. "Blaming others and sulking is the easiest thing to do." He paused. "I didn't mention the most important reason Russia needs us. *On the other side* of the border, there are at least as many, if not more, vampires dreaming of turning our land and people into a free source of both fossil and human energy. And I know this not from posters or newspapers but as a professional intelligence officer." Pavel Andreevich looked regretfully at his disheartened nephew. "Maybe you're right about leaving if you're so doubtful about your service. But don't rush. Let's first see how we can help *him*"— and he pointed at me — "since you dragged this fellow here."

"It's him who dragged me here!" Andrei replied with a grin.

"You, my dear sir, have arrived to save the world from vampires, no more, no less, if I understand correctly?" The colonel's good-natured irony was directed at me with a smile, and I nodded. "Do you know the Russian proverb, 'One man in the field is no warrior'?"

"Yes, I'm already familiar with it," I replied. "That's precisely why I'm here. I'm counting on you and your nephew, Pavel Andreevich."

"You see, son, it's too early for you to run away from the system!" Pavel Andreevich paternally patted the captain on the shoulder. "It'll be easier to fight vampires with some legal help."

"I don't really believe in them yet," Andrei grumbled, continually forgetting he was in a room with two telepaths.

"Surely, that can be fixed!" the colonel said, ready to move mountains. "After all, we'll help him unlock his potential, right, Yan?"

"Maybe later," I replied vaguely, and quickly concealed the reason for my hesitation. I didn't want to disappoint the doting uncle. When it came to paranormal abilities, Nature had clearly decided to take a break with his nephew, or perhaps the nephew was suppressing Nature with his cynicism. With a mindset like Andrei's, and without a genetic connection to the descendants of Lemuria, the chances of developing paranormal abilities were close to zero. One way or the other, it was time to get down to business.

"Right now, I'm interested in Khatyn and the executioners who burned its residents in 1943. Among them was a vampire I need to find and..." I hesitated, not even wanting to think about murder. "... possibly eliminate. He must have been their commander, and he's still alive."

"How do you know he's alive?" Andrei interjected with a hint of challenge.

"Not me, but our mutual acquaintance Cassandra and other seers."

"Cassandra? How intriguing!" Pavel Andreevich exclaimed. "*The Greek* Cassandra**?"

Andrei chuckled, recalling the whimsical prophetess. "No, they are just namesakes!"

"We were hoping you could help, Pavel Andreevich," I said. "I know that you partially blocked the memories of the local population. Will you agree to restore some to their original state?"

"Well, we didn't block them, we just slightly altered the memories…" the retired colonel clarified. He sighed. "It's possible, of course, given the looming political upheavals… but it won't be of much use."

"Why not?" Andrei and I asked in unison.

"Because to succeed, you need the name of your vampire. Otherwise, in the vastness of our country, you'll get nowhere, even if you manage to extract the perpetrator's image from someone's memory."

"Why couldn't I get anywhere?" I still didn't understand the problem. After all, we had managed to track down the colonel himself! I completely forgot that my luck had only worked thanks to Jim's random recollection of a document with the name "Pilatov" written in it.

"Just think how good this bastard must be at covering his tracks if he's been doing it successfully for forty years!" Uncle Pasha insisted. "The victims only glimpsed the executioners, and they didn't know any names at all, you can trust me on that. We scanned all the witnesses before modifying their memories. So, even if we unlock them, they won't help much, while plenty of filth will come out. And dealing with that mess won't be your responsibility, Yan, with all due respect…" The colonel gestured at Andrei, implying that the fallout from restoring the memories of Belorussian villagers who had survived the German occupation would fall on people like the captain. I didn't fully grasp what kind of consequences he meant, but I decided not to get distracted.

"Think about it," the colonel continued. "Of the six surviving witnesses to the Khatyn tragedy, only four are still alive. They were children at the time and perceived the horrors of war through a child's mind, much like you did, Yan." Pilatov Senior paused, giving me time to process his words. "Are you following me?"

"Yes," I confirmed.

"Furthermore, these children survived only because they managed to hide. So, the chasteners didn't see them, which means the survivors didn't see many of the criminals either. The ones who undoubtedly shared drinks with your vampire were his fellow vampires. That's who you need to find to dig into their memories!"

"Exactly!" Andrei agreed, raising his index finger. "We need to dig up interrogation records of former collaborators. It's so simple!" This earned him an approving smile from his uncle.

"Knowing the names, Andrei can track down the executioners through already existing court cases, and from there, you can identify your vampire," Pavel Andreevich said. "One thing's for sure: if the criminal is still alive, he's walking free, because people like him don't end up in camps here." The colonel ran his fingers across his neck, illustrating the alternative. Then he gave me a patronising pat on the shoulder. "The path was established long before you showed up, Yan! The case records are kept in the Belorussian KGB archive. You'll need official access to retrieve them. I could help with that…"

"That'll be such a hassle!" Andrei groaned.

"Or maybe we won't need official access…" I countered with a wink. I disappeared and then reappeared to show them a quicker way into the archive.

After a brief pause, Pavel Andreevich said, "Yes, but you'll need the captain's help to sort through the papers…"

"Well, he already has teleportation experience!" I laughed, noticing Andrei's grimace at the thought of this new mode of transport. I tried to reassure him. "Don't worry, you'll get used to it!"

Andrei snorted. "They've married me off without asking!"

"Today's Saturday, which means the archive is closed. Can you manage to do it in two days?" Uncle Pasha asked, rubbing his hands together.

"I don't know… I hope so," I responded. I had no idea.

"Then you'd better hurry!"

The captain, barely keeping up, asked, "There must be a ton of documents on Khatyn, right?"

"Absolutely!" confirmed the colonel. "I didn't read them myself, but I was briefed when we worked with the population in the fifties and early sixties. Even back then, there were seven volumes."

"Seven volumes!" Andrei groaned and looked at me in despair. "We won't finish quickly then… We'll need more than two days to find this… whoever you're looking for. And there's nothing to do there during the daytime, even on weekends, since we'd be there unofficially. Oh, and I must go to work on Monday!"

"You were given the task of warning me, right?" Uncle Pasha objected.

"Well, yes…"

"I'm sure you'll be able to use this to take a vacation. Your superiors think I'm sick and are unlikely to refuse. And I'll be able to confirm that you came to me and told me everything that was due. That's what we'll do." Andrei seemed delighted to hear

Uncle's advice, and Pilatov Senior said to me," It's very convenient that your Cassandra friend left, so I won't have to lie, saying that she didn't show up here."

This was a purely human speculation, which I would never have thought of, and which once again proved how difficult it would be to act in the world of homo sapiens without their help. Having thanked the experienced scout, I approached the captain and asked:

"Well, shall we repeat the journey?"

He rolled his eyes in resignation and meekly extended his hand to me, but suddenly Uncle Pasha stopped us with a cry of "Wait!" He ran to the kitchen and returned with three translucent plastic bags, which he carefully folded and solemnly handed to his nephew.

"One for now, one for the return trip, and one extra, just in case. Don't vomit all over the Belorussian archive. Good luck!"

And with that, we teleported to Minsk.

---

*Chekist: intelligence officer

**Cassandra is the name of a character from ancient Greek mythology, a Trojan princess gifted with the power of prophecy.

Chapter 10. In the Labyrinths of Memory

Twilight was already settling in when Captain Pilatov and I found ourselves in a park near our destination. Although my passenger didn't have to use his uncle's plastic bags, the captain's sensations after teleportation were far from pleasant. I could say the same about myself, as the air in the heroic city of Minsk was anything but clean and fresh. It was oversaturated with gases unfit for breathing, not only carbon monoxide and carbon dioxide, to which I was just starting to adapt somehow, but also some other repugnant emissions, presumably from factory chimneys. Yet the atmosphere pleased the eye, as if unaware of the pollution in its lower layers. In the west, the sun, partially obscured by high-rise buildings, coloured a fiery border on the sparse, feather-like violet clouds, while in the east, the bottomless maw of the Universe was slowly and inexorably swallowing the sky.

Couples strolled through the park, showing little interest in the heavens' beauty. Most of them held hands, and the more uninhibited ones embraced and even kissed on benches, ignoring the disapproving glances of solitary walkers who were leading their large, small, and tiny dogs by leashes fastened around the poor creatures' necks. I had never seen animals so crudely restrained, and when I asked Andrei about it, he replied, "It's the right thing to do! To stop the dogs from biting or attacking passersby, or those ones over there." Swallowing envy, the captain who was still single gave a barely noticeable nod toward a couple tightly pressed against each other on a bench we had just passed.

Like any homo liberatus, I wasn't at all bothered by those. On Lemuria, the desires of the flesh were unrestricted by place or age. There, in the lap of Nature, such couples would likely have been sitting naked. However, at the sight of dog collars and leashes, I was overcome with indignation.

"But these animals are highly suggestible. You only need to tell them, or, at worst, command them! I'm sure even homo sapiens could handle that."

"Well..." Andrei stretched the word uncertainly. "You're right, and most can manage, but not all. Besides, dogs are usually kept on leads more to prevent strangers from getting frightened if an unfamiliar animal, especially a big one, comes running up to them."

"How can anyone be afraid of dogs?" This news astonished me. "After all, humans call themselves *the kings of Nature*! What sort of kings are you if you're afraid of even creatures that are easier to control than any other animals?"

"Dog owners, of course, have control over their own pets, but strangers don't always manage. Still, you're mostly right. Only a few people are afraid of dogs. But why does this bother you so much?"

"I've never seen a living being so restricted in its freedom, and in such a ridiculous and cruel way!"

Andrei smirked ironically. "*You haven't seen our zoos or prisons yet!*" Then, he asked, "Not even predators?"

"Strictly speaking, a dog is a predator too!"

"Exactly!" The captain exclaimed. "Then, how do you defend yourselves if, as you claim, you live side by side with wild nature? Say, if a lion or a bear wanted to eat you?"

"Homo liberatus can negotiate with any living creature by influencing them through suggestion and telepathy. We learn it from early childhood and do not need to restrain or kill anyone or physically defend ourselves in any way."

"Are you saying you could even negotiate with a lion or a crocodile?" my companion asked with a sceptical snort.

I smiled. "What difference does the species make?"

"Can you demonstrate?"

"Where would I find a lion here?" I said, pretending not to understand.

"Then give an order to that Newfoundland over there!" Throwing me this silly challenge, Andrei jabbed his thumb over his shoulder at a shaggy black dog with an apathetic expression ten steps behind us. The dog was being led on a leash by a frail teenage girl in jeans and a long jumper. She was daydreaming about her attractive classmate, whom she hoped to meet during this evening walk in the park. The giant shaggy pet reached up to the girl's waist and was at least twice her weight. The dog was trudging reluctantly beside her along the path while dreaming of rolling around in the enticing silky grass on the lawn to the right. However, sensing that the beloved owner's thoughts were floating far away from him, the loyal creature made no attempt to satisfy his simple canine desire for joy.

I stopped and, without looking back, began to communicate with the fastened-to-the-leash and bored-to-death Newfoundland, and Andrei turned around to see what would happen. At first, the dog stopped, rooted to the spot, and did not move, despite the girl's prodding. Then, unexpectedly for everyone except me, of course, the shaggy fellow plopped down on the dusty asphalt and rolled on his back, raising his heavy paws. Having rolled around to his heart's content, the giant pet stood and shook his greyed-with-dust fur coat quite spectacularly right on his owner, who did not have time to jump away. Then the animal ran around the poor girl, who, in her confusion, dropped the leash. Having made three turns clockwise, the Newfoundland abruptly reversed and circled her again three times.

"Rothschild! Stop it!" the fragile teenager shouted in a panic. "Sit! Sit, I said! Rothschild, are you crazy? Sit! Paw!"

The usually docile dog ignored her. Onlookers had already gathered around, not offering any help as everyone feared the dog had canine rabies. So my apparent indifference would not seem strange to anyone, I also turned to face what was happening and noted that my companion was barely holding back from laughing out loud. I left the dog alone a minute later. The Newfoundland stopped the performance as suddenly as he had started, instantly calmed down, and, as if nothing had happened, stood at the foot of the tearful girl, the giant's face returning to its earlier expression of boredom. We imperceptibly separated from the crowd and moved on.

"Fascinating!" Andrei exclaimed, finally allowing himself to laugh for quite a long time when we walked away. "Only I feel sorry for the girl. She was really scared!"

"You asked me for it!" I smiled sadly. Andrei stopped short, and I added, not even trying to hide my condemnation, "That's how it always is with you. First you act, then you think. As a result, you harm yourself and others. You are light-minded creatures. And that's on top of the vampire problem!"

"That is true," the captain agreed with a guilty look.

We strolled along the central avenue of Minsk. I admired its whitewashed cleanliness, the gradually lit nocturnal lights, and the straightness of the lines. It was not at all natural, but still… If only the air weren't so godlessly polluted!

When we reached the KGB building, its grand entrance adorned with massive white columns, it was already completely dark. Floodlights illuminated the entire facade, sending up bright beams and making it impossible to approach the wall unnoticed.

"This human creation is quite new," I remarked.

"Yes, new," the captain agreed. "The Nazis destroyed Minsk to the ground during the war, so the entire city had to be rebuilt. You could say Belarus rose from the ashes like a phoenix."

Andrei paused, admiring the monumental structure, which exuded a certain oppressive grandeur. Suddenly remembering something, he added, "And do you know what's ironic? This building was reconstructed by German prisoners of war. What an excellent use of their labour! How would you put it? Our people transformed destructive energy into creative energy."

"And thus, restored balance," I added. My companion had made me smile.

"Well, maybe to some very minor extent."

"Have you been here before?"

"Never had the chance," the captain replied, tilting his head back to assess the difficulty of an unauthorised entry into the fortress. He scratched his head. "Though Uncle Pasha has, many times. We should've asked him how to find the archive in this palace. How did I not think of that?"

"But I did."

"When did you manage to ask him?"

"I had a look through your uncle's memories. He didn't block me out, so it was like reading an open book."

We had to move around the corner of the brightly lit building to teleport inside. The archive's enormous interior had no windows, and we found ourselves in pitch darkness. The impenetrable silence felt unnatural yet blessed after the deafening clamor of the central avenue. While Andrei was still getting his bearings, I tried to get a sense of our surroundings.

Before us stretched a labyrinth that held the people's history, their feats and betrayals, crimes and punishments, and since this history was documented on paper rather than preserved in the memory of a living being, I, like a homo sapien, had no access to this neatly stacked knowledge other than through reading. In short, this was the domain of the KGB captain, who was well-versed in paperwork.

Soon Andrei stopped feeling nauseous and pulled a thin, elongated object from his pocket. The object turned out to be a source of light. The captain always kept a torch at the ready. That was why, despite being unable to see in the dark, he had no objections to a nighttime visit to the archive! The thin beam of light from the device barely allowed my companion to make out what lay a couple of metres ahead, whereas I, due to the sharp contrast between the light and the darkness, could no longer see anything else properly.

“How are we supposed to find what we need?” I asked.

“It’s simple — alphabetically! Follow me,” Andrei replied nonchalantly.

So, we set off on a journey between the shelves. The captain directed the torch beam mostly at the labels until we reached the letter K, where we found boxes marked *Khatyn* occupying several shelves.

Andrei scratched his chin, eyeing the hefty volumes appraisingly. I, on the other hand, froze in awe. My vampire’s name was hidden among hundreds, even thousands of painstakingly gathered protocols, reports, notes, and memos — and even then, there was no guarantee of finding him!

“Right,” the captain finally declared, “there’s no way we can get through all this in one night or even two! Digging through papers here and now is completely pointless.”

He pulled the far-left box from the top shelf and spaced out the others so its absence wouldn’t be noticeable, then took some of his uncle’s spare plastic bags from his pocket. Just as we were about to carefully pack up our haul, a switch clicked, bright fluorescent light flooded the room, and a wary male voice came from the side of the entrance to the archive.

“Who’s there?”

Having been busy with the boxes, we had failed to notice the earlier click of a key turning in the door's lock somewhere at the far end of the document storage room. Andrei hurriedly turned off the torch. The guard's footsteps could already be heard approaching, and there was no time to teleport without leaving traces of our presence.

My companion’s face paled and twisted into a panicked grimace. With nothing better in mind, he seemed ready to resign himself to a hopeless game of hide-and-seek in this labyrinth of human memory. The captain had already started to move, leaving the box of Khatyn documentation on the floor. Andrei tugged at my sleeve, trying to lead me away, but I held him back, pressed a finger to my lips, and gestured for him to stay behind me with the papers.

The whole manoeuvre took only a few seconds, and a moment later, the guard's figure appeared at the end of our row of shelves. He only saw an empty passage between the shelves and a clean, pale green wall at the other end. I must say, the guard was conscientious. He decided to walk through the narrow corridor between the shelves and missed us only because we had pressed ourselves to the shelves and to each other as closely as possible. Had the guard been a Lemurian, he would easily have heard the drumbeat of fear hammered out by the heart of Captain Pilatov, who had entered the archive at night and without written authorisation, like a spy. And if he was found, then… For a homo sapien, Andrei controlled his fear surprisingly well, but those moments of waiting felt like an eternity to him.

At last, the guard convinced himself that the noise among the shelves had been his imagination. He switched off the light and the click of the key in the lock signalled the all clear. Quietly but efficiently, we stuffed the folders into the three transparent plastic bags, and Andrei whispered with relief, "Right, let's fly back."

"What about the rest?" I was puzzled.

"Remember this place," my accomplice replied, grinning. "You'll have to come back more than once to take as much as you can carry" — he pointed at the remaining materials on the shelves — "and put back what you're finished with." Now his finger moved to the bags full of papers. "Until we find what we need."

"Me?" I was shocked and stared at the seemingly endless stacks of human history. "Alone?"

"Of course." Andrei rolled his eyes. "I wouldn't survive that many teleportations!"

"But you're so good at navigating this maze!" I protested, thinking, *"It's worth a try."*

Andrei, seeing through my clumsy attempt at manipulation, laughed quietly and assured me with barely concealed superiority, "Don't worry, you'll manage!"

***

The house of Pilatov Senior was a perfect place for examining secret documents. Firstly, there were no unwanted eyes. Pavel Andreevich generally did not entertain idle guests, and now he had asked the neighbour who helped with the housekeeping not to come for the time being, citing a visit from his nephew. Secondly, Uncle Pasha was an experienced intelligence officer who understood our work well, having encountered it before. And finally, since no one had yet been informed about the miraculous recovery of the dying hypnotist, it was easier for Andrei to maintain the cover story of visiting a sick relative while staying at his uncle's house.

The following day, the captain called Colonel Sviridov and requested official leave to spend time with his dying relative, an honoured member of the security services. At the same time, he suggested, he could remain on standby in case the "magical lady" —Cassandra — decided to show up after all.

"All right, stay there," came the reply from the other end of the line. "You can file the paperwork later."

Captain Pilatov was surprised at how easily he had received approval, and without any objections too. He did not know that his superior had undergone a suggestion session in the style of homo liberatus.

And so, the work began. Both officers, Pavel and Andrei, set about helping me with great enthusiasm. The elder was especially keen, and not just out of gratitude for his recovery. Having always concealed his views, which strayed far from traditional materialism, from his Party comrades, Pavel

Andreevich saw special meaning in his return to life. He believed he had been healed for a purpose. Thus, I gained a loyal assistant skilled in unravelling mysteries born of the sapiens' matrix.

Before we unpacked the first bag of archival trophies, Uncle Pasha produced a small black case, a decommissioned mini camera from the KGB.

"This is no longer cutting-edge technology," the retired spy said, placing the tiny device on the table, "but it will still help us capture the most important details..."

Sorting through archival documents covered in decades of dust turned out to be a tedious and painstaking task, one that, I admit, greatly irritated me. So, this was how homo sapiens compensated for their lack of astral and mental connections! Yet another meaningless activity into which they poured their energy and ever-dwindling time! Now, I had to do the same too.

We fairly divided the folders into three piles, but I had an advantage since I had access not only to what I personally fished out of this sea of dusty cellulose but also to what the other two uncovered. I was grateful for their participation because I knew that without assistance experienced in the human matrix, finding the right path in this labyrinth of memory would have been overly challenging.

In the first folder I opened, I found the minutes of a partisan commanders' meeting. On the present list, there was the commander of Uncle Vasya's Detachement, in which my recent acquaintance, the director of the Khatyn memorial, had fought.

29 March 1943. *

Scanning the hurried notes written by someone's hand on a torn-out page from a notebook, I read aloud:

"'Major Voronyansky... Cease overnight stays and halts of partisans in villages, even for individuals, as this provokes the enemy's barbaric reprisals against our population. Many examples can be given, even in our case: 184 people burned alive in the village of Khatyn...'"

"So, the partisans must have finally decided not to spend their nights in villages after the tragedy in Khatyn!" I thought. *"Now I understand why Matvey carries such a crushing sense of guilt... But wait..."*

"A hundred and eighty-four?" I repeated. Where I grew up, the violent death of even a single living being was an unthinkable sacrilege, yet here I was, learning that vampires had taken thirty-five more lives from my native village than were mentioned during the tours in Khatyn! How could that be?

I felt such grief, as if the tragedy had happened only yesterday.

The colonel, who had been poring over the protocols in front of him, looked up. "You misunderstand, Yan. The partisans couldn't have known the exact number of people killed in the village. The figure here is probably approximate."

"A *figure*?" That sounded utterly bizarre! What shocked me even more was the complete lack of drama in the colonel's voice. I was at a loss for words.

The retired hypnotist studied my silence intently for a few moments, then finally added, "Hmm. It will be hard for you with such a reverence for life."

"What's wrong with all of you?" I was too outraged to find the right words. "Though, I suppose I should have known..."

"You see," Uncle Pasha said as gently as he could, "there's a kind of built-in defence mechanism in the human psyche. What you're feeling right now drains your energy, and it's destructive." And he was right, because after my surge of indignation, I felt a slight weakness. "A person, consciously or not, prioritises their own health and well-being, trying to preserve strength."

Pavel Andreevich looked sadly at his nephew, who was waiting in silence, completely failing to understand the reason for my anger.

"That's why people, although they create countless reasons for grief for themselves and others, simply can't mourn forever, especially for strangers. No matter how horrific, lives lost in any tragedy turn into numbers for us in forty years, if not sooner." He glanced again at the captain. "Unfortunately. So, you'll have to get used to it, Yan. For instance, this document lists already a smaller *figure*." And the colonel began reading from the notes.

"'Report by the Pleshchenitsy District Commission on the burning of the residents of Khatyn by German fascist invaders. 28 October 1944.

"'We, the undersigned members of the Pleshchenitsy District Commission for the accounting of atrocities committed by German fascist invaders during their period of occupation, including…' Let's not worry about the names for now…" Uncle Pasha skipped a few lines. "'… hereby state that on 22 March 1943, 150 German soldiers and officers arrived in the village of Khatyn, Pleshchenitsy District, Minsk Region, BSSR. They surrounded the village and opened machine-gun and rifle fire upon it, then herded the villagers into the barn of Joseph Kaminsky. The barn was set on fire with the people inside.

"'When the elderly and the women in the barn began breaking down the door to escape, the German fiends opened fire with machine guns. As a result of this atrocity, 157…'" Pavel Andreevich paused for my benefit. "See?" He continued reading. "'… elderly, women, and children burned to death in the barn. The Germans also burned down the village, which consisted of 27 houses. This report has been prepared accordingly. A list of the burned victims and surviving witness' testimonies is attached. Commission Chairman Yasinovich, commission members…'"

Out of the corner of my eye, I saw the captain reach for the mini camera, but before he could take a picture, Pilatov Senior swiftly pressed the nephew's hands to the table with his palm.

"Hey, easy there! Save the film! We only photograph what we don't already know!"

I could not get the numbers out of my mind. "It's not one hundred and forty-nine here either. It's one hundred and fifty-seven!"

"This document is from 1944!" the colonel said.

"So what?"

"Well, this protocol was probably one of the first!" Andrei interjected. "Back then, they probably didn't know about all the survivors."

It's worth noting that everything Uncle Pasha explained to me so thoroughly was already obvious to the captain. Only now did Andrei, who had been fidgeting impatiently during our conversation, finally realized — albeit belatedly — what my issue with the numbers was.

"They must have been taken in by other villages, and the investigators probably found them only after the war." Flipping quickly through the stack of papers, Andrei added, "There are hardly any individual witness statements about Khatyn in the first folder. Look, just this one, dated a day before the previous document. 'Witness Statement of V.A. Yaskievich. Pleshchenitsy, 27 October 1944. Year of birth: 1930…' Meaning he was fourteen at the time of the testimony. It looks like the boy simply was nearby," the captain explained. "And the other children were even younger.

"'Regarding the matter at hand, I testify: On 22 March 1943, around 150 people — German soldiers and officers — entered our village of Khatyn. They surrounded it from all sides and opened fire with machine guns and rifles. After that, they stormed the village, drove the residents into the barn of Joseph Kaminsky — I don't remember his patronymic — locked the door, and set it on fire. When the men started breaking down the door, they opened fire with machine guns. Thus, 150 people —

children, women, and elderly — were burned alive in this barn by the hands of the German fiends.

"'Among them were my parents — my father, Anton Antonovich Yaskievich, aged 50, and my mother, Yelena Sidorovna Yaskievich, aged 51 — my brother, Viktor Vladimirovich Yaskievich…'

"Eight names in total," Andrei clarified, skipping over the rest. "'So, out of ten family members, only two of us survived. My sister, Zosya (Sofya) Antonovna Yaskievich, born in 1934, also survived. When the Germans started driving people into the barn, she ran to the farmstead…'"

"Regarding the matter at hand..." I repeated silently to myself. *"So what eight-year-old Sonya Yaskievich went through, hiding in her aunt's potato cellar, doesn't count as relevant since nothing about it was mentioned in the report?"*

"It absolutely counts!" Pilatov Senior said, responding to my thoughts. "But there were hundreds like Sonya back then. Can you imagine the chaos the few survivors' lives were thrown into both during and immediately after the war?" Pavel Andreevich paced the room, sipping lukewarm tea he had earlier set aside on the mantelpiece, away from the writing desk. "A person who's lost their home and family was like a needle in a haystack. All the witnesses of the tragedy were left homeless and scattered, staying with relatives or acquaintances in nearby villages, often quite far away from Khatyn. Only after the war were the surviving children gathered in an orphanage. And minors were hardly likely to be actively interrogated as it would have forced them to relive the horrors they had endured. They, like the entire population after the Nazi occupation, suffered from post-traumatic stress disorder. That was, in fact, the official reason for our… well, you know… hypnotherapy…"

Meanwhile, Andrei was drawn to another document.

"There's testimony here about the burning of another village — Osovy. For example, witness M.K. Poletyka's statement, dated 30 October 1944," he said, struggling to make out the handwriting of an unaccustomed-to-essays peasant woman. "'I can tell you as an eyewitness what the German punishers did. In May 1943, the Germans arrived in our village. All the residents hid in the forest, trying to escape those monsters and tormentors, but the chasteners ordered everyone to return home. We spent the night at home, and in the morning, at about seven o'clock, they started rounding up partisans' families and driving them into a barn outside the village.

"'That morning, four Germans came into my house and wouldn't let me leave. They gathered young and old and locked them in the barn. Then they gathered everyone else in the street, lined them up, and set the barn full of living people on fire. I managed to slip away and hide. When the Germans left the village, I ran to the barn, where people were burning.

"'My brother's wife and her two children burned there. In total, 50 people were burned in the barn. Three more children, aged 7 to 10, were shot while trying to escape. That day, 53 people were killed.'" Having finished reading, the captain set the yellowed paper aside. "You see, Yan? The same thing happened in Osovy as in Khatyn, like a carbon copy, except for the *numbers*. Witnesses only name the victims, as in their family members and neighbours, but not a single perpetrator!"

"I told you," Pavel Andreevich said, "executioners don't introduce themselves to their victims."

Only now was I beginning to understand how right Uncle Pasha had been when he claimed that his "patients" were unlikely to shed light on my search. It turned out I had been chasing the hypnotist in vain… Or had I? Is anything ever really done in vain? It remained to be seen why he had met with the residents of the affected villages. The old scout had done a good job of keeping the details of that "therapeutic" operation out of his consciousness, even when it was at the centre of the conversation.

"There is also a brief mention of the Riga Trial in 1946 here," Andrei said, interrupting my thoughts. "Bruno Pavel confessed that he gave the order to burn down Khatyn. Is this what you're looking for?" I was about to show interest and leaned over the table to take the sheet from the captain's hand, but he continued. "For some reason, there are no protocols from there…"

I leaned back in my chair, disappointed.

"The Riga Trial was one of the first," explained Pavel Andreevich. "Only German officers were tried there, and the case was overseen by a military tribunal, so the documents should be in their archives, not the KGB's. Anyway, it's pointless to go digging there."

"Why?" Andrei and I asked in unison.

"All the war criminals were sentenced to death back then, and we're looking for a living vampire, aren't we?"

"Yes," I agreed, and the captain at once made a dubious yet optimistic conclusion:

"Then the circle narrows significantly! Most punishers were either executed or are serving time, right?"

"I'm sure not all of them," replied the colonel, pressing his lips together, "but there's nothing here so far." He looked concerned and pondered again how cunning and intelligent my opponent must have been to avoid exposure for all forty years since the war. Of course, that's assuming he hadn't moved abroad like some other traitors… But Pavel Andreevich was not one to rush to conclusions and merely said aloud, "The next trial took place in the early sixties. The documents are in the archive," and he made a dismissive gesture in my direction.

For more than a week, I had to haul boxes and folders from the Belorussian KGB archive to Pilatov's house at night, then return them and bring new ones in their place. Each batch of papers was neatly spread out on a sturdy, long desk in a spacious study. In his dressing gown, Uncle Pasha sat sideways in the leather master armchair facing an English-style fireplace, his back to a wall covered in a slightly faded light-green tapestry. Andrei and I sat on the opposite side of the table in guest chairs upholstered in the same light-green tapestry fabric. The chairs had elegantly curved legs and black wooden armrests and were equally as comfortable.

All this antique luxury had survived from Pilatov's noble ancestors, untouched by commissars because the doctor, Andrei's grandfather, had been held in special regard. The study doubled as a library, so the other walls were lined with volumes of scientific, literary, and historical works covering everything that had fascinated this unusual family of homo sapiens for generations. I had never been in a human library before, and I couldn't shake the feeling that our work progressed more smoothly surrounded by these folios, as if fragments of the scholars' and thinkers' souls lived within them. As if their great minds, longing for an audience, whispered hints and clues in our ears.

In the investigation protocols from 1961, we found testimony from the only adult who had survived the Khatyn massacre. I had heard about him during the tour. His six-metre statue, a monument raised in memory of a life miraculously saved, towered in the centre of Khatyn.

"'31 January 1961.

"'Senior Investigator of the Investigation Department of the KGB under the Council of Ministers of the BSSR, Captain Murashko, interviewed Joseph Josephivich Kaminsky, born in 1887, a native of the village of Gani in the Logoisk district of the Minsk region. J.J.Kaminsky is from a peasant background, a Belorussian, a citizen of the USSR, has no Party membership, has a primary education, with no prior convictions, and is married, a pensioner, and resides in the village of Kozyri, Logoisk district.

"'The interview began at 12:25 p.m. Kaminsky was warned about the responsibility for refusal to testify and for giving false testimony under Articles 134 and 136 of the Criminal Code of the BSSR. Signature — Kaminsky.

"'Quesrtion: What language would you like to give your testimony in?

"'Answer: I will give my testimony in Russian.

"'Question: Where did you live, and what were you doing during the German occupation of 1941 to 1944?

"'Answer: During the German occupation, I lived in the village of Khatyn, Pleshchenitsy district, Minsk region, until 22 March 1943, having moved there from the village of Gani when I was still a child. After German punitive troops burned down Khatyn, I was treated for wounds and burns at the Bogdanovka farmstead near Logoisk and later in the town of Logoisk until the Soviet Army liberated the area. Before Khatyn was destroyed, I worked in agriculture, but after being injured, I did not work anywhere. I have been living in the village of Kozyri since 1944.

"'Question: Describe in detail the circumstances of the ruination of the village of Khatyn.

"'Answer: On Sunday, March 21, 1943, many partisans arrived in Khatyn. I do not know the name of their detachment or brigade. After spending the night, most of them left the village early the next morning while it was still dark.

"'Around midday on Monday, 22 March 1943, while I was at home in Khatyn, I heard gunfire near the village of Kozyri, located 4 to 5 km from Khatyn. The gunfire was intense at first, then ceased, and shortly afterward resumed. At about 3:00 p.m., the partisans returned to Khatyn and settled down for lunch. An hour or an hour and a half later, the Germans began surrounding our village. A battle broke out between them and the partisans. Several partisans were killed in Khatyn. After approximately an hour of fighting, the partisans retreated, and the German soldiers began collecting carts and loading them with property. They only took Stefan Alekseevich Rudak from the village as a cart driver. He (Stefan) later died at the front in 1944 to 1945. The rest of the villagers were herded into a barn about 35 to 50 metres from my house. That was my barn.

"'Six punishers entered my house. They spoke Russian and Ukrainian. Three of them were dressed in German uniforms, and the other three wore grey overcoats. All of them were armed with rifles. My wife, Adelia, and our four children, aged 12 to 18, were at home at that time. I fell to my knees. They asked me how many partisans there were. I replied that there were six people, but that I did not know who they were, whether they were partisans or else. I was then asked if I had a horse and told to harness it.

"'As soon as I left the house, one of the chasteners struck me on the shoulder with the butt of his rifle, called me a bandit, and ordered me to harness the horse faster. The horse was kept at the yard of my brother, Ivan Josipovich Kaminsky, who lived across the street. When I entered his yard, I saw that my brother was already lying dead on the doorstep of his house. Apparently, he had been killed during the earlier fighting. I harnessed the horse, and the troops took it. Then, two of them drove me and my brother's son, Vladislav, to my barn.

"'When I entered the barn, about 10 people, including my family, were already there. I noticed they were not wearing clothes and asked them why. My wife, Adelia, and my daughter, Jadwiga, replied that the chasteners had stripped them. More people continued to be herded into the barn until it was completely packed, so tightly that it was impossible to raise one's arms. The barn measured 12 by 6 metres, and about a hundred of my fellow villagers were forced inside.

"'From inside the barn, through the open door as people were being forced in, I could see that many houses were already on fire. I realised that we were going to be executed and told the others in the barn, 'Pray to God because we are all going to die here.' At that moment, one of the punishers standing at the door responded, 'Oh, you trampled icons, burned icons — now, we will burn you.'** He spoke Ukrainian and was tall, thin, wearing a grey overcoat, and armed with a submachine gun…'"

I stopped reading and stared blankly ahead. So those words had really been spoken! And exactly as I remembered them! My heart started pounding so hard that it felt as if it might explode in my chest. This surge of energy propelled me to my feet, and I began to walk back and forth in the study room. For a few seconds, both Pilatovs stared at me in astonishment.

"Why are you pacing like that?" Andrei finally asked.

"I *remember* those words! About the icons!" I said, struggling to catch my breath, which had quickened from the agitation. "So that language was Ukrainian?"

"Definitely!" the officers confirmed.

The captain seemed about to add something, but I pointed at the papers scattered on the table. "Read the rest of it, Andrei! Please! Questions later!"

So, he continued from where I had left off.

"'Those words of the chastener stuck in my memory, especially since the barn was packed with innocent civilians, many of whom were young children, even infants, and the rest were mostly women and the elderly. Just recalling them brings forth a horrific image of this monstrous act of human extermination in the village of Khatyn, among whose inhabitants I found myself. The barn was already burning, or rather, it had caught fire even before I told the people inside, 'Pray to God,' along with other words, as mentioned earlier. The people doomed to die, including members … of my own family… were crying and screaming desperately.

"'When the executioners opened the barn doors, they began shooting the civilians with machine and submachine guns, and other weapons. Yet the gunfire was almost drowned out by the cries of the people. My fifteen-year-old son Adam and I ended up near the wall. The… bodies… of those who had been shot fell on top of me while the still-living thrashed about in the crowd like waves. Blood poured from the wounded and the dead. The burning roof collapsed, and the horrific, frenzied cries of the people… they grew even louder. Beneath the roof, the burning people screamed and writhed so violently that the structure seemed to spin. I managed to crawl out from under the bodies and burning people and make my way to the door. At that moment, the executioner I mentioned earlier, the Ukrainian one, was standing at the barn entrance. He fired his submachine gun at me and wounded my left shoulder. The bullets seared my skin, grazing several parts of my back and tearing my clothes.

"'My son Adam, already badly burned, somehow managed to escape the barn, but he collapsed after being shot… about ten metres away. Wounded, I lay motionless, pretending to be dead so that the executioner wouldn't shoot me again. However, part of the burning roof fell onto my legs, and my clothes caught fire. I began crawling out of the barn again. Raising my head slightly, I saw that the executioners had already left. Near the barn, there were… heaps of bodies… killed and burned. Among them lay Albinas Yetka, bleeding from his side. Since I was close to him, his blood flowed directly onto me. I tried to help him, pressing my hand against his wound to stop the bleeding. He was dying, his body was completely burned, and his… face and skin were gone. Yet he still said, 'Save yourself!' upon feeling my touch.

"'Hearing Albinas's dying words, another punisher approached from somewhere. Without saying anything, he lifted me up and threw me aside. Although I was half-conscious, I didn't move. Then the executioner struck me in the face with the butt of his rifle and left. My back and hands were badly burned. I lay there barefoot, having kicked off my burning felt boots while crawling out of the barn. I was lying in the snow, in a pool of blood mixed with melted snow. Soon, I heard the signal for the executioners to leave. When they had gone some distance, my son Adam, who was lying about three metres away, called me, asking me to pull him out of the pool of blood. I crawled over and tried to lift him, but I saw that he had… he had… been cut in half by the machine-gun bullets. My boy managed to ask, 'Is Mum alive?' Then… he died.

"'I don't remember all the other bodies near the barn, but I do recall seeing Andrei Zhelobkovich, who was also killed. His wife and three children, including an infant, died there as well. I couldn't stand or move, but soon my brother-in-law, Joseph Yaskievich, who lived about one and a half kilometres away, came and took me home, almost carrying me the whole way. By then, the village of Khatyn was completely burned down. It was the evening of 22 March 1943, after nightfall. The executioners had set fire to the barn and started shooting people around 5 or 6 p.m. When Joseph Yaskievich, who died four years ago now, was leading me away, I saw two bodies lying outside the village, but I don't know who they were.

"'Afterwards, I received treatment at my relatives's home in the hamlet of Bogdanovka and later in the town of Logoisk. Once I recovered, I didn't work anywhere and stayed with my relatives. Thus, on 22 March 1943, the German punitive forces completely burned down the village of Khatyn and its 187 inhabitants…'" Andrei read, emphasising this number as he looked at me, "'were either shot or burned alive. According to Stefan Rudak's accounts, 15 people were killed near the village of Khatyn, while the rest were shot or burned in that barn.'

"The partisans' report recorded the total number of Khatyn's victims," the captain explained to me before he returned to the document. "'As for the chasteners, I only remember the details I've mentioned. I can add that there were few Germans in Khatyn at the time. Most of those that I saw in my house, on the streets, and near the barn spoke Russian and Ukrainian. Given how much time has passed, I wouldn't be able to identify them now.'"

When Andrei finished reading, I had already gotten to my chair and was sitting there with my head in my hands. Yes, blacksmith Joseph Kaminsky had seen far more than little Yasik. He had seen everything.

"Ah, you could have extracted so much from this memory, if only done skilfully!" Uncle Pasha said, echoing my thoughts in frustration. "And there would have been enough of the criminals' portraits too!"

One thing the colonel did not voice aloud: all the witnesses who had undergone the hypnotherapy were deprogrammed at the time to give testimony in judicial investigations and then returned to their earlier state of partial oblivion. However, it had been too dangerous to subject old Kaminsky to hypnosis again because of the onset of his age-related illness. After the trial, the poor man had to be left alone with his memories. That was why the former blacksmith kept returning to Khatyn so often for the rest of his life. And it had been more than thirteen years since Joseph Kaminsky died, so we now had to make do with these sheets of testimony from the unfortunate old man. Although detailed, they were not very useful for our investigation.

"There was also Anton Baranovsky," the colonel added, "probably the only child, apart from Yan, who was in that barn and survived. He too saw many of the punishers' faces. Hear this." And Pavel Andreevich read aloud from the document in front of him. "'When the battle began between the partisans and the punitive forces, I went to my uncle, Iodko Kazimir, where my mother and sister were. During the battle, we lay on the floor and locked the door.

"'As soon as the shooting in the village stopped, someone knocked heavily on the door. We did not have time to open it before the punitive forces smashed it in with their rifle butts. Three or four men stormed into the house. The first one was armed with a rifle, and the others had submachine guns. They were all dressed in German military uniforms. I do not remember the colour of their uniforms or their insignias. The first man, speaking Russian with a distinct Ukrainian accent, harshly ordered us out of the house, using obscene language. When we started to leave, one of the men ordered my sister Maria to stay behind.'"

"I can imagine why!" Andrei interrupted, but the colonel, without taking his eyes off the protocol, just sighed.

"Yes," he said, and continued reading. "'I cannot remember the features of the men who entered the house due to the time that has passed…' In 1943, Anton was eleven years old," concluded Pilatov Senior. Then, he fell silent for a while as he pondered, and we waited expectantly, listening to the thunderous ticking coming from the old grandfather clock. Finally, Pavel Andreevich read the note on Anton Baranovsky's witness protocol. "'Died in Orenburg in December 1969 under unexplained circumstances: suffocated in a barracks that caught fire during the night…'"

Suddenly our captain's stomach let out a loud and unambiguous growl, to which the older generation could not help but respond sympathetically. We exchanged glances, rose from our seats and headed to the dining room, leaving the protocols in the office. The youngest and hungriest of us went to the kitchen to heat up yesterday's bachelor soup with pasta, which I refused to eat because of the chicken leg floating in the broth. Instead of soup, I was offered last year's vegetables, and the captain even took the trouble to chop a salad and dress it with sunflower oil. Turning up my nose from this would have been rude and pointless, so I just tried to chew the fibre while distracting myself with conversation.

"What irony!" Andrei remarked sadly once he felt capable of thinking about something other than lunch. "Khatyn still caught up with Anton Baranovsky. Eighteen years later. Was that a coincidence?"

"I'm not sure actually," admitted the old intelligence officer, rubbing his clean-shaven chin. "Not sure at all. Something here does not add up! Anton writes that he doesn't remember any features. But he would have remembered if he had seen one of those bastards face-to-face... That's exactly the *suggestion* we gave to witnesses of Nazi crimes in Belarus. And Anton saw those four men up close."

"Wait, wait! So exactly why did you alter the population's memories on such a large scale? And what specifically were they supposed to forget?" the captain finally dared to ask.

Instead of answering, Pavel Andreevich quoted the protocol left in the office from memory. "'After forcing us out of the house, the executioners, speaking Russian with a Ukrainian accent, ordered us to go to Joseph Kaminsky's barn...' Do you get it now? With a *Ukrainian* accent. Which we also read about in Kaminsky's testimony."

"Well, at least I now know what language was spoken by the only punisher I remember," I replied, not yet realising the significance of what the colonel had pointed out, but he objected forcefully.

"I could have told you that anyway."

---

*Here and elsewhere in the text, testimonies, protocols, and reports related to the actions of the 118th Schutzmannschaft police battalions in Belarus in 1943-44 are cited verbatim from the collection of documents "The Murderers of Khatyn," Fifth Rome Publishing House, 2018. The original edition is published in Russian. Here, the reports are translated into English by M.V.

**"Oh, you trampled icons, you burned icons — now, we will burn you." In the original document, this phrase is quoted by J. Kaminsky in Ukrainian.

Chapter 11. The Geography of Betrayal: Part 1

Now be silent, I said, if you wish,
You vile traitor! Through me,
Your shame will be forever strengthened in the world.
Dante Alighieri, *The Divine Comedy*

"A Ukrainian collaborator? What a surprise!" Andrei exclaimed sarcastically, rising from the table to clear the dishes. "There were plenty of traitors who saved their skins by serving the fascists wherever the invaders had set foot. Although, strangely, this one isn't local…"

"That's exactly the point!" replied Pavel Andreevich. "The murderers of Khatyn and other Belarussian villages wiped off the face of the earth were mostly Ukrainians. That's been proven long ago."

"How's that?" protested the captain. He had been about to take the plates to the kitchen but now sat back at the table with this question. "Everyone knows that Khatyn was burned by the Germans!"

"That's just the version for ordinary Soviet citizens," Uncle Pasha countered. "Investigations over the years revealed that although the orders came from the German command, the population of Belarus was exterminated by policemen, and not local ones, either. Hitler's forces avoided traumatising their soldiers' psyches unnecessarily."

Andrei raised his eyebrows, spread his hands, and laughed. "Could they still be traumatised?"

"Don't laugh," Colonel Pilatov said, admonishing his nephew. "Motivation is a key factor in war, as in anything else. Do you think only vampires fought for Hitler?

"Of course not," Andrei responded. "I sincerely hope there aren't as many vampires in the world as there were soldiers in the Nazi army!"

"Exactly. Most of them were ordinary German lads, brainwashed with Nazi ideology and encouraged by peasant greed, but they still were normal people. Many went to Eastern Europe hoping to snatch a piece of farmland on the conquered territories. However, everything has its price. It's one thing to kill an armed enemy with whom you're on equal footing — and tormenting defenceless civilians is entirely different. That's no longer war, it's genocide, which, to put it mildly, demoralises any mentally sound person. Genocide requires a certain type of character."

"I agree," Andrei replied, now serious. He stood and took the dishes away to wash them right away. The captain disliked unfinished tasks.

Meanwhile, Pavel Andreevich asked me, "Tea?"

I nodded and he followed his nephew into the kitchen. Uncle Pasha believed Andrei didn't know how to brew tea "properly." I remained at the table, staring blankly at the grey window and remembering how a wave of energy, sweeping and consuming, had rolled towards the men in uniform as they tightly surrounded *that* barn. A three-year-old child, even a homo liberatus, would not have been able to withstand such a force. Little Yasik had barely understood the cause of the chaos and wasn't frightened, thanks to his nature. Yet every cell of his tiny being had absorbed the pulsating charges of fear that radiated from the villagers, who were driven into the enclosed space and doomed to die. That insatiable tide of human terror would undoubtedly have destroyed me if not for the strength of my mother's body. Any adult Lemurian knows that the volume of directed energy flow always equals the receiving side's capacity to absorb it. So, it turns out that the pain and fear of the victims were consumed, at least by most of the punishers standing outside.

Pilatov Junior appeared in the doorway and beckoned me into the living room. I made myself comfortable on the sofa to wait for Uncle Pasha and his tea, and the young officer sat down at an aged, light-wood piano. Andrei lifted the lid, and his fingers began to dance along the black-and-white keys lightly and confidently, producing *music*. Since early childhood, I had not heard this soulful human language, more truthful than any other, singing of both heartache and unrestrained joy. A language that resonates even against one's will. A language of pure emotions, in which everyone hears their own meaning!

The flaw of beautiful sounds caught me off guard while I was immersed in my memories. Once again, just like when the bell had tolled at the site of the burnt-down Khatyn house, my chest tightened, a lump rose in my throat, and for the second time since my return to Earth, unbidden tears welled up in my eyes…

The painful yet longed-for melody broke off as suddenly as it had begun when Pavel Andreevich entered the living room with a tray. The colonel carried a large clay teapot filled with his signature hot brew. Andrei cut the music off mid-phrase, closed the piano lid, and went to the cupboard for porcelain cups. Then, arranging the cups on a small table, he flopped down onto the sofa and sprawled out comfortably next to me, completely unaware of the impression his music had made upon me. After the minimalist austerity of the Moscow KGB dormitory, the captain was simply enjoying the modest yet refined and homely comfort he had known since childhood. Uncle Pasha, however, noticed the moisture glistening in my eyes and, smiling to himself, thought, *"Welcome home, son."* As he poured the tea, he continued the conversation we had started over lunch.

"So, during the investigations — and there were several — it was revealed that an entire security battalion was sent to Belarus. It was mostly composed of Ukrainians who had switched sides to join the Nazis."

"OUN members?" Andrei guessed, his eyes widening, not from surprise but because he had taken a sip of hot tea and scalded himself.

"Partially," the former intelligence officer replied curtly.

I didn't understand. "Who?"

"The captain means the Organisation of Ukrainian Nationalists. O-U-N," Uncle Pasha explained. "Which, by the way, still exists, although it's banned in our country and therefore operates underground. They" — he nodded at his nephew — "monitor OUN members and try to catch them red-handed, but not too successfully. However, in the West, and especially in Canada, the organisation is completely legal."

I was hearing about this for the first time. "What do they do? What do they want?"

Pavel Andreevich pressed his lips together. "They crave to create a Ukrainian state, to put it simply."

"And why is that forbidden?"

"I hardly know where to begin!" the former Chekist smirked wryly. He cleared his throat and took a deep breath. We were in for an after-dinner lecture.

"Perhaps I should start by saying that fertile Ukraine's lands lie at the crossroads of many routes. This territory has been contested by established states from *all sides*, but neither Poland, Hungary, Romania, Russia, nor later the Soviet Union have ever been willing to give up their claims to it in favour of the Ukrainians."

"Why not?"

The uncle and nephew exchanged looks tinged with something like pity, astonished by my political ignorance.

Andrei snorted. "For a state to give up territory as an act of goodwill? That's never happened in history! Never. A territory is surrendered only under duress, like after losing a war, for instance..."

"Correct," Pavel Andreevich said. "It's especially complicated with the Ukrainians. They are the descendants of Cossacks, the free people who roamed with weapons in hand for centuries, seeking fortune along the edges of several countries, along borders and in no man's land. Hence the name 'Ukraine.'*

These free Cossacks eventually settled, developed a unique culture, and began calling themselves Ukrainians, but they never managed to unite into a single state, perhaps due to a lack of cultural and historical unity, as they adopted the traditions of whichever country's border they drifted to and never developed a clear sense of belonging. At least, not yet…"

"Do you think they will manage in the future?" Andrei asked.

"We'll see…" the former intelligence officer replied evasively. Giving voice to the anxiety that had been troubling him for days, he added, "Big changes are coming…"

The essence of the problem seemed clear to me: this was precisely how animals that lived in herds and pride behaved. So, I rephrased the problem.

"In other words, Ukrainians were trying to secure the land they inhabited, to provide resources for their subspecies, but other subspecies had so far proved stronger."

Uncle Pasha stared at me in surprise, then burst out laughing. "Spot on! See, Captain, how simple it all is?" He winked his brown eye. "Although 'subspecies' is quite an unusual term for a nation. And besides… whether they all belong to one subspecies or multiple is still up for debate. They don't even all follow the same religion. Western Ukrainians are Catholics, like their closest neighbours, the Poles, Romanians, and Hungarians, while those in the East follow orthodoxy, like the Russians."

"Religion isn't a biological characteristic," I countered quite seriously, but Andrei still giggled.

The usual after-lunch conversation in the Pilatov family was an excellent opportunity to understand why homo sapiens complicated the natural struggle for survival so much. In my eyes, everything looked simple, even somewhat primitive.

"So, the OUN wants to secure resources for their subspecies?" I said. "That's natural, even in the animal world!"

“Perhaps so, but it all comes down to methods, doesn’t it?” replied Pavel Andreevich. “You’re trying to equate humans with animals, but people don’t like that comparison.”

“Why not? It’s true!”

The colonel smirked. “Good question! For thousands of years, we’ve convinced ourselves that reason fundamentally distinguishes us from the rest of the fauna.”

“And that’s also true,” I said, “but it doesn’t eliminate either your biological nature or ours.”

“We prefer not to think about it,” Uncle Pasha said sarcastically. “Instead, we philosophise,” he added, taking a jab at his nephew. “Humanism is the most widespread philosophy in Europe, isn’t it, Andrei?”

“Humanism, which claims that homo sapiens hold the highest value?” I clarified, recalling information I had obtained from the Unity.

The colonel nodded and Andrei explained. “Humanism declared us the kings of Nature. Perhaps that’s why it has remained popular for so many centuries.”

“Why do you need to be the kings?” I asked, curious.

“It makes it easier to claim all the resources!” the captain blurted out, surprising even himself. The colonel looked at his nephew with pride. “Believing in one’s own superiority is simply profitable. Furthermore, it’s also the foundation of nationalism and racism. It all fits together!”

“So, homo sapiens declared themselves of the highest value, thus permitting themselves to dominate other species. Next, they began the competition among their subspecies,” I translated. “Predatory animals are quite prone to eliminating competition in territorial struggles. However, as you said, humans have a reason, given by Nature, to cooperate and negotiate for survival. Otherwise, they risk degeneration and extinction.”

“That’s exactly where the contradiction arises,” Pavel Pilatov agreed. “According to the humanist philosophy, every person is valuable." He had finished his tea and was pacing the room to stretch his legs. "In this light, the desire for 'subspecies preservation' doesn't justify killing other humans, such as peaceful Polish or Jewish civilians in the territories that OUN members sought to claim at the beginning of this century."

"So, they tried to eliminate other resource contenders, as animals do," I translated again. "That's exactly how large predators fight for territory."

"Predators? Oh yes!" Pavel Andreevich picked up the thread. "Terrible people once led OUN. They bared their teeth at their neighbours, those who, as you put it, interfered with their claim to resources in their habitat." My "simplified" view of homo sapiens' history amused the colonel, though he couldn't deny that lofty national ideals, like any product of the human brain, have biological origins. "Unfortunately, not all homo sapiens are even humanists. Nationalism pays better for our vampires."

"And only in the USSR did Ukraine become a political entity first!" Andrei said with such smugness, as if partial political autonomy for Ukraine were his personal achievement. "And for the first time in history, it gained the territories the OUN had fought for so long!"

"You don't know history so well!" the former intelligence officer countered. "The Ukrainian state was set up earlier by OUN figures and lasted eight months, from April to December of 1918. But I don't blame you for missing *minor* details. The twentieth century saw so many territorial changes that it's easy to get lost." Uncle Pasha pitied his nephew's lack of education. Some topics discussed in Pilatov's parlour couldn't be found in school or even university textbooks. After all, it's impossible to be interested in information you don't know exists! So, the colonel relented and ultimately confirmed Andrei's point. "But you are right. Soviet Ukraine did eventually acquire almost all the territories claimed by the OUN in 1918, and even more after the Great Patriotic War."

“So, the OUN has no purpose now!” Andrei boasted. “Ukraine is the richest republic in the USSR!”

“That wasn’t always the case. Many lives were lost for today’s prosperity, and not just in Ukraine, but at present, yes, it’s hard to call Ukrainians oppressed. Soviet power unlocked the republic’s economic potential. Khrushchev even passed the Crimea — the country’s biggest health resort — to them. Just live and be happy! Politically, the republic is far from independent, but Ukrainians don’t lack power if they want it! Half the Politburo** consists of them, which, frankly, in and of itself is a bit worrying. No wonder those documents” — Uncle Pasha waved towards the study where the Khatyn files were laid out — “are still classified. And yet, the OUN hasn’t disappeared.”

“What more do they want?” I asked.

“Power, I suppose,” Pavel Andreevich replied.

“Why do they need power?” In Lemuria, where Unified Consciousness governs everything, power is unnecessary. Yet some homo sapiens are willing to spend their entire lives pursuing control over their kind! We never understood this.

“Why?” the uncle and nephew exclaimed in unison, staring at me in bewilderment. The colonel even paused mid-stride. I tried to explain. “Why seek power if you have everything you need, with little risk of losing it?”

“Well… there’s always the risk of loss, at least potentially,” Andrei countered.

“That’s why you’re so consumed by eternal anxiety!” I thought. *“The fear of losing!”*

Pavel Andreevich picked up on my thoughts. “Yes. Out of that fear, a person wants more than they have. And the need for control arises automatically to keep and multiply the possessions. Hence, the value of power…”

“So, for our opponents in the West, gullible and vain Ukrainian emigrants are a real treasure,” concluded the captain, trying to steer us away from the silent dialogue in which he couldn't participate.

"Indeed," Uncle Pasha agreed. "Without them, the OUN would have no purpose nowadays, precisely because of the peaceful and relatively prosperous lives of ordinary Ukrainians, those who don't aspire to power."

He kept pacing back and forth, and to be honest, his constant motion was beginning to annoy me. The second I realised my irritation, the colonel gestured for us to follow him and headed to the study, intending us to return to our investigation. Andrei and I rose and trudged after him. From the study room, we heard the colonel continue.

"If you want my opinion, the OUN's struggle was and always will be doomed to failure."

"What makes you so sure, Uncle?" asked the captain, yawning as he slumped heavily into a chair by the desk. He felt sleepy after lunch.

"Because their goals are shortsighted, even romantic."

"Romantic?" Andrei repeated with a laugh. The idea of romantic nationalists woke him right up.

"Exactly. A romantic guy thinks, 'I'll fall in love, get married, and be happy!' And he pursues his chosen one, doing foolish things like climbing up to her balcony with a rose between his teeth."

The captain chuckled, picturing some bloke in wide Cossack pants scaling a drainpipe with a red flower clenched in his mouth.

"However," the colonel continued, "if this romantic hero never considers how he'll build a future family life, such love is unlikely to have a future."

"Maybe he doesn't even want to get married!" Pilatov Junior interjected mischievously.

"That too. And that's exactly what the OUN is like as it flirts with the nation, promising some ephemeral independence from who knows what and even aspiring for dominance! They wave slogans about freedom like those roses between teeth. In reality, it's just an overly prolonged courtship phase. I'm not against the idea of freedom at all, but promising freedom to a nation is like offering a rose to a woman — it can easily turn out to be the cheese in a mousetrap."

"Now I get it!" said the captain. "It's an unusual comparison."

"The Ukrainian nationalists have never presented a clear plan for how they would care for their people if independence were gained," Pavel Andreevich continued. "And ordinary citizens, those who make up the nation, would first and foremost want to live normal, peaceful lives, at least no worse than those they live now as part of the USSR. Independence won't guarantee their well-being at all. It's abstract. You can't spread it on bread, just as you can't feed a family with roses. It is not serious. A smart woman understands this, and so should a smart nation..."

"What if you asked Ukrainians right now whether they want independence? From the USSR, for instance?" Andrei squinted as he asked.

"I'm sure the majority would say no!" the KGB colonel replied.

"In other words, the OUN has no plan for peaceful living?" I asked. "They're fighting against oppression by their neighbours rather than for the happiness of their people? And beyond that, whatever happens, happens? Is that it?"

"Psychologists suggest negative mindsets lead to failure," Andrei said in the tone of a young professor, making the colonel and me smile.

"Judging by their reliance on vague phrases and reckless methods, OUN leaders seem to crave not so much independence for their nation as power for themselves, probably so they can have the freedom to oppress others," Uncle Pasha remarked. "I wouldn't be surprised if they were even willing to exploit and sacrifice their own fellow Ukrainians. They'd likely reveal their vampiric nature immediately if they ever gained power. That's the first point."

"And is there a second?" Andrei asked.

"Of course," Pavel Andreevich nodded. He leaned back in his chair and steepled his fingers. "Caught between several so-called 'oppressors,' these hetmans*** first take one side, then the other, switching between East and West. They always chase the bigger and better deal. Simply put, they don't aim to free the nation or truly care about it. They swap masters, breaking agreements with previous ones. And the funniest part is they end up losing everyone's trust."

"A bitter kind of comedy," Andrei said.

"So, they've been going round in circles for about five hundred years," the colonel continued. "When Mazepa defected to the Swedes in the 18th century, Peter the Great even awarded him the Order of Judas in absentia. And Mazepa's descendants, the Cossacks' leaders, that is, still wear that award."

Andrei rubbed his chin with his fingers. "I knew about Mazepa, of course, but I never thought about him on such a global scale… So, what does this mean? That Ukraine's geographical position made its people traitors?"

In response to this blunt interpretation of history, Pavel Andreevich suddenly slammed his wrinkled hand on the documents resting on the desk so hard that a small cloud of dust rose from the papers. The captain even jumped in his chair.

"Don't you dare!" the retired Soviet spy shouted. He was almost choking with rage. "There's no such thing as a nation of traitors! A nation is made up of individuals, just like yourself!"

Andrei and I stared at the colonel, shocked by his abrupt transformation. His gaunt cheeks, wasted by illness, had suddenly sharpened, and his face, ravaged by recent suffering, took on an implacable, harsh expression. This was the face that had terrified the witnesses I had spoken to. Pavel Pilatov rose from his chair and paced the room again.

"Like a tiger in a cage!" Andrei thought.

"And don't you dare blame the Ukrainians for the destruction of Khatyn!" the colonel said, continuing his tirade in a thunderous voice. "A gang of sadist vampires was at work in Belarus, the monsters with no nationality, the traitors not to any specific country but to human nature itself!"

"Well said," I thought, and the old man added in a low, ominous voice:

"And they'll all end up in the ninth circle of hell.****" Andrei and I looked at him blankly, and the colonel, noticing our confusion, gave his ill-educated nephew a piercing look as if nailing him to his seat. "Read Dante!" Then, he fell silent.

Pavel Andreevich stopped by the window and stared at the raindrops sliding monotonously down the glass. Andrei and I dared not speak. The monumental antique clock's chime in the office's corner made both Pilatovs flinch.

The colonel said, this time more calmly, "If there were any OUN members among the executioners at Khatyn, they certainly weren't fighting for their nation's independence. They were trying to grab as much as possible, either material goods or subtle energy."

"What independence?" the captain responded cautiously. "From the testimonies of former Schutzmänners, it's clear as day," he said, jabbing a finger at the interrogation protocols spread out on the desk. "The Germans didn't see them as equals. They simply used them. I wouldn't be surprised if, had the Nazis won, all those security battalions, having outlived their usefulness, would have followed their victims straight to the crematorium."

"Who knows?" Uncle Pasha's voice held a note of uncertainty. "In any case, the brutal murder of women and children, strictly speaking, not even Russians, Poles, or Jews, is a rather questionable way to promote the ideology of freedom and independence."

"Ah! I think I understand why you altered the population's memory!" Andrei said, finally catching on. "For political reasons, right?"

"What reasons?" I asked.

"Well, look: Ukraine and Belorussia are parts of the same state, the union of the fifteen republics," Pilatov Junior explained. "If ordinary Belorussians remembered that a third of them had been killed by Ukrainians during the war, they'd blame all Ukrainians. The state would fall into interethnic strife and collapse. Isn't that right, Uncle Pasha?"

"Yes," the colonel confirmed. "Most affected witnesses testified that the police spoke Ukrainian or Russian with a Ukrainian accent. Many remembered this detail, but naturally, no specific names were mentioned. Such information does more harm than good..."

"Wait a minute, what do you mean by blaming 'all Ukrainians'?" I saw no logic in this.

"Do you know how the masses think?" Pavel Andreevich asked instead of answering. I didn't. "Everyone judges based on their own experiences. That's how it is!"

"Exactly!" the captain chimed in.

"So, the truth about traitors from punitive battalions would inevitably cast a shadow on others, even those Ukrainians who fought heroically against the Nazis. However, the inhabitants of occupied Belorussia didn't see the latter with their own eyes. What they did experience was the mass suffering inflicted by punishers who spoke Ukrainian. Do you grasp it now?"

What I was beginning to grasp seemed incomprehensible. Homo liberatus simply do not need to agonise over the question, "Who is to blame?" Nature itself expels anyone who violates its laws from Unity, leaving pure souls in peace.

"Yeah... National conflicts were worse than a bomb for the Soviet Union," Andrei reasoned. "And if it came down to choosing... Peace was, of course, more valuable than chasing some aging traitors in hiding. A real peacekeeping mission is a preemptive action!" he concluded, gazing at Uncle Pasha with admiration. "And what a massive undertaking! How on earth did you manage to pull it off?"

Colonel Pilatov finally decided to reveal the truth he had kept secret for years. "Back then, we had an entire group working on it. We travelled around villages and small towns, went to secondary schools and universities, and 'talked' to people. We did a thorough job. To this day, the whole country is certain that the crimes committed on Belorussian land were the work of the Germans… that is, only the Germans."

"That kind of manipulation wouldn't have worked with the Lemurians," I remarked. "Although I'm starting to understand why you resorted to hypnosis sessions. You were trying to maintain balance."

Pavel Andreevich shot me a sidelong glance and curled his lips.

"Balance… Yes, in a sense." The old intelligence officer, who had paused by the window, resumed his pacing around the study. This time, memories long imprisoned by his will were driving him. The hypnotist himself was clearly not in a state of harmony.

"I remember it well!" he exclaimed in agitation. "There was no other way to keep the peace in the western part of the country. The 118th Battalion had nearly two hundred collaborators, and Dirlewanger's Battalion about the same, though indeed, that one partially consisted of Germans. Elite cutthroats too. So, four hundred armed punishers burned and ravaged about six hundred peaceful Belarussian villages. It would have been grossly unfair to blame *all* Ukrainians for the atrocities committed by a handful of their compatriots — and that's exactly what could have happened had the memories of ordinary Belorussians remained untouched! Even a KGB captain couldn't resist generalising!" Uncle Pasha said, pointing an admonishing finger at his nephew, who shrank back in embarrassment. "In the first decade after the war, indiscriminate accusations against Ukrainians were already beginning to spread in Belorussia. Pain is blind… There was no other way to protect Ukrainians from such injustice and the whole country from internecine strife. We had no choice.

"The head of the Ukrainian SSR was the first to sound the alarm. Khrushchev valued his loyalty and listened to him. And so, the general secretary gave the order to take measures… quietly. It was in his personal interest too, as Khrushchev himself was Ukrainian. If the Belorussians had started telling the truth about how the leader's compatriots had shot, tortured, and burned half their republic, Khrushchev probably wouldn't have stayed in power for as long as he did. Our department was tasked with fixing the situation. We had good specialists. Now all the witnesses point to the Germans… Well, almost all of them."

"What do you mean by 'almost'? Were there exceptions? Didn't you encode everyone?" I asked, startled.

"No, there were no exceptions," replied the colonel. "It's just that our programming was purely generic. It didn't include forgetting specific individuals… so if citizens happened to encounter some traitors they had met during the war in person, the memory would automatically activate."

"Wow!" the captain marvelled. "Ingenious!"

"Thank you," Pavel Andreevich said with a smile of false modesty. "Gradually, criminals were still found and brought to justice, but only on an individual basis, without publicising their nationality."

"I see," said Andrei. "And how did the Ukrainian policemen end up in Belorussia?"

"Oh, that's a separate story!" The former intelligence officer gave a bitter smile. "The Nazis understood ethnic psychology very well since their ideology was based on the supremacy of the Aryan race. They recruited thugs from prisoners and defectors, grouped them by nationality to foster a sense of brotherhood within the security battalions, and ordered the execution of Jews at Babi Yar***** to bond these 'brothers' with blood. Then Nazis sent Ukrainian police forces to another republic. To Schutzmänners, Belorussians were not their own people..." Pavel Andreevich paused. "You see, Yan? The national idea becomes all the more absurd, the harder vampires try to justify their thirst for energy."

Andrei snapped his fingers. "Aha! Now I understand: the German soldiers were 'protected from trauma' because the dirtiest job was done by the Ukrainian battalions!"

"The German command was exceptionally skilled at manipulation. Archives hold plenty of examples and evidence," Uncle Pasha said, reaching for a copy of a letter from the first microfilm. Andrei had spent the day before developing and printing the photographs. "Here it is. The original is in German. This is the translation," the colonel explained. "'An order from the chief of the Security Police and SD of the Reichskommissariat Ostland concerning the organisation of anti-partisan operations in the General Commissariat of Belorussia. Minsk. 18 November 1942.

"'All intelligence commanders are to immediately relay, *verbally*, to all noncommissioned officers and soldiers. The Reichsführer-SS has assigned Obergruppenführer Bach the task of combating partisan bands in the General Commissariat of Belorussia. Obergruppenführer SS Bach has delegated to me the responsibility for necessary police measures...'" Pavel Andreevich looked at our expectant faces over his glasses. "Now, somewhere here..." he said, raising a finger and scanning the long text filled with standard military communication phrases. "Aha, here it is. 'I draw attention to the fact that entire villages are often *under the yoke* of partisan *bands*, so the residents should not be held accountable for their past behaviour. What matters is how they acted during the operation against the partisans. I emphasise the significant responsibility involved in such decisions. Political and propaganda factors must be considered…'"

Andrei stared at Uncle Pasha in confusion. "So, the German command didn't plan to exterminate the local population entirely? I always thought they aimed to *cleanse* the territory by eliminating the locals!" The word "cleanse" made me shudder, but I restrained myself and didn't interrupt.

"See? You fell for it too!" Pavel Andreevich said reproachfully. "Most likely, Andryusha, there was a plan for 'cleansing,' but the 'master race' needed obedient servants on the conquered territories. The most submissive cowards could have been spared. After all, slavery exists in the mind of the slave no less than in that of the master. Any relationship between people happens only when all parties involved agree to it."

"Oh come on!" Andrei protested. "What if there's no choice? What if people are forced into slavery?"

"There's always a choice — sorry for the cliché," Uncle Pasha retorted passionately. "All oppression is based on fear of death or pain, but history knows enough examples of people choosing struggle or death over slavery. So yes, you can force someone to obey temporarily, but not for long. It's far more reliable if they act as if it's in line with their own beliefs. Coercion through fear depends on consent rooted in fear, while manipulation through persuasion relies on controlling beliefs — that's all. What do you think about this, Yan?" He turned to me. "After all, your race doesn't know slavery, does it?"

I knew about oppression and fear both from the older Lemurians and my vague childhood memories of the war — too many for one day.

"Exploitation of one's own kind is the primary sign of vampirism," I replied. "Andrei and I discussed this recently. Coercing a homo liberatus physically is impossible, and manipulating us is also futile because we hear not only words but also thoughts. That's why we consider ourselves free compared to your species." I didn't want to dishearten my companions since they were part of the human history they were discussing. Homo sapiens are slaves of their system, without exception. They cannot avoid taking part in it, so I saw no point in dwelling on what couldn't be changed. I simply suggested, "Let's return to the investigation. I feel we're on the right track! Isn't that so?"

Pavel Andreevich, who had caught fragments of my unflattering thoughts about humanity, initially did not respond. However, after a few moments, he finally made an effort to continue.

"Judging by the number of people killed and villages burned, it turns out that either the elderly, women, and children living there were all 'bandit-communists' —"

"Hmm, especially the children!" Andrei interjected sarcastically.

" — or the direct perpetrators, the police, didn't care about orders from above. Again, either the executioners had their own goals, different from those set by the Germans, or they simply took pleasure in the sight of torture and murder… I would say, 'Think what you like,' but in this case, it is precisely the motives we are trying to understand if I'm not mistaken."

I nodded, agreeing with the colonel's train of thought. Andrei reached for the report his uncle had read and scanned the document.

"'Entire villages are under the oppression of partisan gangs.' Seriously?" he snorted.

"Technically, if one wishes, any version of events can be disputed, especially without witnesses. And even then… testimonies can be interpreted in one's favour," remarked the former intelligence officer.

"I doubt the German command sought to clarify the details with the population of the occupied territories," said the captain, and I suddenly remembered:

"The locals helped the partisans voluntarily! That is certain. I recently spoke with Aleksandr Zhelobkovich, and not only that, I also referred to his memories directly. So, the German dispatch was not true!"

"The German dispatch was written for German officers, the living people who needed to be motivated and kept under the illusion of righteousness," Pavel Andreevich explained with a smirk. "What could be more noble than protecting the civilian population from bandits? Of course, not all German soldiers realised that the 'bandits' were locals 'oppressing' their own villages and families. And even if some Germans suspected as much, they still went along with the legend, because the genocide in which they had to participate needed justification."

"Interesting," the captain said. "What about that guy, the one responsible for fighting the partisans in Belorussia?"

"Bach," Uncle Pasha answered, and sighing sadly, added, "Like the great German composer…"

"Yes, him… Do you think he believed that Belorussian villages suffered because of partisans? Or did he just say that to convince his subordinates?"

"I think both."

"How so?" I asked.

"You see, most people can detect lies intuitively — through facial expressions, gestures, and even speech patterns," explained the hypnotist. "Therefore, only a propagandist who believes in their own propaganda can be successful at their job, as from their perspective they would not be lying."

This idea seemed bizarre to me. "How can someone convince themselves of something that isn't true? That's madness! Stupidity!"

"You see, when spreading propaganda helps achieve important goals such as career advancement, fame, or even financial gain, hypocrisy — a very human form of psychological defence — steps in," Pavel Andreevich explained. "And so, the propagandists ignore even glaring contradictions between their beliefs and reality."

I couldn't hold back. "Are they fools?"

"Well... how shall I put it?" The old spy smirked. "In a sense, you're right. Most likely, such people lack critical thinking, and the smarter ones rationalise and use pseudo-arguments. But what a result! The average listener struggles to discern where reality ends and brainwashing begins, if the propagandists have been brainwashed before attempting their jobs."

"Or they made an effort to brainwash themselves for the cause!" the captain chimed in.

"That happens too," Pavel Andreevich nodded in agreement. "When people say that everyone believes their own truth, they usually mean exactly that. Everyone believes a truth that benefits them!" The colonel gave his nephew a meaningful look, hinting at the captain's hidden ideological doubts, then recited:

The scholar, peer of Galileo,
Was no less clever than Galileo.
He knew the Earth revolves around the Sun,
But he had a family to protect.

"Yevtushenko!" Andrei said, finally having the chance to show off a bit of poetry knowledge.

"And admit it, the poet expressed it very well," the colonel noted, smiling at his nephew approvingly. "*On both sides of the border*, people turn a blind eye to whatever is too inconvenient to notice. Many Soviet propagandists, especially ordinary ones, truly believe in the imminent victory of communism, ignoring the burning issues of our reality."

"Absolutely!"

"On the other hand, Western politicians are convinced that communism is a plague, mistakenly equating it with dictatorship. Yet Marx wrote his works in Germany and England!" Uncle

Pasha looked at my confused expression. "Sorry, Yan, I got sidetracked. I think you'll figure it all out gradually. I just wanted to say that there can be no real victors among propagandists — only temporary ones. These people often lie, including and especially to themselves... Bach and his officers most likely preferred to turn a blind eye to the brutal extermination of Belorussian civilians, even if they didn't give direct orders for it."

"And the perpetrators, apparently, had their own interpretations of the orders!" Andrei remarked sarcastically.

"Depending on whose orders, I suppose..." the colonel replied ambiguously. "And many of them were undoubtedly moral degenerates, which you" — he nodded at me — "call vampires. Especially the commanding officers. Killing on orders and giving orders to kill are two very different things."

"Really?" I was surprised. The psychology of a murderer was a mystery to me and hardly an appealing subject, but studying it was necessary to understand the nature of vampires.

"Only a psychopath who values other people's lives as nothing can give an order to kill. Such a person is indifferent to or even enjoys others' death and suffering," explained the former scout. "Whereas a soldier on the battlefield often kills out of fear of being killed. Later, most traitors justified their crimes this way in court. I think their fear was indeed overwhelming, and their psyche was geared towards survival at any cost, even if it meant throwing children into the fire."

"Unfortunately, such people truly exist," the captain clarified grimly. "Although until danger strikes, they..." He sighed. "... *we*... don't even realise what we are capable of."

"Yes, but identifying such people in peacetime isn't difficult," our more experienced companion replied, trying to cheer up his nephew. "Potential traitors always take the winner's side, or anyone who throws them a bigger bone, for that matter.

A natural analogy would be a jackal, which is also indiscriminate and often feeds on the leftovers of a larger predator to survive."

"It's more complicated with people, though," Andrei smirked. "One side wins today, another tomorrow. Easy to miscalculate!"

"Those who sided with the Nazis did miscalculate," emphasised Pilatov Senior.

The captain glanced again at the document signed by a subordinate who shared the surname of a great composer.

"I wonder what exactly they reported to this Bach about their 'exploits'?"

Pavel Andreevich picked up another photograph of a report translated from German.

"Here it is, 'from the commander of the 118th Police Security Battalion to the SS and police chief of Borisov District about a partisan attack on the battalion near the village of Guba and the destruction of the village of Khatyn near Pleshchenitsy… Signed: Kerner, Major of the Schutzpolizei.' We know this Kerner well, though he's no longer alive," Pavel Andreevich added, casting me a quick, mischievous glance. "Don't worry! Kerner wasn't the only one in charge."

Scanning the text, he picked out the key sections.

"'… reporting the following: On 22 March 1943, telephone communication between Pleshchenitsy and Logoisk was damaged by gangs, that is, partisans. At 9:30, two platoons of the First Company of the 118th Police Security Battalion were dispatched to guard the repair team and clear possible roadblocks…' This was the battalion formed in Kiev from Ukrainians. We know it from the trials of the 1960s and 1970s," Pavel Andreevich interrupted to clarify, "we" meaning the KGB. "'It was commanded by Hauptmann of the Schutzpolizei, Velke.' Here, Kerner reports events leading up to the burning of Khatyn."

"So Velke wasn't going on leave?" I asked, recalling my conversation with the museum director. The colonel looked at me over his glasses.

"I don't know. I doubt it matters," he replied, and continued reading.

"'About 600 metres past the village of Guba, they encountered workers felling trees. When questioned, the workers said they hadn't seen any bandits. About 300 metres further on, heavy machine-gun and rifle fire was opened from the east. In the ensuing battle, Hauptmann Velke and three Ukrainian policemen were killed, and two others were wounded. After a short but fierce fight, the enemy withdrew eastward towards Khatyn, taking their dead and wounded. Following the Ukrainian platoon commander's orders, the battle was halted due to insufficient forces to continue the operation. On the way back, the mentioned workers were arrested in the forest under suspicion of aiding the bandits. Soon after, near Guba, some of them attempted to escape. As a result, 23 were killed by our fire, and the remaining detainees were taken to the Pleshchenitsy gendarmerie for interrogation. Since their guilt couldn't be proven, they were released.'"

"Justice!" Andrei scoffed. "Did the Germans, or whoever... the Ukrainians, these policemen, really think that those declared innocent would leave with gratitude in their hearts after watching their comrades being shot?"

"Everyone judges others by themselves," the former intelligence officer responded with a grin. Then he read on. "'To pursue the fleeing enemy, larger forces were deployed, including units of the Dirlewanger's SS Battalion. Meanwhile, the enemy retreated to Khatyn, a village known for its pro-bandit sympathies. The village was surrounded and attacked from all sides. The enemy offered fierce resistance from every house, so heavy weapons like anti-tank guns and mortars had to be used. During the battle, many residents were killed, along with 34 bandits. Some died in the fire. Most residents had, in any case, left Khatyn days earlier to avoid association with the bandits…' How interesting!" Pavel Andreevich noted indignantly. "They herded the entire village into a barn and burned them alive, yet not a word about the barn in the report, although the author personally commanded the execution. 'Residents left the village.' That's an outright lie!"

"Paper doesn't blush," the captain muttered bitterly. "And clearly, no one bothered to verify it."

"Of course not! 'Villagers along the highway could see everything.' They surely saw it and testified later. The bastard didn't manage to kill them all!" Uncle Pasha shouted, finally losing his composure. Now both the old and the young Chekists were reliving the events described in the report as if they had happened yesterday and here, not forty years ago and a thousand kilometres away.

"How modest," Andrei carried on. "Not a word about burning people alive or shooting everyone who tried to escape!"

"So Kerner didn't write anything about that in the report?" I asked, simply surprised.

"He probably meant it under 'died in the fire'!" Pilatov Junior quipped even more indignantly. "You can't fault him!"

"Covering his backside before his superiors while posing as a noble warrior!" Pavel Andreevich explained with disgust. "I noticed the German authorities requested details about Khatyn several times, yet this scoundrel took three weeks to fabricate this. Look at the date: the 12th of April!" He waved the sheet of photo paper as if Kerner were hiding between its typed lines.

"How did he get away with it?" the captain wondered.

"Easily. Look who the report is addressed to. The same Bach. Obergruppenführer Bach's real surname was Zelewski."

"A Pole?" Andrei asked. "How do you know, Uncle Pasha?"

"Am I not a scout? A Pole, yes, but born in Germany. He changed his surname to pass as a true Aryan, which he wasn't.

Borrowed it. The freak probably liked classical music!" Pavel Andreevich shuddered as if he was about to vomit. "By the way, Auschwitz was established under his direct supervision. So, this Zelewski, this fake Bach, was clearly a bloodthirsty vampire who relished the war."

While Pavel Andreevich spoke about the Polish vampire posing as a true Aryan, my outrage boiled over.

"Poles and Germans? Russians and Ukrainians? What absurdity! You're no different from each other! You're all homo sapiens, equally human, none better than the other! A master race and a race of slaves? What nonsense! Revolting. Mindless!"

Overcome with emotion and fearing my energy might harm my companions, I teleported out of the study without waiting for their stunned responses.

What exactly enraged me? Forced to peer into the most repulsive corners of human history in search of *my* vampire, I realised something so clearly that it became unbearably painful for me: ideas of national exceptionalism had been exploited for centuries by homo sapiens to provide resources and to muffle the primal fear of deprivation. The philosophy of superiority, whatever form it took, justified the extermination or suppression of competitors, thus serving the most primitive animal behaviour that was unworthy of a being endowed with seven chakras!

How could people fail to understand that every war they waged was fought between equals stuck at an instrumental stage of development and that the victory of a particular subspecies called "a nation" was nothing more than a temporary illusion? How didn't homo sapiens see that mutual extermination hindered their evolution?

Even before my return, I was aware of humanity's self-destructive games, but I had had no idea things were so critically out of hand on Earth.

---

*The word “Ukraine” is derived from the Slavic root word “krai” – a margin, edge.
**Politburo (Political Bureau): the highest political body of the USSR
***Hetman: here, military commanders who were, in fact, the leaders of Ukrainian Cossacks and the decision-makers acting on their behalf
****The Ninth Circle of Hell: in Dante’s *The Divine Comedy*, the place of punishment for traitors
*****Babi Yar (Kiev): a site of mass massacres conducted by Nazi forces at the end of September 1941. Victims included 34,000 Jews, Romani, communists, and Soviet war prisoners.

Chapter 12. The Geography of Betrayal: Part 2

It was miserable outside. The unpleasant dampness crept into every crevice, leaving not a single patch of space dry. Murky cold droplets hung from the light green leaves scattered across the bushes lining the palisade. Having gathered enough weight, they fell into the rain-beaten grass. The ancestral home of the Pilatovs gazed silently at the dreary landscape through its tear-streaked windows.

In an irritation I had never experienced before that day, I burst out of the gas-heated house, completely forgetting about temperature regulation, and the drizzle, swept down from the dismal grey clouds, quickly cooled my anger to a shivering ache. My entire body was trembling with chills by the time I reached the garden. Its emptiness felt unwelcoming among the soaked fruit trees. I took off my shoes, approached a magnificent apple tree, and placed both palms against its slick trunk. All garden inhabitants had hidden away, trying to escape the persistence of the penetrating rain. No one seemed willing to join me this time, so I replenished my strength alone.

After some time, I managed to balance my body temperature, and the spring rain no longer felt like Nature's lament. My thoughts settled into the desirable equilibrium. Barefoot, I paced through the wet grass, pondering how my new friends' ancestors had lived in this harsh world. How they had hidden from the scorching sun, the cold rains, and the bitter frosts, not even guessing the existence of lush tropical lands. How they had learned to create fire and then come to rely on it utterly. Could the ancient inhabitants of old Lemuria have evolved into homo liberatus in the inhospitable and unpredictable climate of the temperate zone? After all, on the island, they had fed on Nature's abundant gifts year-round and spent their time on experiments and inquiries without worrying about tomorrow. However, here everyone seemed preoccupied with the hardships ahead: humans gathered supplies, some aminals changed their fur for masking colours, while others hibernated through the cold season, only to wake up and start storing fat for the next winter. When one's existence is so often under threat, there is likely little time for finer pursuits.

Reasoning through the way homo sapiens ended up in their vicious circle did not make things easier, but it did help me to be more tolerant of their weaknesses.

Finally, I returned to the house. My spontaneous escape had given the Pilatovs a breather. The uncle and nephew were now calmly drinking tea in the kitchen. In response to their questioning looks, I simply waved my hand, letting them know that I let my steam out. Then Pavel Andreevich said, "I think we should stick to the main issue rather than drowning you in our musings, Yan."

"I'm not so sure," I replied. "I've learned a lot from your reflections, too. It's just..."

"What you've learned, you don't like," the colonel finished for me, smiling sympathetically.

"In a way."

Andrei rose from the table and cleared the cups. "We're wasting time!" He then headed to the study to bury himself in dusty papers again. We followed.

After half an hour of silent document sorting, Pavel Andreevich spoke again.

"Now, to the point. The German command used the 118th and Dirlewanger's Battalions for the filthiest jobs. Dirlewanger's was a mixed unit, made up of Germans and traitors from our people." At the word "our," young Pilatov snorted, but Uncle Pasha, ignoring this, added, "Mostly Ukrainians, too. Importantly, almost all the punitive forces were not locals, so the victims of the atrocities committed by the police in Belorussian villages neither knew their executioners by name nor invited them in for tea. Here's what the defendant Grabarovsky testified to during the 1961 trial.

"'All the residents who didn't manage to escape were driven out of their homes and herded to a barn. Whose barn it was, I don't know. I can't recall how many people I personally drove to that barn, but I know I brought families there more than once. When all the residents of Khatyn were gathered at the barn, they were forced inside and then shot there on German orders. I was armed with a rifle and also fired at the barn with people inside. After shooting the civilians, the barn with the bodies and the entire village of Khatyn were burned down. I didn't set fire to the barn or houses myself. I don't remember who did. I don't know the names Kaminsky, Yetka, or Zhelobkovich…' See?" Colonel Pilatov broke off, turning to me. "Here is what should interest you. Although most Nazi lapdogs tracked down by our agents after the war were sentenced to death, some managed to have their executions commuted to long prison terms. To earn their lives back, so to speak."

I didn't understand. "What do you mean by 'earn'?"

"Through collaboration. This time with KGB," explained Pavel Andreevich with a note of disdain. "Those detained during the investigation eagerly named their former comrades in arms. They hadn't changed. They were happy to sell out their fellow Ukrainians, hoping to save their own skins. Some succeeded. So, you'll mostly have to fish for information from the testimonies of these scoundrels."

"This one gave a lot of names," I said, showing a protocol I had recently taken out of the folder. "'I. E. Tupiga, (Dirlewanger unit) Minsk, 13th of June, 1961. After the battle with the partisans, we destroyed the civilian population in the village. Possibly, as Grabarovsky suggests, it was in Khatyn, but I do not remember the name of the village. I also do not remember under what circumstances the civilian population of this village was destroyed or what exactly my role was in this atrocity…'"

"Look at that! This one's lost his memory too!" Andrei sneered contemptuously.

"Denial is a common interrogation tactic," Colonel Pilatov explained. "This trick is well known in investigative circles. Claiming not to remember creates a chance that no further evidence against you will be found. In the end, you can always 'suddenly' remember later... Didn't they teach you that at the KGB school?"

Andrei flushed and retorted defiantly, "They did, but I rarely get to apply my knowledge!"

The colonel shrugged and rolled his eyes at his nephew's childishness while Junior Pilatov added, "In any case, this guy's tactic of forgetting wasn't particularly successful."

"Why is that?" I asked, curious about how things worked among intelligent beings who couldn't hear each other's thoughts.

"It's simple logic," Andrei explained. "This defendant's service in the punitive battalion is already indisputably proven, and not denied by him, right?" I nodded. "So, the only reason this... what's his name? Tupiga... might not remember his own and his comrades' actions in Khatyn is if there were many such Khatyns on his way! If it had been a one-off case, forgetting it would only be possible due to memory impairment... or hypnosis. You didn't plant such a suggestion, did you, Uncle Pasha?"

The hypnotist flashed a disdained expression and shook his head.

"Well, then this Tupiga is indirectly admitting that he participated in burning down not just one but many villages. Idiot. He really is a *tupiga*. That is, dullard," concluded the captain victoriously. Seeing that his logic hadn't particularly impressed us, he added with a sigh of disappointment, "There are lots of testimonies like this. Look, memory's labyrinths become even more elaborate in their selectivity," Andrei lifted another protocol from the table. "'M. V. Maidanov (Dirlewanger unit) 08.05.61... I do not recall such facts as the villagers firing back at us. However, there were firefights with partisans in many places in the forests. Such settlements were usually burned down by us, and the inhabitants were exterminated. As for killing Soviet citizens in individual houses and barns through shooting and burning, such cases were individual, as I have already testified in previous interrogations. Perhaps this also applies to the village mentioned by the other witness. Usually, civilians rounded up in separate houses and barns were shot by our platoon's punitive troops, who had machine guns and submachine guns, whereas those with rifles were rarely involved. I was one of the latter…'"

"So, he remembers having a rifle, but after that, falls into amnesia. Astonishing!" the captain commented, then continued reading. "'… I do not deny my involvement in committing atrocities in the village of Khatyn. However, I do not remember shooting at a barn with people inside. I led people to the site of the massacre, specifically to barns, in many villages. Most likely, I gathered people in the barn and set the buildings on fire in this village too. What the punitive troops named by Grabarovsky did, I do not remember.' At least he remembers Grabarovsky!"

"And Grabarovsky named many," Pavel Andreevich noted, still holding the earlier document, but Andrei raised his index finger, demanding to finish.

"'Grabarovsky correctly states that the following took part in this punitive operation with me: Sakhno, Yurchenko, Surkov, Shinkuvich, Yalinsky, Sadon, Zayvy, Umanets, Pogachyov, Stopchenko, Maidanov, Bagriy, Gudkov, Radkovsky, Kiriyenko, Mokhnach, Romanenko, Ivanov, Maidanuk, Slynko, Tereshchenko, Rozhkov, Doloko, Zlan, Makeev, Evchik, Bakuta, Godinov, Goltvyanik, Tereshchuk…'" Andrei stopped reading. "My god, there could be dozens of names here! We'll drown in this and still not find the one we need! Which one of them are you supposed to eliminate?"

I shook my head, looking at my friend. “Eliminate.” Of course, Captain Pilatov himself had never hurt a fly in his life, but how casually it sounded coming from the mouth of a homo sapien! Was it not tragic enough that the mere possibility of killing a stranger neither surprised nor disturbed people? Or that murder stood at the hearts of the most thrilling plots invented by their writers for entertainment? At moments like these, a sense of hopelessness crept so close to my heart that I felt the urge to abandon the mission, return to sapien-free New Lemuria, and help my brethren build a world better than the one that had taken shape on Earth…

The colonel's insistent voice brought me back to reality.

“We should focus on the living witnesses. At least their testimonies can be checked and clarified.”

“Exactly!” I agreed. Dealing with the memories of living people was far easier and faster for me than working through papers.

“You need to go back to the archives, Yan,” said Pavel Andreevich. “Here, we have the materials of a major trial against former punishers conducted in 1961, and another process took place in the seventies, and its files might prove even more useful since that information is somewhat more recent, and many new names surfaced then. These witnesses are more likely to be still alive…”

“I don't understand,” Andrei said. “So before their names surfaced, the war criminals were just walking free? Fifteen, maybe even nearly thirty years after the war?”

“Not exactly. The NKVD knew very well that people, who ended up serving the Nazis, did so after being captured. Those Soviet citizens agreed to cooperate with the enemy, some out of fear, others out of conviction. Naturally, our security agencies couldn't investigate the history of every former prisoner of war. After all, our staff were human too, and they couldn't read minds! Well, almost no one could.” He glanced at me sadly and spread his hands. The carefully concealed loneliness of this gifted homo sapien briefly escaped the mental prison where Pavel Pilatov kept his unruly thoughts and feelings.

With an effort of will, the colonel forced the fugitive emotion back into the cell of unwavering control and firmly concluded, "That's why all former prisoners were automatically suspected of betraying the Motherland and given the same punishment — twenty-five years in a labour camp. Many innocent people, already tormented in German camps, were condemned to further suffering in domestic ones, side by side with genuine traitors."

"So, they just locked everyone up without distinction?" Andrei seemed outraged.

Uncle Pasha frowned. *"The thirst for justice... Ah, youth!"* he thought. *"Minimal knowledge but endless opinions. Judging others' decisions is far easier than making them!"* Out loud, however, the old man replied in a deliberately even tone. "Of course, investigations were conducted, but, as I said, the workload of filtering those returning from Europe immediately after the war was simply overwhelming. Evidence was often impossible to obtain, so only those with irrefutable alibis remained free. When Stalin died, and Khrushchev declared an amnesty in fifty-five, many criminals were released alongside the innocent."

"As always in our society, one size fits all!" the captain interjected.

Uncle Pasha shot him a disapproving look, thinking that someone working in state security should understand the complexities behind each investigative error. Still, he left his nephew's remark unanswered, unwilling to be distracted by a pointless argument.

"After the amnesty, some traitors managed to lie low for about five years," Pavel Andreevich continued. "But then... well, they lived among people. I've already mentioned that witnesses' memories were triggered when they recognised the faces of specific criminals, haven't I?" Andrei and I nodded. "Survivors of the occupation sometimes ran into former collaborators. Interestingly, this often happened by coincidence. For instance, the notorious Meleshko was caught because someone recognised him from a newspaper photograph, as a Hero of Labour*, no less! From these accidentally identified criminals, the investigation threads often led to others..."

When we finally went through all the materials from the last Khatyn trial, we discovered that forty years after the war, over half of the fifty folders holding the cases of traitors lacked notes, indicating the death of the suspects. In a haze, I stared at the piles of pages filled with confessions written by executioners — confessions that had bought life for the very monsters who, on the twenty-second of March, 1943, had stood outside *that* barn, listened to the dying screams of my fellow villagers, and shot anyone who tried to escape the flames... And the vampire I was searching for was most likely the author of one of these confessions! But which one?

Eaten up by impatience, I hurried my companions. "What now?"

"Now," Colonel Pilatov replied, looking at me sympathetically over his glasses, "Andrei will read the testimonies, and you will write down all the names he mentions."

"What for?"

"We'll see whose name comes up most often," Pavel Andreevich said, placing on the table the files I had brought from the archive the night before.

The colonel's suggestion didn't seem particularly useful to me. He followed his intuition more than any logical method, but he was good at it... So, I obediently armed myself with a pen.

"All right," Andrei began. "'Petrychuk I.L. Protocol dated the 31st of May, 1973. The distance from my post to the barn, where civilians were herded, was approximately 250 metres. At about that distance, I saw...'" Andrei jabbed his index finger at the sheet of paper under my hand and ordered, "Write! 'Smovsky, Vasyura, Kerner, Vinnitsky, German, Naryadko, Luckovich, Lakusta, Katryuk, Dumich, and Knap among the executioners present at the barn. It was these executioners who opened fire on the barn with people inside. I remember that fire was opened with a mounted machine gun in long bursts. There also seemed to be explosions of grenades near the barn or further away in the village. Almost simultaneously with the gunfire, the barn with the people inside caught fire. The doomed people began to scream… Their cries… echoed throughout the village.'" Andrei paused and asked, "Did you get the names?"

I nodded, trying my best not to dwell on the meaning of what I had just heard, and Andrei picked up the next folder and began reading again.

"'O.F. Knap. The twenty-first of March 1973. I remember clearly, as if it were today, that those who took part in the operation and personally fired at the villagers locked in the burning barn included the battalion's chief of staff, Vasyura; the deputy commander of the First Company, Meleshko; as well as Lakusta, Pasechnik, Pankiv, Ilchuk Zhora, Katryuk, Kmit, Filippov, and Luckovich. Smovsky and Vinnitsky were near the barn but did not fire at it.' As if that makes them less guilty! 'I don't remember whether the commanders of other companies in our battalion were near the barn or if they fired at anyone. After the barn roof collapsed, the groans, cries, and weeping of the doomed ceased. The First Company, which had been stationed in a cordon around the barn, was ordered to withdraw and head towards Pleshchenitsy…'"

Andrei paused, skimming to the top of the page. "Wait, here. He even lists ranks and positions. Write this down!" he told me. "'Battalion Commander Smovsky, Chief of Staff Vasyura, Commander of the First Company Vinnitsky, his deputy Meleshko, Company Sergeant Slizhuk, Platoon Commanders Lakusta, Ilchuk, Pasechnik, section commanders Katryuk, Kmit,

Pankiv, interpreter Luckovich…' All the leadership in one place!" The captain sounded pleased. "Unbelievable how much effort this Knap put into remembering so many details! Yan, are you keeping up?"

The names in different testimonies really did repeat, and I began to understand why it was necessary to write them down each time. Andrei continued reading.

"'Sakhno S.V. Dated the eleventh of June 1974. I cannot say whether Vasyura and Meleshko participated in gathering the villagers. But I saw Meleshko when the villagers were being driven towards the barn. Meleshko, along with other executioners, was moving towards the barn. I later saw Vasyura near the barn when the people were already locked inside. He was with Smovsky, Kerner, Vinnitsky, and some Germans. Meleshko was there too.' Write this down!" Andrei reminded me again when he noticed I was distracted. "'I don't know who gave the order to open fire. I didn't see whether Vasyura and Meleshko fired at the people. The executioners' bullets killed those who tried to escape from the barn. I didn't see anyone survive. Among the dead were many children and teenagers. In total, the executioners killed no fewer than a hundred villagers of Khatyn.'"

The captain waited until I finished another list. It was my first time writing by hand, which was a painfully slow and clumsy process. Yet I welcomed this minor inconvenience, as it distracted me from the harrowing details recounted by the former policemen. When I finally managed to complete notes, Andrei read aloud from the last folder he had selected.

"And finally, 'Lozinsky I.M., Minsk, the twentieth of June, 1974. While in Khatyn, I saw the Chief of Staff Vasyura, Smovsky, Vinnitsky, Kerner, and Meleshko in the village. They gave subordinate commanders orders to herd the villagers into a barn. By their command, the police of the First Company were driving people out of their homes and into the barn en masse.

Kerner, Smovsky, Meleshko, Vasyura, Vinnitsky, other officers, and Germans stood behind the line. Then one of them gave the command to fire, and rifle and machine-gun fire was opened on the barn filled with people. Among the other punishers in the line, Pankiv and Litvin from our platoon were also firing towards the barn.'"

The captain caught his breath.

Pilatov Senior looked at my scribbles and said, "These five are mentioned more often than the others: Kerner, Vasyura, Vinnitsky, Smovsky, and Meleshko. They seem to have been in command at Khatyn, judging by the earlier testimonies. I'll save time and tell you about the already infamous Oskar Kerner, the German commander of the 118th Ukrainian police battalion. I came across information about him in one of the earlier documents. Kerner was arrested by the French in 1945 and beaten to death by Polish security unit soldiers."

"I can't imagine why!" the captain commented.

"Yes, the old fox was cruel and cunning, but even he couldn't escape. In any case, Kerner would hardly have lived to this day: he was well over fifty in forty-three. We can rule him out."

We began impatiently rifling through the folders, searching for the files on the other commanders listed. My heart was pounding twice as fast as its normal rate, my body trembling with anticipation at the increasingly real possibility of finally looking *him* in the eye. Both Pilatovs Senior and Junior were no less feverish. After several days of studying the archives, the KGB officers fully embraced my mission. The hunter instinct, inherent to male homo sapiens, especially those in intelligence service, spurred my assistants on, making us full-fledged comrades.

When we gathered the files on all the former policemen on the list, the captain took the top folder and began reading hungrily.

"Here... 'Konstantin Smovsky... commander of the 118th Battalion. After taking part in punitive actions in Belarus, he ended up in Germany and, in May 1945, appearing before the Western Allies' court, declared himself a fighter for Ukraine's independence, which helped him avoid extradition to the Soviet side… Could it be him?"

"So," I said, "they forgave the murder of hundreds of defenceless women and children just because he was a fighter for Ukraine's independence? How does that justify the killing of innocent people?"

"Don't be surprised!" Pavel Andreevich retorted with a grin. "Just say the word 'independence' to our Western partners and they will willingly turn a blind eye to murder and violence, especially if someone's independence weakens a strong adversary. People like Smovsky are very useful to them."

"What use did they get out of Smovsky?"

Instead of answering, the colonel continued reading aloud. "'… settled in West Germany, where he became the founder of the Union of Ukrainian Soldiers. After the defeat of the Banderite* gangs, with whom Smovsky had maintained contact, he moved to the United States, where he was actively involved in Ukrainian émigré organisations. He was even granted the rank of general-coronet.' Does that make it clear now?"

I shook my head, still uncertain.

"How can you not get it?" Pavel Andreevich said. "If the Banderites had prevailed in Ukraine, it would have fundamentally changed the situation in the Soviet Union and perhaps even led to the collapse of the union itself — and that's precisely what the overseas government was striving for!

"But weren't the USA your allies in that war?" I asked.

A burst of Homeric laughter erupted in the office. It wasn't the first time my naivety had amused the uncle and nephew, who, given their professions, knew all too well the true worth of such alliances.

Finally, the retired colonel patted me on the shoulder and said kindly, "You have much to learn before taking on our vampires, son! Of course, there's no denying that they're humanity's greatest enemy, regardless of skin colour, nationality or citizenship, but how do you plan to operate in the human world without understanding politics? I'm convinced there are far more vampires among politicians than ordinary citizens *on both sides of the divide*. In fact, I strongly suspect that politics itself is their creation..."

Meanwhile, Andrei read aloud in a subdued voice. "'Died in Minneapolis in 1960,'" then set Smovsky's file aside. "Not the one we need."

"Next," Pavel Andreevich said. "Vinnytsky Iosif. Settled comfortably in Canada. A figure in the Ukrainian diaspora..." But after glancing at the end of the document, he added, "Ah, no: 'died in Montreal.' Now, Katryuk, who didn't make your list, is also in Canada, the OUN's main roost. Still alive, but hard to reach."

"Why is it hard?" I asked, surprised.

"The Canadian authorities refuse to extradite him to us. Perhaps you can deal with him, Yan?" Laying Karuk's file on the table, the colonel skimmed through it once more. "But if you're looking for the one who gave the orders for burning and shooting, then I think you need someone else... This one was merely a squad commander — not a big fish. Let's look at other files. Here's Slizhuk Ivan, an active member of the OUN émigré community, also still alive and free. A company sergeant... Another small fry!"

I read the next name on the list. "Meleshko Vasily..."

"Already punished! All these documents" — Andrei picked up a hefty stack of folders and shook them in the air — "are from Meleshko's trial. He's executed."

"Ah, is he the one identified from a portrait in the newspaper?" I recalled.

"That's him," the captain smirked. "So much for not believing in fate!"

And I added, "Nature restores balance, even when people forget about it."

"Those 'heroes' had their idea of balance, by the way," Pavel Andreevich remarked sceptically. "I've already said that such types usually jump onto the heavier side of the scales. When the Germans were driven out of Belorussia, the 118th Ukrainian Battalion joined them in East Prussia and were transferred to France later. By then, things were already looking grim for the Nazis, so the collaborators decided to abandon their masters and switch to the French."

"Oh, I see. For balance, probably," Pilatov Junior quipped. "Their involvement in the French Resistance is mentioned in every file!"

"In 1955, during the amnesty, their service with the French partisans helped many former collaborators gain their freedom," Pavel Andreevich explained. "It was Meleshko who suggested switching to the French. He already realised back then that it could help his case later. A far-sighted scoundrel! Look here: 'By the end of 1944, the entire 118th police battalion had joined the French Resistance and fought against the Germans as the Second Taras Shevchenko Ukrainian Battalion, a part of the 13th Demi-Brigade of the Foreign Legion.' Quite the balance, wouldn't you say? And when Meleshko later worked as a Soviet agronomist, he often met with young pioneers*** and told them stories of his exploits in France — though he wisely kept quiet about Belorussia..."

"How did he even dare to return to the Soviet Union?" Andrei asked indignantly.

"Our government demanded the repatriation of Soviet citizens from foreign authorities after the war, so many returned home, though by no means all. Over half of those who served in the 118th Ukrainian Battalion remained in the French Foreign Legion. It's quite possible that those vampires also continued their bloody deeds there."

“Bloody deeds in the Foreign Legion?” The captain was surprised. “Are you certain, Uncle Pasha?”

“No, I can only speculate,” the colonel explained. “In 1955, for example, the Foreign Legion was directly involved in suppressing anti-colonial uprisings in Algeria. Brutal SS-style measures were used against both Algerian partisans and civilians. The French themselves were horrified. Do you see the connection? It’s quite likely that the hardened lads from the 118th Ukrainian Battalion were sent to Algeria and might have employed the ‘skills’ they honed while hunting Belorussian partisans…”

“Or perhaps they simply couldn’t stop,” I added.

“So it’s not certain whether the former Ukrainian executioners fought in Algeria or not?” Andrei pressed. “Were you already serving back then, Uncle Pasha?”

“No, I have no idea but a general knowledge of modern history. I was working in a different area,” the old intelligence officer replied. “It’s just… the pattern is too similar, and I don’t believe in coincidences. In my experience, most so-called coincidences only appear that way because of limited access to information and our inability to see the whole picture. Tracking those who joined the Foreign Legion was much harder than following those who returned to the USSR. There was no point too… Anyway, never mind them. Who else is on our list?”

Only one name remained unchecked, and I read it aloud with dismay.

“Vasyura.”

“Let’s see what we’ve got on him,” the old scout said, still hopeful.

We couldn’t find a separate folder on Vasyura. Andrei found only a few handwritten sheets attached to Meleshko’s file.

“Testimony of a… witness?” the captain said, stumbling in surprise. “‘G.N. Vasyura, 20 November, 1973…’ Hmm… The handwriting is almost calligraphic!" He skimmed the two pages quickly and began reading aloud.

"'I joined the 118th Police Punitive Battalion in the autumn of 1942. At that time, the battalion was stationed in Kiev. After completing propaganda school in Wust Rau, Germany, I was sent along with a group of graduates to Kiev under the jurisdiction of the Kiev Police Department. From the Police Department, seven of us, former Red Army commanders Meleshko, Korovin-Korniyets, Kozynchenko, Bilyk, Franchuk, Kovalchuk, and myself, were assigned to the 118th Police Battalion, which had already been formed by then. All of us were appointed to officer positions, mainly as platoon commanders. I was appointed commander of the First Platoon of the First Company.'

"I don't get it." The captain paused. "Everyone refers to him as 'the Battalion's chief of staff..."

"Keep reading," Uncle Pasha advised. "Maybe Vasyura climbed the ranks in the German police force."

"All right," Andrei agreed, and continued. "'Korovin-Korniyets was appointed chief of staff of the battalion, and Kozynchenko became the battalion's weapons technician. While serving in the battalion, I soon met other commanders: Vinnytsky, commander of the First Company; Shudra, commander of the Second Company; and Naryadko, commander of the Third Company. I also met the battalion commander, Major Smovsky. I don't know the first names or patronymics of these colleagues.'

"He's clearly trying to play innocent," the captain remarked. "'I also got to know the squad leaders, Lakusta and Katryuk, who served in the First Platoon of the First Company. I can't remember any other squad leaders. I learned that, alongside Ukrainian commanders, the 118th Police Battalion had a German commander, whose name was Kerner. I don't know his first name or patronymic. He held the rank of major in the German army. Each company and platoon also had German supervisors to whom the Ukrainian commanders were subordinate, even though these Germans held lower ranks.'

"They're the master race, after all!" Andrei couldn't resist, glancing at me nervously, wary of triggering another outburst of irritation. "And it seems the Ukrainian commanders thought it was normal. What I can't understand is this: they didn't like Russian communists, even though the communists created all the conditions for their development, and certainly without any racial discrimination. Yet the fascists treated Ukrainians like second-class people — and no complaints!"

"Well, maybe that's why some wanted to return to the USSR after the war, despite everything, rather than stay and serve the French?" I suggested.

"I don't think we'll ever be able to figure that out," Andrei began to speculate. "Maybe they were returning to their families, hoping everything would blow over..."

"Keep reading!" the colonel interrupted sternly.

Pilatov Junior grunted in disapproval but obeyed and continued reading Vasyura's testimony.

"'All the Germans kept their distance from us, the commanders, always occupying separate quarters. They received instructions and orders from Kerner and passed them on to the companies and platoons. Often, the Germans didn't even inform Battalion Commander Smovsky about their actions. In effect, there were two headquarters within the battalion: German and Ukrainian. Almost all the decisions of the Ukrainian headquarters were coordinated with those of the Germans. Only in matters of security organisation, communication between units, maintaining discipline, and minor appointments within the battalion, did Ukrainians decide independently.'

"And where does he call himself the chief of staff? Nowhere?" Andrei repeated the question. "'The 118th Police Battalion had about three hundred men, and at the time, I knew many of them by name, especially in the First Platoon of the First

Company, where I served as platoon commander for a time...' For a time... And what did he do after that?"

Uncle Pasha let out an angry but oddly amusing growl. He had finally become annoyed by his nephew's rambling. After all, Vasyura was the last name on the list, and if the first mission's vimpire wasn't him, then our investigation had hit a dead end. Andrei glanced nervously at the colonel's tightly pressed lips and focused on the details of Vasyura's testimony without further comments.

"'Now, more than thirty years later, I have forgotten many of the policemen's surnames. Of those I do remember, it's only by surname. I can't recall anyone's first name or patronymic. The surnames I remember among the rank-and-file policemen are: Skrypko, who was always the battalion's clerk and only went on punitive operations when the entire battalion was deployed; Vuss, I think Pavel, who was always Battalion Commander Smovsky's orderly; Egorov, the groom and coachman for the horse assigned to Smovsky; Pidzharyisty, the battalion's food and supply clerk; Lutyuk, the battalion's cashier and records manager; Aleksandrov, the battalion's signalman; Chizhik, the battalion's barber; Antonenko, a policeman from the third company; Spivak, a policeman from the First Platoon of the First Company; Schneider, a machine gunner — I don't know which company he belonged to — he was killed by partisans on the same day as the German Velke; and Topchiy, a policeman — I don't remember his platoon or company. I can't name anyone else... I don't know if I would be able to recognise any former policemen now, as more than thirty years have passed.'"

Andrei stopped reading. Pavel Pilatov looked troubled while we waited expectantly.

"Interesting..." the former spy finally said.

"What? Uncle Pasha, don't keep us in suspense!" Andrei and I both could barely hold back our impatience.

"Such detailed testimony — and it's absolutely useless!" Pavel Andreevich began to reason. "And not a single word about this witness's own actions. Straight out of a textbook! That Vasyura clearly knew how to answer a prosecutor's questions."

"That, by the way, was written by Vasyura himself, not from his dictated words," said Andrei, turning the page. "And here's more, in a different handwriting, recorded by the investigator. Let's see…

"'Question: What was the purpose of forming the 118th Police Battalion?

"'Answer: Back when we were in Kiev, we were told that the battalion was created to combat partisans in the occupied territories.

"'Question: Were there any cases of police officers from your battalion being executed in Pleshchenitsy?

"'Answer: I remember, around January 1943, there were two cases of police officers from our battalion being executed for connections with partisans. The first time, three officers were shot, and the second time, one officer, along with some civilians. Who exactly carried out the executions, whether it was the Germans or the police themselves, I don't recall. Specifically, the three were shot by the Germans, but as for who shot the officer with the unknown civilian, I can't remember.'"

Andrei stopped reading aloud but kept flipping through the pages, scanning the printed text with searching eyes as if he had missed something.

"Well? Go on!" the uncle urged him.

"That's all…" the captain said, his voice wavering.

"What do you mean?" the colonel and I exclaimed in unison. I added, "And where are the questions about Khatyn?"

"They're… not here…" Andrei mumbled even more uncertainly. "Nor is there any confession that Vasyura was the chief of staff of the 118th Battalion."

"Wasn't he accused? Was he only called as a witness?" Pilatov Senior pressed on.

"It seems so..." his nephew replied, sounding even less certain.

"That name appears in the interrogation of nearly every executioner! And you're saying there's no case file, no sentence against Vasyura? Are you sure?" Andrei simply shrugged. "How could they not open a case against someone whose active punitive role is mentioned so many times in such a high-profile trial? I don't understand!"

All three of us started going through the folders of indictments again and again. A good hour and a half passed before Pavel Andreevich gave up and drew a conclusion:

"There's nothing else about Vasyura. Not even a photograph."

"There's this," the captain said. He opened a white envelope attached to the printed sheets. Inside was a single sheet of paper. Part of the text was typed, while another part was scribbled in handwriting so messy it seemed impossible to read.

"A medical certificate. It's a doctor's handwriting, I see!" the captain laughed.

Then the uncle and nephew dove into deciphering the doctor's scrawl, until finally Andrei announced, "Lung cancer! The date on the medical certificate is a week before the one in Vasyura's testimony. Ah... Maybe that's why he wasn't accused? It's a terminal illness, after all. And the location is Velyka Dymerka. Was he interrogated there?"

"Wait, but Vasyura isn't listed as deceased, is he?" Pavel Andreevich interrupted. "Though that type of cancer is the most aggressive. People die from it within six months at most... Something's off here, I sense it!" His eyes gleamed with a hunter's excitement.

I asked the main question. "Do we know where he is now? If he's still alive, of course."

Andrei checked Vasyura's testimony. "There's only an address from 1973: the village of Velyka Dymerka, Brovary District, Kiev region. It seems like he was interrogated at home, as a sick man, probably. If Vasyura miraculously recovered, I think we'll find him there. His place of work is Velykodymersky State Farm. The position is deputy director for economic affairs. Wow!"

"So it won't be hard to find him?" I asked eagerly, barely able to contain my urge to act.

"If he's alive, yes!" the captain replied. "In any case, we need to go and check!"

Uncle Pasha was the only one who hesitated.

"Interesting," he finally said. "Shadow chief of staff, deputy director of a state farm. He's always in secondary roles... This Vasyura is like some kind of grey cardinal! If he hadn't died or retired, he might still hold the position and be a respected man. We need to tread carefully. It isn't the 1930s anymore!"

Despite his caution, Pavel Andreevich was practically glowing with hope. He deliberately paused for dramatic effect, and, savouring our expectant and tense expressions, finally squinted his mismatched eyes, looked me over appraisingly, and asked, "So, is it warm in your Lemuria? What do you wear there?"

"Only light tunics," I replied, not understanding where the colonel was going with this, as he seemed to be hiding his thoughts for effect.

"Hm, I suggest you familiarise yourself with the fashion of the far north. I bet you've never seen snow!"

"Only in early childhood, in Khatyn."

"Well, you'll be reminded of it before the snow melts. Early May in Komi is practically winter. Andrei, find the addresses of the colonies where our friends Sakhno, Knap, and Lozinsky are holidaying," Uncle Pasha ordered, bolting up.

The captain buried himself in the folders at once while Pavel Andreevich went upstairs. I followed him. The colonel opened a massive dark wooden wardrobe with thick wall tiles and pulled out a quilted jacket, a winter coat with a karakul collar, and a sheepskin coat. I picked up the names of these warm clothes from his thoughts. After inspecting the karakul-collared coat, Uncle Pasha hung it back on the hook, and we returned to the study room carrying the quilted jacket and sheepskin coat.

"You'll go together," he announced. The nephew's teleportation experiences didn't inspire much confidence in the uncle. "But no guerrilla tactics! Enter through the main gate. Andrei will show his ID and organise an official interview. While he's asking questions, you, Yan, will pick the minds of the right prisoners. That way, you'll figure out who Vasyura really was and whether he's the one you're looking for."

Meanwhile, Pilatov Junior had finished writing down the addresses of the colonies, asking, "And you, Uncle?"

"I'm not your nanny!" the colonel quipped. "I'll command from central headquarters."

Feeling accomplished, Uncle Pasha stretched luxuriously, clearly preparing to move his favourite massive armchair to the window overlooking the garden and take a nap as soon as he sent us off to the far north.

---

*Hero of Labour – the award given to the most productive workers in the USSR

**Stepan Bandera – the far-right leader of the radical militant wing of the Organization of Ukrainian Nationalists

***Pioneers – the children's communist organisation in the USSR

Chapter 13. The Last Victim of Khatyn

No man chooses evil because it is evil — he only mistakes it for happiness.

Mary Wollstonecraft Shelley, *A Vindication of the Rights of Men* (1790)

Although Pavel Andreevich was unaware of my ability to adapt my body temperature to any environment, warm clothing turned out to be handy — as a disguise. To the uninitiated, it would have been odd to see someone standing unperturbed in a light sweater, head tilted back, in front of massive double-leafed metal gates amidst a white tundra under wet snow blown by a howling wind. These gates were the only way for a homo sapien to get past the towering brick wall, crowned along its entire length with rings of metal wire bristling with ominous spikes.

As if responding to my thoughts, Andrei also tilted his head back and said, "The zeks here would give anything for the ability to teleport!"

"Zeks?"

"People serving sentences in prison," he explained, then added, "It's better if no one sees you at all. It will be easier for me to arrange a meeting with Stepan Sakhno on my own. I too work for the security system, after all." And he touched the KGB identity card in his inside pocket.

I obediently vanished from sight and examined the premises while the captain spoke to the prison officers at the checkpoint crisscrossed with metal partitions. In this grim, enclosed space, every step echoed lifelessly. The grey ceiling, hanging almost directly overhead, reminded me of the slabs of graves where people entomb their dead, preventing their souls from merging with the world and thus condemning them to ultimate death. Apparently, free homo sapiens fear the dead no less than they fear criminals.

People like to say that such places are "chained in stone," but there wasn't even any real stone here, the stone that makes up sheer cliffs kissed by the breath of the ocean, the stone that carries Earth's riches, absorbs the sun's warmth, and returns its accumulated heat to all living things at night. The prison shell was built from Nature's materials yet they had been mutilated by blending, heating, and shaping. Neither inside nor out did I find a single stick of growth breaking through the earth, nor was there any earth visible at all. Nature had been completely expelled from the place, so a regular energy exchange was impossible within these walls.

It struck me that punishment for crimes against the laws of homo sapiens was a cruel, grotesque parody of how Lemurians paid for disrupting harmony. People take it upon themselves to judge offenders and then banish them from both society and the natural world despite their ignorance, or maybe, precisely because of it.

And within these concrete walls, there was no source of energy except other homo sapiens. Whoever ended up here for long enough had every chance of turning into a vampire, even if they weren't one before imprisonment. To make matters worse, most human criminals eventually returned to society, and if they grew accustomed to taking energy from others while in prison, they continued draining Nature further once free.

Tiles, bricks, concrete, asphalt, plaster, iron, dark-green paint covering the walls and bars — all this was reflected in the sullen faces of the guards, whose work seemed akin to punishment itself, the only difference being that they had the right to spend their free time outside the colony and participate in the natural exchange of energy, provided they recognised its necessity. If not, it was unlikely that prison staff could resist the temptation of wielding power over living beings and avoid turning into the very vampires they guarded.

Unseen, I followed Andrei and the impassive prison officer into a room divided into two halves by a partition of painted iron bars. A table stood in the centre, split in half by this barrier. On the other side was another door, and from it emerged a prisoner clad in a dark blue quilted uniform. From Sakhno's file, I knew he was only sixty-four, though the body of this gaunt homo sapien appeared worn out as if it belonged to an eighty-year-old. The prisoner's face resembled the concrete floor of the prison, while his pale bluish lips and sunken eyes were lost in the hollows of deep wrinkles. Nevertheless, those eyes darted about nervously as soon as the inmate heard why the KGB captain in civilian clothes was visiting.

"I'm investigating new details regarding the destruction of Khatyn, and I'd like to ask you a few questions."

"What? Again?!" The little man's voice rang with feigned indignation mixed with a fear that even Andrei noticed. Stepan Sakhno had fought in the punitive detachment during the war and spent over ten years in a high-security colony for that, so he knew perfectly well how to survive among vampires. He could no longer boast the youthful strength he had in the 1940s, but instead, he had learned to preserve energy through restraint, through calm and steady behaviour. Yet now, the former chastener and seasoned convict was overcome with turmoil. For a brief moment his memory flared with an image: an angry man pinning Sakhno's neck against a dark wooden wall with both hands as though trying to strangle him.

"At present, we are particularly interested in the command structure of the 118th Police Battalion," Captain Pilatov explained.

"I've already given testimony many times," replied the prisoner, leaning back in his chair and squinting appraisingly. Undoubtedly, he still had secrets to hide, but Sakhno quickly realised the visitor wasn't interested in his sins. Therefore, the zek soon calmed down, and the vision of the mysterious strangler faded from his mind.

"I've read it," Andrei said, "but our investigation is now focused on the senior officers who are still alive. Did you know men named Slizhuk, Katryuk, and Vasyura?"

"Yes, all three served in the 118th Battalion," Sakhno confirmed with deliberate detachment.

"What role did these commanders play in the executions and punitive actions in Belarus?"

"Well, I can't really remember now who was in charge of what…" the prisoner said, stalling. "Slizhuk… I honestly don't remember what he did. Katryuk was, I think, a section commander, but not in our unit. Vasyura… he was the chief of staff. I remember him well." At the mention of Vasyura, the former collaborator's voice no longer sounded simply detached. It became lifeless.

The images flickering before Stepan Sakhno's inner eye bore no resemblance to his dry responses to the officer's questions. This was exactly what we had aimed for. I stopped listening to the sluggish dialogue and focused on the former executioner's memories instead.

Our convict seemed to shrink inwardly when speaking of the chief of staff. His memory conjured up the image of a young officer whose handsome face was as expressionless as if it were carved from cold marble. Vasyura turned, piercing Sakhno with dark, hellishly malevolent eyes, and Stepan shuddered with terror. The former collaborator's recollection of the chief of staff always returned to the exact same moment. On that day, Sakhno had arrived at the headquarters to report the failure of an order. He imagined all sorts of dreadful punishments for the failure since Vasyura was notorious for his cruelty towards enemies and subordinates alike. Sakhno had escaped unscathed only because the commander had already been informed of the failure and knew that Sakhno wasn't to blame…

"In Vasyura's 1973 testimony, he stated that the battalion had two headquarters: one German and one Ukrainian," Andrei said. "Kerner commanded the German staff, while the Ukrainian chief of staff merely carried out his orders. Do you have anything to add to his testimony?"

Sakhno smirked crookedly. "Yes, he followed orders that he was giving himself."

"Could you clarify that, please?"

"Erich Kerner was already well past fifty," the prisoner answered reluctantly. "And I think he was often ill. Vasyura, on the other hand, was young, fluent in German, and had higher education in communications. He was even better than Kerner!"

"Better?" Andrei repeated in surprise.

"Stronger, I mean," Sakhno clarified, shivering as goose bumps ran down his arms. "So, if you're looking for who was making the real decisions, it should be Vasyura."

"And why didn't you mention this during Meleshko's trial?"

"Because back then, they only asked me about Khatyn, where the entire command staff was present. I didn't know exactly who gave which orders," the former collaborator shrugged. Sakhno wouldn't admit to himself that even in the seventies, when he was finally tried for treason, he had still feared the bloodthirsty commander more than the Soviet investigator. By then, his fear was groundless and irrational, yet no less real. "So, Vasyura remained free?" the prisoner asked, perking up. Upon receiving a confirming nod from the captain, he remarked with unhidden envy, "And yet, he's no less guilty than I am, that's for sure. I don't understand how he managed that..."

At the end of the conversation, Sakhno disappeared behind the heavy metal door, dragging his feet and shuffling them along the concrete floor. As for me, having learned enough about Vasyura, I nevertheless followed the former executioner into the camp, burning with curiosity to find out what had so greatly frightened him at the start of the captain's visit.

But I had to wait until evening. Upon returning to the prison-life routine, Sakhno's mind transformed into a calculator. He became occupied solely with weighing his energy expenditures and minimising them to preserve his meagre resources. One could hardly blame a longtime inhabitant of a settlement cut off from Nature. The zek had mastered the art of survival and, despite his impoverished circumstances, managed to covertly draw energy from the inexperienced younger inmates who squandered it. Only after lights-out, when the barracks fell silent and his fellow zeks settled onto their hard bunks, did the elderly convict's mind finally relax and surrender to memories.

Sakhno had been afraid for as long as he could remember. Despite the vagueness and fragmentation of his childhood recollections, it became clear to me that fear had taken root in this wandering soul lost in darkness from a very early age. Born during the civil war's famine, death, and lawlessness and raised amidst the devastation that followed, the child did not care who was in the right. Styopa* quickly realised that his tiny life was unimportant to both the Whites and the Reds. At times it seemed to him that it mattered little even to his parents, who cared equally for their many offspring and their calves and piglets, showing interest in neither's feelings. His taciturn, exhausted mother gave birth often, and nearly half of her infants did not survive the hard times. Two younger sisters lived to the ages of three or four before dying one after the other from illness or malnutrition — Stepan never found out the true reason. He only remembered their still, sharp-featured, pale greenish faces peeking out of the crude wooden boxes nailed together by his father. These were then sealed shut with rough lids and buried in deep graves at the village cemetery. The boy was five at the time, and his fear of being put in a similar dark hole became his most horrifying nightmare. No one paid any attention to the child's fears because everyone was afraid in those days. In response to the world's indifference, Styopa learned to ensure his survival and well-being at any cost, disregarding others just as others disregarded him. Even in his old age, he still considered absolutely any act committed in pursuit of this ultimate goal a good deed. Nothing and no one were worth the risk of ending up in a grave prematurely and rotting away to bones. Stepan was glad he had never known the joys of fatherhood because he would never have sacrificed anything for a child. During his time in the SS, he had killed other people's children more than once without hesitation, simply following orders.

In truth, Sakhno did not crave blood — it was yet another war that thirsted for it. As a healthy twenty-year-old lad, he had no chance of avoiding participation. So, Sakhno joined the Red Army, was sent to the front, and surrendered to the Germans at the first opportunity. In 1941, it seemed their victory was just around the corner. To survive, he agreed to collaborate with the Nazis and was relieved to spend several months in their propaganda school, far from the front lines. Later, he was assigned to an auxiliary police unit formed in Kiev. Sakhno was pleased to be stationed far from the real carnage. Moreover, the police were given weapons, which meant they could defend themselves.

Being transferred to Pleshchenitsy to fight Belorussian partisans, whose courage and desperation were legendary, became the most unpleasant and terrifying surprise of his life. On such an assignment, the chances of dying were at least as high as on the front lines. Worse still, a traitor like him could be killed from around any corner in the rear, so there was no room for relaxation or loss of vigilance, not even for a moment.

Stepan saw partisans everywhere. Their accusing, threatening faces seemed to peer out from all the shuttered window embrasures in town and from every bush along the forest roads. Not even in his hungry childhood had he been so afraid! Power over the defenceless was the only thing that created an illusion of safety. Nurturing this illusion, the young policeman committed insane, dirty, and brutal acts. The fear retreated in the frenzy, though only briefly.

Raping terrified and doomed women, for some reason, helped best of all. Sakhno and his "brothers" developed the habit of visiting a Jewish settlement, where they indulged in such activities almost daily, without consequences. Sometimes they even hunted down the daughters of Abraham, who had tried to hide from their unwanted attention. This proved an excellent distraction from his thoughts of dying himself. The rape raids continued until all the Jews had either fled to the forests or been executed on the orders of Nazi superiors.

...One day, when he was eight years old, Styopa dealt very cruelly with a neighbour's cat for stealing his food, which was scarce for both people and animals at the time. For this, the older boys cornered him to teach him a lesson. Out of fear, the little executioner flailed his fists blindly and managed to leave the nearest "teacher" with a black eye that remained shut for a week, so the village bullies decided to stay away from the crazy boy. Styopa remembered this for life, and grown-up Sakhno confronted the partisan threat in the same manner — only now he was armed. He fired indiscriminately, not only at every partisan but also at anyone suspected of aiding the invisible fighters' survival in the dense forests and treacherous Belorussian swamps hated by both the Germans and Ukrainians. His behaviour, driven by self-preservation, was interpreted as bravery by his superiors and earned him their praise.

The superiors... they were no less terrifying than the partisans. The senior officers, both German and Ukrainian, were a different breed. Sakhno was not the only one to feel this difference and fear them accordingly. In his mind, he divided the commanders into "ideologues" and "bloodsuckers". Smovsky and Vinnitsky, for example, were ideologues and believed that by supporting the Germans, they were fighting for Ukraine's independence from the Soviets. Something about this logic did not quite add up. Stepan could not understand how submitting to Nazi Germany or burning Belorussian villagers alive could help Ukraine achieve independence…

But he did not ask questions. He did what had to be done.

Styopa held no interest in political debates among former OUN or UPA** members. He quickly realised that it was best not to get involved with ideologues. It was enough to pass as one of them by staying silent, nodding in agreement with their freedom speeches, and speaking the Little Russian dialect, that is, the Ukrainian language, in the presence of the clean-shaven, education-loving Vinnitsky, the cutthroat Smovsky, who sported a Cossack hat and Hitler-like moustache, and their politically savvy comrades who formed the backbone of the 118th Ukrainian Battalion.

Far more frightening were the others, those indifferent to politics, who feared nothing and grew intoxicated by the sight of blood. The bloodsuckers had initially sided with the victorious Germans for the sake of power, but when they realised the Nazi army was rapidly losing its strength, the cunning, eggheaded Meleshko led the entire battalion over to the French saboteurs, who were fighting against the Nazis. The bloodsuckers' lack of conviction made them somewhat like Styopa, yet he feared them more than the German Nazis, Ukrainian nationalists, and Soviet partisan communists combined. The bloodsuckers were unpredictable. They did not care whom they tortured or killed and never missed a chance to revel in human suffering.

Now the convict tossed and turned on his bunk, thinking, *"Why did that damn captain have to come?"* Forty years after the war, when the routine of police service had faded, dissolving into the minutiae of prison life, the most horrifying memories became even sharper in their stark loneliness. Now disturbed, they drove away any hope he had of sleep. Worse still, they turned into nightmares. While Styopa was in a daze, the chief of staff of the punitive forces appeared to him as a demon of cruelty.

Once, Vasyura had knocked out the teeth of two subordinates who had drunk vodka at an inappropriate time, then forced them to lick their own blood off the floor. Another time, two comrades suspected of ties to partisans were executed on his orders. As for the partisans who fell into the hands of the chief of staff and his friend, the interpreter Luckovich, they turned into shapeless lumps of flesh. Styopa had seen this with his own eyes.

He and a company chief had entered the battalion headquarters. The chief went to see Kerner, and Stepan began looking for Vasyura, who was not in. When he asked where the chief of staff might be, someone pointed to a house in a small alley and said he was there, conducting an interrogation. Styopa headed there. He saw Vasyura and the interpreter Luckovich torturing a Belorussian lad with ramrods in the presence of a German intelligence officer. The lad looked just over twenty or so, Styopa thought after glancing at the remnants of youthful skin that had not yet been slashed and torn by the torturers' whistling metal rods. The young man's face was so disfigured by bruises and swelling that it was impossible to discern where his eyes, nose, or mouth were.

The suspected partisan did not scream. At each blow, he let out a dull groan, his body arching unnaturally before slumping down again. It was then that Styopa mentally branded his commanders as bloodsuckers. With each new wave of pain inflicted on their victim, Vasyura and Luckovich grew more frenzied and even seemed to stand taller. When Stepan entered the house and froze, mouth agape and eyes wide at the sight of the bloody mess the suspect had become, the two tormentors seemed to revel even more in their gruesome work, feeding off the horror of their audience. Although the lad was already unconscious and clearly incapable of giving up any information, Vasyura and Luckovich continued with the "interrogation." Meanwhile, the third man, the German, did not look at the scene at all. Turning his back to it, he stared out the window as if lost in unrelated thoughts.

After standing there for a while and realising that his superiors had no intention of stopping the torture for his sake, Stepan decided to leave and return later. He still remembered how he bolted out of the house, his heart pounding wildly, and how he had wanted to run away, hide somewhere in the swamps, and live as a hermit just to get as far away from the bloodsuckers as possible. Gulping fresh air outside like a fish thrown out of the water, he headed for headquarters and resolved to wait for his fearsome superiors there.

Luckovich was the first to arrive. Engaged in conversation with Meleshko, he approached the headquarters' hut. Stepan was sitting on the porch, and as the two men drew level with him, he overheard:

"Well done, Vasyl! And your lads too!" Catching his subordinate's proud, grateful look, Luckovich patted his fellow butcher on the shoulder. "The radio operator will come in very handy. The pup Vasyura and I interrogated just died," the interpreter said, adding a foul curse and spitting on the ground.

"Permission to leave?" asked Meleshko, taciturn but clearly pleased with himself.

"Granted. Go and rest," Luckovich replied with a wave of his hand. And, already gripping the door handle and nodding to invite the waiting Sakhno inside, he called out to the departing Meleshko. "Hey, Vasyl? What's the radio operator like? Is she pretty?"

Meleshko turned, stretched out his fist with his thumb up, and the interpreter, baring his teeth in a predatory grin, glanced at the barn where they kept the new suspects and those who had survived the interrogations.

In his childhood, Sakhno tortured a cat for stealing, and men like Vasyura, Luckovich, Meleshko, Kerner, and Dirlewanger had likely done the same for fun. Whether they were Ukrainians or Germans, it did not matter. Stepan had encountered butchers of all nationalities during and after the war. In the high-security prison camp, such men had been gathered from all corners of the vast country. There too, beatings to the point of blood — sometimes of death — were common, as well as rapes or making the weaker inmates lick the floor… It was not so much the deprivation of freedom as the forced coexistence with these freaks that had been Stepan's punishment for his cowardice and the crimes it had led him to commit.

After the war, part of what was then the Taras Shevchenko Second Ukrainian Battalion had remained in service in the Foreign Legion, so Sakhno hadn't known that Meleshko had returned to the Soviet Union until he was summoned for interrogation in the early seventies. Stepan himself had wanted to leave the Army and its hardships as soon as possible, but staying in France as a civilian didn't work out. He was repatriated to the USSR and, in the filtration camp, told the NKVD about the French partisans without mentioning Belarus, just as Meleshko had taught. Finally released in 1955, Stepan moved to Siberia, hoping to disappear into its vastness. He had long yearned for a quiet, settled life where safety wouldn't just be a luxury. And in Kuybyshev, life really did start to improve.

There was no shortage of work in the industrial city. With the status of a former front-line soldier, eventually granted to Sakhno after Khrushchev's amnesty, earning respect wasn't difficult. Stepan had always been highly aware of his dependence on others, so he tried to stay in the good graces of whomever he worked for, behaving exactly as required. To live by Soviet standards, it was necessary to be proper. Stepan did this well — he didn't even need to pretend! Why would a simple man, who had never reached for the stars, hate a government that had given him a life he couldn't have dreamed of in his manure-covered hungry childhood?

Fitting into Soviet reality wasn't hard — it had been created precisely for men like him. So then why did the ideologues from the 118th Ukrainian Battalion fight against it? This question occasionally crossed Stepan's mind, but deep analysis was never his strength. Yet, when Sakhno's candidacy for chairman of the factory's comrades' court was proposed, he couldn't help but appreciate the irony of the choice made by his trusting colleagues.

Sakhno met Lusya at the factory. She was much younger than him and listened to his stories about France like they were fairy tales from a distant kingdom. Her wide, trusting eyes melted the hardened heart of the former chastener. Although Stepan had abandoned all hope for eternal life on the threshold of the first looted and burned Belorussian home, Lusya seemed both his pass and his guide to paradise.

Did the former police executioner repent? Was he tormented by guilt for the infants murdered during the war? If that had been the case, Sakhno wouldn't have been able to tie his life to someone as pure and naive as Lusya. No. The atrocities committed during the war now seemed unreal, as though they had happened to someone else — perhaps a character in an old black-and-white movie. Stepan decided that he had simply been unlucky until now and that destiny had finally granted him the happiness he had longed for. Most importantly, he felt safe for the first time in his life.

But not for long. His sins wouldn't let him into heaven.

The year 1969 turned out to be unfortunate. Sakhno and his wife had finally farewelled their dream of having a child, and the problem lay with Stepan's health, as if Nature was punishing him for his past misdeeds with women. Thirty-five-year-old Lusya looked sad, casting reproachful glances at her respected war-veteran husband, though she dared not complain. However, unaware of the true divine plan, Stepan's cowardly soul secretly thanked God for not burdening him. To take a break from family routine, Sakhno volunteered to accompany a shipment to Orenburg, more precisely, near the city, to a new oil well for which their factory was supplying equipment.

It was December. The journey got off to a bad start. Stepan and the heavy KAMAZ truck driver had to wait out several snowstorms, then crawl along snow-covered roads so slowly that it seemed skiing would have been faster. They travelled for several days, stopping at tiny roadside hotels that were far from European standards. The accommodation staff didn't put in much effort, knowing their trucker clients were undemanding. The driver, Vasya, was indeed happy with everything, but the same couldn't be said for his forwarder. Sakhno kept recalling the dollhouse cleanliness of the Provence motels, and nostalgia for the foreign life that he had never had swept over him like a ghost of Christmas past throughout the nearly weeklong journey.

At last, they reached their destination, unloaded the KAMAZ, and stopped to rest… in a barrack. This time, Sakhno could no longer hide his frustration. Having entered the barrack, he once again regretted signing up for this adventure, especially before the festivities.

"Damn women. All troubles come from them!" he growled.

This amused the driver, to whom Stepan had complained a lot about his shaken family life during the trip. The temporary living quarters for the shift workers were a step below even the roadside motels in the hierarchy of accommodations. The toilets were outside, posing a health risk in Siberian December, but the barracks themselves were heated by hot stoves, and the mouthwatering smell of fried eggs and onions spread around in the evenings. The canteen served simple but plentiful free lunch. That's where the two men headed the next day.

"So, Vasya, do you think we'll be home for New Year's?" Sakhno asked, rubbing his hands over a steaming bowl of cabbage soup.

"Don't worry, we'll make it to your sweetheart in time!" the trucker replied with a wink. "Bet you miss her already."

Stepan glanced at his companion with mock anger. At that very moment, a driller — a sturdy, fair-haired man, fortyish, with a beard touched with grey — was passing by their table towards the serving counter. He suddenly stopped, stared at Sakhno, and turned pale as death. Stepan looked at him questioningly while Vasya blurted out cheerfully, "What's wrong, mate?"

The man only swallowed hard and, saying nothing, walked stiffly to the counter, which emitted the smell of canteen food. Vasya made a face and, unseen by the oilman who had turned away, twirled his pointing finger near his temple while the former policeman felt something sink and collapse into a cold, black void inside him. Sweat broke out on his forehead. The strange subject sat beside another oil worker, diagonally opposite Sakhno. He ate slowly, fixing a piercing stare on Stepan, who could barely swallow a bite. The man's face looked unfamiliar, but Sakhno had learned to trust his instincts. He stayed on alert all day, but nothing happened until the evening.

In the dim, moonlit darkness of the Siberian night, someone was waiting for Stepan on his way back from the toilet. A figure in a padded jacket and felt boots stepped out from the wall shadow and pounced on him. In an instant, the strong hands of the oilman grabbed the defenceless former executioner by the lapels and pinned him against the barrack logs.

Anton Baranovsky, for it was he, finally let out the anger that had built up all day — and over many years.

"Don't you remember me, you bastard? How many people like me did you burn in barns?"

"What are you talking about, brother? What barns? Burned who?" Sakhno stammered, sweating in terror despite the frost. "You've got the wrong man! Let me go!"

"No, scum, I haven't got the wrong man!" Anton growled, keeping the murderer of his family locked in his iron grip. "Do you remember Khatyn? How you and your mates drove us out into the street? There were four of you. I still see your ugly faces in my nightmares!"

Stepan was trembling violently. "What are you talking about? I fought in France!"

But Anton, ignoring these feeble protests, kept shaking the soul out of his tormentor.

"And my sister, Maria, do you remember her? The one you... before burning her alive in the barn... Do you remember?"

The memory of the young girl's untouched body, her ankles reddened from desperate resistance, her smooth, almost childlike thighs helplessly spread apart and gripped by Stepan's rough hands. Her fair hair loosened from its braid in a hopeless struggle. How could he forget? It was he who had ordered her to stay behind in the house when the rest of the family was driven out. Her brother's eyes, filled with a thirst for vengeance, were so much like hers, light blue, wide with terror and pain, pleading for mercy...

Then the chairman of the workers' tribunal was once again reborn as the boy Styopa who had lashed out with his fists to save his skin. And with that came his false sense of confidence.

"Get off me!" Stepan snarled, shoving the former Khatyn boy away with force and anger. "You've got the wrong man! Get lost!"

Anton stepped back. "Oh no, I recognise you, and your filthy barking too! That's fine. We'll let the militia sort it out tomorrow, and then the KGB will get involved. I'd strangle you myself, but I don't want to go to prison for you, scum!"

The oilman suddenly turned around and strode away, determined not to change his mind.

Meanwhile, instead of returning to his barrack, the former sergeant of the 118th Ukrainian Battalion followed his enemy discreetly at a safe distance. The growl of machines working the night shift at the oil well conveniently drowned out the crunch of snow beneath his felt boots. Even though it was already late in the evening, there was no guarantee that the miraculous survivor of an old crime wouldn't share his discovery with one of his comrades that night. Leaving such an urgent problem unresolved until the morning was as good as signing one's death warrant.

Sakhno circled the enemy's barrack for a long time, peering into its dimly lit windows. Through gaps between the intricate frost patterns on the glass, he saw that the enemy had no opportunity to speak to any of his neighbours, as they were already sound asleep in their bunks. The enemy himself stayed awake for a long time. With his head in his hands, he sat at the table under the faint glow of a desk lamp, squeezing his eyes shut and opening them again, clenching his fists and running his fingers through his hair repeatedly as if trying to banish the flood of terrifying, unforgettable memories.

A snowstorm began. Stepan didn't feel the cold, just as Anton Baranovsky's family hadn't felt it when they were driven outside in their underclothes. His heart was pounding wildly with fear making him hot, just as their hearts had. The former punisher was secretly glad for the storm that promised to hide the traces of his manoeuvres. Finally, past midnight, the enemy switched off the lamp, approached the bed in the far corner of the barrack, and eventually, after sitting there for a while, pulled back the blanket and lay down.

Propelled by the wind, Sakhno ran back to his barrack, hoping the driver had already fallen asleep. Sure enough, the man was snoring like a pig. On tiptoe, the forwarder crept to the table, constantly glancing at Vasya, afraid to wake him. Stepan grabbed the truck keys and matches lying there, then stuffed a few empty kefir bottles from the entryway into his pockets. He left the barrack again and trotted towards the KAMAZ truck. With meticulous care, he siphoned a little reserve petrol from each canister, ensuring the fuel shortage wouldn't be evident to the driver. After that, he glanced around nervously and headed towards the log cabin, where the danger lay dormant…

The commotion caused by the sudden fire of mysterious origin didn't reach the guest barrack immediately. Burly Vasya shook supposedly sleeping Sakhno by the shoulders, rattling him like a reed.

"Oi, Stepan, wake up! There's a fire!" the young giant bellowed, eager to rush to help and fully convinced his partner would join him.

Stepan woke up slowly, making a deliberate effort to appear groggy.

"Why are you yelling like there's a fire?" he grumbled.

"But there *is* a fire!" Vasya roared, dashing outside and shouting "Catch up!" from the doorway. He grabbed a bucket and buttoned his padded jacket on the run.

The burning barrack was extinguished, but the workers inside succumbed to carbon monoxide poisoning. The one who had been sleeping in the corner where the fire had started died of asphyxiation. Had this episode come to light four years later, when the chairman of the Factory's Comrades' Court was finally arrested following a tip-off from a vigilant Kuybyshev Chekist, Stepan would now be lying not on these bunks but in the ground, with a couple of law enforcement bullets in his chest. Fortunately for the arsonist, the investigation was focused on war crimes and was simultaneously dealing with several traitors to the Motherland. In exposing them, Sakhno had proved more useful than his former comrades from the 118th Police Battalion…

The convict stretched contentedly on his hard bed. Life went on. Despite its twists and turns, he was still not rotting in a dreadful box in a deep hole in the ground. This thought comforted him, as always, and finally, Stepan fell asleep.

---

*Styopa – the diminutive of Stepan

**Ukrainian Insurgent Army (or UPA): a Ukrainian nationalist partisan formation founded by OUN in October 1942

Chapter 14. The Land and the Peasants

Studying the inner world of the petty vampire engrossed me so much that I completely forgot about the KGB captain's inability to teleport. When satisfied with my curiosity, I finally tuned in to Andrei's thoughts and found him sprawled across a blanket on an uncomfortable bunk in one of Syktyvkar's dingy hotels. He was staring at the pages of a book he had bought on a whim, but inside, he was boiling with righteous anger, which prevented the meaning of the printed word from reaching his mind. As soon as I appeared before my companion, whom I had carelessly abandoned to fate, he jumped up, lunged at me with his fists, and yelled, "You Lemurian bastard!"

Fortunately, I managed to immobilise his fist before it reached my eye. He froze awkwardly with his arm raised mid-swing, which only enraged him further, while I bought myself time to apologise before any blows could land.

"I'm sorry! I really am! I got carried away and completely forgot that I needed to bring you to the city first."

"Let me go this instant, you scoundrel!"

"Do you promise to behave yourself?" I knew full well I was at fault, but I couldn't help laughing. The captain's furiously bulging eyes, already usually protuberant, now seemed to almost pop right out of their sockets.

"I promise!" Andrei rasped, although not very convincingly. Finally able to move, he slumped into a chair and sulked, crossing his arms over his chest. I felt sorry that my oversight had drained my friend's energy, although it was not entirely without benefit, as the temperature in the cold hotel room had risen noticeably.

"Do you have any idea what I had to go through?" the captain said. "You whispered that you'd be right back and then vanished! And there I was, like an idiot, sitting opposite the duty officer in a penal colony in the middle of nowhere, unable to explain why

I was sitting there. A high-security prison isn't exactly a waiting room. Questions arise! What else does an investigator from the capital need here after finishing his business? And how did he even get to the colony in the first place?"

"So, what did you tell them?"

Andrei waved vaguely. "I said I hitched a ride."

"And how did you get to the city?" I finally thought to ask.

"Ah, now he's curious!" the captain snapped. "On their truck. Luckily, they sent a lorry to Syktyvkar for supplies today and the weather calmed down, but I had to entertain the driver with stories about Moscow for two hours on the way!" Having let his anger out, Andrei fell silent and stared gloomily at a corner of the room, at the greasy cream wallpaper decorated with small brownish-pink flower patterns. His thoughts were bleak.

"Why do you think you'll definitely have to resign now?" I asked.

"Because you've compromised me! If I travelled from Moscow on official business, I should have been brought and taken back by an official vehicle. God forbid they get suspicious, call my superiors, and make inquiries! How will I explain to Colonel Sviridov my unauthorised trip beyond the Arctic Circle? He thinks I'm visiting my uncle in Veliky Novgorod and waiting for contact with extraterrestrial civilizations there. And what will I say then? That I have actually made the contact?"

Given homo sapiens' inability to teleport, the sudden appearance of an ordinary KGB captain in several distant locations across the USSR within a short time could indeed seem suspicious. Now, I saw the seriousness of my blunder, which was, of course, due to my inexperience in the human world. Homo sapiens, it turned out, kept secrets even from those with whom they shared a common cause! If Colonel Sviridov started asking questions, Andrei would have to reveal the existence of homo liberatus and explain my mission, which, in turn, would unravel a web of complications. So, failing to look after my friend might also have created a potential problem for myself.

Meanwhile, Andrei softened. "Alright, it's my fault too. I should have planned a better cover story and discussed transportation options," he sighed heavily. "There's just so much going on..."

I felt sorry for him, and ten minutes later, Captain Pilatov slept in his comfortable bed at Uncle Pasha's house. I didn't wake the host on our arrival. Compared to Syktyvkar, the May night in Veliky Novgorod felt like heaven, and I fell asleep in the garden under my favourite apple tree. That's where Colonel Pilatov found me in the morning when he stepped outside for fresh air, pondering how to apply his miraculously restored health to putting the ancestral home in order. He was dressed in knee-length dark green shorts and a white polo shirt, planning to combine a survey of the necessary work with some exercise.

My sudden awakening came at the colonel's hands: Pavel Andreevich was shaking me by the shoulders with considerable force. When I opened my eyes, I saw his face contorted with anxiety.

"Hey, Yan! What's wrong with you, son?" Uncle Pasha was panicking. "And where's Andrei?"

"Everything's fine..." I mumbled sleepily. "That's enough, stop shaking me!" The colonel was so zealously trying to bring me to my senses that he almost shook my astral body out of my physical one. No one had ever used force on me before — even during the fire in Khatyn, my mother had managed to shield me from the shoves and blows of executioners. The new sensation was so unpleasant that I even felt nauseous. I had to put up an energy shield to make Uncle Pasha finally remove his hands and step back.

"Andrei is in the house," I reassured my worried friend. "We got back last night and didn't want to wake you. I was just sleeping."

"But why in the garden, on the ground? There are plenty of spare rooms in the house. You know that!"

"You have a power spot here, Pavel Andreevich." I was now fully awake and glad to have the opportunity to finally inform the garden's owner about the valuable resource he unknowingly possessed.

"Where?" he asked, puzzled.

"Right about where you're standing now," I said, pointing to the spot where the tree emerged from the ground.

"Under the apple tree?" The colonel peered at the base of the trunk as if he were hoping to see the power with his human eyes. "What nonsense."

"Not at all. I'll even say more: if you spent just half an hour a day here, my help in curing your illness probably wouldn't have been needed."

"Why didn't you say so earlier?" Colonel Pilatov protested, and justifiably so.

"I meant to, but I got caught up in the investigation and never found the right moment," I admitted.

"So, I just sit under the apple tree?" the old man asked enthusiastically. "Meditate?"

"Yes, you know how to do that," I replied without the grandeur he was expecting. "Just take off your trainers. You need to be barefoot. You'll live to a hundred!"

Pavel Andreevich left his footwear to the side, sat beside me, leaned against the marvellous apple tree, and closed his eyes. The old man thought about how he had nearly died of cancer, yet the cure had been right under his nose. How despite all his experience and knowledge, which he once thought would suffice for several lifetimes, the world was still full of mysteries worth living for even beyond a hundred years, if possible. I stayed silent too, admiring his orange aura that grew and filled with vibrant healthy hues. Two neighbours' cats turned up and rubbed against the colonel's legs, and one even climbed onto his lap. My old acquaintance the hare cautiously appeared from a bush and tickled my friend's ankle with its delicate whiskers.

Pavel Andreevich opened his eyes. "What on earth is this?" The cats didn't really surprise him, but the fearless hare was extraordinary. However, as soon as the old man spoke, the bunny zipped back into the bushes.

"Oh, that's my old friend," I said, waving after the fleeing rascal. "You've created a strong energy flow with your desire to live to a hundred, and the animals wanted to share in it."

The colonel, who had never kept pets, hesitantly stroked the cat snuggled against his stomach and asked, "So, how long do I have to sit here?"

"I think that's enough for the first time," I said, getting to my feet and offering him a hand. "Especially since I can't wait to tell you what we discovered in Syktyvkar, and it's better done behind closed doors."

Andrei, exhausted by teleportation and other twists and turns beyond the Arctic Circle, slept until noon. While he rested, I shared with Uncle Pasha the information I had extracted from Sakhno's mind.

"Not bad at all," the retired colonel approved. "You'd be priceless in espionage! If all our agents could read information like that..." He rolled his eyes mockingly towards the upper floor, where Captain Pilatov was still asleep.

"If everyone could do it, there wouldn't be any need for spies," I retorted, and the old man just spread his arms comically, having no comeback.

"We should sort out Baranovsky's murder in Orenburg, but that can wait. Sakhno is already in custody," Pavel Andreevich reasoned. "So, it's Vasyura after all... Are you sure? You only met one of the former Schutzmänners. What about the others?"

"I have no more doubts. There's no need to waste time on the rest."

"Then, I have something to boast about too!" With these words, Pavel Andreevich went to his study and returned with a thin sheet of paper, rolled into a tube, which he handed to me. "Here, it came by fax."

I took the paper from his hands and began reading aloud.

"'Report on the deputy director for eco…'" I stumbled. The printed text was unclear in places, and I struggled to decipher it. "I can't make it out!"

"Economic affairs!" Pavel said.

"Aha…" I attempted to continue. "'… economic affairs of the Velykodymersky collective farm Vasyura Grigory Nikitovich, born 9th of February 1915.

"'April 1985, village of Velyka Dymerka, Bro… Brovarsky… district, Kiev region…'" I stopped, exhaled, and blinked to relieve the strain.

The colonel took pity on me. "Alright, let me do it!" He snatched the paper from my hands, put on his glasses, and continued almost without faltering. "'Vasyura Grigory Nikitovich has worked at the Velykodymersky collective farm for 30 years, starting as an ordinary bookkeeper in 1955. His higher education, extensive life experience, initiative, excellent managerial skills, and pronounced organisational qualities soon allowed Grigory Nikitovich* to take up the position of chief accountant, as his desire for continuous learning and improvement manifested in tangible results. Grigory Nikitovich is a qualified and development-oriented employee primarily responsible for the farm's high profitability and prosperity.

"'In 1965, Comrade Vasyura assumed the position of deputy director for economic affairs. His achievements are evidenced by several accomplishments in this key role for the collective farm. Grigory Nikitovich implemented a complete overhaul of the enterprise's accounting processes, efficiently updated agricultural and domestic equipment, commissioned significant agricultural facilities, and actively participated in the construction and commissioning of both a secondary school and a hospital. Thanks to Comrade Vasyura, the collective farm achieved high performance figures, managed resources more effectively, maintained valuable personnel, and acquired modern equipment, enabling timely work completion.'

"That's a capable man, one cannot deny that!" remarked Colonel Pilatov. "Apparently the Germans appreciated it too…

"'Comrade Vasyura maintains a strict mentorship style and high standards with the staff, motivating many employees to work diligently, improve performance, and pursue career growth. The team under his leadership is disciplined, socially protected, and operates under safe working conditions.

"'Grigory Nikitovich places great importance on working with young people. As a veteran of the Great Patriotic War, he regularly meets with schoolchildren, supporting the teachers of the Velykodymerska Secondary School in their noble mission of fostering patriotism among the younger generation. Furthermore, Comrade Vasyura is an honorary cadet of Kalinin Military Communications School in Kiev.

"'Grigory Nikitovich is an example of hard work and determination for the collective farm staff. He continues his professional activities despite having reached retirement age. Comrade Vasyura has been repeatedly awarded certificates of merit and was honoured with the Veteran of Labour medal.

"'This character reference is provided at the request of the military enlistment office regarding the nomination of Grigory Nikitovich Vasyura for the Order of the Patriotic War in honour of the fortieth anniversary of victory over the Nazi invaders.

"'Signatures of the Velykodymersky collective farm managers:

"'Yatsenko Anatoliy Tikhonovich/Yatsenko — Head of the Village Council of the Velykodymersky collective farm.

"'Bocharov Anatoliy Borisovich/Bocharov — Deputy Head of the Village Council of the Velykodymersky collective farm.'"

When the colonel finished reading the reference, I asked him, "Where did you get this from?"

"It's not about what you know but who you know!" he replied, winking conspiratorially with his brown eye.

It turned out that while Andrei and I were freezing in the far north, the retired officer had not been idle. He called the Brovary District Military Enlistment Office and obtained this reference on Vasyura using a few old connections. By a strange coincidence, the former chief of staff of the 118th Ukrainian Police Battalion had just demanded the Order of the Patriotic War.

"How can one demand an award?" I wondered. "Isn't it supposed to be a token of gratitude given by society? That's what I was told at least!"

"You were told correctly," Pavel Andreevich agreed. "But in this case, the award is commemorative."

"Commemorative? How so?"

"It honours the fortieth anniversary of the Victory to all veterans. It seems our subject was somehow overlooked. Honestly, with a past like his, it's quite foolish to risk exposure for vanity!"

Pilatov Junior appeared in the doorway, behind the colonel sitting on the sofa. He yawned and stretched first upwards, then outwards, as if spreading invisible wings, then leaned against the doorframe with his arms crossed. Andrei was dressed in the same sagging tracksuit he had been wearing when I had carried him from the Moscow dormitory to Uncle Pasha's house. Pavel Andreevich noticed my gaze and realised we were no longer alone. He turned, assessed his nephew's state, and remarked, "You don't look too sharp!"

"You try teleporting to the Arctic Circle and back!" replied the captain with mock grievance. "Give me a day in the sun and I'll be as good as new." Then he prompted to change the topic. "What did I miss?"

Uncle Pasha handed him the character reference for Vasyura. "Here."

Andrei skimmed through the copy of the text. "A Labour Hero and model worker, huh? This reference is almost too perfect! Interesting… Is it from the enlistment office?" He pointed to the paper and, receiving a nod from the colonel, suggested, "We need to find out why Vasyura wasn't on the awards list in the first place. Give me a day to recover, and we'll head to… what's it called?" He checked the reference again. "Velyka Dymerka and Brovary."

Pavel Andreevich rose from the sofa, put his arm around his nephew's shoulders, and led him outside to meet the wonderful apple tree. As he was leaving, he turned and winked at me again with his brown eye, promising not to waste the day but to focus on planning how to track the vampire.

Later that evening, we decided that the captain and I would pretend to be representatives of a production company interested in partnership with the Velykodymersky collective farm. This would lead us straight to the deputy director for economic affairs. We found a fine classic business suit for Andrei in the colonel's wardrobe. When Uncle Pasha was younger, he had a similar build to his nephew. As for me, being slimmer and shorter than the Pilatovs, I had to visit the town shop, which resulted in a less elegant, off-the-rack suit. To complete the look, I had to accept a hideous tie, which made me sympathise with Cassandra's discomfort during our visit to Lubyanka. At least I didn't have to wear heels!

"How badly must she have wanted a child from me to endure so ridiculously restricting outfit?" I thought. A pang of unease hit my heart, but I brushed it aside.

The following day, we landed at a short dust-covered concrete railway platform reeking of machine oil. From there we were to walk to the Velykodymersky Village Council to familiarise ourselves with the area and avoid the locals' suspicion. I thought it an excellent idea to observe Vasyura while "undercover," as scouts say, to better assess how powerful this vampire was, whether he was aware of his strength, and what kind of relationship he had with his surroundings.

We didn't have a map of the area, but Andrei was confident that we could find our way by asking around, so his first move was to question the station cashier. She turned out to be a plump, busty woman with a double chin, unnaturally tiny bleached blond curls, and lively, inquisitive brown eyes that darted about in her broad, sweaty face. Her railway uniform seemed ready to burst as a dark blue skirt and light blue blouse clung too tightly to her fat body that was rapidly bidding farewell to its youth. She was just a little older than the captain but looked old enough to be his mother. While I was looking around, the cashier was eyeing a well-dressed handsome man, my companion, with interest and flirting clumsily as she explained the directions.

"When you leave the station, take the concrete road so you don't get lost. Just go straight and straight" — she raised her thinly plucked eyebrows and pointed with a sausage-shaped finger — "until the road turns left. Then you turn left too and keep walking until you reach the centre. Everything's there: the village council, the shops, and the school…"

Joining the conversation, I matched her tone. "Thank you very much!"

"You're so-o-o welcome!" replied the cashier in a shrill soprano, baring her rodent-like teeth in a sugary smile. I grabbed the captain by the sleeve and led him away from the woman devouring him with her eyes. Next to my companion, I looked utterly unremarkable, but honestly, I was glad to in this situation. We finally escaped from the station and walked along the cracked concrete road lined with fresh but already dusty grass.

"Where did you get such a knack for languages?" Andrei asked with a laugh, referring to my Ukrainian addressed to the cashier.

"Well, we don't really have language barriers."

"How does that work? Do you learn every language?"

"No, we just understand them. I'm not entirely sure how, but I think it comes with telepathy, which is the first practical skill any Lemurian learns," I explained. "You read the thoughts and desires of any living being and respond in the language of their thoughts."

"Can a homo sapien learn to do it?" the captain asked enviously.

"It's possible, though it'd take time and concentration… For your kind, cracking languages is usually difficult, because you built the Tower of Babel instead of building yourselves…"

We continued the rest of the journey to Velyka Dymerka in silence. Andrei pondered my words, and his face took on that familiar, hopelessly philosophical expression. After spending just under a month side by side with a one of the homo liberatus, the thirty-three-year-old officer had begun to suspect that humanity's general underdevelopment might be the root cause of his dissatisfaction with himself and even the sense of inadequacy that had plagued him for years. Like most people, Andrei tended to take easy options and was already beginning to construct a mental excuse to reconcile himself with this sense of inferiority, as there seemed no way to reach the level of the Lemurians anyway. Knowing my friend well enough, I didn't interfere with his dive into another bout of melancholy. After all, the only thing that really mattered was that he was still walking beside me and had never refused to help, often sacrificing his energy and comfort for the sake of my mission.

Soon I stopped paying attention to Andrei's thoughts and focused on the dull features of central Ukraine's farming land. In their struggle against extinction, homo sapiens had cleared away the dense, game-filled forests of mushrooms and berries that had thrived here just a couple of thousand years ago, mutilating Nature in the process. The area was now open, clean-shaven for agriculture, and looked unnaturally bald. On either side of the road stretched ploughed and planted fields. Some were covered with green sprouts while others were black with rich, fatty soil dusted with some chemical substance that, due to the dry spring, had not soaked into the chernozem but instead rose into the air on the wind, making it hard to breathe. Tall trees that formed narrow windbreaks looked like forlorn dwarfs against the vast expanse of farmland. The dusty concrete path, also coated in grime, led us across the fields to a narrow-paved road. We took turns stumbling over small potholes in the asphalt, which near the village gave way to a hard-packed dirt road. There, the slightest movement of wind, feet, or wheels raised a cloud of dust, so a yellow-grey haze hung in the air, never settling before the next disturbance.

A tractor with a blue cabin and an empty trailer roared and clattered past us — and that was the worst part: visibility on the road vanished completely. There was no air to breathe because of the stinking diesel fumes and the grey dust that instantly clogged our nostrils and covered our clothes, shoes, hair, and sweaty faces. When we finally emerged from the hellish cloud, Andrei looked at the sleeve of his uncle's diplomatic suit.

"Couldn't we have teleported?"

"Would you really prefer two teleports in a row?" I asked in genuine surprise.

"Right now, yes!" barked the captain, and began feverishly brushing himself off, swearing loudly. I sighed but agreed with my companion that walking along the country road was not the best idea. Following his example, I also began brushing myself off, though without the swearing. In short, neither of us liked it here already.

It was eleven in the morning when we finally entered the village in our tarnished suits. The streets were almost deserted, apart from a couple of bicycles that passed us by with baskets tied to their handlebars. The owners of this unsteady transport glided quietly over the rutted dirt road like melancholic ghosts. First, a man in a worn grey jacket and a battered cap rode past. He was about my age but looked almost elderly. Moreover, he reeked unbearably of alcohol and sweat, the odour of which made it clear he was suffering from liver damage. The man paid us no attention. However, a thin woman, around forty, in a grey cotton dress with her hair slicked back into a meagre ponytail, rode by a minute later and glanced curiously at the two city-dressed young men. She too carried on her way. When the dust from the second bicycle's wheels settled a little, it became quiet again, the only remaining sound coming from the invisible, ever-present pigeons that continued to coo, celebrating their recently hatched offspring.

The sun blazed unseasonably hot. Fresh young foliage lent patches of vibrancy to the dull landscape, but even in the bright daylight — or perhaps because of it — a stranger walking through the village felt an oppressive sense of loneliness and inexplicable loss. These feelings were exacerbated by the endless impenetrable wooden fences painted dark green or sky blue. It seemed that if you collapsed and died in the middle of the street, you would simply be left there as prey to wild and domestic animals. Such thoughts weighed heavily on the captain.

On the other hand, I was struck by the stark contrast between the neglected, rutted street, overgrown with unsightly weeds along the edges, and the well-kept plots Andrei could not see behind the fences. Clearly the locals strictly distinguished between what was theirs and what was not. Beyond the fences, not a single patch of land was left idle: vegetables were planted in the rich, freshly tilled soil with geometric precision. All this abundance, well watered and fertilised with animal dung rather than chemicals, was just beginning to sprout, promising to yield appetising fruits in time. The patterned leaves of carrots were already green, and cucumber and courgette stems had sent out tiny snakes of tendrils spreading along the beds. Pink tops of early radish peeked from the earth, spring onions reached upwards in neat rows, and the warm air carried the fragrant scent of fresh dill and parsley.

In almost every yard, several varieties of fruit trees were in bloom, and the farthest corners were overgrown with thorny raspberry bushes, making trespassing from a neighbour's property fraught with painful scratches. The fences dividing the yards themselves were as tall and sturdy as the outer ones, but these were left unpainted, simply nailed together from wooden planks blackened with age. The same scene played out in every garden: in the only still-vacant patch, some middle-aged or older woman was bending double with her skirt tucked up and burying small oblong pinkish-brown tubers in the ground. The garden mistress would occasionally straighten up to wipe sweat from her face, then return to planting potatoes.

Many untended fruit trees grew along the edges of the street. Some had already shed most of their petals, while others still delighted the eye with white and pink blossoms.

"Fruit trees by the roads — that's what I love about Ukraine!" said Andrei. "Pity it's not summer now, or we could have gorged on cherries, apricots, or apples while trudging through the village."

"Don't they have this in your area?"

"Sometimes, but not often."

"Why, I wonder?"

"I don't know... Maybe the soil up north isn't as fertile. Or maybe people there worry less about thieves than they do here..."

"What do trees have to do with that?"

"Kids want apples sometimes, and they might sneak into a neighbour's garden to get them," Andrei explained. "But if the apples grow right on the street, there's no need for theft. Though that's just my guess since I'm no village dweller."

"Why do they even need those fences between gardens? Why can't they just share one big orchard?"

Andrei laughed. "You have no idea about private property, do you? Like you've come straight out of communism!" Seeing my puzzled expression, he clarified what he meant. "Everyone makes their own jam!"

"What's jam?"

"Er..." My companion wrinkled his brow, searching for the right words. "Scientifically speaking, it's fruit and sugar subjected to heat."

"Ah, sugar..." The memory of its unpleasant, unnatural sweetness made me grimace. "I see. That's not found in Nature in its processed state that you use. And it shouldn't be."

"During the war, sugar was more valuable than gold."

"There shouldn't be wars either!" I snapped. Even the thought of humans killing each other was repugnant! Andrei spread his hands, partly agreeing with me and partly indicating that he couldn't change anything. I understood he was right and forced myself to change the subject. "In the village where your uncle lives, I hardly saw any tall fences... Just some stakes, mostly symbolic."

"Look behind the fences, into the private yards. I'll bet anything they're immaculate!" It turned out Andrei knew a thing or two about rural Ukrainian life.

"Already had a look," I replied with a smile. "You're right."

"Local people are known for their devotion to property," Captain Pilatov explained with a wry grin. "Maybe that's why there were more anti-communists here than anywhere else. Greed doesn't fit into our bright future."

I did not appreciate his irony. "Property is the main weakness of *all* homo sapiens, with minor variations. Not property itself but the sense of security that comes with ownership. It's directly proportional to the amount owned."

"It's like a crutch!" said Andrei, raising his index finger.

"Exactly," I agreed. "A crutch may help you move, but it's no real leg!" Andrei nodded in agreement, and to liven up our dull walk, I elaborated. "In the same way, property requires energy and time. It needs to be maintained. It must be controlled. Energy, of course, can be restored, but time… time is irreplaceable because it's limited by your biological cycle. *Time is your life*. A very short life."

Andrei stood on tiptoe and craned his neck to peer over a light-blue fence that was lower than the others. Beyond it, a weary red-faced woman was toiling away in the vegetable garden. Almost in a whisper, so she wouldn't hear or notice us, the captain said, "It seems here, property consumes far more energy than it provides."

"Addiction to property is exactly what stalled your evolution," I replied sadly. I was no longer looking in the direction in which he indicated. Everything was already clear to me. "If homo sapiens had learned to manage natural energy flows, they would have gained direct access to the Earth's resources and stopped viewing the ownership of things as the main means of survival."

"So, to stop wasting our lives on accumulation, we must stop worrying about a lack of resources. And to stop worrying, we need to know how to attract them…"

"Through energy control!" I finished.

"Yes. Learning to control energy takes time — the time we spend accumulating and safeguarding resources. It's a vicious circle!" the captain concluded. "Do you think we have any hope?"

"I think you don't, at least in the near future," I answered honestly.

"What about people who already have everything and don't need to work? Surely they can devote time to developing such practices!" my naïve friend exclaimed.

I sighed. “It’s not so much about having or lacking resources as it is the fear of losing them. As far as I know, wealthy homo sapiens fear even more than the poor because they have more to lose. The moment trouble looms, they’ll abandon all their spiritual practices and throw themselves into saving their assets, dedicating the rest of their lives to it if necessary. And some keep building their wealth even when they could already afford to never work again. It’s hard to imagine anything more pointless! Accumulation turns into an addiction. At their core, homo sapiens are slaves to fear, and as long as that remains so, freedom will be nothing more than a dream, no matter how loudly they shout about it. Sadly, fear is embedded in your DNA, and we can’t change that.”

“Why not, by the way?” Andrei asked. “You can influence conception, can’t you?”

“We can influence the process of conception, but not its outcomes. DNA is an extremely complex biological system, and a single change could trigger a chain reaction with unpredictable consequences. Most likely, those consequences would be disastrous, like any interference with Nature. You already have stories about such failures. Frankenstein, for example… We don’t try to change Nature. We negotiate with it. Do you see the difference?”

“Not really,” Andrei admitted.

Seeing people sweating behind fences as they planted potatoes filled me with an unusual sense of hopelessness — hopelessness to help them. It’s impossible to pull someone out of the monotonous, small-minded swamp of peasant life when they themselves consider their existence on a tiny patch of land… if not happy, then at least stable and secure.

“I feel especially sorry for peasants,” I added.

“Why them in particular?” Andrei asked.

“It’s simple. These people work themselves to the bone and force the land into a deal. They give it their strength but also make it work unnaturally hard. Peasants believe that, after all their backbreaking labour, they have the right to demand a return from the earth in the form of a harvest, but the land never asked them to impose so much energy. In any case, owning it is your most laughable illusion. The earth takes the remains of its 'owners' when they die while it carries on living. So, who owns whom really?"

We were absorbed in our conversation, hardly noticing we had reached the centre of the village. It was a small square entirely clad in asphalt, with a few stunted trees huddling in its corners. This place was called the "centre" not only due to its geographical position in Velyka Dymerka but also because it was intended to serve the practical needs of the residents. Around the perimeter, there were single-story boxes with doors and signs that read *Household Goods*, *Industrial Goods*, *Grocery*, *Bread*, *Pharmacy*, and *Tyre Repair*. The asphalt near the entrance to the latter was covered with dark stains of engine oil accompanied by cigarette butts discarded underfoot. The rest of the square appeared cleaner.

We entered the door marked *Grocery*, hoping to procure something edible and ask a few questions. But my hopes of finding food were dashed immediately. Aside from neatly stacked pyramids of metal tins containing the ever-present canned sprats and glass jars filled with fruit boiled to a rubbery consistency, nothing was remotely consumable. A dark-haired saleswoman seemed to be dying of curiosity at the sight of two strangers. She wore a presumably white apron and cylindrical headwear of the same colour. She resembled the cashier we had met earlier at the station with her plumpness and cloying friendliness toward strangers. Andrei now asked the woman about the location of the village council, and from behind the counter came her melodious reply in Surzhyk, a blend of Russian and Ukrainian.

"It's just around the corner, the big white brick building. You can't miss it." She paused, then, unable to contain her nosiness, asked, "Who are you after?"

"We need the deputy director for economic affairs," the captain replied, trying to sound official.

"Oh, he's not at the council today! He'd be at the school, giving a speech. My lad said they've got an assembly for Victory Day."

"Thanks a lot, beautiful!" Andrei said, brightening up. "One more question: do you have any kind of hotel here?"

"A hotel? Well, there is one," the woman giggled, "but I wouldn't recommend it…"

Having scanned her mental picture of what passed for a hotel, I tugged on the captain's sleeve and, looking him in the eyes, said, "She doesn't recommend it!"

Andrei nodded and turned back to the assistant.

"Or could we maybe rent a room from someone for a couple of days?"

"Oh, there's plenty of that!" She then bellowed towards the entrance, startling us both. "Timofivna! Would you take a couple of gentlemen in?"

We turned to see a short, wiry woman, sixtyish, entering the shop. She carried a homemade cloth bag and, though still sturdy, had clearly lost the full figure she might have possessed a decade ago. Her dried-up frame sagged mournfully under a dark dress with tiny faded flower patterns. A knot of her greying hair was covered by a headscarf tied at the nape of her neck.

"Who are they?" the elderly woman asked, stepping inside.

"They're from the city, here on business with Vasyura, but they'd better not stay at his place."

"Why is that?" the captain interjected.

"His wife's ill, and besides…" The assistant shuddered at the thought of anyone living in Vasyura's house. Timofeevna sized us up from head to toe, calculating how much to charge.

Already aware that she had a large vegetable garden, I preempted her deliberations. "Ten a day will do. And we'll be having meals as well."

Timofeevna gave me a look of slight surprise but didn't dwell on my accurate guess. Instead, she asked, "How long for?"

"As long as it takes," Andrei replied evasively, and added politely, "If it's no trouble. We'll pay upfront."

"All right." The woman gestured invitingly after purchasing the matches and salt she had come for. "Come along, lads. We'll have to stop by the market since you want meals…"

Andrei grabbed two bottles of Kuyalnyk, handed me one, and took a greedy swig from the other.

Vera Timofeevna sniffed disdainfully. "What do you need that Kuyalnyk for? The water from our well is better…"

"We'll try that too, Timofeevna," the captain replied with a charming smile. Then, as if casually, he asked the assistant, "What time's the event at the school? We'd like to pop in, just out of curiosity."

"Two o'clock, I think," came the uncertain reply.

"Two o'clock it is," our new landlady echoed. "My lad said he won't be coming to mine after school because of the assembly."

"Her grandson," I explained to the captain. The elderly woman raised her sparse greying eyebrows, mildly surprised, but refrained from commenting on my ability to guess details again.

"Well, then we've got a couple of hours to settle in," Andrei said, checking his watch. "Via the market, of course. And we'll help you carry the bags."

Vera Timofeevna was a shrewd woman guided by practical experience. She had survived the occupation of Dymerka. When the Nazis took her eighteen-year-old husband to work in Germany, she was heavily pregnant and learned of his death only after the war. It turned out that Eugen had twice escaped on his way to Europe to return to his family. The first time, the guards recaptured him and put him back on the train. The second time, they shot him. Seventeen-year-old Vera was left dependent on relatives with a baby in her arms. She never remarried due to the postwar shortage of men. The war had also taken her two older brothers, and she stayed in her parental home, which she eventually inherited.

Her beloved son Georgy studied agronomy in Kiev, returned to Dymerka as a promising young man, started a family, and built a large modern house like a proper manager. Despite her solitary life, Vera Timofeevna considered herself lucky — well, luckier than many, at any rate.

Unlike the village shop that lacked a decent selection of fresh vegetables, the Velykodymersky market offered plenty of cabbage, potatoes, carrots, and thick-skinned apples, albeit from last year's stock. The new harvest was still far off, but the abundance of fresh radishes, greens, and early strawberries delighted the eye. It was not entirely clear to whom all this produce was sold, as most of the locals grew the same crops in their gardens. According to Baba** Vera, the locals only came to the market for what they were missing, while people from apartment blocks in urban areas did the bulk of the shopping.

Timofeevna bought half a sack of potatoes, dried beans, a head of cabbage, some other vegetables, herbs, and a slab of pungent smoked pork fat without asking our preferences. The captain rubbed his hands in anticipation, took the bags from her, and suggested cheerfully, "Is that a borsch on the menu? Should be ready by evening!"

"That's right, sonny," Vera Timofeevna replied with a good-natured grin. Incidentally, she worked as a cook in the local canteen. By sheer coincidence, she had a day off only because a celebratory dinner for the district authorities was planned that evening at the local restaurant, and she had been invited to serve as the event's only chef.

"But I'm hungry now," Andrei complained plaintively.

"Come on, darling, we'll sort something out at home," replied the kind woman.

The fridge in Baba Vera's kitchen was packed with culinary delights, mostly prepared from animal carcasses. My companion's face lit up with salivating anticipation. Such a variety of meats was rare even in Moscow shops, and after paying Timofeevna for three days in advance, Andrei pounced on the homemade sausage, that is, pork meat and fat mixed with herbs and spices and stuffed into pig intestines. Baba Vera quickly fried it in a pan with an incredible amount of fat. Watching this process and smelling the frying meat almost made me sick. Of course, I had realised already at the market that only Captain Pilatov would be dining there.

While Andrei feasted and chatted with the hostess, I stepped outside through the back door for fresh air. The sight of the garden and orchard was pleasant, but in the climate of the central region, these vegetables and fruits were only beginning to sprout and were not edible yet. However, I needed to eat something, and there was no time for teleportation elsewhere, so improvisation was necessary.

I spotted a couple of carrot seedlings pushing through the soil, removed my uncomfortable shoes, grasped the green stalks near the earth, and, speeding up the energy flow to the plants, pulled out two long, bright-orange roots. I rinsed them under the outdoor tap by the back door and relished their juicy sweetness. I repeated the procedure several times and then headed toward the nearest apple tree for dessert. I found a white blossom tinged with soft pink already pollinated by a busy bee and cupped it in my hands. The flower quickly turned into a green fruit and grew before my eyes. When a large apple lay in my palm and I admired its perfection, waiting for the sweet flesh beneath the crunchy whitish-red skin to ripen fully, Baba Vera suddenly shrieked behind me, "Oh dear heavens!"

I turned around and saw Timofeevna, wide-eyed and open-mouthed, watching my manipulations. I had to leave the ripe apple on the branch for the moment and rush to help the poor woman, who was slowly sliding down the wall. I brought her back inside and sat her on the nearest chair. "I'm so sorry!" I said. "I should have warned you that I don't eat meat…"

"Meat… Yes… I see…" she echoed faintly, but then she suddenly sprang to her feet and hurried back to the garden, to my apple. Strictly speaking, according to the laws of homo sapiens, it was *her* apple since it had grown on *her* land.

The captain and I followed Baba Vera outside, where we found her examining the branch covered in spring blossoms with a single ripe fruit at the end.

"What kind of miracle is this?" Andrei asked quietly with a smile, not particularly surprised. "Can you do that too?"

I had to explain. "Yes, but I don't do it often. There was no time to teleport to the tropics."

"How do you do that?" our hostess asked, having finally found her voice and ignoring my mention of teleportation.

"By controlling energy flows, Vera Timofeevna," I replied matter-of-factly, and then finally dared to ask, "May I eat this apple now?"

The mother of Velykodymerka's agronomist nodded in astonishment and only managed to ask, "What kind of flows?"

"You see, dear Vera Timofeevna," my companion began smoothly, well versed in handling the public, "where this young man comes from, people spend their time not toiling but maximising the development of their minds and bodies. So, if someone wants an apple, they just grow one themselves, right there and then…"

"And can he grow potatoes too? Or beetroot?"

"Potatoes, carrots, and beetroot too," listed my charming friend, taking her arm and leading her back inside to give me a chance to finish my dessert.

"Imagine how much could be grown for sale!" Timofeevna murmured in awe, calculating the profits a quick and seemingly effortless harvest could yield. "And how many times a year can you do this?"

In her own way, Baba Vera was not without imagination. At once she envisioned neat piles of fresh fruits and vegetables, beautifully displayed at the market in the off-season, envious glances from neighbours, and the pleasant rustle of banknotes in the many pockets of a special market-day apron that had a separate compartment for each denomination. She also pictured a new pigsty with a couple of plump dwellers — the dream she had so far been unable to bring to life due to a lack of time, money, and helping hands.

Timofeevna's flight of fancy was interrupted by Andrei's rather shocking statement. "They have no agriculture, no land ownership, and no trade. They don't need any of that. With such talents, they can live day by day."

So, everyone dreamed of their own paradise.

Having finished my food, I returned to the kitchen. "That's true, Andrei, but we prefer to consume Nature's gifts when they ripen, and turn to growth acceleration only when unavoidable, like now. I think we should hurry if we want to hear *Comrade* Vasyura's speech."

The courteous captain thanked our hostess for the delicious meal and stepped outside the gate with me.

"I think Baba Vera's having an existential crisis," Andrei remarked, glancing back at the house. "Shouldn't you erase her memory?"

"Erasing memories is impossible, my friend. That's pure science fiction. At most, you can block some memories with hypnosis," I replied with a sigh. I was reluctant to use suggestions on our hostess, as her sharp mind could still be helpful. "I don't think it's necessary in this case. Vera Timofeevna understands that no one would believe her story about a guest with superpowers, and the prospect of being labelled a mad chef is highly undesirable as such a reputation might result in being fired."

Faced with such sound reasoning, the KGB captain could not argue.

After stepping through the gate and looking around, we teleported closer to the school, risking being noticed in this unconventional mode of travel but lacking the time for another dusty walk in Velyka Dymerka.

---

*Variations of patronymic names' spelling reflects the variety of different speakers' background and situations. Thus, the patronymic Nikitiyevich signifies the use of the formal Russian language, and the variations Nikitovich and Mykytovich point at the use of so-called Surzhyk and Ukrainian language, respectively

** Baba (from "babushka"): refers to a grandmother or any woman of similar age and may be applied to any woman in colloquial speech

Chapter 15. The Vampire's Story: The Ideal and the Real

As soon as we walked into the school building through the main entrance, a petite woman hurried towards us. She was wearing a crimson silk triangle tucked under the collar of her white blouse and tied at the front in a neat square knot. "A pioneers' leader," Andrei guessed, recalling his own childhood and the undergraduate girl in a pleated navy skirt that fell just above her rounded knees. Those lovely knees used to drive the teenage Pilatov crazy… The woman who approached us was much older than the one from his memories. Andrei realised this from the fine, dry wrinkles on her face, visible only up close. Her blond, straight, and slightly sparse hair was cut sharply to end just below her pointed chin, where her slender neck began. Her pale lips, thin as a thread, barely outlined eyebrows, and general faded appearance gave the impression of a person who had lost her colours under the scorching sun. Only her large, deep, and anxious blue eyes seemed to compensate for lack of joy on her thin face. This woman, dressed like a schoolgirl, lingered for a few seconds. Looking up at us, she asked in a high, almost childlike voice, "Are you here by invitation?"

Andrei shook his head, and the pioneers' leader, without another word, disappeared into the chaotic movement of white shirts adorned with bright drops of red ties.

I had never seen so many children before! The two-story school building buzzed with their voices like a beehive. Kids darted up and down the stairs and ran through the foyer, hurrying to finish their tasks before the assembly began. Gradually, the triangular crimson drops merged into one flow, moving towards the assembly hall, a spacious room filled with rows of seats connected to form bulky structures of four chairs each. This was where the ceremony was to take place.

The hall welcomed newcomers with the expressive singing of a deep baritone that overpowered the buzzing voices. However, the singer himself was nowhere to be seen, and the music emanated from two electronic devices positioned at the corners of the stage.

This Victory Day
Smells of gunpowder.
It's a celebration
With grey at the temples.
It's a joy
With tears in the eyes...

The song's lyrics and the singer's voice, though recorded, moved me almost as deeply as the captain's piano playing at Uncle Pasha's house. Homo liberatus have little art as we enjoy the voices of Nature above all and can share the products of our imagination with anyone without needing to materialise them. Most importantly, thanks to our perfected exchange of thoughts and energy, we are rarely overwhelmed by the same emotions that inspire homo sapiens to create their greatest masterpieces. Aching for something lost or unattainable troubles Lemurians very rarely, simply because there are too few goals in the world that we cannot achieve. And grief over untimely death is more the subject of legends than an inevitable reality for my kind — after all, our loved ones live for a few centuries and don't fight each other. Even mild sadness is uncommon among homo liberatus. All except me. Perhaps that's why the song, born of human suffering, touched me so deeply. Something stirred within me again, and I tried to swallow the lump in my throat and stop the tears that had welled up at the worst possible moment.

Meanwhile, Captain Pilatov glanced around, observing the crowd, completely unaware of my inner turmoil. He wasn't paying attention to the song, which he knew by heart, as it had echoed across the country every spring for as long as he could remember.

The spacious hall quickly filled with pioneers. Between the rows of chairs and the entrance, there was a small poorly lit area free of furniture. A few adults who had also arrived without an invitation stood near us, leaning against the wall, blending into the group of unofficial guests to avoid attention. In the festive commotion, no one cared about the two strangers anyway.

Perhaps the only one who noticed our presence was a stocky reddish-haired man who moved about, aiming the lens of a Zenit camera alternately at the stage and at the chattering young audience. Having accidentally brushed against me, he apologised and granted me a disarming warm smile. With a quick glance, the man with the camera noted Andrei's perfectly tailored suit and my gypsy appearance, both of which were rare in these parts. Thus I met another worthy representative of homo sapiens. I liked Ruslan Batalov immediately. Every movement of the young man radiated bright, sunlit energy, and his eagerness to share it was almost excessive. My interest in this new character distracted me from my own emotions, and I promised myself to find an opportunity to get to know him better, especially since, as a native of a neighbouring village, Ruslan might prove useful to our vampire hunt.

A sudden chill swept in from the entrance to the hall. In the doorway stood a tall old man, his slender, stooping frame neatly clad in a grey suit adorned with a couple of medals pinned to the lapel. Beneath his jacket, an immaculately clean white shirt was visible, its collar spread open in the absence of a tie, revealing an Adam's apple as sharp as a thorn.

The newcomer moved slowly, but without shuffling. He did not use a cane, yet he looked weary and seemed utterly indifferent to the ever-bustling pioneer leader who flitted around him anxiously, trying to show respect to the honoured guest who was known for his sternness. He glanced down at the small woman only occasionally, and with disdain, like one might look at a yapping dog underfoot. That made her even more flustered.

"He's an unpleasant type," Andrei remarked in a low voice. "Is that Vasyura?"

"It is," I replied curtly, struggling to suppress my tremor of excitement. I was almost certain that this was the vampire I had been hunting for so long!

My vampire.

My temples pounded with the awareness that from this very moment, I could crush the monster that had executed my mother, crush him like a filthy louse! I was incredibly fortunate to see Vasyura for the first time in the presence of three hundred innocent children's souls. For their sake, I managed to keep myself under control, though just barely. That's why my response came out even drier than intended.

"He's sucking energy as he walks. Poor leader…"

This time Captain Pilatov noted my feelings, and he turned his gaze on me, impressed by my composure.

I gritted my teeth and muttered, "Don't ask." After all, killing was far from the purpose of my mission.

The old man seated himself at the centre of the stage behind a long table draped with a red cloth. He swept his gaze across the audience with a hostile, predatory expression. *"He's looking at the children like a boa at rabbits!"* flashed through the captain's mind.

The narrow lips of the former commander of the punitive battalion curled into a scornful sneer, but such a blatant display of evil anticipation didn't surprise anyone in the hall. Everybody in the village knew about the "complicated" personality of the deputy director of economic affairs, although the pioneers and their teachers had no inkling of energy vampires. Some even said that the lazier workers occasionally got a punch in the face. While such methods weren't exactly in line with Soviet standards, the straightforward heirs of Cossacks who resided in Velyka Dymerka were not well versed in legal matters, and a "fatherly scolding" from a war veteran did not offend them, especially since it was always "for a good reason." As a result, these chastised workers would inevitably improve their efforts, earning a bit of extra money, which in turn pleased their wives. Moreover, thanks to the farm's high productivity, achieved in no small part through such disciplinary measures, Grigory Nikitovich Vasyura was highly respected by the district's administration, which saw the benefits for all. When it came to the interests of the village, Vasyura knew the right people and the right things to say. In other words, the locals viewed him as a reliable and solid fortress wall. They respected him and chose not to dwell on the old man's harsh character or his contempt for anything that moved.

"Dear children!" squeaked the pioneer leader into the microphone, addressing the suddenly hushed hall. "Today, at our celebration assembly, we once again welcome the honoured guest, our fellow villager, a veteran of the Great Patriotic War and a Veteran of Labour, Grigory Nikitovich Vasyura!"

She clapped her hands with exaggerated enthusiasm. The children also clapped, but without enthusiasm, rather in a rote, rehearsed manner. In the back row, a teenager with a shaved nape, dressed in a crumpled but clean white shirt, leaned towards the ear of his companion, whose unruly hair covered his ears, and whispered, "He'll talk about the signalman's heroism and the French partisans again. It's the same every year! Boring!"

"Yeah," responded his dishevelled freckled friend. "I hope it ends quickly! I need to feed my granddad. Mum's gone to town and left him with me for the whole day."

"I bet your Granddad Ivan would tell a better story if he could. About partisans," the one with the shaved nape said sympathetically.

"Yeah… It's a pity he's been lying silent since before I was born…" agreed the freckled boy with a sigh.

At that moment, a young teacher standing by the wall made a comically angry face and shushed the troublemakers, wagging a slender finger at them. They closed their mouths and turned their eyes to the stage with expressions of dull obedience on their sun-tanned faces. An expectant silence fell over the hall.

Finally, Vasyura, without rising from his chair, began to speak slowly.

"I greet the younger generation," the old man said. At the beginning of his speech, he had just enough strength for one breath. His thin, pale lips, tinged with blue, barely moved, and his voice was so faint and creaky that, despite the dirty-brown hue of his aura and the incident with him draining energy from the fussy pioneers' leader, I briefly doubted whether we had found the right man.

"Grigory Nikitovich!" the leader said, addressing the guest speaker in an elevated tone. "Tell us about your struggle against the Nazi invaders so that the young pioneers always remember the price veterans paid for the peaceful skies over our heads."

"Well then..." replied the vampire, pretending to need time to think, though he was about to deliver the same annual speech as always with only minor variations.

Then I, at last, began my mission. Putting emotions aside, it was a great stroke of luck not only to have tracked down Vasyura but also to have arrived in Velyka Dymerka on the day of his public appearance. It provided me a perfect opportunity to study the vampire as if in a laboratory. I tuned into the mind of the former chief of staff of the punitive detachment to scan his thoughts and memories during his address to the pioneers.

And I will say in advance that the results of this experiment exceeded all my expectations!

The old man cleared his throat with a disgusting croak. Slowly, as if reluctantly, releasing the words from the narrow, wrinkled slit of his mouth, he began.

"Even before the war, I graduated from the Kiev Military School of Communications, after which I was sent to the Baltics to serve in my specialty."

Before attending the school of communications, Vasyura had briefly worked as a teacher in his hometown Chyhyryn. He had an aptitude for academics and a great desire to control others. Vasyura never understood where this urge came from, but it stayed with him throughout his conscious life, sometimes growing so unbearably intense that it drove him to acts even he found strange. In childhood, the only creature under Grisha's command was a dog of an unknown breed, Polkan, whom the young master trained to exhaustion and punished harshly even for the smallest flaws. Young Vasyura felt inexplicable exhilaration at the sight of the large animal cowering miserably, pressing its muzzle to the ground under the blows of its merciless master.

Pragmatic by nature, the young vampire realised that education was the key to power and that seven years of mandatory schooling would not suffice. So, he completed ten years, focusing on mathematics and languages, especially German, which was highly regarded between the First and Second World Wars. The teaching profession seemed the most obvious choice, as Vasyura had often felt dependent on teachers in his childhood. However, school disappointed Grigory: the pay was low, and the ability to control students was limited by regulations from the Education Commissariat. In addition, corporal punishment was strictly forbidden ever since communists had taken power. Yet the young vampire, spreading his wings, craved thrills. He dropped out of part-time teacher training and entered the military school.

"When the war began, I was already commanding a unit," Vasyura croaked. "Our division was stationed in Latvia and took part in the battles for Liepāja. This small coastal border town was a strategic position. Still, at the time of the fascist invasion, our division was only half-staffed." His voice began to strengthen, its metallic ring gradually replacing the feeble creak of old age. "Moreover, experienced conscripts had been discharged in the autumn of 1940, and in their place, we received young recruits who had not been fully trained by the summer of 1941. We also lacked good tanks and had to make do with light vehicles…"

As the audience's attention focused on the speaker, the movement of an invisible force, imperceptible to the human eye, took on a vectoriel direction, and the seventy-year-old vampire, like a magnet, became the centre of attraction for bioenergetic flows that had been chaotically swirling around the hall before his address began. Vasyura paused and took pleasure in surveying the children, frozen in fear like animals confronted by a dangerous reptile.

This strange homo sapien, however, was unaware that he was committing an act of vampirism. Vasyura simply knew that the undivided attention fixed upon him always made him feel invigorated, and he used his public position to seek out any opportunities to receive that attention. So, he was fully conscious of his power over the audience, savoured it, fed on it, and it was abundantly clear why this old man came here every spring… Like any person deeply dependent on an external substance, the vampire had no compassion, no shame, nor any other human values. Nothing existed for him but thirst and the single goal of satisfying it.

"Near Liepāja, there was a fighter aviation regiment flying outdated planes," Vasyura continued, becoming increasingly animated. The wrinkles on his face smoothed out before the audience's eyes. He seemed to grow ten years younger. "New planes were expected, but they didn't arrive in time, and the regiment also lacked pilots. They said some of them were still undergoing training… That regiment was destroyed in the first German raid, and Liepāja was left without air support. The enemy outnumbered us by a third and was much better equipped. So, our defensive position was no better than that of Brest Fortress, whose tragic fate you all surely know." The vampire's face twisted into a malicious grimace, and he added, without hiding his disapproval, "In short, our commanders were too trusting. They didn't expect an attack, didn't prepare… even though the Germans were at our borders already."

"How do they even let him say things like this to schoolchildren?" the KGB captain whispered in surprise, referring to the veteran's anti-Soviet jab at the Army leadership. "We'll need to alert the local authorities…"

I cast a sceptical glance at my friend, who was unaware of the vampire's friendship with those very same local authorities.

Still, Andrei was right: Vasyura's last words betrayed a hatred for the regime that had forced him, such a charming young officer, to fight for a weak army. To this day, Vasyura had no doubt that his switching sides to a stronger army and taking revenge on his "offenders" had been fully justified.

Similarly to Andrei, many in the hall felt uncomfortable. On Victory Day, such a bitter critique of Soviet command seemed out of place. Yet in this rural community, the deputy director's outbursts were often excused as resentment against Stalin's regime, which had "unjustly" imprisoned him "for being captured." Still, some couldn't help but shift uneasily, giving more energy to the vampire than they would during ordinary passive listening.

Thin strands of children's energy continuously stretched toward the dirty-brown aura of the gaunt old man and disappeared there, as if into a black hole. For the first time, I witnessed an act of vampirism with my own eyes. Vasyura was so powerful that even I, standing in the opposite corner of the hall, had to put up an energy shield to avoid becoming one of his donors. To his credit, Andrei resisted the vampire's power quite well until I realised the necessity to extend the protection to him too.

The speaker took a carafe from the table and poured water into a faceted glass. The aging vampire's hand was now steady, and his movements were as precise as a young man's. He drained the glass in one gulp, as if washing down a rich, spicy meal, grunted with satisfaction, and, becoming more engrossed, continued.

"A signalman's feat isn't as noticeable as a soldier's on the battlefield. What's heroic about a telephone operator repairing a line damaged by enemy fire, one could say?" Vasyura theatrically raised his voice on the rhetorical question. "However, if the line isn't repaired, communication between units breaks down, and the army can't act in coordination. Often, the outcome of a battle depends on timely message transmission, especially when resources are scarce." The old man looked at the young pioneers demandingly, wanting to ensure they were still paying attention. Their eyes were fixed on him, but that didn't necessarily mean the kids were listening. Some, to their good fortune, only pretended to be attentive, while thinking about their own little businesses. The vampire, of course, couldn't know this for certain, but he suspected it. Irritated by his inability to control the thoughts of the obediently seated pioneers, he exhaled with a short growl, pulled a disgruntled face, and resumed speaking, this time even more dramatically.

"Signalmen often had to go out several times to find broken wires crawling under fire along the laid cables. Here you sit safely" — he pointed his bony index finger like a gun at the front row, finally capturing the full attention of the wide-eyed pioneers — "but there, anyone could be killed at any moment by a sniper or a stray bullet! Many of my comrades died like that. At the start of the battle, I was at the command post, but when we ran out of men, I took the tools and went to find the broken wire myself. That's when I was concussed and lost consciousness..."

The old man fell silent and glared at the audience like a hawk, as if accusing them of having inflicted his concussion. I scrutinised his face and listened to his recollections. So far, he had told the absolute truth. Vasyura was no coward, and as I stood in the opposite corner of the hall, I faintly noticed one peculiar trait of this vampire: the part of his brain where fear arose in ordinary people seemed somewhat numb. It was not functioning properly. This variation in homo sapiens was news to me, which meant that no one among the Lemurians knew about it either! Such a phenomenon demanded a closer investigation, both at a shorter distance and with other samples. Sakhno, the zek, was the exact opposite: it was fear that had turned him into an energy thief and miser. As was the case for a true homo liberatus, the anticipation of discovery outweighed my hatred for the executioner, and I began watching Vasyura with even greater interest.

One could easily imagine how much energy human army lost at the start of the war due to fear of death, the agony of wounds, and the torment of dying! *Vasyura was still thrilled by memories of his first battle when, as a young vampire, he had experienced such a euphoric surge of excitement and sensations so vivid and incomparable that nothing had ever stimulated his bored mind in the same way before. Similarly, someone remembers a uniquely delicious dish prepared by a skilled chef, craving that taste over and over yet never quite recapturing it. No doubt, euphoria in his first battle had been caused by the novelty of unlimited feeding, but Vasyura had chased after that initial experience ever since. The power that the Nazis unleashed in 1941 had opened endless opportunities for their ally to witness human suffering and inflict it himself. Yet the sense of novelty comes only once, and Vasyura had never managed to recreate that day, no matter how hard he tried. Still, in pursuit of that elusive cocktail of sensations, he matured as a vampire...*

For several seconds, the speaker scanned the hall with the gaze of an eagle, searching for prey. He tried to catch at least a trace of his comrades' fear in battle, but mild discomfort from the prolonged pause was the greatest suffering his patiently silent audience of peaceful Soviet village children could offer.

That was all Vasyura had to make do with! He was frustrated but not surprised. The elderly bloodsucker often regretted not staying in the Foreign Legion. Who could have imagined that the French, having suffered under the Nazis, would permit the torture and punishment of Algerian guerrillas with no less cruelty than the Nazis themselves had allowed in Belarus in '43? Who could have foreseen that Khrushchev's Thaw would weaken the fear that had practically hung in the air during Stalin's era? The world had truly turned upside down...

A couple of feeble claps broke the tense silence. Those were triggered by the youngest pioneers, who were hearing Vasyura's story for the first time. Their more experienced mate quickly hushed them in a whisper. "Wait, he's going to talk about imprisonment and the French partisans!"

The speaker managed to catch that. He threw a piercing glance at the careless child and continued his story, emphasising each word and relishing the sight of the boy guiltily drawing his head down between his shoulders.

"Yes, I was captured. Wounded. Unconscious." Vasyura paused meaningfully. "I ended up in a concentration camp in the area of Schirmeck. We were worked to the bone and barely fed there, but I was young, strong, and managed to survive until '44."

It was a lie, delivered in a tone that brooked no argument. *For that three-year period, Vasyura had constructed a mental ghetto where memories lived as though they were scenes in an adventure novel, exciting but seemingly fictional, bearing no resemblance to the senior lieutenant of the Soviet Army he impersonated during meetings with youth. He had invented a different wartime story, replacing the original as casually as one might rearrange books on a shelf. Whenever the conversation turned to his dealings with the Germans, Vasyura's accounts sounded as convincing as a performance by a talented actor. Both the lies and the mental manipulations were fun for the vampire, though they meant no more to him than shuffling a deck of cards.*

"Then, during the repair of tracks blown up by partisans, a few of us managed to escape. This happened near the French-Swiss border. We knew the French Resistance, the Maquis, was fighting the fascists nearby. My comrades and I decided to flee and join the guerrilla war in France…"

Vasyura remembered too well how it really happened.

On a stifling July night, in a dimly lit wooden hut, the senior police officers debated how to proceed. The Nazi army was retreating hopelessly, and in the morning, the 118th Schutzmannschaft Battalion were informed that they would be transferred through Poland to Prussia and from there to France within two days. The Ukrainian lads, who had committed plenty of unsavoury acts and among whom Vasyura was the eldest, sat around a long table covered with a faded floral linen tablecloth. On the table stood empty metal cups that had held tea, but there was no one to refill them, as the local servants had been sent away to ensure that nothing said here would leak to the Germans. There was no time for vodka that night either. Sweating profusely, the men argued in heated whispers in a mix of Western Ukrainian dialect and Surzhyk. Some jumped up, gesticulating wildly, as though compensating for their inability to swear aloud.

"What do we need Germany and France for? We barely understood them here. What will it be like there?"

"Ah, if only I could go home and set up my farm. My hands are aching for the soil."

"Who's going to let you farm, you moron? The war's not over yet. At best they'll send you to the front. Getting shot at day and night isn't the same as guarding. At least with the Germans there's less risk…"

"But they don't see us as human beings…"

"How do you think the Soviets will think of you if you stay here? SMERSH will sniff you out in no time, and it'll be the wall for you! If not, then it's the front line with that ogre build of yours. The penal battalion even. What will you do? Hide in basements? We have to go with the Germans."*

"And do what there? Die with the Fritz? They've already lost the war."

"We'll see when we get there..."

"What about our families?"

"You think you'll help them by staying here? If you're not at home, you're either captured or missing, and if you're not at the front and not listed in partisan units, then what have you been doing all this time? Mark my word, they've got records of all the partisans. They'll find out about you soon, and then it's the gallows for you, and your family will be branded as traitors forever. We need to disappear for a while. There's no other way but to go abroad."

The cunning Vasyura listened in silence, reflecting while feeding off the energy released by his frightened comrades. He held a low opinion of his fellow officers, especially the illiterate ones who whined about their mums and dreams of returning to peaceful lives. The chief of staff knew perfectly well that the best option was to go to Europe with the Germans and see how things played out. The only issue was leaving his wife behind. His vacation shortly after the destruction of Khatyn had borne fruit: now, Nina had a six-month-old daughter, living proof of the spouses' wartime reunion. This, in itself, was evidence of his collaboration with the Germans.

"Stay in Latvia," he wrote to his wife. "But you must move somewhere away from Liepāja before the Red Army arrives. Don't return to Leningrad, though. Your relatives will ask questions about the child if they think I'm missing in action. Settle somewhere no one knows you. Don't give details, and, most importantly, keep quiet. Sell the things that I brought and

sent to you earlier if necessary. That'll be enough for a while. When the Reds arrive, try to find work. With your language skills, you can teach or work as a translator. Teaching is better. It pays less but earning the respect you need is easier.

"I've enclosed a gift for our daughter with this letter. I hope to see her when I return. And make sure you burn all my letters."

They had been moved west through northern Poland rather than through Warsaw, where another division had become bogged down in fighting. The daredevils of the 118th Battalion felt incredibly lucky to remain far from the front line, as their main adversary here seemed to be the summer heat. Over two weeks, they were transported on thirty railway carriages from Iława, first to Germany, then to Strasbourg, and further into Burgundy. The journey was long and tiresome. The officers' carriage was cleaner and more spacious than the one reeking of smoke, sweat, and boots where soldiers travelled. Yet even in this luxury, the heat was unbearable.

The Ukrainian lads' desire to serve the Germans was fading by the day. Those who had joined out of sheer fear for their skins no longer wished to fight and had agreed to go to Europe only because they feared reprisals from the Reds. However, the nationalists, who had been fighting "for freedom," motivated by resentment against the communists who had dispossessed their wealthy families in the 1930s, bore no grudge against the French. As for Vasyura, he was almost certain that had he stayed in the USSR, he would have found a way to rise. Yet as a vampire, he was subconsciously drawn to the anxiety that periodically swept through his comrades and the terror of random victims he could prey upon during the journey. By then, the twenty-nine-year-old SS officer fully realised how much human suffering excited and amused him, though he never understood the root of this fascination, even until his old age. The likes of Vasyura — his friend Luckovich, the platoon commander Meleshko, and a whole pack of dim-witted privates — were drawn to the scent of blood, but on the territories, liberated from the fascists, blood would no longer flow in the same unchecked torrents they had grown accustomed to while hunting partisans. With the retreating Nazi army, the vampires moved westward, but even there, they could no longer feast as they had in Belarus. Eventually, these bloodsuckers grew weary of serving the Germans too.

Then the language issue popped up. Idling in Poland for a few days had been quite fun. The Ukrainian lads roamed the markets, where they understood almost everything the locals said, or wandered through villages in groups of three or four with their rifles to grab food and vodka. However, their looting pleasures were banned upon entering Germany, and they could only speak to each other there. To make matters worse, the senior officers were read an order stating that they would be sent for military retraining upon arrival at their destination. Instead of gratitude, this provoked panic. Most had risen to higher ranks due to their zeal as punishers rather than their qualifications. So, these men had never mastered foreign languages and were afraid to be separated from their brothers in foreign lands.

Vasyura observed his subordinates' inner turmoil with interest. The language problem did not particularly concern him as he knew Russian, Ukrainian, and German well, and understood some French. When they reached France, he was even taken off the train for a day and driven in a special vehicle to assist in an interrogation.

The handsome Ukrainian officer was brought in to charm a young compatriot, a former model who turned out to be a Russian princess by birth and an anti-fascist underground fighter by occupation. Vasyura's task was to extract as much information as possible about her Maquis comrades and, ideally, persuade her to collaborate with the Germans. Such an unexpected instruction given to the Ukrainian punishers' chief of staff before entering the interrogation room caught him off guard. Playing the role of the good cop had never been part of the vampire's repertoire — Vasyura derived far more pleasure from wielding a ramrod. He still hoped that the mask of an irresistible man, which had once so deeply impressed the young Nina, would work there too. However, Viki, raised in Paris and married to a Russian prince in exile, greeted her "near compatriot" with such an icy, aristocratic disdain that it forced Vasyura to retreat to the corner of the room to handle a sudden surge of rage.

Meanwhile, the German interrogator posed what seemed like a reasonable question.

"I don't understand why you resist Germany, which is fighting against the communists. After all, it was because of the communists that your family lost its place in society and was forced to leave Russia."

The daughter of Russian emigrants replied with the same noble dignity.

"The goal you are pursuing in Russia is the destruction of the country and the extermination of the Slavic race. I am Russian, even though I have lived my whole life in France. I will betray neither my homeland nor the country that gave me refuge."

Her last words were directed most of all at Vasyura's burning eyes, which glared with hatred from the corner of the interrogation room at the bruised and battered princess model. Displays of reckless heroism were nothing new to the vampire, as Belorussia had been full of patriots devoted to their homeland. He considered such people to be holy fools. These idiots, who valued ideals above their own lives, controlled their fear too well, which tormented Vasyura with an agonising thirst and a maddening sense of dissatisfaction. Born unable to participate in the natural energy exchange, the vampire could not comprehend that a healthy person's love for their homeland stemmed from a genetic connection to the energy of home. Like a predator clawing prey from its den in a frenzy, Vasyura usually *became enraptured with forcing the fools to suffer and fear. Yet during the interrogation in France, constrained by his subordinate position and unfamiliar role, he neither extracted information from Vera Obolenskaya** nor received a chance to make her suffer. That day remained a splinter in the vampire's memory for years...*

The Schutzmänners were brought to France not for combat but solely for security and partisan suppression. It was assumed that the policemen would continue in Burgundy as they had in Belarus, but the commanding officers completely ignored the soldiers' sentiments. Whether the leadership denied the complexity of feelings and motivations in these "lower race" mercenaries, assuming their fear of Red Army reprisals would be enough to keep them loyal, or Nazis simply buried their heads in the sand as defeat loomed, the fact remained that they gravely underestimated Ukrainian cunning and adaptability.

The French, in turn, treated the Ukrainians quite favourably, especially after realising the policemen had little desire to fight for an almost defeated army. Shortly after arriving in Burgundy, a resistance agent undercover proposed that Vasyura's compatriots join the Maquis. There was little debate among the brothers, as the Schutzmänners had long resented their masters — for treating them as near humans, for making them repair railways like forced labourers, and for threatening to separate them from their comrades. Concerns about the future also troubled the traitors, and fighting alongside the French resistance offered hope of redemption.

Thus, a "few Ukrainian brothers," namely the entire 30th SS Grenadier Division, deserted the German camp on the night of August 27th, 1944.

Tell part of the truth if you want your lies to be believed. This event became the foundation of the tale that Vasyura had been telling the pioneers for years.

"Around half past two in the morning, we ventured deeper into the forest. After that, everything went offtrack. We were unfamiliar with the area and took the wrong road. We missed our rendezvous with the French resistance agents, members of the Maquis, whom we had managed to contact through one of their men embedded in the German forces. We wandered around for several hours before finally reaching a village, where a local resident connected to the resistance helped us locate the partisans." Vasyura poured himself another glass of water from the decanter, downed it in one gulp, and continued. "The French Resistance fought no less dangerously than the Belorussian or Ukrainian partisans. You could even say it was an international struggle — so many of our countrymen were involved that entire units were formed from them. We were assigned to the Second Ukrainian Battalion, named after Taras Shevchenko. Wherever you served, your social circle was very limited. You knew only those you interacted with directly and no one else. So, we mostly kept to our fellow countrymen and rarely dealt with the French. Most Ukrainians hardly knew the language, so that was somewhat of an advantage," Vasyura added, using the truth again.

The French Resistance army was full of all sorts of people. Choosing the lesser of two evils, the former Schutzmänners tried to stick together, showing no interest in anyone or anything outside their group and their welfare, as usual.

What followed in the vampire's tale was a passage memorised from an interview with a Belorussian partisan, published in a newspaper many years ago. The essence of guerrilla warfare is timeless, so this part of the story always went down well, even though Vasyura's experience as a fighter on the invisible front was far less extensive than his experience exterminating such fighters.

"At first it was mainly railway warfare," he lied brazenly. "We blew up trains carrying weapons and supplies to the

Germans and destroyed water towers at railway stations. In short, we did everything we could to make life harder for the enemy. At the same time, our men studied maps of the area and familiarised themselves with French weaponry. We prepared ourselves for anything that might be useful behind enemy lines."

The material, stolen from old newspapers, had nothing to do with the veteran's true history. The fact was that the Taras Shevchenko Second Ukrainian Battalion was formed on the 27th of August and disbanded on the 28th of September 1944, leaving the brothers neither the desire nor the time for partisan exploits in unfamiliar territory.

"Barely had we familiarised ourselves with the situation and the surroundings when, on the third day, we were already tasked with a difficult operation," Vasyura said, continuing his lie. "We had to blow up a railway line located seventy kilometres from our main base. We covered that distance on foot in a day. We took everything we needed for the operation — ammunition, explosives, and so on — and set off at nightfall. About seventy partisans went on that mission. After a day and a half, we reached the railway tracks."

"That's it," the vampire thought. *"The more numbers, the better! Numbers always sound convincing."* And he carried aloud:

"When we arrived, we were given clear instructions..." Here Vasyura paused, casting a glance of subtle mockery around the room. Had his listeners been more attentive, they might have wondered who and in what language could have thoroughly briefed Ukrainian lads in the Alps, but neither the young pioneers nor their teachers were particularly sharp-minded. They simply swallowed the vampire's fables. A smirk of satisfaction flickered across Vasyura's face. No one had ever interfered with his feeding off the pioneers' energy.

"Each partisan received a specific task and knew exactly what to do. Railway guards were also involved in the operation and later joined our partisan detachment," he added. Again, in all the years Vasyura had been feeding the youth this story, not once had anyone questioned how French guards ended up integrating into a group of Ukrainians who didn't speak the language! "The military guard at the railway bridge was swiftly neutralised. As a result, we could operate unhindered along more than two kilometres of track."

The vampire had no suspicion of strangers being present in the hall, nor was he concerned about such a possibility. In his old age, Vasyura had completely ceased being cautious.

Meanwhile, besides Captain Pilatov, who was within the field of my energy protection and therefore raised his eyebrows in surprise at every inconsistency in the veteran's story, there was another sceptic in the hall. Journalists did not attend the assemblies of the Velykodymerska pioneer squad every year, but that day, a reporter had been sent from the district to cover the veteran's meeting with the younger generation to mark the anniversary of the Great Victory. Ruslan Batalov had come to the village school purely by chance, replacing a sick colleague. He had not even informed the senior editor about the swap. From the very moment Vasyura appeared in the assembly hall, Ruslan felt an inexplicable but strong aversion to him. The reporter, although acting on intuition, managed to shield himself quite effectively from the vampire's manipulations, and entirely on his own!

The speaker, meanwhile, congratulated himself on yet another successful performance. With brazen confidence, he continued the stolen newspaper account without a single reference to the original source.

"Our actions to blow up the railway were well organised," he said. "People were positioned so that the mining and ignition of the charges occurred simultaneously along the entire length of the target. We had no more than half an hour for the operation, but despite such a tight timeframe, the enemy still discovered us.

As a result, the mining took place under enemy fire, which came from the nearest station. We allowed one train to pass, then managed to plant explosives under the rail joints and detonate four charges. The operation was carefully planned, which allowed us to retreat successfully. All partisans gathered at the designated meeting point within a very short time. We completed the task successfully, although by the end of the operation, we had lost twelve comrades in battles with the enemy. We had wounded men too. However, the enemy suffered four times as many losses, a large section of the railway was disabled, and a bridge was destroyed. Consequently, the railway remained out of service for a very long time. Later, we learned that all partisan units from local areas had participated in the operation." The vampire spoke with exaggerated pathos, overacting considerably while his audience fell into a hushed silence.

Vasyura poured himself more water, took only one sip this time, squinted, and peered into the hall. When the new oppressive pause became unbearable for everyone except the veteran himself, he shot a demanding glance at the timid pioneers' leader crouching at the corner of the presidium. She hesitated as he glared with such contempt as if she were one of the hens clumsily loitering on the outskirts of Dymerka. Then, the small woman flinched and hurriedly blurted out the question from the script.

"Grigory Mykytovych, what were your daily routines as partisans like?" Half-dazed, like most of Vasyura's audience, she'd forgotten to switch from Surzhyk to a formal literary language and had spoken in a rural patois.

The vampire rewarded her with a deliberately encouraging grin and delivered another well-rehearsed answer. "Life in the partisan unit was far from peaceful. We often had to face German machine gunners head-on. Although the enemy frequently outnumbered us, we partisans emerged from battles with relatively few losses." Vasyura jerked his chin forward in a nervous motion that was entirely at odds with the confident tone of his speech, as though his sharp cheekbones threatened to pierce through his shaven, taut, bluish skin. The speaker's voice seemed to live a separate life apart from his face.

"Food supplies were also a challenge," the impostor continued. "We gathered fruits and berries. We hunted with rifles but tried to do so as rarely as possible to avoid the Germans hearing gunshots in the mountains and locating us. While we occasionally managed to obtain meat, we often went without bread and salt for days. Why? Because such supplies were very hard to procure. We couldn't stay in one place long enough to receive airdropped supplies, and airdrops couldn't feed so many fighters anyway. Procuring food locally was also difficult because of the large number of partisans, although the local population supported us and provided much help… And the Germans feared every bush!" Vasyura chuckled, recalling his cowardly comrades like Sakhno. "They would only move during the day, along main roads. In areas occupied by Nazi units, they faced constant unpleasant surprises from us. They always mined their positions and fenced them with barbed wire. But our men never lost heart and continued to crush the enemy at every step, with few losses for the partisans and heavy losses for the enemy," the vampire said, triumphantly concluding his lies.

The pioneers' leader clapped enthusiastically, urging the kids to admire the bravery and ingenuity of the partisans in general and the guest in particular. The audience had no choice but to clap too. Vasyura, having finally finished quoting tales lifted from partisan folklore in newspapers, rounded off his story with just enough truth to reliably conceal his crimes against people and Nature for forty years.

"On the fourth of September 1944, we prepared to take the Morte-Pontarlier Road. Lieutenant Fyodorov and Colonel Peti discussed plans for the upcoming offensive on Pontarlier. The night was tense. Every one of us knew we would face battle early in the morning. But the partisans were well prepared to meet the enemy. The Germans were armed with light tanks, artillery, mortars, and machine guns. We, however, had only grenades and submachine guns. The enemy outnumbered us three to one in manpower. Over the day, we repelled three attacks. After driving them back for the third time, we retreated deeper into the forest, where the rest of the unit and the wounded awaited us. We withdrew not because we lacked the strength to hold our ground but because the position was no longer suitable. By the evening of the fifth of September, Lieutenant Fyodorov's third company and the French partisan forces liberated the city and captured around three hundred Germans. In this battle, private Bronislav Luzhinsky was killed, while Junior Sergeant Lukinyuk and Private Mikhail Tokar were seriously wounded."

"The first time he's mentioned names!" Captain Pilatov noted to himself.

"On the ninth of September, the first and second companies of Negrebetsky liberated Damblain. After the war, the locals erected a monument in honour of the city's liberation." Vasyura made another strange movement with his chin. Inwardly, he regretted never having seen that monument. "On the twelfth of September, Fyodorov's company, along with a company of the French army, fell into a German ambush near Mauchamps and engaged in battle. We found ourselves in a triple ring of encirclement, which we managed to break through only after two days, and with great difficulty. Fyodorov commanded the retreating troops. Eight soldiers from our battalion received awards from the French command, and on the twenty-eighth of September, at the request of the Soviet embassy, the French disbanded the battalion." If the audience had dared, they would have clearly heard the hatred in the veteran's voice. "The Shevchenko men, after surrendering their weapons, departed for Marseille. The French authorities offered the fighters the choice of either remaining in the Foreign Legion or returning to the

USSR. One hundred and sixteen people returned home." The speaker paused briefly and inwardly added, *"And a significantly larger number joined the French army!"* Then he curled his lips and continued aloud, "Thus, at the end of 1944, our partisan chapter was over..." Vasyura's face contorted, and in an utterly icy tone, he concluded, "What happened next is no longer a story about war. Thank you for your attention." He narrowed his eyes and fell silent.

The young and adult listeners remained silent for a few more moments as if crushed by a heavy press during the vampire's speech. Then, everyone applauded, and the forty-year-old pioneers' leader rushed up to Vasyura.

"Thank you, Grigory Nikitovich, for your interesting and educating story!" she squeaked in a shrill voice, eager to be heard by all. "The Motherland will never forget your feat and the feat of your comrades in arms who fell in battles for our Soviet Motherland! Let me thank you with this commemorative gift for our peaceful sky above!" She hastily handed a bouquet of red flowers, coarsely serrated petals, and a small red box to the former destructor of Belorussian villages. Then, the woman clapped in frantic delight.

The song "Victory Day" started again, and the best students, honoured to congratulate the veteran, stepped onto the stage. Each of them handed him bouquets of carnations, and Vasyura basked in the rays of recognition with a face frozen like stone. In truth, he was sickened with the feral desire to snap the necks of those red ties. I, too, felt nauseated — with disgust.

"I'll be outside," I told Andrei, gesturing towards the exit. I barely managed to wait until I could finally get some fresh air. I moved away from the porch and leaned against a tree that grew about a hundred metres from the main entrance.

What now? For an hour I had seen the world through the eyes of the vampire who had made me an orphan. It felt as if I had been to hell. The memories of a mutated homo sapien, who had cruelly tormented his own kind, burned my soul. I was again dizzy with the temptation to go back and crush him like a louse, even in front of a crowd. I was huffing. I tried to control myself, but instead, I was inexorably losing strength, and I could do nothing about it for the first time in my life! I felt ill and began to understand that I, too, risked becoming the vampire's victim. Unable to retain the energy draining out of me, I channelled it into the young oak tree that I was embracing with both hands. Its buds were just beginning to swell, but within seconds, the tree burst into beautiful carved leaves and became covered in green acorns.

"Are you all right?" someone asked behind me.

I turned and met the perceptive gaze of the man with a camera.

---

*SMERSH (an abbreviation of Russian "death to spies!"): the name of several independent counterintelligence organisations in the Soviet Union during World War II

**Vera Obolenskaya, née Makarova: daughter of Russian immigrants and a member of the French Resistance, awarded the Order of the Patriotic War, 1st Class, posthumously in 1965

Chapter 16. Vampire's Lair

Batalov, the journalist, was the only one who, standing on the school porch, noticed how the bare crown of the oak tree had suddenly burst into lush summer greenery. Driven by curiosity, he approached the tree, which continued to sprout leaves and acorns as if viewed through time-lapse photography. Drawing closer, Ruslan saw me leaning against the oak with my eyes closed and forgot the marvels of Nature at once. He hurried over, grabbed my shoulder, and asked, "Are you all right? Do you feel unwell? Should I call an ambulance?"

"No, no, I'm fine... thank you."

I opened my eyes and shook my head but didn't move. For a few seconds, Ruslan stood hesitantly, keeping his hand on my shoulder. He didn't want to abandon someone whom he saw as a weak person, and his concern helped me recover and regain my strength. What intrigued me most was that this young homo sapien had shared his energy with me effortlessly, as though Vasyura's performance had left no impact on him.

"I suddenly felt drained after the veteran's speech," I admitted, and Ruslan sympathised.

"I saw you in the hall," he said. "You stood on your feet the whole time, and it was stuffy in there!" He patted my shoulder. "And that Vasyura... heavy presence. He looked at the kids like a snake at rabbits. Like a vampire!"

I nearly jumped in surprise. "Interesting comparison!" Ruslan had no idea that my reaction was to his insight rather than his clever metaphor. Batalov clearly had potential, as humans say, but rushing to "initiate" a journalist could lead to undesirable consequences for the mission. Even the prematurely green oak tree was an embarrassing slip on my part. Performing "miracles" so close to a homo sapiens crowd was unwise.

So, I floated a trial balloon. "Anyway, most of his story was a lie."

"What do you mean?" Ruslan asked, his sharp grey eyes suddenly sparkling with curiosity.

"It's simple. Vasyura served the Nazis in a police battalion and commanded the burning of Khatyn."

Ruslan's jaw dropped. Vasyura was a well-known figure, respected in Dymerka and the entire district. Ruslan sat cross-legged on the grass beneath the oak, peering up at me.

"And the evidence?"

"There is evidence," I said, removing my shoes and lowering myself to the ground beside him. "Look, here comes Andrei Pilatov, a KGB captain. We're investigating this together."

"Unofficially for now," Andrei specified, approaching us and quickly grasping the topic.

"Meet Ruslan Batalov..."

"A journalist," Andrei finished for me. For some reason he was in high spirits.

Our new acquaintance glanced between us in surprise. "How did you know my name? And that I'm a journalist? I didn't have any identification on me!"

In fact, heading to the Velykodymerska school for a routine report, Ruslan had deliberately left his press badge behind, hoping to work quietly. Some of the young female teachers knew him from village club dances where, in his school days, he often accompanied a girl named Anya. That felt like a different life now... At this moment, Batalov dreamed of breaking the story of the century and felt rather embarrassed covering a school assembly.

"Am I part of the investigation too?" he asked with a mixture of hope and caution. Andrei and I chuckled in unison.

"Not yet," my companion reassured him. "But who else would run around the hall with an expensive camera during an event?"

"And have such good vampire-proof armour!" I added half-jokingly, deploying a still poorly mastered human skill — lying. "Your name is in the papers."

The poor guy's bewilderment turned to suspicion. Blessed with a sharp intuition, Batalov sensed something off about me.

I quickly tried to reassure him further. "Don't worry, we're not crazy, and he really is a KGB captain."

Andrei supported my words by pulling out his ID and holding it before Ruslan's eyes until the journalist sighed in relief.

"At least the KGB captain must be normal!" he thought.

"My name is Yan. I'm from Belorussia, and this case concerns my family."

"All right, guys," our new acquaintance finally said, "other questions later. What evidence do you have that Vasyura served the Nazis?" The looming sensation was already buzzing in the journalist's brain like an irrepressible drill, drowning out all irrelevant thoughts.

"Plenty of evidence!" Pilatov exclaimed. "In the trials of traitors in the 1970s, there were testimonies not only from Vasyura's fellow soldiers but also from himself, openly admitting to collaborating with the Nazis. However, unlike other witnesses, Vasyura never mentioned that he held a commanding position in the police battalion used for hunting partisans. The only question is why his testimony was buried."

"That's very strange indeed," Ruslan agreed. "And the documents?"

"They're in the archives where they belong, but we have copies," Andrei said, waving the folder he carried everywhere.

"Hmm..." Ruslan rubbed his hands together, deep in thought. Nobody hurried him.

"If you're right, exposing this scumbag is a holy cause! But we must act carefully. Vasyura has friends in high positions."

"That's what my uncle says, too," Andrei agreed. He landed opposite us on the lawn, risking his fancy suit.

"And your uncle is…?" Ruslan asked.

"A retired KGB colonel," Andrei explained proudly.

"Ah," Ruslan snorted ironically. "Then we'd better listen to the uncle! What else does he advise?"

"To visit the vampire's lair and scout it out," I interrupted before they could puff out their chests further. "We need to split up. By the way, what's got you so excited, Andrei?"

And the captain finally shot his story out. "Well, after the event, I decided to introduce myself to the headmaster —"

"You shouldn't have done that," I interrupted, shaking my head. "It would've been better not to talk too much about the real reason for our appearance in Dymerka."

"Oh, but I should have! Vasyura's eldest daughter works at the school as the deputy head, and the staff clearly don't have much love for her or her father. So, the headmaster didn't hold back, even though our conversation was unofficial. And yes, he promised to keep our chat confidential, so don't worry." The captain glanced in my direction. "That's how I found out that the deputy head's father was involved in dodgy dealing with construction materials when the school and the village council were being built. Word is, Vasyura has a huge house in the village."

"Well, the headmaster's house isn't too shabby either!" Ruslan remarked. "Maybe he's holding a grudge against Vasyura for something else. Or against the daughter, since she's his deputy… You got all this from the headmaster in just half an hour?"

"Yep!" The captain nodded confidently and gave a self-content smile. "Seems like the man had a lot to get off his chest but he does not dare to talk to the local authorities, being afraid of Vasyura's cronies."

"I see… Still, the right credentials can achieve miracles!" the journalist said with envy. He'd heard plenty about Vasyura but had never had the chance to speak with the old man in person.

Besides, his editor in chief didn't exactly encourage curiosity about officials of any rank. More often than not, Ruslan's boss would glare and hiss, "Stay out of it!"

"That's not all," Andrei continued. "I was leaving the headmaster's office, which is next to the staff room, and overheard two teachers gossiping in the corridor. I pretended to be studying the honours board, and here's what I caught. One said, 'Vasyura was passed over for the Order of the Patriotic War at the recruitment office, and he went ballistic! He's not exactly dripping with medals!' And the other replied, 'What order? He did time in prison!' The first one said, 'Well, they say he was only imprisoned because he was captured... That's long forgotten. Anyway, the old man was furious and requested to be awarded too. He even made the kolkhoz* chairman write a reference letter!' And we've already got a copy of that reference!" the captain finished cheerfully.

"So what?" Ruslan asked, not getting the point.

"Don't you see?" Andrei jumped on his feet and started pacing back and forth on the grass, gesticulating excitedly. "You said that Vasyura has connections, right?"

"Well, yes..." both Ruslan and I answered.

"And the conscription department is run by military officers!"

"So?" The journalist still didn't get it.

"They retire at forty-five!" Andrei said, looking smug.

Finally, Ruslan began to catch on. "If Vasyura had contacts there ten years ago, they've probably been replaced by younger officers by now, the ones he possibly hasn't had time to butter up."

"Well done, Andrei!" I praised, silently admitting I never would've picked up on that detail myself. "I think we should start there!"

"Guys, let me join your team!" Ruslan pleaded. "I've been to the conscription department in Brovary many times. As a journalist, it'll be easy for me to navigate and talk to the right people without drawing attention to you, especially if your investigation's unofficial — only for now, I hope…"

Andrei and I exchanged glances, and since Batalov had also made a good impression on him, the captain said, "Sure, come aboard!"

Because of the Victory Day celebrations, the part of the operation Ruslan had offered to handle was postponed until Monday. We gave him copies of the protocols from the Belorussian archive, which sent the journalist into rapture. He was to review the folder's contents over the long weekend and visit the recruitment office on Monday.

"This is going to be explosive!" Ruslan kept exclaiming as he scanned the documents, then hurrying off to catch the next train.

But before leaving, the journalist turned, waved to us, and, glancing at the curly canopy of the oak tree, thought again, *"Strange, really!"* thankfully without connecting the early appearance of acorns to our presence. A minute later he was already absorbed in planning the strategy for the new investigation.

Captain Pilatov, noticing where our new companion had looked, raised his head, grinned, and said, "Oh! Acorns! Your doing?"

"It happened by accident," I explained.

"And him…?"

"He saw them but didn't get it. Humanity's problems are far more important to him than Nature's paradoxes."

"Fair enough," Andrei concluded contentedly.

We returned to the flat to question Baba Vera about Vasyura's banquet, but she'd already left for that evening's side job. We decided to split up: I would study the vampire more closely while Andrei would head to Vasyura's house to meet his family.

I later learned everything that happened there from Captain Pilatov's memories account. That visit turned out to be life-changing for him, and someone else too.

***

The vampire's lair was surrounded by a tall fence made of sheet metal, painted in a maroon-brown. *"Like some kind of bunker!"* thought Andrei as he approached Vasyura's yard. The gates for vehicles and the smaller pedestrian gate were also made of metal and looked impenetrable. The house was entirely within the yard, so only the top part of the front wall, built from the same white brick as the village council and the school, was visible, along with the grey-tiled roof with a dormer window.

Andrei pressed the button of the electric doorbell above the gate and waited. No one answered. He pushed the button again and then once more. Finally, there was the sound of a door opening somewhere deep within the yard, and a minute later, the bolt clicked.

The vision appeared in the slightly opened door, leaving Captain Pilatov thunderstruck. A delicate creature of about twenty or twenty-two, with deep and sorrowful golden-brown eyes, looked up at him questioningly. She wore a simple white cotton dress, clean but unpressed. This was Vasyura's younger daughter. She was flushed and breathless, having run out of the house in haste. A strand of her light-ash curly hair had escaped from under a simple plastic headband, falling along her temple and down her slender neck, making her look especially touching and defenceless.

For several seconds, Lyuba studied the uninvited guest, looking puzzled and somewhat disappointed, before asking impatiently, "How can I help you?" Her voice and manner exuded confidence and determination, which quite clashed with her fragile appearance. The posh phrasing of the question, unexpected in the speech of a Ukrainian village girl, also surprised the KGB officer. Finally, Andrei gathered his wits and remembered to show his ID.

"Captain Pilatov… Andrei."

Lyuba glanced at his credentials briefly, then let him into the yard and, with a beckoning gesture, ran back to the house. The visitor easily caught up with her thanks to his long strides. Despite his confusion about her hurry, the captain couldn't help but notice the quality of the interior. The family's wealth was far more evident here than outside the house. All the doors were made of walnut wood, with frosted glass inserts that had recently become fashionable. Thick carpets covered the floors, even in the hallway. The walls, adorned with expensive beige wallpaper, displayed several exquisite engravings, just as unexpected in the home of a collective farm worker, even a senior, as the urban formality of his daughter's speech.

"I thought the ambulance from the district had arrived so quickly," the girl said, explaining her earlier disappointment as they moved. Without enquiring about the visitor's purpose, she pointed him towards an open door leading to a large, well-furnished room on the ground floor. "You'll have to wait. Mum's having another attack!"

"What's wrong with her?" Andrei asked. Instead of heading to the sitting room, he followed the girl up the stairs to the mezzanine, where Vasyura's wife lay dying.

"Cancer… She's suffering terribly. I can't leave her. My father and sister went off to their banquet," Lyuba said. Pausing for a few seconds before the door to the attic room, she turned to Andrei. Seeing that he was about to follow her inside, she raised her anxious eyes to him and added in a hoarse voice, "So maybe it's even good you've come. It's scary here alone."

"I was hoping to speak to your mum… Confidentially…"

"Speak?" Lyuba hissed. "I told you, she's unwell!"

"I understand," the captain replied peaceably, but inwardly he pitied the girl. "*She looks so exhausted and on edge,*" he thought. "*Probably from lack of sleep.*"

"Don't tell Mum who you are. You'll only make things worse!" she instructed. "Say you're my friend from Kiev."

Andrei already realised that he was unlikely to get any answers to his questions from Vasyura's wife, but he still followed the vampire's daughter into the triangular attic. Compared to the affluent furnishing downstairs, everything here looked poor. A small, homespun rug lay forlornly on the bare floorboards. On a wooden bedside table, a few useless medicine bottles glistened. A small table covered with a colourful cloth held a large glass jug and a faceted glass filled with water next to a plate of untouched, long-cold dinner. A dim light shone from a pre-war green glass lamp, a rare survivor.

Lyuba's mother lay on the narrow single bed, fading away. Her cheeks were sunken, and her skin stretched over them like thin, pale grey parchment. The woman's eyes were closed, but the regular grimaces of pain twisting her face showed she was not asleep.

"Why is she put so far away?" Andrei whispered, panting slightly from climbing to the third floor. "If she needs urgent care, it might be too late by the time someone gets here!"

Lyuba waved her hand hopelessly. "Father decided so!" Her voice again carried a note of anger, and she added bitterly, "He doesn't want her to be an eyesore. He has 'an important job,' you see. 'Can't afford to be stressed or overworked.' He hardly comes here, and Galka doesn't care either. They've sucked all the strength out of Mum and dumped her on the nurse."

"And you?"

"I'm finishing my teaching degree in Kiev. Mum forbade me to drop out," the girl explained, stroking her mother's hand with strained tenderness. "I visit often, but only for her. The nurse won't be here during the holidays, so I have to manage everything myself."

Feeling her daughter's touch, the sick woman opened her eyes just barely. Her bloodless lips moved as she saw the stranger, and the young people caught her whispered question.

"Who is this, Lyubochka?"

"This is... my friend, Mum," the girl replied, suddenly realising she hadn't remembered the visitor's name or surname. She stared at their guest in panic.

"Cap... sorry, Andrei Pilatov," he said, stepping in to help. "Nice to meet you." He glanced at Lyuba and, secretly pleased with his role as her suitor, dared to add, "At last..."

"Nina Vladimirovna!" the girl whispered.

"Nina Vladimirovna," the captain repeated.

The dying woman's deeply sunken eyes, once blue but now drained by pain and almost transparent, lingered on the visitor for a few moments. It seemed she was summoning her last bits of strength to cling to this tormenting world and take part in the destiny of her beloved youngest for the final time. At last, Vasyura's wife spoke to Lyuba in a barely audible voice.

"A good man..." she said, and then, slowly shifting her gaze to Andrei, she pleaded, "Promise..."

"Anything."

"Take care of Lyubochka," the sick mother breathed out. "Take her away... far away..."

"Mummy, what are you saying?" the girl interjected. "How can I leave you?"

The dying woman closed her eyes, too weak even to shake her head in refusal, and whispered, "Not long... left..." Then, almost inaudibly, she pleaded with the visitor again. "Promise!"

Just then, the doorbell rang with an abrupt buzz, and Lyuba startled.

"That's the ambulance! Stay here!" she said and ran to meet the paramedics.

Suddenly Nina Vladimirovna's eyes flew open. She grasped the visitor's hand with unexpected strength and sputtered, burning the last spark of life in a feverish plea directed at him.

"Andryusha, save my girl! Take her away! Grigory, her father, is a terrible man... She mustn't end up like me..."

Captain Pilatov, as much as he pitied the dying woman, simply couldn't miss this one chance to hear Vasyura's wife's confession.

"What about her father?"

"He's monstrous... A true vampire... No one knows... he tortured people, killed them... I never told anyone... for my daughters' sake! Never... But I must... before I die..."

Andrei sat down carefully on the edge of the bed and gently asked, "Who did he kill?"

"People... Innocent people... During the war. He... served the Germans... I know..." The woman struggled to breathe, gasping for air, yet determined to finish. "He came home... on leave... in an SS uniform... Brought back... things... He would still kill... if he could... He killed me, see? Save Lyubochka, I beg you! Her sister... takes after him... but Lyubochka is a good girl..."

Footsteps and voices echoed from the staircase. Following Lyuba into the room, a short, middle-aged woman appeared.

"You keep the patient too far away from the entrance!" she said with a reproachful tone, still trying to slip into the sleeves of her white gown.

Nina Vladimirovna gripped the captain's hand with her freezing fingers and rasped, "Promise you'll take her away!"

Seeing Andrei's nod of agreement, she sighed with relief, and a peaceful smile froze on her pale, emaciated face. Forever.

"Mum! Mummy! No!" Lyuba screamed in anguish, running to the bed and grabbing the motionless body by the shoulders. Then she turned to the paramedic. "Do something! Help her!"

The doctor approached the bed, took the thin, almost transparent wrist that hung over the edge of the narrow bed, held it for a few seconds, then grimaced and shook her head.

"It's too late. Nina Vladimirovna is at peace now," she said, sitting down at the table to fill out the death certificate. "Where are the husband and eldest daughter?"

"At a banquet, I suppose," Andrei replied, painfully aware of how absurd his words sounded.

"Someone needs to call them home," the paramedic said impassively. She looked questioningly yet firmly at the stranger. "And who are you?"

"A friend of Lyubov Grigoryevna's," the captain answered evasively.

"Can you go and get the family?"

"Yes, but a little later," he said, glancing sideways at Lyuba, who was trembling over her mother's body. From that moment on, the happiness and sorrows of this girl, with her tearful golden-brown eyes, mattered more to him than the rest of the world.

When the doctor finished her paperwork and left, Andrei led the deceased's daughter outside, almost forcibly. They sat on a bench under a tree. Lyuba rested her head on her hands and stared blankly down at the concrete path leading from the gate to the porch.

The yard appeared desolate. In the twilight, extensions added to Vasyura's once-little house over time looked like the tentacles of a giant octopus, its glowing window eyes reflecting the last rays of the fiery-purple sunset. Each extension ended in a triangular attic disguised as a roof, and only tiny windows betrayed the existence of additional living spaces. Captain Pilatov was well aware of how officials in cushy positions enriched themselves. Once again, he noted the outward simplicity and even drabness that carefully masked the owner's wealth.

The vegetable garden was small, growing only greens that required minimal care. Unlike their neighbours, the family of the deputy director of the farm did not engage in gardening. Vasyura likely considered digging in the dirt beneath his dignity while his wife and daughters, schoolteachers, had no time for it.

There was little growth in the yard, just a couple of apple and apricot trees, scattering white petals on the concrete paths rarely swept since Nina Vladimirovna became bedridden. A large brick garage, big enough to fit a medium-sized lorry, loomed disproportionately over the rest of the property. A wide asphalt driveway led to it from the iron gates, and barely noticeable against the fence in the far corner of the yard, almost apologetically, stood a pitiful wooden shed painted green.

Pilatov observed all this from the bench, where Lyuba sat beside him. The captain wanted nothing more than to comfort the girl, but he felt no hollow words of condolence could match her loss. His sudden love for the vampire's daughter prompted him that simply being there was the best thing he could do for her.

Finally, Lyuba took her hands away from her face. "You know, I have no one left."

"What about your father? Your sister?" the captain asked, though unsurprised. The answer was obvious from Nina Vladimirovna's last words, but Andrei wanted to hear it from the girl herself.

Lyuba shook her head sorrowfully. "They hate me… I don't even know why…" She paused. "Maybe because I'm not like them…" She broke off, letting out a choked sob. "Actually, they hate almost everyone. Mum was the only one who ever truly understood me… And now there's no one!" Tears began to flow silently down the poor girl's cheeks again.

Andrei moved, wishing to take her hands in his but not daring to touch her without permission. Instead, he unexpectedly blurted out, "You have me!"

Lyuba drew back and, raising her tear-filled eyes framed by long, dark lashes clumped together with moisture, whispered, "But I don't even know you!"

"That doesn't matter. You will. In time," Andrei promised, feeling like a rock with the whole world as his foundation. He wanted nothing more than to become the cornerstone of happiness for this orphaned soul.

"You came here to find something out," the girl said with a heavy sigh, trying to pull herself together. "What was it?"

"I already found it out. Your mother told me."

Lyuba frowned, sprang up from the bench, and clenched her fists as though she was about to smash Pilatov's nose.

"Did you interrogate her while I went to get the doctor?" she exclaimed.

"I didn't have to, honestly!" the captain explained, waving his hands in alarm to get her to sit back down. "She told me herself exactly what I came here to find out."

Still breathing heavily, the girl froze, arms crossed, staring at Andrei suspiciously. After a moment, she asked, a little calmer, "Is it something I don't know about?"

"I think so… At least, your mother clearly didn't want to say it before you."

"Then why did she trust *you*?" Lyuba asked as she sat back down, still doubtful. Her mother had been her closest friend. Lyuba couldn't imagine Nina Vladimirovna keeping secrets from her. "Did you tell her who you are?"

"Of course not," Andrei said with a shake of his head. "I think it was a secret she had kept her whole life, but she didn't want to take it to… eh… you know. And I just happened to be there."

"And you? Will you tell me?"

Andrei didn't answer right away. After a moment of thought, he said, "It's a very complicated matter. It concerns your father…" He hesitated to reveal the whole truth about Vasyura's crimes. It was the wrong time. "Of course, you're the first person who has the right to know, and I promise you will, but let's talk about it later. Perhaps, once the funeral arrangements are in place…"

Lyuba shrugged, nodded, and slumped. "Alright…"

Satisfied that the girl had calmed down a little, Andrei walked off into the darkness and, through the poorly lit village lane, headed to the restaurant to pass the sad news to Vasyura and Lyuba's sister. Meanwhile, the vampire's younger daughter returned to the house to spend a few last moments alone with her unfortunate mother.

---

*Kolkhoz: a cooperative collective farm operated on state-owned land in the former Soviet Union

Chapter 17. The Coven of Grey Cardinals

Vera Timofeevna was already working in the restaurant with her assistant, preparing a festive banquet table for an event of ambiguous status. The gathering seemed to be private, as Vasyura himself always invited the same select guests. The skillful cook's son, the chief agronomist of the state farm, had never been honoured with such an invitation. And thank goodness for that, thought Baba Vera. The state farm director, Vasyura's superior, had also never been seen here as far as Timofeevna could remember. Yet for some reason, the food for the feast had been purchased using the farm's budget rather than the deputy director's personal funds. From Vera's thoughts, I gathered that this banquet had become almost a tradition, always held on the anniversary of Victory Day, although no toasts were ever raised to Victory or in memory of fallen compatriots.

Vera Timofeevna had been catering this event for many years. She had plenty of reasons to dislike the guests who gathered there, but her pragmatic soul was drawn to the attractive remuneration, despite having to feign deafness and blindness. Also, Baba Vera was afraid to refuse, knowing full well the price of dependence on those in power, regardless of the ideals they professed. So, the seasoned chef did her job diligently and kept any doubts to herself.

The kitchen was hot, with pots bubbling and pans sizzling. I observed invisibly as Timofeevna wielded knives and graters like a juggler, occasionally issuing commands to her assistant, Zoya, a downtrodden-looking woman of about thirty. Due to her extreme incompetence, Zoya was not allowed to cook and focused on cleaning, washing dishes, and other minor tasks instead. She had been instructed not to leave the kitchen until the dinner was over, after which she was to go straight home. Zoya attended this evening shift every year, too, because the management ordered it. Her husband, who never tired of reminding her that the family needed money, did not mind. In fact, he happily sent her off to any evening job, occupied himself with private affairs during her absence, but then took all the money she earned and hid it somewhere. Zoya, for her part, barely saw any of the money, though this fact somehow escaped her comprehension. In the village, her lack of wit was almost legend. It seemed as if her thoughts were moving in one direction along a dark, narrow corridor and were limited only by this mental tunnel. She regarded the "important bosses" attending the banquet as demigods and took pride in being chosen to serve them. Her extreme intellectual limitations prevented her from imagining anything beyond what she could see, so her mind could not form a picture of what might happen after dinner, reducing the risk of gossip to zero. Vera Timofeevna, who valued working in a clean environment, understood that speculation about Vasyura's "gathering" was unwelcome, so she always invited this quiet, dim-witted assistant.

Wanting to familiarise myself with the setting and find a suitable place to confront the vampire face-to-face, I left the kitchen and proceeded down a short corridor leading to the banquet hall. The corridor walls were lined almost entirely with wide metal shelves stacked with various utensils. Beyond a door clad in plain plywood with a small viewing window was a spacious banquet hall. Low-hanging decorative beams intersected in several places among its high ceilings. Heavy burgundy curtains, tied back with elaborate ropes woven with gold threads and ending in large tassels, framed the windows over light though almost opaque drapes. On the hall side, the plain plywood door with the window was clad in oak veneer with beautiful woodgrain patterns, recently refreshed with varnish that still gave off an unpleasant smell.

A long table set for thirteen guests gleamed on polished parquet flooring. About a dozen attractive young women in spotless white aprons and matching starched caps over neatly styled hair bustled around it. None of them were local, and it took me only a few minutes to figure out why…

In the corner opposite the door with the window, a frail young man, the Komsomol* leader of Velyka Dymerka, was setting up music equipment. He was going to great lengths to climb the ranks of authority, although he did so in a rather peculiar manner. This vampire with piercing drill-like eyes was known among event organisers for assembling an escort service from Komsomol "activists." Like him, these girls aspired to a resource-rich future and, in pursuit of it, provided various services during private gatherings. Although Vasyura was not a Party member, he wielded inexplicably considerable influence in the district, so the Komsomol leader was also making every effort to ascend here. Having finished setting up the sound system, he approached the activist waitresses and asked briskly, "So, girls, is everyone here?"

"Yes, Vasyl Vasylych," several coquettish voices responded.

"Ready for the event? No antics like last time?"

The girls exchanged glances and shook their heads vigorously, eyes wide. The Komsomol leader scrutinised his team with an inquisitorial stare, making a few of the activists feel queasy. Satisfied that there were no unfamiliar faces, he flashed a syrupy smile, gave the nearest girl a slap below the waist, and said, "Good girls. Get to work!"

The "antics" Vasyl Vasylych mentioned had occurred recently. The Komsomol escorteers had indeed been promoted for their services periodically, so replacements had to be found. Last time, one girl brought along a friend who was just as naive as she was pretty. The newcomer proudly accepted the offer to "help at a Party meeting" but failed to grasp the full list of duties implied between the lines. When a balding, pot-bellied vampire began groping her with his sausage-like fingers, she slapped his face and ran to complain to Vasyl Vasylych. The Komsomol leader explained the Party's shocking expectations to the poor girl in the simplest terms. She burst into tears and flatly refused to join the bosses in the sauna. Shortly after the incident, the unfortunate beauty was given a forced "promotion" to Vorkuta. Keeping the incident under wraps had been so exhausting for the Velykodymersky Komsomol leader that even the despair and depression of the girl exiled from sunny Ukraine to the far north could not replenish his energy… Vasyl Vasylych felt happy that this time, the banquet was staffed with "battle-tested warriors," so he could relax and enjoy what he considered pleasant and useful company.

I stepped outside and only then noticed that the light-yellow single-story building, squat and adorned with decorative white borders, had two wings. To the left of the main entrance was the restaurant with a utility room, while to the right was something resembling a small hotel. I peered inside and found several cozy rooms furnished with comfortable sofas, plush armchairs, small tables, and elegantly lit floor lamps with luxurious shades that softened the harsh electric light. Each room had a large bed. There was also a sauna in the same wing, the source of the Komsomol activists' excitement. Vasyura proved to be a more than hospitable host, and although he was unlikely to enjoy all the pleasures offered to guests here, he clearly had not lost his strategic thinking. The solid building on the outskirts of the village was not built yesterday. It was used periodically as a retreat for visiting officials, while the residents of Velyka Dymerka had no free access to it. I drew these conclusions from the thoughts of Vasyl Vasylych, who organised such gatherings rather often.

Vasyura arrived first in a blue Zhiguli, along with his eldest daughter Galina. He looked way more cheerful than when I'd seen him enter the school auditorium. Almost at the same time, two housekeeping managers of neighbouring collective farms turned up. The men exchanged handshakes rather reservedly, although they were bound not only by years of acquaintance.

These guests were about Vasyura's age. They had also collaborated with the Germans during the war, though not with as much dedication as their Velykodymersky friend. Both, too, had served five-year terms in labour camps and were released under Khrushchev's amnesty. Like Vasyura, they preferred to stay in secondary roles, which had not prevented all three from executing so many profitable joint ventures over the past twenty years that none of them could complain about an insecure retirement.

Galina approached and greeted her father's mates. She was in high spirits. The father of a misbehaving boy had been summoned to the school straight after the pioneers' assembly, and the deputy headmistress had scolded them both in her office. She savoured both the shame and anger of the parent and the terror of the unfortunate offspring, who could foresee the harsh punishment that the drunken, non-pedagogical kolkhoz mechanic was sure to inflict on him afterwards. School life provided plenty of such emotional outbursts, ensuring Galina Grigoryevna, a veritable vampire, never suffered from an energy shortage. Her skin was perfectly smooth at forty-one, and her black eyes glistened with the same contemptuous coldness as Vasyura's.

Two formidable shrews, slightly over fifty, arrived in their cars. One was a stout woman, the warehouse manager of the dairy plant, and the other was a thin, sharp-nosed lady, the deputy chief doctor of the Brovary hospital. The three ladies withdrew inside the restaurant to while away the wait for the banquet in the bar. Next came the former deputy head of the Brovary military enlistment office, a retired major, still quite robust. He was an old friend of Vasyura and a notorious bribe-taker, thanks to whom the Soviet Army had been short of many conscripts whose exemption certificates were produced via the aforementioned medical matron.

The deputy chair of the Brovary District Executive Committee and the deputy head of the Construction Department arrived in one car. These longtime accomplices had orchestrated numerous schemes involving the illegal resale of building materials, thus siphoning off district funds, which had, in turn, deposited generous layers of fat around their bellies. With their help, Vasyura profited handsomely from the village council and school construction in Velyka Dymerka, resulting in the extensions to his house.

The guests from Kiev were the last to arrive. A comparatively recent acquaintance of the banquet host, the vice-rector of the Kiev Pedagogical Institute pulled up in a red Moskvich. He sprang out of the car and grasped Vasyura's cold, wrinkled hand with both of his.

"Very glad to see you in good health, Grigory Nikitiyevich!" the professor trilled in a piercing falsetto. "How is your beautiful daughter?"

"I should be asking you that," Vasyura smirked, furrowing his brow. "After all, I entrusted her to you!"

"But you knowwww…" the vice-rector began to fawn.

"Yes, yes, I know," the old vampire waved him off. "You have plenty like us. Just joking."

Five years earlier, during entrance exams to one of the republic's top universities, this professor had received a car boot full of premium-quality fresh pork from Vasyura. Although the vampire's daughter had scored highly enough on her exams without any help, and the gifts to the institute's management were likely unnecessary, her father had decided to play it safe. He had his hidden reasons.

As Lyuba was growing up, everything in the house began to change. The younger daughter was slipping out of the despot's control, and the wife quietly supported it. Vasyura could not tolerate that, as he considered them both his exclusive property. The vampire ceased to cherish Nina Vladimirovna and began to treat her like a broken machine destined for the rubbish heap because she "encouraged the rebel". Vasyura insisted that bribe-givers might push out even the best candidates by offering the gift to the vice-rector. In truth, he sought to make his daughter feel indebted and thus keep her under his control. The professor had enjoyed the pork fillet so much that a few other representatives of Velyka Dymerka's golden youth, far less talented than Lyuba, were admitted to the Kiev Pedagogical Institute over the next four years. These protegees of the vice-rector, indeed, occupied places that rightfully belonged to others in the competition-based free education system.

In a slightly worn blue Zhiguli arrived the retired vice-rector of the Kiev Military Communications School, Vasyura's former classmate. Lieutenant Colonel Gubko had never seen the front line during the Great Patriotic War. He had managed to build a career in the rear instead. He was unaware of his friend's service in the SS, but his sixth sense told Gubko that Vasyura's past was at least as murky as his own. Perhaps out of vampiric solidarity, this bald blimp continued, even after retiring, to help his friend pose as a hero and receive honours. Thanks to his efforts, Vasyura held the title of Honorary Cadet of the school and appeared before future officers as a veteran at least once a year, feeding on the high-quality energy of healthy young men. Gubko himself preferred to stay in the capital even after retirement. He particularly enjoyed visiting shops, where citizens had lately been queuing for butter and sausage. He loved to inhale their depression deeply and feel an instant surge of energy. Yet a lot of the food for this lazy, pot-bellied man came directly from Dymerka, bypassing the shops, so Gubko knew about shortages only from rumours and queue observations. With the help of the construction department duo, he had built himself a dacha in nearby Pukhovka, on the Desna River, where he visited only in bourgeois style to fish and have a barbecue. Vasyura was a frequent guest there.

Vasyura's old classmate glanced around the banquet hall from the doorway, rubbing his hands in anticipation of the feast.

"A splendid spread, as always, Grigory Nikitovich!"

"We share what we have," Vasyura replied with feigned ease.

Among the delicacies displayed before the ghuests, there was far more meat and fish than vegetables, partially because it was not the season for them but also because of the host's desire to flaunt his means. This vanity was evident in the smug grin that repeatedly touched the corners of his thin lips. On the table, a flat dish showcased an elegant spiral of sandwiches topped with expensive red and black caviar, the kind one could acquire only through special connections. Smaller plates displayed a variety of thinly sliced sausages and cheeses, garnished with canned peas and fresh herbs for decoration. Simultaneously with Gubko's arrival, Baba Vera's masterpiece — a freshly slaughtered suckling pig — was brought in, filling the hall with the mouthwatering aroma of spiced, roasted meat, which made the vampires already seated at the table salivate.

Vasyura's circle consisted of carefully chosen individuals. They were not people but levers, preferring to operate in the background similarly to the host. He did everything he could to keep his coven of grey cardinals under his firm control. Though the attendees had known each other for quite some time, there was no spiritual bond among them strong enough to foster genuine friendship. Instead, they shared a connection reminiscent of spiderwebs, positioned so closely to one another that any desired prey was inevitably ensnared. Even spiders need their kind! They band together to make draining the resources out of their victims easier. Throughout the banquet conversation, the auras of Vasyura's guests intermingled, releasing slimy threads of greyish-brown energy that coalesced into dark tumours of dense nodes and ligaments. The air in the hall grew thick with the stench of parasitism, overpowering even the nauseating scent of the finely sliced meat delicacies devoured by the vampires.

The host needn't have worried about losing his connections. His guests were of the same breed — energy siphons of varying strength and appetite: vampires and vampirettes, fledgling vampires and vampire spawn. They fed on the strength of homo sapiens, nibbling away here and there, their need for a pack as vital as it was for hyenas. Vasyura, however, stood among them as a vampire lord. His eyes, so black they seemed devoid of pupils, pierced like daggers. Everyone knew that refusing this charismatic old man invited a sensation akin to falling into an abyss. In truth, none of those present even considered contradicting the host. Deep down, each regarded him as extraordinary and sought his favour, even though some ranked higher than the deputy director of a collective farm in the social hierarchy. Naturally, none of the attendees knew about host's SS past. As for Vasyura, he had met vampires far stronger and more insatiable than himself during the war and afterward in the Soviet camp. Like a battle-hardened wolf, no longer capable of power struggles, Vasyura contented himself with this local pack that he could easily dominate, even in his twilight years.

"So, godmother," he said, addressing the hefty manager of the dairy warehouse, who was devouring cervelat sausage like Scylla devours sailors, "do you have anything left from the last batch?"

"Almost all gone," Nelli Borisovna replied. She had just stood up and stretched across the table for another delicacy. "How much do you need, Mykytovych?"

"Just a couple of crates," Vasyura muttered through his teeth, casting a disdainful glance at her ample bosom, clad in a light-burgundy high-necked velvet blouse adorned with garish sequins.

"Drop by after the holidays. We'll figure something out!" she promised with a cheerful grunt, plopping back into her chair.

The warehouse manager had been selling butter on the side for about five years. Following the authorities' direction, this butter was supposed to remain in warehouse refrigerators instead of being sent to grocery shops for ordinary Soviet citizens. When the expiration date of the perishable product approached, it was just written off. Nelli Borisovna devised a simple but highly profitable scheme: using intermediaries like Vasyura, she found middlemen who bought the butter well before its expiration date and resold it at double the price to other shadow retailers, who in turn sold the scarce product at the market at triple the price. Soviet citizens — or now, rather, the wives of high- and mid-ranking seniors — willingly paid inflated prices for ordinary butter to avoid queuing.

Thus, the energy of cows, milkmaids, creamery workers, and buyers was seamlessly converted into cash, which filled the pockets of three categories of vampires: Nelli Borisovna, the middlemen, and the shadow retailers. All thanks to an unspoken directive from above forbidding the sale of butter to ordinary workers at government-set prices. Why such a directive existed, the warehouse manager had no idea, but she didn't trouble herself with details, preferring to seize the opportunity rather than "let the product go to waste." Deep down, she even thought she was doing a good deed! All it needed was discretion about the premature clearance of the refrigerators and prompt documentation of "expired" goods. Nelli Borisovna always reserved a little extra for her own connection. She understood the value of the coven perfectly, ensuring its members could always count on her butter.

Vasyura grimaced, looking at the storekeeper's lips, greasy from smoked salmon, and gave a confirming nod to her invitation to drop by after the holidays. Just then, an activist girl serving at the table approached him and said in a honeyed voice, "Grigory Nikitovich, someone's asking for you. Will you go out yourself, or should I invite them in?"

“Who’s asking?” hissed the host.

“Some man,” the girl stammered uncertainly, stepping back half a pace as though scalded. “Young… dark-haired. A stranger. Doesn’t seem local.”

“What for?” Vasyura was still deciding whether to send the uninvited visitor away personally or through the waitress.

“He says it’s important..."

The uninvited visitor was me. Having observed the entire company of vampires well enough, I finally decided to confront the former SS officer with his impending reckoning so that he wouldn’t doubt it was coming. Vasyura strolled unhurriedly to the porch. He was bored at the banquet and curious to see who might dare to turn up to the gathering uninvited. Besides, the old man hoped to savour the stranger’s embarrassment, whom he planned to rebuke for disturbing the peace of a distinguished individual. He looked around, and, seeing no one either at the entrance or in the car park, shook his fist towards the bushes and let out something between a growl and a hiss.

“Damn jokers! I’ll get you!”

Yet he was in no hurry to return inside. Instead, he sat down on the low stone railing of the porch and watched as the May night thickened. Twilight, when darkness creeps over the world imperceptibly, when all living things settle to rest and lower their guard from exhaustion, when it’s so easy to trap a half-asleep animal or catch a person unawares — he had loved this time since the war. In recent years, Vasyura had taken to tormenting his wife, worn out after long school days, until he squeezed the last drop of life out of her.

Recalling the satisfaction and sense of fulfilment that came with the sight of Nina Vladimirovna’s tears, the vampire even rubbed his hands in pleasure. He was sure no one was watching him, let alone reading his mind. Meanwhile, I had been standing nearby the entire time, listening to the stream of consciousness and observing him, but I showed myself only when Vasyura was about to return to the banquet hall. I appeared an arm's length away from the old man, who flinched in surprise and pressed his hands more firmly against the railing. Yet neither physically nor mentally did Vasyura feel the fear one might expect from a homo sapien in such a circumstance.

"So, this is the chief of staff of the 118th Schutzmannschaft Battalion," I said, staring into the vampire's black eyes.

He still wasn't afraid. In fact, he seemed almost interested, and replied impassively, in the same icy tone that usually made his victims shrink into themselves, "I don't know what you're talking about, young man. And who are you, anyway, to speak so rudely to an old man?"

"I'm Yasik from Khatyn, which you, filthy vampire, destroyed in '43!" I stood straight, shielding myself with a reliable energy barrier.

"What Yasik? There was no Yasik there!" the former SS officer protested, then, realising he had just confirmed everything in his surprise, flew into a rage and pointed towards the road.

"Get lost, you hooligan, or I'll call the militia!"

The old man was furious, but he still managed to size up his opponent and coolly conclude: *"Nah, too young! He's lying and wants something, of course."* He pointed to the road again, trying to burn me with his hateful gaze, which usually worked for him without fail. Instead of answering, I turned invisible and reappeared in front of the former executioner.

"Go ahead, call them!" I replied, keeping my voice light. "Let them think you've finally gone mad with rage."

"Who are you?" Vasyura demanded, finally realising that neither his black glare nor commanding tone worked on me. That he was facing a superior opponent. Most surprisingly, fear still did not come to the vampire. Instead his mind began to simmer with excitement, as if at the start of a thrilling game. I decided not to change tactics.

"I am your reckoning."

All my life, I had dreamed of raising the pain of my childhood loss above my mother's murderer like an axe and seeing the vampire's face twisted in terror. Yet now, as I uttered the long-awaited threat, I felt as though I was hearing myself from the outside. My voice sounded calm, almost casual, and the words fell like cold shards of ice. The energy shield prevented the vampire from overpowering me, but it also protected me from myself, for giving in to hatred before this freak would be like letting him bite off my finger.

Like all his compatriots, Vasyura had been raised with materialistic views. He didn't believe in divine punishment and certainly was unable to immediately accept a new reality where an opponent could turn invisible and do who knows what else. The former chief of staff had no doubt my appearance and disappearance were just a trick, but his quick, calculating mind grasped that my promise of reckoning was no joke.

"So, will you kill me right here?" he asked defiantly. A devilish smirk twisted the thin line of his wrinkled mouth.

"Make you a victim? No, you don't deserve that, bastard!" I replied. "First, everyone will know about your crimes."

"You can't prove anything, whelp!" snarled the former commander, growing even more enraged.

"Others will prove it, and I won't even be here!" To make my point, I vanished and reappeared again before the furious old mutant. "Just know this time you won't escape justice. *Adieu*!"

I finally disappeared from the vampire's view, leaving him to ponder the troubles looming over him. For some time, Vasyura sat on the porch railing, reflecting unperturbed on the challenge thrown at him. There was no doubt that excitement and danger rather entertained him. Maybe that's why my desire to kill him had vanished. The homo liberatus curiosity proved stronger than human hatred once again. It had turned the child wronged by fate into an impassive observer, a scientist. And I was glad. After all, the essence of my mission was primarily to study the nature of vampires, their strengths and weaknesses.

Even during my visit to the village school, I had noticed Vasyura's brain differed from that of other humans, and this meeting at close range only confirmed it. The monster existed due to a distinct mutation that made homo sapiens incapable of love or empathy, paralysing his spiritual life and blocking the natural energy exchange. Yet even as a seventy-year-old man, he sought thrills. Thrills, not feelings. It turned out I had just given my mother's executioner a life-or-death chase to participate in, all the more exhilarating for it being his last. Although the vampire was still betting on wriggling out as always. His enemy's clear superiority turned defence into Vasyura's favourite game — a game without rules, granting a carte blanche for any means.

To once again avoid facing punishment for his crimes, Vasyura needed Valerian Krotovsky, a retired deputy head of the Investigative Department of the Ukrainian KGB. Valerian Karpovich, as always, was among the guests invited to the annual banquet, but today, for some reason, he was running late.

Just then, as if on cue, his white Volga rolled up to the restaurant.

"Speak of the devil!" thought Vasyura. He was far from superstitious. Like a true player who kept a poker face no matter how the cards fell, the vampire did not move from his perch on the porch railing. He merely greeted the latecomer with a dignified wave of his bony hand.

"You're late today, Karpych!" the former Nazi rasped with feigned carelessness as soon as the guest swung his long, crane-like legs out of the spacious car. "The storekeeper's already eaten nearly all the salami, and the neighbours will soon finish off the vodka."

"Good evening to you, Grigory Mykytovych!" Krotovsky's voice rattled like dried peas in the darkness. "Never mind, never mind! No one will starve here. You're a magician. You could feed everyone with a single fish!"

"Come on, let's go, let's have a drink," Vasyura gestured, inviting the retired lieutenant colonel inside. "I need to talk to you," he added, catching the inquisitive glance of his old acquaintance, whose ears pricked up at once. With a casual nod towards the restaurant, Vasyura said, "Later, when those lot crawl into the sauna."

The arrival of the last guest shed light on the miraculous transformation of the punitive detachment's chief of staff, a sadist and vampire, into a relatively innocent witness to the crimes of his comrades in arms during earlier trials revolving around what happened in Khatyn. Krotovsky's acquaintance with Vasyura began in Kiev shortly before the 118th Battalion was deployed to Belarus. Using the local police, the Nazis were hunting down and deporting Ukrainian youths to work in German factories. Vasyura, then only a junior officer, showed up with two soldiers to take the sixteen-year-old Valerian, and his mother crawled toward them on her knees, promising to do anything if only they would spare her son.

Valerian was the late-born child of a single mother, a teacher of Ukrainian and German languages, and her one and only joy. Vasyura knew that schools were typically full of all sorts of gossip, so he decided that the teacher could be a useful informant. She agreed but performed poorly. Her son, however, proved to be most resourceful. He adored playing spy games and had a real talent for surveillance. Keen observation ran in his blood, and it didn't matter to Valerik who the target was.

Krotovsky knew nothing about his father. The mother refused to speak about this matter, kept no photographs, and had no mementoes, but she was never surprised by her son's talents. From this, the young sleuth concluded that he had inherited them, along with a surname that didn't match his mother's, from his unknown parent.

Even before the Nazis arrived, the boy entertained himself by uncovering the secrets, sins, and weaknesses of his peers, their parents, and even many teachers. He spied on everyone without specific purpose and shared information rarely and selectively, only when it offered him a benefit. Naturally intelligent, Valerian realised that a reputation as a snitch carried no rewards, so he refrained from overusing the power of knowledge. What thrilled him was owning the information itself.

The spying demanded by Vasyura offered not just benefits but survival, freedom from deportation and the chance to stay with his mother, the only person he trusted, although like Vasyura, the boy lacked the ability for love. The young spy quickly gained the trust of the underground resistance and often acted as their messenger. He was so cautious that the partisans never figured out the source of their leaks. Those who realised it later in the Gestapo torture chambers carried the secret of the young "mole" to their graves, which never awakened a shred of guilt in Valerik.

When Kiev was liberated from the Nazis, the shrewd young man did not follow them but finished school with top marks and enrolled in intelligence training. He later married by the Party's order and began serving the Soviet state. Although Krotovsky's shallow soul lacked patriotism, he understood and followed the game's rules: to keep doing what he loved, that was, spying, he needed to be an exemplary citizen and show loyalty to the country.

Only his mother knew about his exploits for the Third Reich, but she died soon after the war. Everything was going well until 1973, when Valerian Karpovich, by then a deputy head of the Investigative Department of the Ukrainian KGB, came face-to-face with Vasyura. The latter had been brought to Kiev for sorting out some formalities before being sent to Grodno. Vasyura was to be questioned in the Meleshko case, which involved too many witnesses of his own deeds at the 118th Battalion. So, things looked grim for the former chief of SS staff.

Valerian Karpovich didn't know what his "benefactor" had been up to since the battalion left Kiev in 1942, while Vasyura remembered exactly how Krotovsky's career began. The former SS officer recognised his former informant at once but didn't show it publicly. Instead, he offered such an evil look that the lieutenant colonel decided to help Vasyura avoid involvement in the Meleshko case without waiting for more explicit blackmail threats.

Always thinking several steps ahead, Krotovsky called in favours from contacts in Minsk and Kiev and arranged for the "terminally ill" witness to be questioned at home. The case was quietly dissolved, and their debts were settled, binding the two vampires for life. Neither felt burdened by the connection as they were cut from the same cloth.

While Krotovsky remained in service, he regularly received pleasant gifts from Velyka Dymerka. After retiring, he finally divorced his wife and settled in a lovely flat in relatively quiet Brovary. He stuck to Vasyura like an old dog to its master. Their relationship stayed the same, as though the former KGB deputy was still a sixteen-year-old errand boy for the charismatic Nazi officer. Krotovsky never rebelled though. Like the other minor vampires in Vasyura's circle, he instinctively regarded Grigory Mykytovych as a higher being.

Vasyura interpreted my words "Others will prove it!" correctly and once again counted on the former mole's contacts to shield him from punishment, at least by ordinary humans.

As the banquet host led Krotovsky to the table, I heard familiar footsteps in the darkness. At the far end of the concrete path leading from the dusty village street to the restaurant's porch, a tall man with a military bearing appeared. It was Andrei, carrying news of Nina Vladimirovna's death. Unfortunately, I had not heard his thoughts earlier. I had been too busy watching the vampires and was blocking out all distractions. As soon as the captain arrived, I realised it was already too late to save the poor mother of his beloved, for time is beyond the power of homo liberatus.

---

*Komsomol: The Communist Youth Organisation

Chapter 18. Love*

For the farewell ceremony, Nina Vladimirovna's body was moved to the village club's foyer, as Vasyura refused to turn his den into a "thoroughfare." Lyuba spent the following day by the coffin and did not cry only when distracted by mournful errands. I had ample time to observe her.

On the evening of the banquet, the strong vibrations in the air caused by Captain Pilatov's raging hormones informed me of changes in his personal circumstances even before he reached the restaurant. I understood my comrade had unexpectedly acquired a mission of his own. Knowing Andrei's sensitive nature, I wasn't really surprised by this abrupt shift. I could manage without his help by that time, but I felt responsible for my friend. After all, he wouldn't have met this girl if I hadn't dragged him to Velyka Dymerka. I wanted to entrust the captain, as humans say, into good hands — and a vampire's daughter could turn out to be anything! So, I decided to thoroughly study the object of the young officer's serious intentions.

Luckily, there was no cause for concern. Having approached Lyuba, I felt relief and a pleasant warmth, as if the girl exuded a summer sea breeze. As though Nature had balanced the father's devilish malice with the daughter's angelic kindness. Yet that day, her pure soul was overshadowed by the grief of losing her closest relative and her fear of the future. The vampire's daughter was in her final year at a pedagogical institute and had already been assigned a job at the Velyka Dymerka school, thanks to her father's efforts, which had been presented as care. Lyuba was right in thinking that Vasyura considered her his property and trapped her in this way: the law required a young specialist to work for three years at their assigned location. Living in the hated house without her protective mother meant dependence on the despot's will. Apart from her father and sister, Lyuba knew of no other relatives. Vasyura had forbidden his wife from contacting her Leningrad kin, and his own family was never mentioned, as if they didn't exist. Thus, as far as they knew, the vampire's children had no grandparents, aunts, or uncles.

It wasn't just about her father, though. Lyuba had been born and raised in Velyka Dymerka, but throughout her not-so-long life, she had felt like a fledgling that had hatched in a serpent's nest by mistake. People in the Ukrainian village were, to put it mildly, pragmatic. Sincerity was a rare commodity among the Dymerka residents, at least towards Vasyura's daughter. The father was feared and disliked for his harsh nature, yet he influenced everything happening in the collective farm. Almost every neighbour tried to curry favour with the manager, lavishing flattery on his youngest daughter. Lyuba, however, always felt repulsed and irritated by their cloying praises. Most of the time, she felt they said one thing to her face but thought another. All except perhaps a few teachers, as she was the smartest in her class.

Vasyura's younger daughter studied effortlessly and for the pleasure of learning, while few of her classmates believed in the joy of knowledge. Village kids willingly copied her work, but behind her back, they called the girl a swot and a snob, which was far from the truth. Things became particularly difficult as the children grew older: their talking with Lyuba had all but ceased in the middle of the eighth grade. She would enter the classroom, sit at her desk, and feel an invisible heavy cloud pressing down on her neck, draining all joy like a parasitic squid and plunging her into despair. To her classmates, bullying the deputy director's daughter seemed risky, but ignoring her was safe enough. Yet their parents would greet her sweetly on the street. "Hello, Lyubochka! Would you like an apple?" Eventually it turned into an undeclared boycott when no one in the class spoke to her for two months.

Only Aleksey, her desk mate and a loner by nature, remained indifferent to both the collective mood and her academic achievements, for Aleksey was hopelessly in love with

Lyubochka. Their class teacher noticed this and seated them together until the end of school, which was a wise decision. For Lyuba, it was a relief that, out of male pride, he never begged to copy her work during tests. In turn, the mischievous loner eventually caught her passion for learning and genuinely improved his performance. Thus, love, like an electric conductor, connected Aleksey to education.

But the boy had a unique talent of his own: even as a teenager, he could see through people as if his brain had an inbuilt sensor. It was Aleks who opened the girl's eyes to the root of her troubles. One day, on their way home from school, Lyuba cried out in despair, "Why does no one talk to me? And they look at me like an enemy… What have I done to them?"

"They envy you," the boy replied, trying to sound unemotional.

Lyuba was taken aback. "Envy?"

"That you're a top student, that the teachers like you, and that your father's the boss," Aleks explained.

"But is that a reason not to talk to someone?" The naive schoolgirl was stunned.

Aleks only shrugged and confirmed the obvious. "For them — yes."

The solution turned out to be laughably simple. After that conversation, Lyuba tried not to excel too much at her studies and earned a couple of B grades that term. The plan worked better than expected: as if by magic, her classmates let go of their disdain, and the not-so-excellent student soon gained a couple of friends to spend breaks with instead of standing alone. For obvious reasons, these friendships were not the kind to share problems with, especially those related to her father. Her only true confidants were her mother and Aleks.

Much to her father's displeasure, Lyuba spent increasingly more time with the boy, whom Vasyura blamed for her academic "slip." Aleks was the first to die. Shortly after their final exams, he drowned in the river under strange circumstances. And now, her mum was gone too…

Having extracted all this from the whirlwind of Lyuba's mind as she mourned by the coffin, I deeply regretted not saving Vasyura's wife. Although, even if I had been there during Andrei's visit to the vampire's house, it could have been too late anyway, as the tumour had fully consumed the poor woman. It turned out that the charming, enamoured KGB captain was Lyuba's only chance to escape the snake pit. A chance the girl herself had not really considered. And although Andrei lingered nearby the entire time, looking for an opportunity to speak with her before the funeral, Lyuba seemed to avoid him. In truth, her thoughts were dragging through a hopelessly dark tunnel, so her tear-filled eyes, fixed on the ground, simply did not see the captain.

Due to the hot weather, the funeral was organised quickly, and by the next day the entire village had gathered at the cemetery to bid farewell to their beloved teacher. Andrei and I trailed at the back of the procession, trying to avoid being noticed by Vasyura. Captain Pilatov deemed it wise not to encounter Lyuba's father. Even back at the restaurant, he had simply sent word of Nina Vladimirovna's passing through a waitress.

The Headmaster of the Velykodymerska school, where Vasyura's wife had worked for over twenty years, delivered a rather heartfelt speech at the graveside.

"Today, we bid farewell to Nina Vladimirovna. This is an irreplaceable loss of a wonderful person who, like no other, knew how to comfort both children and adults." The principal paused, took a deep breath, and added to himself, *"... whose blood her husband and Galka sucked."* And he continued aloud. "And how to forgive. And most importantly, to love no matter what." At these words, Lyuba stifled a sob, and tears streamed down her face again while the principal went on.

"Forgive us too, Nina. Even if your name fades into the corners of our memory, the kindness you gave to adults and children will remain in their hearts and bloom again..."

Galina, the vampire's elder daughter, flinched at these final words. Her mother's "pointless" kindness and selflessness had caused a rift between them. Vasyura, meanwhile, stood with a face as impassive as a plaster statue, and the villagers mistook this for the grief of a stern veteran. Or rather, they wanted to believe this because admitting the truth would have been too uncomfortable: behind this impassive mask, there was hollowness.

The old man had long considered his wife a spent and discarded asset whose fate no longer concerned him. He had met the young student Nina shortly before the war during a work trip to Leningrad. A tall and imposing young officer with an eagle-eyed gaze, he had no difficulty charming the nineteen-year-old professor's daughter, raised on classical literature. Due to her inexperience in matters of love, she allowed him not just to charm but to enslave her. Nina dissolved entirely into the strong, charismatic man, while the vampire cherished her as a good owner who cherishes valuable property.

He calculated that the naive beauty from an intelligent, noble family would produce well-bred children and raise them accordingly. Vasyura knew human weaknesses. On the third day of their acquaintance, he arrived at the professor's house with a ring and a luxurious bouquet, asked for the girl's hand, and immediately received her parents' blessing, as their main weakness was faith in human decency. Vasyura married her and took Nina to the Baltics, but not before secretly writing an anonymous denunciation of her father. Soon the professor was arrested, and the Soviet Army lieutenant forbade Nina from contacting her family to avoid tarnishing his reputation. After the war, Vasyura insisted that if she wrote to them, his service with the Nazis would surface, along with questions about the birth of their elder daughter. Thus, the Russian language and literature teacher from the Velykodymerska School never learned what happened to her father in the camps or to her mother and sister during the siege of Leningrad.

The poor woman spent her entire married life under her husband's absolute control. Yet she never complained. She even kept forgiving Vasyura's wrongdoings, following the Russian proverb, "Husband and wife are one Satan," even when she began to realise how truly close Grigory was to that very Satan.

Nina Vladimirovna's loyalty to her husband remained unwavering, despite all the "unusual" actions he committed, many of which she knew about or suspected. Her dedication held their strange marriage together, as Vasyura fully understood how uniquely patient Nina was. She had only failed him in one regard by indulging the rebelliousness of their younger daughter. In the vampire's eyes, this completely negated his wife's lifelong devotion. When he realised that Nina Vladimirovna was not on his side in friction with their daughter, the vampire flew into a rage and began tormenting his wife with heavy criticism. He later resorted to physical violence, too — something he had never previously done to her. She burned out like a candle. In the vampire's view, she had received her due, and he felt not a shred of regret. So, while neighbours and colleagues bade farewell to the deceased, Vasyura simply grew bored, passing the time by contemplating how to subdue his defiant daughter. When the school principal finished his speech, Vasyura scooped cemetery soil into his bony palm and, with a disdainful grimace, carelessly flung it onto his wife's coffin.

My gaze shifted between the endlessly sobbing Lyuba and Andrei's face, full of sympathy yet forced to stay on the sidelines, unable to offer his beloved a shoulder to lean on. I whispered to Captain Pilatov:

"You really need to get her out of here as soon as possible." Seeing my friend's uncertain gaze, I dispelled his doubts. "I've been observing her. I think she'll agree when you explain."

"It's good to have a friend who can read minds," Andrei mused. I smiled and patted his shoulder. Love is the highest value in both our worlds and the unbroken thread that links homo liberatus with humans.

"She's a lovely girl. A pure soul, a bright aura, despite all she's been through here," I whispered, causing the captain's face to light up with a happy smile that was utterly inappropriate at a funeral.

There was no time for delay. The wake was being held in the school canteen, which could accommodate almost the entire adult population of Velyka Dymerka. Andrei caught up with Vasyura's daughter on the way there. She shuffled along, dragging her feet like an old woman. The tracks of tears shed at the cemetery had not yet dried on the girl's face. In the chest of the enamoured captain, his heart pounded with such intensity that it sounded almost louder than his whispers.

"We need to talk," he said, as if in passing, trying not to attract attention.

"About what?" Lyuba asked mechanically, looking down.

"About something very important... concerning you..." Andrei stammered.

Vasyura's daughter twisted her lips apathetically and kept walking in silence.

"About what I learned from your mother," my friend added hesitantly.

"What a wimp!" I thought. But then the captain, keeping pace with her, finally mustered all his courage.

"Forgive me, Lyubov Grigoryevna. I understand this isn't the best time... but please believe me, it might be too late after..."

Lyuba suddenly stopped and looked intently up into the face of her recent acquaintance. Her swollen, tear-streaked eyes became more focused and even flickered with a spark of hope.

"Alright," the girl agreed. "Let's meet by the school, near the garden, in an hour or so. Everyone will have had a drink by then, and I hope nobody will notice I'm gone."

"I'll be waiting!" Andrei exclaimed in a joyful whisper before quickly slipping away into the crowd.

An hour later, the captain paced outside the school windows like a wild animal. He was going to confess his love. To convince the girl of his sincerity. To reveal that her highly respected father was a former Nazi collaborator who would most likely soon stand trial and be executed. And finally, to propose marriage and an immediate move that would practically be an escape. By all means, it was no easy task, and my attempts to support Andrei with the certainty that Lyuba liked him too did nothing to boost my friend's confidence. The KGB captain's heart still threatened to leap out of his chest, and a leaden lump seemed lodged in his throat. The fear of rejection refused to release its grip.

"She'll probably say she won't marry the first man she meets! That's perfectly natural! A girl like her wouldn't trust a stranger... And I just want her to be happy! How do I prove my intentions are more than serious?"

Anxiety made him feverish, and each fresh wave of trembling sent his teeth chattering uncontrollably. The young man's nervous energy drained almost as much strength as I had spent curing his uncle's cancer, though with far less benefit. Energy simply seeped out of his body, vanishing into the already warm twilight of May. I felt sorry for my friend. Humans can never be completely sure of their lovers' feelings. They doubt, even after hearing confessions of love. And when it comes to speaking those words, they overcome the fear of rejection, losing energy that could otherwise save lives.

For homo liberatus, things are different. Thanks to telepathy, mutual love is never a secret. We receive answers instantly. We do not mistake mystery for love or substitute substance with uncertainty. Free from fear, Lemurians are unafraid of rejection or fading feelings, and even unrequited love leaves us clear-minded thanks to our ability to keep hormonal balance. When rejected, we feel no torment because we don't measure our worth by reciprocated love since a single failure is trivial compared to the grandeur of Nature! We don't even know jealousy, which for humans stems from the same fear of loss and defeat.

Lyuba was running late. At last, she appeared, wondering what was so urgent. Nervous trembling tormented her just as it did my companion. She liked the captain very much, although guilt about thinking of a man on the day of her mother's funeral gnawed at her and embarrassed her even more. Lyuba imagined her future in the darkest colours. The KGB officer, who had unexpectedly offered her help at the moment of Nina Vladimirovna's death and who, as it turned out, remained nearby, was like a saving beam of light appearing at the end of a dark tunnel. Lowering her eyes and trying not to show too much interest, Vasyura's daughter did not notice how Andrei's face lit up at her arrival.

"Sorry to keep you waiting," Lyuba began, though my companion had never once blamed her for his long vigil outside the school windows.

"Polite, unlike her father!" flashed through Andrei's mind. "Not at all!" the captain hurried to respond. "I'm grateful you agreed to spare me some time at such a difficult moment for you. But..." Andrei took a deep breath, attempting to swallow the lump in his throat that kept him from speaking coherently, and finally managed to squeeze out, "What I need to say is important for both of us."

Hearing the word "us," Lyuba momentarily forgot to breathe and looked questioningly at the young Pilatov, a spark of hope in her golden-brown eyes.

"Will you marry me?" he blurted out.

Lyuba gasped, parting her dry lips in surprise. The energy surging in the captain's heart swept through her in a powerful wave, blossoming into joy in her soul, but in the next instant, doubt and the fear of making a mistake surged coldly, drowning out the happy "yes" that had been ready to escape her lips.

Invisible, I watched their conversation unfold, discovering ever-new sides of homo sapiens. It turns out that their men resemble Lemurians in love. Andrei recognized his soulmate at first sight and, having imprinted on her, was now ready to do anything to make her happy. I'd felt the same way when I first saw Polina. On the contrary, a love confession from a stranger and a sudden proposal seem to evoke bewilderment and fear in human women.

"Can someone fall in love so quickly?" they wonder. *"What kind of person is he? What can he do? What does he fear? What are his strengths? His flaws? What awaits me and our future children if I say yes? I don't trust him, not yet..."* These questions buzzed in Lyuba's head like a swarm of bees, distracting her from what she truly felt next to this man. She could only manage a hesitant murmur.

"But I barely know you…"

Of course, it's unfair to blame female homo sapiens for hesitation and the need to test their chosen partners. For them, it is a matter of survival — after all, motherhood in their species requires support. Lacking the art of telepathy, women demand not only proof of the ability but also a sincere desire to provide care and protection from men.

The young people, Andrei and Lyuba both, were very serious. Both felt the same, and both were tormented by insecurity. I, invisible, watched this absurdity and tried my best not to startle the lovers with laughing air — so comically pointless did this two-sided storm of hormones and energy appear to me. Though despite the uncertain response, there was no trace of protest in the girl's voice, so the captain, sensitive from love, felt encouraged.

"I understand your confusion and apprehension, Lyubov Grigoryevna… Lyuba… I understand that perhaps you do not feel the same way about me simply because you haven't had time to figure out your feelings." Andrei gazed into her eyes, which were studying him tensely. "I fell in love with you the moment I saw you in the doorway of your father's house, but believe me, if it weren't for the circumstances, I would never have frightened you with such a hasty proposal." Andrei spoke as though a dam had finally burst within him. "I would have invited you on dates and surrounded you with attention and care. We would have walked under the moon along the riverbank and talked a great deal. I would have given you flowers… white roses… And only after seeing that you loved me too, after you knew everything about me and felt safe with me, would I have dared to confess my feelings and ask for your hand." He breathed deeply and finished helplessly. "But now… forgive me… I must rush things so ridiculously… It's just necessary!"

"What necessity are you talking about?" Lyuba asked quietly. "Does this have to do with your first visit to us? The conversation with…" Her voice trembled "… with my mother?"

The captain nodded.

"Tell me! Now!" Vasyura's daughter demanded, now, her voice ringing with steel, and Pilatov, sitting beside her, tensed inwardly. I, however, smiled and thought that Lyubochka would surprise us all yet.

"It is a very frightening truth…" Andrei began. He kept asking himself whether her fragile shoulders could bear yet another heavy burden. There was no way out now, but the captain hesitated for another second. "Yes, I'm afraid you do need to know." He drew in a deep breath and finally said, "Alright. Evidence has been found of your father's service with the fascists during the war."

The girl's eyebrows shot up and she objected almost too quickly. "No, no, he escaped from captivity and fought in the French Resistance! And he was in a Soviet camp for being captured!"

"Unfortunately, that's not the whole truth," Andrei countered in a low voice. The last thing he wanted was to be the bearer of such news. "Vasyura was captured in forty-one and joined the French Resistance in forty-four. Your sister was born..."

"Mum was pregnant just before the war!"

"According to her passport, your sister Galina Grigoryevna is two years older than she really is. She was born in early forty-four, after your father visited the occupied city of Liep*ā*ja on his leave, while serving in the German security police."

Lyuba's eyebrows rose incredulously. "Does Galina know about this?"

"I'm not sure," the captain shrugged. "I don't think so..."

"Then how do *you* know?" Vasyura's daughter demanded.

This entirely reasonable question was a real test for my friend. It was hardly the right time to reveal his acquaintance with a telepath who had direct access to her father's thoughts!

Hesitating for a moment, Andrei evasively answered. "The investigation is still unofficial, conducted by a private individual... My acquaintance... He found out. But it is certain!" Realising he was treading on shaky ground, the captain shifted to a more concrete topic. "But that's not the main thing... From early forty-two to August forty-four, your father served in the 118th Schutzmannschaft Police Battalion, formed from Ukrainians who had sided with the Nazis. He commanded the battalion headquarters. The KGB has testimonies from other policemen, Vasyura's former colleagues. Many testimonies..."

Stunned as if struck by lightning, Lyuba stared at him for a few seconds, then jumped up and paced back and forth along the path in front of the bench, wringing her hands.

"Unfortunately, that's not all either. I'm sorry, it's difficult to talk about this... with you..." Andrei struggled to speak — the words seemed to freeze on his tongue. "But I must. To protect you."

"Stop stalling! Speak!" the girl exclaimed, waving her hands.

"Alright..." Andrei looked around cautiously and finally whispered, "Grigory Vasyura commanded the burning of several Belorussian villages, including Khatyn... and... personally tortured and killed. Not only partisans but also innocent women and children..."

"Enough!" Lyuba interrupted him indignantly. "This is all disgusting! Why should I even believe you?" The young man faltered, his face turning crimson. Confiding such horrific details about her father to the woman he loved was no less repulsive than the details themselves.

"I'm so sorry..." was all he could say. "I saw the interrogation records of the punishers with my own eyes. My friend has photographic copies, and if you want..." The captain was referring to the folder handed over to Ruslan and thought he would need to borrow the documents from the journalist for a day or two to show them to Vasyura's daughter.

Lyuba stopped pacing along the path. She stood still and stared at Andrei with wide-open eyes. The distressed look of my love-struck friend did not lie. Besides, the girl knew her father's cruelty too well and understood better than anyone else that everything mentioned by the KGB captain could very well be true. Memories of her childhood in Vasyura's house swirled through her mind like a grim kaleidoscope. There was the shattered, bleeding head of a striped kitten hurled against the wall. Lyuba had brought him in from the street. The "flea-ridden" creature's only crime had been entering the house without the head's permission... Then there was the number of guard dogs, none of which survived in Vasyura's household for more than a year, until eventually, the family stopped keeping them... There was the red-purple bruised eye and the grotesquely contorted mouth of a farm tractor driver who had lost a tooth. Due to a hangover, the man had failed to show up for work during the busy summer harvest... There was her mother, applying cooling compresses to the blue-brown bruises on her thighs and forearms. The scoundrel beat her with anything he could find but never touched her face, deliberately, so that his wife would not be suspended from her job at the school... And then there were the four walls of Lyuba's room, locked from the outside after the teenage girl had bravely attempted to protest her father's methods of asserting control over everything that moved. Vasyura never regretted anything, never acknowledged his actions as cruel or unfair — he was merely "teaching."

Lyuba had long since stopped believing the village tale that her father's harsh character resulted from everything he had been through. After all, he was not the only one who had returned from the war, spent time in prison, and had to adapt to civilian life. What kind of life would it be if all war veterans were like Vasyura? The cruelty of her perpetually angry and harsh father had always traumatised and perplexed her, but it still seemed like mere background noise, as if it was something secondary to a larger picture. Yet there was no foreground to that picture. At the centre was a gaping void, as though several key pieces of the puzzle were missing. And Captain Pilatov had just helped complete the image.

"Let's say you're right," Lyuba finally said in a calmer voice. "If there was evidence, why wasn't he convicted earlier?"

"That was our main question as well!" Andrei replied. "All these years, Vasyura was protected by a contact... from the KGB, and we've only just found out who." He looked at the vampire's younger daughter, his heart gnawed by anxiety.

Pilatov was convinced that the girl, his only chance for happiness, now saw him as an enemy tarnishing her father's name. Without any hope of forgiveness, the captain concluded, "Nina Vladimirovna knew about her husband's crimes, although not the details. While you were out meeting the paramedic, she told me about it. She didn't want to take it... with her... but she couldn't bring herself to tell the children either." Then, gathering his courage once again, he added, "And she also asked me to take care of you."

Lyuba sank onto the bench and covered her eyes with her hands as if struck down. She sat there for a long time, torturing the captain with her silence. Andrei waited in agony but without a word while the girl wrestled with her thoughts. Lyuba had inherited her grandfather's professorial poise and her father's immense psycho-energetic strength, albeit with a different disposition. She was perhaps one of the few, if not the only one, who had dared to defy the old vampire in recent years. Clearly, Vasyura had left his younger daughter alone only for the time being, and Lyuba had long dreamed of escaping both him and the detested Dymerka. Marriage seemed like the perfect opportunity, but wouldn't disappearing just before her father's arrest be an act of betrayal? Then again, was it truly so shameful to betray a traitor? On the other hand, she hardly knew this Andrei... But could anything be worse than life with Vasyura?

Lyuba looked at the young man's face again — love was unmistakably written there. She had no idea yet how much the KGB officer was risking by intending to marry the daughter of a former Nazi. And then she heard her own quiet voice, sounding so alien, break the heavy silence.

"I believe you. I agree to marry you."

Overcome with joy, Andrei grabbed her slender fingers in his large, soft palms and pressed them to his lips, still not daring to go for a real kiss — and Lyuba suddenly felt better.

"And where is your comrade?" she asked. "The one who is leading the investigation?"

"He'll be here shortly," Andrei replied, silently begging me not to appear out of nowhere in front of the already overwhelmed girl. So I pretended to arrive from around the corner of the school building, and the captain, with a sigh of relief, introduced me to his beloved. "Meet Yan. His family suffered in Khatyn."

"Pleased to meet you," I said, smiling at my friend's fiancée and joining the conversation without any unnecessary explanations. "You need to take Lyubov Grigoryevna away before the official investigation begins." Answering Andrei's unspoken question, I patted him on the shoulder and added, "I'm very grateful to you, but now I can manage with Ruslan's help."

"Are you sure?" the captain asked.

"Undoubtedly! You have other concerns now — a young wife and everything that comes with it..."

I smiled at Lyuba, who blinked in confusion. She didn't understand how I knew about her agreement to marry the captain, given just before my arrival.

Andrei noticed her bewilderment and gave a rather dodgy explanation. "Don't be surprised. Yan is special."

"The main task now is to ensure that Vasyura's fate doesn't affect you," I told the girl, steering the conversation back to practical matters.

"And what about Galina?" Lyuba objected weakly.

"Galina? She..." I tried to answer as gently as possible. "She is very much like your father, isn't she?" Lyuba nodded. "She can take care of herself. I think you know that."

"I do know," thought the captain's fiancée. *"But how do you?"*

"Perhaps Andrei will tell you my story in more detail later," I responded to her unspoken thoughts, surprising her even more.

Andrei chuckled. "I told you he's special!"

It was decided that Lyuba would return to Kiev, where the young couple would give their marriage application to the registry office. Andrei hoped to speed up the process using his KGB credentials. Vasyura's daughter was to take her final exams and receive her institute diploma under the new husband's surname at the last moment to ensure that the vice-rector, the vampire's friend, wouldn't have time to sniff anything out or report it to her father. In truth, the affair was common enough as many of Lyuba's classmates had married during their five years of study.

It was also decided to ignore the assignment to the Velykodymerska school and rely on the captain's service to exempt Lyuba from any legal complications. Moreover, Andrei was aware that the country was approaching such chaos that no one would soon care about minor violations. He was already considering resigning and settling with his wife in Veliky Novgorod at his uncle's house.

Lyuba went home to pack her things. The following morning, she left for Kiev by train to sit her exams without speaking to her father or sister about the hasty marriage. Andrei joined her later, on the train. Thus, my mission lost a fighter, at least for the time being.

---

*The Russian female name Lyubov (the short is Lyuba) is also a common Russian name that translates as "love."

Chapter 19. The Ghost

In the month I had spent on Earth, I had quite a bit of fun seeing the stupor of homo sapiens exposed to the Lemurian race's powers. However, Andrei scolded me for revealing my nature to the vampire, who immediately began pulling strings among his useful contacts to evade retribution once again. According to the captain, this would undoubtedly complicate my task. My friend was right only partially.

The news of Nina Vladimirovna's death did not make Vasyura hurry home from the banquet. After reading Andrei's note, he thought, *"Send the dead to the grave and the living to the table,"* and returned to the hall as if nothing had happened. He addressed his gathering.

"Dear guests, today I must leave you a little earlier than I had planned, but enjoy yourselves, and have fun as usual. Vasily Vasylych, be so kind as to keep an eye on things!" Vasyura casually threw this remark toward the Komsomol leader as he walked out of the hall. He exchanged glances with Krotovsky, nodded for him to follow, and withdrew with the retired spy to one of the furnished rooms. Ensuring that the guests were occupied with choosing further entertainment and that no one was behind the door, the former SS officer sprawled in a large armchair and began.

"Today, just before your arrival, some brat, about twenty-five years old, showed up here, claimed to be a living witness of that incident in Khatyn, and threatened me with retribution."

"That's impossible, Grigory Nikitovich!" Krotovsky sputtered. "If he were a witness, he'd be about fifty!"

"Exactly," Vasyura grumbled, thinking it prudent to keep silent about my ability to become invisible. "So, who is this son of a bitch? Where did he come from, and what does he really know?"

Krotovsky shrugged in bewilderment, and the deputy director of the state farm concluded in a tone that brooked no argument, as if he once again commanded an encircled battalion. “In other words, you've got a job to do, Valerian. Find out about him discreetly and hush it up if necessary.”

“Consider it done, Grigory Nikitovich. Don't worry!” Krotovsky assured him in a sweet voice.

If Vasyura had been able to read minds, he would have discovered that Valerian Karpovich had no intention of lifting a finger. The influence of the former KGB boss was former too. Krotovsky knew perfectly well that all those strings he had pulled twelve years ago to save his old Schutzmann patron had long since turned into fishing rods at retirement dachas. Now the only thing pulling on them was the fish of Ukraine’s ponds.

Krotovsky did not know the new KGB bosses well enough to negotiate trustingly with them about an old, highly sensitive matter without harming himself. It was smarter to lie low, leave everything as it was, and hope that the threats to his pal from some young upstart were just a hooligan prank, which was exactly what Valerian Karpovich did, despite assuring Vasyura that everything had been taken care of. And that was when I finally understood that vampires were incapable of friendship.

***

Nevertheless, I decided to act more selectively and disguise myself more carefully in the future. For instance, it was probably not worth rushing to reveal all the details of my origins to a journalist, a person with access to the homo sapiens’ mass consciousness. On Monday, the 13th of May, I “accidentally” bumped into Ruslan in the park adjacent to the Brovary military enlistment office, near the circular platform where a silver-painted birdlike airplane with a red pentagram on its tail stood frozen in the takeoff position as a monument to the courage of wingless people.

Batalov did not notice me right away. From the private house at the intersection of Chernyakhovsky and Dimitrov Streets, where he rented a room, it was about a twenty-minute walk to the enlistment office, but Ruslan had already been circling the area for two hours with our folder under his arm. During the holidays, he had studied every line of the protocols, which truly amounted to a news sensation. Yet Ruslan was plagued by doubts about the people who had handed him the materials so carelessly and about the documents' authenticity.

He still could not understand how Vasyura had managed to avoid accusations and retribution for over ten years if such serious evidence of the crimes of that unpleasant old man with malicious eyes had been in the hands of the investigation all along. If the protocols in the folder turned out to be forgeries, the journalist risked smearing a respected person and becoming a laughingstock and a blind puppet in someone else's game.

Ruslan was twenty-eight years old, and his career had stalled somewhat due to his excessive enthusiasm and honesty. The editor inchief kept him on staff, acknowledging the young journalist's talent and energy, but Batalov's most hard-hitting articles, produced on the typewriter inherited from his grandfather, a military correspondent, collected dust in the chief's drawer. Much to the author's disappointment, the boss feared losing his position for publishing such materials.

The wind of change that had begun to blow through the country three weeks ago promised new horizons for such tireless truth-seekers as Ruslan. Therefore, he looked to the future with hope, and now more than ever, he could not afford to stumble.

"Out for a walk?" I enquired, trying to make my voice sound casual. Ruslan snapped out of his thoughts, his reddish eyebrows shooting up in surprise.

"And what brings you here?" he asked.

"I'm looking for you, Ruslan Bogdanovich," I admitted. "I wanted to see what conclusions you've drawn from this material" — I pointed at the folder under his arm — "and whether you are still interested in the topic."

The journalist scrutinised my face with his honest grey eyes. He still hadn't decided whether it was worth dealing with me.

"It is!" I said. I couldn't hold back.

My companion's jaw dropped. "Are you reading minds?"

"A little," I joked, realising I'd given myself away again. I quickly steered the conversation back on track. "You're probably wondering how Vasyura has managed to avoid retribution all this time?" Ruslan nodded and was about to express his surprise again, but I hurried to explain. "My friend Pilatov and I wondered the same thing."

"And? Do you have an answer?" the journalist asked with a hint of sarcasm.

"It's all quite mundane, really," I explained. "Vasyura has a friend in the KGB who's been covering for him this whole time. Andrei and I just figured out who it was. Actually, I came to tell you about it."

"And this protector of Vasyura — is he a big shot?" Batalov asked anxiously, thinking, *"Here we go again! So many bumps in the way that a normal person can't take a straight path without breaking their legs."*

"He *was* a big shot, but he's retired now," I reassured him. "I think the path is clear and fairly straight." I met the journalist's wary gaze again, but luckily, we had just reached the exit of Victory Park, across the road from the military enlistment office. I gestured invitingly towards the building, blocking any possibility of further delay. "Seize the moment, Comrade Batalov!"

"And you? Are you coming with me?" Ruslan asked, still hesitating.

"I'll wait here. Otherwise, I'd have to explain who I am and what I'm doing..."

"Yeah, you'd have to. You haven't really explained that to me, either. Your friend just flashed his ID..."

“I will when I have more time!” I replied, not entirely sure if I’d keep that promise. “What matters to you isn’t who I am, but the documents’ subject matter and authenticity. Isn’t that what you call ‘a scoop’? So go on, comrade reporter, towards your bright future!” Of course, I planned to follow him, but the comrade reporter didn’t need to know that. I wanted everything to unfold naturally, the way it did for homo sapiens.

Ruslan’s heart pounded as he climbed the steps to the enlistment office — not because he was on the verge of a scoop, but because he knew exactly who handled the documentation on military awards there. Anna Druzh. Or, for nearly ten years now, Anna Seliverstova. Anya. The most beautiful girl in their secondary school class, whom everyone had been in love with. Anya couldn’t have been unaware of that, but she was shy, which was probably why she was drawn to him, a bold and straightforward teenager. Ruslan had carried her schoolbag since fifth grade, fought over her more than once, and shared his plans to be a journalist like his grandfather, and the girl had listened, wide-eyed, to the stories of a wartime correspondent that the hero’s grandson enthusiastically retold to her.

Walking through the grubby beige corridors of the enlistment office, Ruslan remembered the day of their first and only kiss — so thrilling for him — as he walked Anya home after the school-leavers’ prom. He pictured the hazel-eyed face of the delicate girl, framed by two heavy black braids, her lips moist, smelling candy-sweet, her slim waist cinched with a wide silk sash over her prom dress. Then, Ruslan dared to kiss her and confess his love, which had already been obvious anyway, and they talked about how they would get married and spend their lives together.

Soon after, Ruslan left for Kiev to take the university entry exams. On his return, he learned about his school sweetheart’s upcoming wedding to a young border guard officer from Brovary, where she’d gone to apply to technical college. For Anya, like many Ukrainian village girls who weren’t aiming for the stars, finding a husband was her life's goal, and marrying a military man was both prestigious and romantic. Having met a determined, handsome senior lieutenant, she had drawn a winning lottery ticket and wasted no time cashing it in, much to her girlfriends' envy.

"Women shouted 'hooray' and threw their bonnets in the air!"* Ruslan had quoted bitterly to his mother, who delivered the unpleasant news. He proudly stepped aside. A first-year journalism student with vague career prospects could not compete with a Soviet Army officer, and he thought it best not to linger, though he hadn't lost his feelings for Anya.

Thanks to his mother's gossip network, Ruslan had always known the couple's movements from border to border across the vast country. Recently, after being wounded while apprehending a trespasser, Major Nikolai Seliverstov transferred back to his hometown, taking up the post of head of the Brovary Enlistment Office. He had even secured a part-time job for his wife there. So, after several restless years, Anya had a comfortable life, a decent job, and time to raise their twins — helping with homework, taking her daughter to music school, and her son to football training, and all close to her aging parents. Her life was a success. And Ruslan? He was just a small-town journalist, hardly impressive by comparison with Major Seliverstov.

Despite the old heartbreak, Batalov felt far less at risk with his school friend than with his colleagues and superiors. He knew perfectly well that the investigation of this still shaky but promising story had to start in Anna's office. Yet speaking truthfully, his thoughts were more focused on imagining how she had changed than on why he'd come. Ruslan approached the plywood door marked *Awards Department* and knocked loudly as if trying to drown out his wildly beating heart.

"Come in!" sang a semi-familiar voice from inside. The visitor pressed the metal handle, pushed the door open, and saw *her*.

"Well, hello, stranger!"

Forewarned about an unexpected visitor over the internal line, the young woman smiled warmly with her pearly pink lips, revealing straight, light-beige teeth. She stood from her desk, quickly met Batalov, and happily threw her arms around her former classmate. Her high heels clicked, and her curvy hips swayed in a tight, uniform skirt.

"Batalov! Ruslan! So, this is what you've become!"

"What?" Ruslan asked, pulling a comic grimace.

"Solid! A real man!" she laughed, remembering the skinny reddish-haired boy who had cuddled her after prom.

"You've changed too," he mumbled, not wanting to elaborate. Compared to the delicate girl he'd held in his memory for ten years, the snow-white had developed appetising curves, to put it mildly, and her soprano voice now had metallic notes like that of an experienced woman. With awkward enthusiasm, Ruslan hugged her plump waist, breathing in the aroma of oriental spice, which also felt unfamiliar. This was no longer Anechka, who smelt like candy, the girl he had wanted to kiss and protect — this was Anna Petrovna Seliverstova, the major's wife.

"How are you? Married? Any kids? Still working as a journalist?"

"No, not married. What kind of family can a journalist have?" Ruslan joked. Anna smiled politely, even condescendingly, having immediately assessed the unimpressive career of her former admirer. He added, "I'm not asking about you because I already know."

"You know?" she said, feigning surprise. "How?"

"Well, I visit my mother often, and she regularly updates me with all the news," Batalov smirked. "Maybe I became a journalist thanks to her genes."

Ruslan pulled another funny face, and he and Anya burst out laughing. In their home village, practically every female could successfully replace a news broadcast. Anna even had tears in her eyes from laughing so hard. The awkwardness melted away. She reached into her handbag, pulled out a handkerchief and a mirror, dabbed at the black mascara starting to smudge, and finally asked, "I heard you're here on business?"

"Y-yes…" Batalov replied, figuring out where to start. "I've been working on an investigation. It's a rather sensitive matter… That's why I'm so glad I ended up talking to you…" She raised an intrigued eyebrow. "Does the name Grigory Vasyura ring a bell?"

Her beautiful eyebrows shot up in surprise. "What a coincidence! Hold on!" Holding up her index finger for him to wait, she returned to her desk, picked up the top folder, extracted a document, and handed it to Batalov. "Here, read this. It came in recently — we haven't even sent it for review yet!"

Ruslan took the sheet, filled with neat, ruler-straight handwriting, almost calligraphic, except for its excessively sharp angles and lines, which made it difficult to decipher.

To the Head of the Military Commissariat, N.M. Seliverstov.

G.N. Vasyura's Statement

I, Grigory Nikitovich Vasyura, Director of Economic Affairs of the "Velykodymersky" State Farm, a veteran of the Great Patriotic War and Labour, and a leading manager in agriculture (a character reference from the farm director is attached), was unjustly overlooked for the awarding of the Jubilee Order of the Patriotic War. I consider this a glaring injustice, ingratitude, and disrespect.

With this statement, I demand a review of the above matter and the restoration of justice.

Best regards,
Signature: Vasyura
*Date: ** May 1985*

"What nerve!" Ruslan just couldn't hold back.

"What do you mean?" the awards department clerk asked. "The tone of the statement is harsh of course, but the old man's resentment is understandable…"

"Hmm, you should have seen this 'old man'!" the journalist responded. "But that's beside the point. Look at what I've got here," he said, handing Anna our folder.

She skimmed the document, her eyes widening as she read further and further down.

"So, effectively, this Vasyura commanded the burning of Khatyn?!" Anna finally exclaimed. The idea that a traitor and Nazi executioner had lived near her folks for years seemed unbelievable to the wife of a Soviet border guard. Even more unbelievable was that a statement from this very criminal demanding an award for defending Soviet citizens was now on her desk! Yet the photographs of protocols before her looked pretty convincing.

"Where did you get this?"

"From the KGB archives in Belarus… apparently…"

"What do you mean 'apparently'?"

"That's where things get strange," Ruslan admitted. "I'm not even completely sure these are copies of genuine documents, and even if they are, they may not have been obtained entirely legally."

"Wait, are you mixed up with criminals?" Panic and disappointment crept into his former classmate's voice. She feared for her and her husband's reputations.

"Of course not!" the journalist said, hastening to reassure her, and noticed Anna's involuntary sigh of relief. "I was approached by a private individual," he explained, "a strange guy, who claims to be a relative of one of the victims in Khatyn… but he seems like he's from another planet!" It had never crossed Ruslan's mind that both claims could be valid. "However, a KGB captain from Moscow accompanied him," Batalov continued, "and showed me his ID, a real one. The captain said he was here unofficially to help his friend as part of the investigation, which is private, 'for now.' They passed this folder to me, specifically because I'm a journalist. I met them by chance at an event where this Vasyura gave a speech. More than an unpleasant character, I must say!"

Ruslan looked expectantly at his attentive listener, who suddenly asked, "This is very important to you, isn't it?" All these years, Anna had felt like a traitor, even though she knew she'd made the right choice for herself, as evidenced by her happy marriage. Ruslan hadn't attended her wedding, nor had he ever shown up when she visited her parents in the village. He clearly hadn't forgotten anything — and now, he was at her workplace asking for help. Anna thought that assisting the still-unsuccessful journalist might serve as atonement and ease her guilt.

Ruslan hesitated. "If even part of what's in these documents is true, it could mean big opportunities for me... professionally." Anna nodded, and Ruslan added, "The problem is that Vasyura is a respected figure around here, so everything needs to be double-checked before anyone makes any public accusations. We must be careful. I think we might need your husband's help."

The awards department clerk stood up from her desk, walked to the window overlooking the courtyard, crossed her arms, and in deep thought, stared outside at the officers smoking and chatting during their break. It was a just cause, but rushing into it recklessly wasn't an option. They could both be in trouble if they were wrong, and so could her husband, Nikolai.

Meanwhile, seated on a visitor's chair, Ruslan studied Anna's profile. Despite a slight double chin, she still looked attractive. He marvelled at how no trace of his old love for her stirred within him, even though she remained beautiful despite her fuller figure.

"Yes, I need to talk to my husband," she finally said. "But not here..."

Right on cue, Major Seliverstov entered the office without knocking.

"Ready to head home? I'm driving to Kiev and can drop you off," he said, clearly in a hurry. Spotting the civilian sitting at her desk, he slowed down. "Oh, you have a visitor? Hello!" He shook Ruslan's hand firmly.

"Ruslan Batalov, journalist," Ruslan said, returning the handshake.

"Have we met before?"

"Only in photos!" Anna replied with a smile, sitting on the windowsill. "My classmate and childhood friend. Remember I told you about him?"

"Really?" Nikolai mockingly widened his eyes. "The one who skipped our wedding?"

"Yep," Batalov admitted with a laugh. "And I apologise for that!"

"You should apologise for having kissed my wife!" Nikolai thought jealously, but said aloud, "Apology accepted. Nice to meet you at last! Better late than never!"

"Shall we invite Ruslan over?" suggested Anna.

"Let's do it!" Seliverstov agreed, accepting an imaginary challenge. "We'll get to know each other better and make up for lost time." He tapped his chin and gave a conspiratorial wink, hinting at the drinks that hadn't been shared at the wedding.

Nikolai was far from foolish and understood that this must be the school admirer of his Anna, the one his mother-in-law had mentioned more than once. The major trusted his wife completely though. Back in the small military border town where he had served before his injury, the community was tiny, women were few, and there was no shortage of dashing young officers in uniform. Anna had attracted more than her fair share of admirers, both secret and open, but the faithfulness of the officer's wife had withstood all the challenges back there, so this sudden appearance of a former classmate, now a journalist, most likely meant he simply needed something, and Anna intended to ask her husband and superior for advice or assistance.

The perceptiveness of some homo sapiens in the absence of telepathic abilities never ceased to amaze me, yet I still felt sorry for the poor major. He couldn't be entirely certain of anything, and despite his logical reasoning, a stinging fear of losing his beloved wife and the family began to stir uneasily in his brave heart. Then again, only someone capable of fear could truly be called brave… Accustomed to facing danger head-on, Nikolai decided to gather intelligence through action.

"I'll be in Kiev today and back late. How about tomorrow evening?"

"Deal!" Ruslan agreed, shaking the hand of the matured snow-white's husband once more. "See you tomorrow then!"

Batalov left the couple behind, and I followed him, pretending I had been waiting outside the recruitment office all along. Ruslan did not really want to talk to me and spoke curtly, hoping to get rid of me as soon as possible. While recounting his visit to the awards department, the journalist made every effort to leave out his personal feelings, as if wringing water from a soaked sponge. I listened with a smile that puzzled him, though politeness kept him from commenting on it. I was tempted to confide in this new player in the mission, but I decided to hold back and to first see what agreements the major and the journalist would reach.

Having a full day of forced idleness ahead of me gave me time to think about Polina. Naturally, I thought of her every time I saw the romantic entanglements of my homo-sapien acquaintances, but until now, the search for Vasyura, the study of his habits and surroundings, and my general observations of humans had kept me distracted from focusing on my own feelings. Polina was still so young by society's standards that I considered it a blessing not to disturb her without reason. Now, bound to a day of inactivity,

I allowed myself to check in on her. After all, she didn't even need to know I was there.

The days were growing longer and warmer. I found Polina sitting on a bench by the lake, the exact spot where I had told her about homo liberatus nearly a month earlier. She gazed at the still water. For the umpteenth time, she was replaying in her mind the moments of our encounter, the most incredible adventure of her young life so far. For fear of being labelled crazy, the girl was afraid to tell anyone about meeting me. Sometimes she even wondered whether her encounter with an alien was nothing but a dream or a product of her vivid imagination. Her mother scolded her for her slipping grades, her teachers were baffled, and her classmates mocked her as a "sleepy fly." Tired of pretending to carry on with her usual life, Polina often retreated to the spot where we had met and where no one disturbed her thoughts and dreams.

Sleepy, however, she was not. Her experience of travelling through space, albeit as a passenger, had awakened her potential, and her capabilities rapidly expanded. This development, still unrecognised by Polina herself, extended far beyond the school curriculum. She had begun to sense the energy flow in living things — and the once-monotonous, shallow world had suddenly become overflowing with new sensations that overwhelmed her. They flooded the girl's senses, leaving her bewildered and unsure how to manage the chaos without help. To those around Polina, however, this confusion made her seem sluggish and distracted.

Now I had a valid reason to intervene in this human's life, to help her spread her wings, so to speak, and to be there for her! I expected it would be far more pleasant than hunting a vampire, but delivering Vasyura to human justice was still my top priority. Only then could I completely free myself from the fate of a murderer. Thus, although my heart longed to stay with Polina by the tranquil lake, I forced myself to resist the urge to appear before her. I returned to Brovary instead.

On the other hand, Ruslan had quite the opposite reaction to the meeting with his school love. He no longer felt his earlier attraction to Anna, nor did he harbour any lingering resentment. This brought him an unexpected sense of freedom. It was as though a door to the past, which had remained slightly ajar for ten years, had finally slammed shut. Ruslan was clearheaded as he prepared to visit the major's home. He understood that he needed to win over the head of the household, so he picked up a bottle of the best cognac his budget could afford. For the rest of the family, he settled on a box of Evening Kiev chocolates. He procured both items through his landlady, who had worked for years as a storeroom clerk in the central grocery shop. A headline immediately formed in the journalist's mind, *How I Searched for "Evening Kiev" in Brovary*, but he wisely abandoned the idea of writing another pamphlet doomed to languish in an editor's drawer. After generously thanking his landlady for sourcing the rare treats, Ruslan stepped through the gate and strode down the dusty pavement towards the opposite end of town, where the major and his wife had made their nest in a high-rise block.

Shaking hands, Ruslan followed Seliverstov through a long hallway into a spacious living room furnished with a plush beige set of a large sofa and two comfortable armchairs as well as a new dark walnut wall unit with a display of crystal glasses arranged in perfect symmetry. A vast carpet with intricate patterns covered the wall behind the sofa. I glanced at it and noticed quite an active life, invisible to the eyes of the owners but seething among the fibres of their carpet. A fully extended drop-leaf table stood by the sofa, laid out hospitably, and the lady of the house was arranging delicacies that her husband had brought back from the capital the day before. Their daughter was practicing scales on an upright piano in the corner of the same room while a muted colour television was on behind her.

Granted amnesty upon the guest's arrival, the girl ran off cheerfully, and Anna made a mental note to ask her husband to move the piano to the children's room. In fact, she also thought it was high time to separate the twins into different rooms, even if this meant she and Nikolai moving into this large one, which so far had served only as a lounge in a rather bourgeois manner.

Anna considered herself happy. She had everything a Soviet woman could dream of — a loving and decently ranked husband, healthy and well-mannered children raised in the fresh forest air, and now, this beautiful state-provided two-bedroom flat almost in Kiev, where the major's wife hoped to grow old. She felt confident inviting former classmates or Nikolai's colleagues with their sweet-toothed gossip-loving wives here. Ruslan also admired the scene of well-being before him. He knew that happy people were usually more inclined to help others.

On the silent television, young men in shorts chased and kicked a ball across a massive field surrounded by several ascending tiers of seating filled with spectators who frequently jumped up and gestured wildly.

"What's the score?" Ruslan asked his host.

"3:1, Dynamo," Nikolai replied cheerfully. "Who are you rooting for?"

"Dynamo!" Ruslan answered, telling the truth as he smiled broadly and set a bottle of cognac on the table.

"That's the spirit!" The major extended his hand to his guest. It was amusing to see how often homo-sapien men exchanged handshakes, especially when trying to demonstrate mutual goodwill. In truth, each harboured a slight wariness of the other, but neither saw the other as an opponent, nor did they wish to.

"You two carry on chatting while I finish up in the kitchen," said Anna, quickly tucking away the box of Evening Kiev brought by the guest from the children's reach before leaving the men to get on. The cognac Ruslan had brought found its way into Nikolai's hands.

"Well, how about a quick toast to new and old friendship?" he suggested. "Or maybe some vodka instead?"

"Vodka's fine," Ruslan agreed, not particularly familiar with cognac-drinking rituals.

"Remember to have snacks!" came Anna's voice from the kitchen. The men exchanged conspiratorial glances and chuckled. The major preferred to keep up appearances, while Ruslan wanted to eat but was too shy to start. And so, the alcohol set on its journey through their unfortunate bodies solitarily. Pouring a second round, the major finally took a piece of herring, and Ruslan followed suit with relief. Nikolai decided it was time to broach the subject.

"So, what brings you here after all these years? Is it business?" He had returned from Kiev late the previous night, and the morning had been filled with the usual chaos — breakfast, getting the kids ready for school, and heading off to work. Anna preferred to delegate difficult matters to her husband, so she was glad to be occupied with daily chores this time.

Loosened by the vodka, Ruslan met his companion's straightforward gaze.

"Honestly, I regret not reaching out to you sooner, Nikolai Ivanovich. I should have put childhood grudges behind me a long time ago..." He hesitated briefly. "Although it seems time has truly healed me." With these words, he returned such an open and friendly look that Nikolai felt reassured. Ruslan placed a folder on the edge of the table. "As for business, this time, it's anything but childish. I've come across these materials..."

Nikolai reached for the folder, opened the first page, and, showing complete ignorance, asked, "What's this?"

Ruslan realised that the awards department clerk had not told her boss anything about the doubts concerning veteran Vasyura. The journalist then briefed Anna's husband on everything he knew about the case, illustrating his account with excerpts from copies of the protocols.

"You see, obtaining official access to study the military archives in an orderly way would take an eternity. And besides, Vasyura is a respected man. I wouldn't want to put myself in a compromising position if all these copies turn out to be forgeries," Batalov concluded.

"And you decided to put me in a compromising position instead!" Nikolai thought as he listened intently. He wanted to retort, but Anna returned to the room at that moment.

"I feel sick at the mere thought that everything in this folder could be true! Can you imagine awarding this *creature* the Jubilee Order of the Patriotic War? Ugh!" she said, shuddering, and then turned to her husband. "And the copies are most likely from genuine protocols."

"What makes you so sure?" the major asked.

Anna perched on the wide armrest of the sofa and, lowering her voice to almost a whisper, as if someone might overhear them.

"This morning, I called the archive and made an inquiry. They told me that since July 1941, Grigory Nikitiyevich Vasyura has been listed as missing in action. Your 'respected man' is nothing but a ghost."

---

*"Women shouted 'hooray' and threw their bonnets in the air!" – a quote from Alexander Griboyedov's comedy *Woe from Wit*, expressing women's admiration for military men.

Chapter 20. The Shimmer of Indigo

The homo sapiens took over Vasyura's case and everyone who learned about his Nazi past through me was determined to act. Both Pilatovs, the colonel and the captain, assured me that the human justice system was fully capable of dealing with a war criminal without the help of an alien. So, for the time being, I decided to step aside and keep my distance from Vasyura to avoid the temptation of taking matters into my own hands. One way or another, I had made significant progress in my mission by understanding what made one a vampire. Would the Lemurians choose to intervene and halt this evolutionary dead-end branch from total domination on Earth? Such a decision required the presence of all my kin, and there were just under three Earth months left until the next Unity. I resolved to spend this time with Polina.

In my absence, the poor girl kept returning to our bench by the lake again and again. Only this water, these bushes, and these trees had witnessed what she had seen, and only they could understand the longing that never left her after having learned about homo liberatus. Meanwhile, the warm May days dragged on endlessly, and Polina spent all her free time sitting by the lake as if glued to the spot in anticipation of a new miracle. She had begun to think that the miracle would never happen again and that her life would consist of nothing but these sickly sweet, monotonously quiet days on the outside and this chaos of thoughts and feelings on the inside. Her elation at my return was all the stronger for my absence.

"Yan! You're back!" A powerful wave of joy sent Polina leaping to her feet. She barely restrained herself from throwing her arms around my neck, and her energy field, compressed daily by a growing tumour of hopelessness, tripled in size at once and turned into a dazzling glow, bright blue with a violet shimmer. It almost seemed that flowers might begin to bloom in her footsteps.

"Hello, my sweetheart!" I thought, but aloud I said with a serene smile, "I did promise, remember?"

"I remember, of course," Polina replied with a sigh, stepping back. "How could I forget? It's just… promises are easy to make…" This young soul had already been tainted by human scepticism.

"I see your faith has wavered," I remarked.

"A little," the girl admitted with another sigh, and returned to the bench. In truth, seeing my appearance out of thin air once again had made Polina question her sanity for a moment. Now she suddenly felt lost, unsure of what to do or say — and she was so endearing in her confusion! Her heart was pounding wildly, her cheeks were aflame, and her little ears might as well have been used to light a fire. I felt both amused and sorry for the poor teenager, doomed to endure such a devastating storm inside her own body. To help her cope with the awkwardness, I got straight to the point.

"Tell me, what do you dream of most in the world?"

Polina, caught off guard by this sudden change of subject, raised her eyebrows in surprise, but I reassured her.

"I'm serious!"

After a moment's thought, she quietly replied. "I'd like… to see the world." Although her light-blonde head bore no resemblance to the gypsy-like Lemurians, Polina's soul longed to soar freely, like the souls of the true homo liberatus that knew no boundaries. The next moment, she remembered the noisy carriages of long-distance trains and the nauseating stuffiness of the old bus, by which her parents used to take her from a remote railway station lost in the steppe to a small village in the Krasnodar region, where her grandmother lived. Polina shuddered. "But I don't like trains. Or planes. Or buses… Or anything that crams people together like sardines in a tin. Ugh!" She looked disgusted. "Do you know what I thought about while you were gone?"

"Of course I do!" I replied, and we both laughed. "You want to travel as easily and quickly as the time I once teleported you straight to your room." Without giving the ever-doubting teenager a chance to say her dream was impossible, I finally revealed the secret of her origin. "The thing is, you carry the homo liberatus gene."

"What? Whose gene?"

Children linked to both our species genetically can be easily identified by their indigo-coloured aura, which, by the age of twenty-five or thirty, usually changes to another shade, depending on their spiritual development. After that, it becomes much harder to trace their connection to us. That was how I had recognised from our very first meeting that Polina carried a drop of Lemurian blood.

Young descendants of homo liberatus among humans never ceased to amaze. The talents of indigo children are as diverse as the shades on a genius painter's palette, from barely perceptible hypersensitivity and fine intuition to powerful "magical" gifts celebrated in folklore. Some hear unspoken thoughts, others foresee the future. Some move objects without touching them, and a select few even master the art of teleportation and astral travel. It's impossible to predict what astonishing mixture Nature might pour into the next vessel of life, so Lemurians only joke, saying that conceiving children with homo sapiens is our way to improve humanity.

We never worry about inheritance. In matters of love, homo liberatus are as carefree as Nature itself. Nature maintains its own balance, and we trust it implicitly. Like a nonchalant experimenter, it shuffles and mixes millions of lives, creating new ones, and then forces them to tackle the challenges it offers.

Until my mission began, very few of us had deliberately sought out our scattered Earth-bound relatives because you never know in what remote backwater or frenzied whirlpool of a megalopolis the next bright indigo flame might flicker. Even so, any Lemurian who had encountered indigo accidentally tried teaching them to feel, understand, and use their gift, for Nature's benefit and out of mere compassion. It had been like saving a stray kitten from starvation and the winter's cold. And yes, there had always been a few enthusiasts who voluntarily devoted their lives to mentoring young "magicians" on Earth, but I was not one of them. I was only interested in Polina.

"Children like you sometimes grow up to become wizards," I began without preamble. The girl opened her mouth in surprise, and I continued with a smile. "For example, Merlin, the greatest wizard in human history, was a son of homo liberatus. His father had to leave the boy among humans simply because the child was born with the gene of fear." Polina stared at me wide-eyed. I fully understood how implausible all this must have sounded to a teenager trapped in the human matrix, but I kept adding fuel to the fire. "And that is far from the only case. It's safe to say that all the great prophets and healers on Earth are our relatives — just like you."

Polina didn't know what to think. She could no longer doubt the reality of a world she had previously read about only in fantasy books, but believing in her own connection to that world was simply too much!

"But… I'm just… ordinary…" she finally stammered.

"Do you really believe that?" I interrupted with a wry chuckle.

She shrugged awkwardly.

"Do you need proof?"

"Well, yes…" Polina murmured.

"All right. Do you remember how we teleported from here to your room?" I asked.

She nodded.

"What did you feel immediately after that?"

Polina closed her eyes, smiling dreamily. "It was amazing! Like soaring high on a swing — and then falling and soaring again!"

"Would you like to repeat that?"

"You don't even have to ask!" she exclaimed enthusiastically.

"Well, there you go. For the bodies of ordinary homo sapiens, teleportation — if they ever experience it as passengers — is a tough ordeal. Something like this," I said, and shared my memory of how Andrei Pilatov had vomited in his uncle's garden after I brought him there from Moscow.

"Ugh!" Polina grimaced. "Good thing that didn't happen to me!"

"That's because you're like me… at least to some extent."

"But how? My parents are normal people!"

"Normal?" I laughed. "Possibly… It might not be about them, but about their ancestors — perhaps quite distant ones. All I can tell you for sure is they are on your father's side."

"So, is my dad…?" the girl asked in bewilderment.

"He has his talents," I replied evasively. "I can't tell you more." Discussing her father's involvement in a secret defence project, something even families weren't supposed to know about, was inappropriate.

Polina excitedly tried to imagine a life full of wonders, which suddenly loomed ahead. New sensations, which had unsettled her ever since the teleportation a month ago, were now beginning to make sense.

"You liked moving through space because it's in your blood," I concluded, then asked without ceremony, "Do you want to learn?"

"You don't even have to ask!" my indigo girl exclaimed again. Yes, the question was truly ridiculous. "I'm ready! Really!" Suddenly she remembered… "Oh! My holidays start in two weeks, and my parents are sending me to Grandma's!"

Polina was so naively and sincerely upset that I laughed until tears came.

The main obstacle to homo sapiens achieving freedom of spirit is their tunnel vision. Each human mind moves along a kind of corridor — some incredibly narrow, others slightly wider. Some, having suffered from their limitations, develop mental claustrophobia and desperately chase after knowledge, trying to push back the walls of their prison, equally ephemeral and impenetrable. Unfortunately, no matter how hard humans try, they merely replace one mental model with another, and none of them, not even indigoes, can break free of a model altogether.

Polina frowned in confusion for a few seconds as she watched me laugh. Finally, she realised what had amused me and began giggling too.

"Grandma lives by the sea, right?" I asked after catching my breath. "That's a perfect place for learning — meditations and practice." Noticing the sour face she pulled at the word "learning," I added with cheerful sternness, "You don't think you can teleport with the snap of your fingers, do you? I'm not a fairy godmother!"

"Of course not," Polina lied, and blushed, catching my reproachful look, and I realised how much patience I would need. I had never considered teaching my calling, and I used to think it was pointless the way some Lemurians fussed over distant relatives found among homo sapiens. Now, as I felt an irresistible pull towards this awkward indigo girl, love wouldn't let me abandon her to face her gifts alone. Reluctantly, I continued disappointing the teenager.

"Spatial travel isn't magic, my dear, and even pure-blooded homo liberatus don't get all their skills handed to them on a silver platter. Lemurians start learning to control their powers little by little, from infancy, and they only master the full range of skills by the age of thirty or forty by Earth's reckoning, sometimes even later. For example, I couldn't manage interplanetary teleportation until I was forty-four. So, don't expect that I wave my hands over your head and then you'll fly free. That only happens in fairy tales made up by ignorant and lazy homo sapiens."

"Pity," thought Polina, glancing sideways at me and snorting.

I smirked and shattered her hopes for easy magic completely. "If you manage to cover a couple of metres to start with, that would be great! Got it?"

Polina pursed her lips and nodded.

"Now go home. On your own. On foot for now. And on your way, think about how you could better use the energy and time you'll spend working your legs, covering… how far is it?" I squinted, estimating. "Let's say, two kilometres." I tried to give my tone a hint of sternness, but my indigo girl unmistakably caught the laughter in my voice. She stuck her tongue out at me and set off, both happy and puzzled, overjoyed at my return and now anticipating incredible transformations. However, the news that mastering "magic" depended primarily on herself sobered her up. Not that my indigo was unwilling to work hard — it was just that doubt at once began gnawing at her teenage soul, poisoned by human fear. She trusted me, but she lacked faith in herself.

I planned to settle down for the night right there by the lake, under an energy dome, but first, I needed to properly assess what I was dealing with.

Late at night, I teleported to Polina's room.

Even in her deep sleep, the poor girl was battling gravity: lying on her stomach, she pressed one bent knee and her left elbow against the mattress, while her right arm hugged the pillow she had buried her face in. I admired her peaceful sleep for several minutes, fighting the desire to pull those grey pyjamas with pink elephants off her uninitiated body and caress her until exhaustion… But that wasn't why I was there.

When I finally overcame my impulse, I ran my hand along the spine of the sleeping girl without touching her, where the indigo glow bordered on the air. Sadly, it was impossible to restore the energy field of this young but already civilization-scarred being artificially, in one session. Not even two would suffice. Deep down, I had hoped my teasing about the coming difficulties and training would turn into a joke!

Polina's biggest blockage was in her second chakra. Then again, blockages in the two lower energy exchange centres in homo sapiens were nothing new to Lemurians. The reason was the same old fear. When energy stagnates at such a primitive level, one can, at best, use only a fifth of their brain power. I had assumed that an indigo child would be different from ordinary humans, but I had to admit, I was too optimistic. Despite her kinship with homo liberatus, she would have to traverse a far more challenging path than the children of Lemuria.

First, I needed to help Polina break free from the shackles of the human matrix, because without cleansing and restoring the red and orange chakras, there could be no hope of mastering even such a basic skill as telepathy, let alone teleportation. Who knew how this would turn out? Judging by the experience of Unity, curing humans of themselves was a thankless task, and sometimes even impossible. Honestly, I would have simply left if I didn't love Polina so much! Although this challenge promised to turn into a tough one, the next day I cheerfully offered her the first exercise.

"Close your eyes and imagine everything that pleases you. It doesn't matter in what order."

The girl stared at me in surprise. She had braced herself for difficulties already and did not expect to hear about pleasure. I nodded encouragingly. Then, my indigo girl closed her eyes and began to reflect. In her memories, fragments of sensations and images from her still rather limited life experience began to whirl like a kaleidoscope.

... warm sea water kissing her feet... The soothing whisper of the surf... A light touch of salty breeze on her face... Soft, moist sand transforming into whimsical constructions under the hands of a little dreamer...

Yes, the seaside promised to be the perfect place for our training!

... The leaves rustling in the solemn silence of a seemingly still but life-filled forest... A sense of dissolving, being lost in this mysterious green hum – a feeling familiar to any Lemurian child.

... Five-year-old Polina sings on a swing in her grandmother's garden. The child's clear voice, untainted by shyness, flows freely in time with thrilling rises and falls, spreading through neighbouring yards and making people smile...

... Vivid scenes from films about love and adventure that the teenage girl has learned to empathise with, imagining herself in the place of the heroes...

... And there she is, walking along a deserted beach next to someone handsome and strong — a tall, broad-shouldered blond guy who, alas, looked nothing like me. His features were indistinct as he had yet to be met, but the sweet excitement that unfailingly gripped Polina's body in that part of the fantasy, where the imaginary prince charming took her hand, felt completely real...

At this improper moment, my indigo girl checked herself, and her thoughts quickly shifted to entirely different joys: she recalled the taste of chocolate and vanilla ice-cream. Then she imagined deliciously soft sweets with condensed milk filling. Then came an airy eclair with delicate cream that melted on the tongue. Pieces of veal, soaked in aromatic spices and tomato sauce, from her mother's signature beef stroganoff. Crispy, golden-brown potatoes with fried onions and shrivelled browned chanterelles. And finally, dumplings with fresh homemade mince, flavoured with garlic and fragrant pepper, drowning in rich sour cream mixed with butter. She imagined all these simple delights so vividly that her mouth even watered.

Ugh! Only now did I begin to grasp the signficance of homo sapiens' culinary culture and understand why they loved their body-poisoning food so much! Culinary pleasures occupied a disproportionately large space in Polina's world, as if she were addicted to a drug that replaced less accessible joys in life. Yet the images she pictured belonged to a cheerful person, undoubtedly capable of experiencing a full range of pleasures, both physical and spiritual.

So why then was my young friend's orange chakra so tightly blocked?

The answer did not take long to find. Suddenly Polina stirred and opened her eyes. She glanced at her small wristwatch and squealed. "Oh! I need to get home!" Without further explanation, she jumped to her feet and started towards the town.

"Wait! Where are you going? We haven't finished!" My attempts to persuade her to stay even a minute longer were swept away by a hurricane of her worry that obliterated any rational argument I could make.

"Mum must be worried sick by now!" my indigo girl shouted over her shoulder, running through the forest.

I had not been so perplexed in all my short time on Earth. It was as if a heavy, crude rock had smashed through the window to the beautiful memories and the much-needed peace in the teenager's soul had been shattered into sharp fragments!

Polina skipped home, her heart leaping out of her chest, blood pounding in her temples. She flew up to the third floor, taking the steps two at a time, flung open the unlocked door, and called out from the threshold, "Mum, I'm so sorry I'm late!"

"Oh thank god!" came a deep, disgruntled voice from the room. "I've been worried sick for an hour now! Where on earth have you been?"

"I'm so sorry, please forgive me!" Polina pleaded as she stepped into the room. "I was wandering in the forest and got lost in thought…"

I was invisibly present during this domestic scene, trying to figure out why my indigo girl had interrupted her meditation halfway through so abruptly. Polina's mother was sitting in an armchair in front of the television. On the square dark-wood coffee table before her was a large plate holding a whole loaf of crispy-crust bread, sliced lengthwise, carefully rubbed with garlic, and barely eaten. Each half of the porous soft white loaf was covered with rather thick slices of smoked pork fat. To me, the only edible thing on the plate was the garlic. All this was washed down with a cup of strong, very sweet tea. This was the nightly ritual meal as the woman waited for her husband, who later in the evening found little joy in a wife weighed down by such a heavy supper. She secretly dreaded getting pregnant "at her age," so she preferred the pleasures of food over lovemaking. I could see how Polina had developed her habit of substituting tasty treats for all other joys of life that were out of reach.

From the woman's thoughts, I gathered that the interrupted dinner irritated her more than her daughter's lateness itself, but the officer's wife considered disciplinary talks to be her primary parental duty. She couldn't "allow the child to spiral out of control," so Polina's mother, as usual, placed her hand over her heart quite convincingly, clearly not intending to grant the guilty girl an easy pardon.

"Lost in thought for a whole hour? How's that even possible? Did a thought about your worried mother happen to cross your mind among the others?" she asked sharply. "And take off your shoes if you don't mind! Don't bring dirt into the flat!"

Polina, still out of breath, returned to the hallway and kicked off her shoes awkwardly, ready to sink through the floor from embarrassment, never mind that it was her responsibility to clean the apartment every week. Sins were rarely forgiven in this household, where punishment was replaced with the constantly stoked sense of guilt with great effect. Polina tried her best not to make mistakes, but more often than not, the opposite happened — her mother always found new reasons to nitpick. "Have you finished your homework?"

"Yes, of course! Everything's done," the girl hurried to reassure. "There wasn't much homework anyway as it's the end of term."

"You'd better be sure," her mother said through pursed lips. "Get changed and brush your hair please. Don't walk around the house looking like a mess. And have your shower before your father gets home."

Polina went to the bathroom, and I, surprised at how shamelessly this woman drained energy from her own daughter, became curious about her mentality. Indigo's mother wasn't a complete energy vampire, but she often suffered from an emotional thirst brought on by the desperate lack of bright experiences in this "wilderness" to which she had followed her husband. Such was the price of a prestigious marriage to a military officer.

It was obvious to me that the girl's hour-long tardiness worried the mother far less than she made it seem to Polina. After all, everyone knew that within a heavily guarded military base surrounded by barbed wire, the dangers of the street for teenagers were practically nonexistent. To be fair to the officer's wife, she grew up in a big city and indeed carried numerous fears, which didn't fit in this small settlement. She feared that her daughter might fall in with a bad crowd, start drinking, take drugs, end up passed around by men, or be harmed by cruel strangers. Bored in the quiet town, Polina's mother often envisioned disturbing stories from urban legends in such vivid detail that their realisation seemed only a matter of time and unavoidable teenage mistakes. She imagined those horrors and desperately tried to instill fear in her daughter, considering it the only means to keep trouble at bay.

On the other hand, this forty-year-old woman could hardly be said to lack pleasure. She rarely felt guilt, which primarily suppresses the orange chakra. At the same time, she criticised others and evoked a sense of guilt in them skillfully, prompting them to make amends by doing nice things for her. Polina's father had been making especially great efforts. His busy service schedule left him with little free time, but he spent most of it eagerly fulfilling his beloved wife's wishes. The woman had turned into a drama queen out of boredom. With her husband often absent, the most accessible and safest form of drama was child-rearing, which she practiced regularly. Polina was brought up to believe the parents lived solely for her sake, and under the pretext of fulfilling her filial duty, the girl was required to treat her mother's nerves and heart with the utmost care. To be honest, that heart was surprisingly healthy considering its frequent tests with pork fat. Polina's mother was always right, at least in her own eyes, and preferred not to notice how different her daughter was from her and other people's children. The girl gave up many of her desires because the mother deemed them harmful or unnecessary. The teenager's anxiety and persistent guilt served as proof that the child's conscience was developing properly, so the sense of righteousness during those hand-on-heart performances was complemented by the satisfaction from fulfilled parental duty.

Thus, the mother truly wasn't letting Polina spiral free, and my indigo girl seemed frozen in the state of a promising, wonderful bud. Sensitive like any teenager, she deeply worried about her "mistakes" and "failures," and didn't let herself become "too proud," meaning she negated her own talents and generally did not think highly of herself. In the end, almost all the energy Polina gained from her restorative time in the forest went towards earning someone's approval. The indigo girl managed to do things her own way only when no one else was around. This was why she preferred solitude. Still, the energy blockages created in her "pleasure chakra" by guilt and anxiety were quite severe.

I returned to the lake in deep contemplation. In just a month of being on my home yet so unknown planet I had won over several adult homo sapiens and tracked down a vampire with their help, but now I suddenly found myself at an impasse. I felt lost before the invisible emotional wall that separated me from a fourteen-year-old girl. And while my tired body was recovering under the protective energy dome, my soul reached out for guidance to that barely discernible point lost among the stars, New Lemuria.

"Dad!" I called out.

Simon immediately responded.

"Hello, son."

He had been watching me all this time, so there was no need for explanations. Now our souls spoke to each other, and in this astral dimension, my father led me somewhere. It was such a relief just to follow without making decisions! Simon and I journeyed deeper into the Lemurian jungles, and with each step, I travelled a day back in time, growing younger and more curious, and then smaller and more inexperienced. After fifteen thousand steps, I was once again a little boy, the one I had been after fleeing the vampire-ravaged Khatyn.

We arrived at a Waterfall of Hope. Its streams glided down gracefully. Each drop of water didn't fall but drifted leisurely through the air, reflecting sunlight in tiny rainbows that little Yasik loved to gaze into so much. Simon carried me into the misty veil of water shimmering with soft colours…

A small, lonely boy, torn away from war, I never questioned how my father and the other Lemurians understood one another without words. After Khatyn's fire, I fell silent for many months, but almost immediately began to hear the inner voices, first of homo liberatus, and soon, the voices of all the living beings that inhabited the planet. It didn't seem strange to me at all. On the contrary, I thought that was the "proper way" and that I hadn't read minds before because I had been little, but now I had simply grown up.

Homo liberatus do not tell their children fairy tales or moral stories. Instead, they simply show them life, setting them free to explore it without constraints, all the while watching closely and always ready to support their little ones. The children are sent to immerse themselves in the world and learn to live in harmony with Nature both within and without. There are no schools on Lemuria. Each newborn homo liberatus becomes the focus of their parents' life for the next ten to twelve years, by the end of which young Lemurians are fully capable of protecting and providing for themselves and begin mastering spiritual practices.

The Earth-born boy had been used to relying on adults. I remembered how, instead of answering questions, my father would simply give an encouraging nod, spurring me on to investigate and discover. Eventually, the answers always revealed themselves without intermediaries, and I developed an understanding of what was right and wrong directly from Nature. Even more than most parents, Simon tried to help me become independent, strong, and wise as he didn't want me to share the fate of Jesus.

I can always rely on my father, even though I outgrew childhood long ago. He remains my best friend. And now, he was pointing me to the path ahead, reviving memories of my own unfolding: I was not meant to be Polina's teacher, but her guide and translator.

Simon knew humans all too well. As we parted, he said, "Your love is the key to success in helping this girl. Don't expect anything good to come from 'magic' born of fear and resentment, but the power unfolded in love will be driven by love."

Chapter 21. Three Moons with Indigo

Homo liberatus do not build castles in the air, which is why we rarely feel disappointed. And worrying about failing someone else's expectations is entirely outside our nature.

It was quite different for Polina: the fear of disappointing her parents, teachers, friends — the whole world! — literally governed my indigo's life. At a mere thought of failure, anxiety would overwhelm and drain her so much that it was astonishing how the poor teenager even had the strength to walk. What a senseless waste of energy!

So, Polina prepared to learn teleportation just as she did mathematics at school — and there she stood, a straight-A student for whom meeting the teacher's expectations had automatically become more important than the art she wished to master. Unwillingly cast as a judge of someone's success, I found myself in a ridiculous trap, while the unfortunate prisoner of a matrix where grades mattered more than knowledge wasn't even aware of her captivity. Discovering a way out of this trap posed a challenge for both of us. All I could do was muster patience and hope that thanks to meditation practice and gradually shifting consciousness, the shackles of Polina's mental prison would weaken. Only then could the healthy energy exchange be restored in this young victim of civilization.

It was nearly summer, and the lakeside grew too crowded. Couples, different ones every evening, often occupied our bench, so while waiting for the trip to her grandmother's, we practiced in a quiet spot in the forest where my indigo girl had loved to go even before we met.

"Answer me this: what is it?" I began, pointing forward with my index finger.

"This? It's a tree," the girl answered, surprised by the question's simplicity. I remained silently expectant, and she added uncertainly, "An oak."

"Good," I agreed. "What do you know about it?"

"Well…" She paused for a moment. "Oaks live long, a hundred years or more."

"Let's say that's right," I responded, trying to keep a neutral expression. "What else?"

Polina hesitated briefly, then quickly recalled, "Of all the trees in the temperate zone, they have the thickest trunks." I grimaced sceptically because the tree before us was young and still rather slender, but the girl, oblivious to my reaction, continued. "Acorns grow on its branches and fall to the ground. New oaks grow from them." My protégé paused and looked at me with a question in her eyes, wondering what more I expected her to say, but I remained silent, deliberately provoking confusion. Flustered, she blurted out, "Furniture… and paper… are made from trees too."

At this point, I couldn't help myself and burst out laughing. "Where did you find all that?"

"I don't know… can't remember," Polina replied, embarrassed and puzzled. "I must have read it somewhere, or maybe they told us at school… or even in the nursery. What's so funny?" she asked, finally feeling offended.

"I'm sorry! Of course, I shouldn't have laughed," I apologised. "You just completely misunderstood my question. I meant, what do you know about *this* tree? You often come here, don't you?"

"Well, yes…"

"Go on! It's more of a rhetorical question. I know it's almost like your friend!"

"That's true!" Polina agreed, and her face lit up with a radiant smile. "All right… I get it. *This* oak is still young. It grows in the shade of other trees, and that's probably why its leaves come out so late. Look, everything else is green, but its buds have only started to swell."

"Well done!" At last, we were on the right track. "Anything else?"

"There's a bird's nest at the top. See it there?" She pointed to a barely visible dark knot of twigs hidden among the thick branches. "It appeared last year. I wonder if anything lives there now…"

"It does," I said, winking knowingly. The girl smiled again but said nothing.

"Is that all?" I asked, and she nodded in confusion. "Tell me, child, why do you always come to this particular spot when you have an entire forest at your disposal?"

Polina had never asked herself this question.

"I don't know. I just feel drawn here I suppose…"

"Well done!" I praised her again, though she didn't understand why. The matrix didn't impart praise for not knowing something. "Because this is a place of power, and you found it all by yourself! And this oak is a conductor of energy despite its youth. Its roots reach deeper into the earth than those of other trees, drawing nourishment from the depths and bringing energy to the surface. Many creatures come here day and night to replenish their strength, and your oak generously shares its energy with the forest dwellers." Having remembered Uncle Pasha's apple tree, I smiled. "That's why its leaves appear late. Out of all the people, it seems only you felt how special this tree was." Polina listened, as if spellbound. "*Oak* and *tree* are merely words that allow you to categorise the world — that's what you tried to do at first."

"But everything I said is true, too!" the girl objected, still offended.

"What's true?" I exclaimed, unable to suppress resentment. When it comes to Earth's Nature, the extermination of forests by humans is one of the most painful topics for Lemurians. "That furniture is made from oaks? A rather sad truth! Who even came up with the idea of stealing trees from Nature to make sitting and storing junk more convenient?"

"People…"

"And people named the trees as well. Mere homo sapiens! Probably to make it easier to learn how to stockpile firewood!"

Polina hunched her shoulders as if she were personally to blame for homo sapiens cutting down trees for millennia to make their trinkets and buildings. I finally came to my senses. "Now now, this has nothing to do with you! Go ahead and hug your friend." The girl obediently moved in my direction. "Not me — the oak!"

"What?" Polina stopped and stared, wide-eyed. "Do you want me to hug the oak?"

"Haven't you ever done that?" I asked with a mischievous wink, and she blushed again. Polina kept forgetting about my direct access to her thoughts, and when she remembered, she felt exposed. "I know that when you're alone, you talk to plants like they're living beings, and you're right to do so. Go on!"

There was no need to repeat the request. Polina approached the tree, took a deep breath, closed her eyes, and wrapped her arms around it, and I immediately wished I could take the oak's place. My indigo girl melted into the tree's powerful energy, blending with it and standing there for a long time, finally free of worrying about my presence. This was, indeed, the best place around for mastering so-called "magic," that is, the ability to reveal and amplify human potential.

When Polina finally opened her eyes and stepped away from the young oak, I said, "Now answer me one more question: who are you?"

This time she didn't rush to reply. All the roles she had been forced to play, like a small, thoughtless cog in society's machine, lined up impatiently in the teenager's mind.

"You're a girl, and you should take care of your looks!" her mother scolded whenever Polina forgot to brush her hair or attempted to leave the house in a wrinkled blouse. The officer's wife worried that the girl's untidy appearance would affect the mother's reputation in the small town, where everyone knew each other.

"You're my daughter, and you should be the best!" her father insisted, expecting Polina to excel at school and heaven knows what else. It's hard to imagine a more absurd motive for achievement than this one, turning a child into a tool for satisfying parental vanity! Luckily or not, my indigo found learning effortless. She was at the top of the class anyway, so extra pressure only created unnecessary tension, subtly squeezing energy out of her.

"You're a top student — you must set an example for others," her teacher repeated, hoping that at least this quiet, intelligent child wouldn't complicate her life. For a naturally humble girl, the "duty" of setting an example was a burden.

"You're a pioneer, and you should show initiative!" the youth leader tried to inspire her, hoping to off-load some work onto the creative child. Polina did organise a couple of themed evenings at school, genuinely wanting to make the world around her more interesting and vibrant, in her own way. And it came as a complete surprise to the poor indigo when the other children saw her as a show-off because of it.

"You're my friend, and you must help me!" whined Lena from next door whenever she wanted to copy Polina's math homework. If it weren't for the pressing issue of assignments, this same envious Lena would have gladly bullied my indigo, whom she secretly called "not of this world," but as it was, Polina's classmates simply kept their distance unless they needed something.

"Should, should, should… But I'm not what I should be for others! And anyway, why should I be?" Suddenly Polina was struck by the obviousness of this thought. The roles imposed by the matrix now seemed small and even somehow unreal. It was an eye-opening moment: the people forcing her into these roles saw her as nothing more than a tool for achieving their goals, which often had nothing to do with what Polina wanted for herself.

I waited patiently for an answer. At last, my indigo girl looked at me with dignity, raised her chin proudly and a little funny, and declared with confidence, "I am a person."

And I replied, "Excellent! You've grasped your first lesson."

Let me clarify. The children of Lemuria begin their growth path by learning about the surrounding world and themselves as part of it. When asked, "Who are you?" they answer, "I am a part."

***

Like my late mother, a herbalist, Polina had a special connection with plants. She very quickly began to sense the flow of life within everything that sank its roots into the earth. Even before we met, she talked to flowers, and after just two days of meditation, she could already distinguish the energy of an oak tree from that of a birch or a pine. Then she puzzled me with a question.

"You don't eat the flesh of living beings, but you eat plants — and they're alive too!"

"That's correct," I said.

"Then why is it that you — I mean, your people — think it's wrong to kill animals but acceptable to pluck and devour plants?" She stroked the ferns beside us. "And don't tell me that apple trees or walnut trees have no souls or feel no pain! Animals can run away from a hunter at least, but plants can't. They're completely defenceless... Cutting them down is even more despicable than killing animals!"

Now that was true Lemurian logic!

"You're right, plants sense everything," I said. "At the same time, by eating their fruits, we cause no pain to the trunk, the stem, or the branches, because fruits are Nature's way of providing nourishment. Their flesh is to plants what mother's milk is to mammals — it's created specifically to feed offspring and therefore given away without pain or regret. A woman or a female animal usually has enough milk to feed their child, but sometimes she has more than enough and can even nourish another's young. When a child moves on to solid food, the mother's breasts still produce milk, which she must release to avoid discomfort.

"Incidentally, Lemurians don't reject animal milk either, but we only drink it after ensuring the animal's young won't go hungry. Want one?" I asked, offering Polina an apple, and she took the fruit, carefully preserved by humans since autumn, but didn't hurry to eat it. The girl brought it close to her eyes and examined its slightly wrinkled skin. "Now you'll eat the apple, and then scatter the seeds on the ground," I encouraged her. "They'll have a chance to sprout."

"Do you eat seeds?" she asked.

"Well… sometimes we do. But, you know, our digestive system is an open one, just like yours." I accompanied the words with a vertical gesture from head to stomach. Polina giggled and took a bite of the apple. "So, by disapproving of cutting down trees while eating their fruits, we're neither contradicting ourselves nor Nature," I concluded.

Communicating and exchanging energy with our green neighbours was a good starting point in training my indigo girl. Polina had already done it intuitively anyway, and I merely encouraged her, helping recognise the source of her bond with the forest. Unfortunately, mastering her own body's abilities proved much harder for the girl. Plants direct their energy in a single continuous flow, whereas humans are far more complex beings and can only control the forces of their physical and subtle bodies after clearing all their chakras of blockages.

When it comes to suppressing, clogging, and blocking their own and others' energy centres, homo sapiens know no equal. Nature gifted them with intelligence, making them richer in it than most of Earth's inhabitants. Yet humans have used this gift not to cooperate with Nature, but to defend themselves against it and to exploit it as much as possible. And even that wasn't enough for them, so homo sapiens began exploiting each other through laws, taboos, morals, and traditions. They invented weapons to keep others in no less fear than their own one, thus locking themselves into an endless vicious circle.

One can only break free from the matrix outside the society that created it. That's why the most enlightened humans are often hermits. However, before we met, Polina's desire for solitude was less about seeking enlightenment and more about escaping a world that bothered her with its coarseness and insensitivity. My indigo girl was still a slave to the polarised dual system. Books and films had filled her mind with ideas of "good" and "evil," school had defined what was "proper" and "improper" behaviour, and her mother constantly drilled into her what was "healthy" and "harmful," despite having rather limited knowledge on the subject herself.

A three-month trip to stay with the grandmother was more than timely. The small seaside village was the perfect place to spend long summer days training and meditating to the sound of waves crashing against the rocks. The old woman — and I call her that purely out of convention since Baba Olya looked barely over sixty and had the energy to outshine a somewhat lazy forty-year-old daughter-in-law — was utterly devoted to her only granddaughter. She was so overjoyed at the child's arrival for the whole summer that she would not even entertain the thought of nitpicking, which could discourage the growing girl from future visits.

The elderly woman was far more tolerant than Polina's mother. Her mind was so occupied with daily concerns that it seemed to stop there. She did not seem to ever think of her past, so I couldn't learn much about it. Not that I tried very hard, since the granddaughter interested me far more than the grandmother.

I settled on the working theory that Baba Olya, aging and likely battered by life in the human matrix, had inherited only a balanced, fear-free disposition and respect for freedom from homo liberatus. She let her granddaughter roam wherever she pleased, only insisting that Polina, who swam like a fish and spent entire days at the beach during every visit, come home before dark.

Polina loved staying with her liberal-minded granny, but accustomed to living under her mother's strict rules, she took the conditions of her freedom far too literally. As soon as the sun's edge touched the horizon, my indigo girl would fall into anxiety instead of absorbing the energy the sea released at sunset so abundantly. I couldn't persuade her that all this worry, this storm in a teacup, was hopelessly pushing us away from the goal. At first, I tried to use gentle persuasion to keep my trainee from rushing off before dark. When Polina jumped to her feet, preparing to leave early yet again, I grabbed her sleeve and asked, "Where are you going? It's still early!"

"Let go! I need to go home!" My indigo girl jerked her hand away, drowning in a wave of irritation, both from my repetitive question and her fear of offending me. Eventually, my patience wore out. There was no point trying to discuss things in the evenings when Polina was in such a frazzled state. I waited till the next morning, and as soon as she appeared on the deserted beach we used for our practices, I said, "We need to have a serious talk. What's happening to you in the evenings?"

"What do you mean?" the girl asked, her cheeks flushing bright red.

"What makes you so anxious when it's time to go home?"

"You know what," Polina replied reluctantly.

"I do, but I want to hear it from you."

She rolled her eyes, heaved a sigh, and mumbled, "Well… I'm afraid of upsetting Grandma if I get home too late."

"And why are you afraid?"

She shot me such an indignant look it was as if I had blasphemed in a church.

"Don't you understand?" Polina exclaimed. "Grandma is old! What if she gets so worried her heart gives out?"

"Is your mother old too?" I knew my questions sounded cruel from a human perspective, but it was the mercilessness of a surgeon cutting into flesh to remove a tumour. That's how it is with homo sapiens: everything beneficial to them is either painful or unpalatable.

"N-no, of course not... Mum isn't old... Maybe a little... But she raised me! She didn't sleep nights!"

"Were you a wanted child?"

Polina looked at me in surprise and, after a short hesitation, replied, "I guess so... Mum always says I was. Why do you ask?"

"Because deciding to bring a helpless baby into the world automatically means accepting responsibility for it and being ready for temporary inconveniences."

Polina nodded. "Y-yes, of course."

"So sleepless nights and caring for a baby are sacred parental duties. You don't owe her anything for that!" Despite my ironclad logic, these arguments seemed absurd to my indigo. She heard me, recognised my reasoning, but her mind rejected the blasphemous claim that her mother had no right to claim gratitude for fulfilling her natural role. Unsure how to respond, the young indigo remained silent, and I reminded her, "Besides, your mother is younger than me."

"Well... you're different!" Polina clung to this justification like a lifeline.

"Exactly!" I agreed with an ironic smile. "I differ in that I can sense the state of cells and tissues in any living organism. And I can say with certainty that neither your mother nor your granny has any hint of heart problems." I hesitated, debating whether to continue, but couldn't resist adding, "Though your father could use some work on his heart instead of hiding the symptoms because he's too afraid of worrying his perfectly healthy wife. How is that fair?"

I stopped to catch my breath and, realising I'd gone too far, immediately regretted my sharpness. Polina stared at me with wide eyes. On top of debunking the myth of maternal infallibility, she now had new worries about her father. I shouldn't have dumped so much on her… Still, what had been said couldn't be taken back, and the only sensible option was to make the most of the moment.

"Can you see how absurd your worries are?" I asked. Polina frowned and bit her lip so hard that her mouth became a thin line. Her world was once again turning upside down. I softened my voice as much as I could. "Don't think your mum is lying when she clutches her heart. She truly believes she could die of a heart attack if she worries too much. However, not everything people believe is true. Do you understand?"

Polina didn't answer, but I knew she was seething inside. I raised my hand in a calming gesture. Her energy, directed against me, was becoming tiring, but there was no other way forward but to lance this boil.

"No feeling is more destructive than guilt. You must get rid of the habit of giving in to it for the slightest reason. Once and for all."

"So, do homo liberatus never make mistakes to feel guilty?" the indigo girl asked sharply, having listened to me with silent distrust.

"Of course we make mistakes, though rarely."

"And what do you do then?"

"Exactly that — we act! We fix things wherever possible, and make amends for any harm — caused unintentionally, since none of us is capable of harming deliberately. Do you understand the difference between feeling guilty and correcting a mistake, between suffering from a destructive emotion and acting rationally?"

"And what if you can't fix something or make amends? For example, if someone dies because of you?"

"Then we let go. Firstly, there is no death in Nature, only transformation. And secondly, not all tragedies remain tragedies when viewed from a broader perspective..." I stopped short. The truth, spoken aloud by my own lips, pierced my heart like a sharp thorn. If my mother had not perished in the fire of Khatyn, I could neither have carried out nor even started my mission.

"And does it not hurt you at all? Do you feel no regret?" Polina asked defiantly, mistaking my pause for hesitation.

"Of course it hurts," I admitted, unable to suppress a heavy sigh. "We grieve for lost loved ones no less than you do, but we are not afraid of justified risks or their consequences, because we are incapable of feeling fear. In making choices, we always follow the guidance of our subtle essence — our conscience. This sets us apart from villains, who act solely to satisfy their base needs. Villains have completely lost connection to their conscience, which makes them the primary victims of homo sapiens' civilization." Speaking of villains, I had vampires in mind, but I still did not want to burden the teenager with talk of my mission. For now, she needed to figure herself out.

Polina shrank into herself. Conflicting thoughts fought desperately in her mind. Following the voice of the subtle essence, as homo liberatus did, sounded wonderful, but what should she do with everything she had been taught so far? And if she abandoned the rules ingrained in her since childhood, how was she supposed to live until she heard that voice of *the true conscience*? I sympathised with her doubts. After all, she was being required to abandon a fundamental principle of the homo sapiens' matrix! Unfortunately, if Polina wanted to uncover and develop her indigo abilities, there was no other way for her but to take control of her guilt and her urge to live up to people's expectations. As for me, I had to be firm. I could not afford to wander in the fog of uncertainty or indulge in petty human games.

"Listen," I said, "all living beings care for their loved ones in one way or another, but that means offering help in times of need, not making unjustified sacrifices. To waste nearly a day's worth of energy worrying about potential misfortunes or apologising for every disapproved action is a violation of Nature's energy exchange. The views, opinions, and feelings of even your dearest people are theirs, not yours. If you want to develop your abilities, you must clear your mental space of everything that destroys it. Sweep it out with a filthy broom. If you can't, then there's no point in continuing this practice."

My words hit Polina like a cold shower. She said nothing but understood me well — I could see it. Until then, the girl had not considered constantly worrying about her mother's nerves harmful to her own inner balance. Now that she had started to think about it, she could not deny the fact that insatiable guilt, like a noose around her neck, had been tightening each year, increasingly cutting off access to her true self. I was indeed asking too much of a fourteen-year-old, but there was no other way to help her. Even to pull someone out of quicksand, you need the drowning person to reach out their hand to the rescuer. There must be a will to live. My indigo girl had to finally choose between her own path and living to please others. And to stop Polina's decision from being blind, I braced myself and added this.

"Before you decide how to move forward, you must know one more thing. Indigo people like you inherit some of the homo liberatus' abilities, but never the full spectrum. And, in truth, I don't know exactly what will come of your training. There will certainly be results because you can sense and understand plants even with your chakras clogged. And that's just a small share of your talents. You will learn a lot, but teleportation is the most complex skill possessed by the inhabitants of Lemuria. It may remain beyond your grasp, no matter how much effort you make, even if you completely change your attitude not only towards your loved ones but also towards the whole world."

"Can't you do something to me... if I fail to teleport?" Polina asked hesitantly. "I mean, you cure cancer, influence cells..."

"That's not the same thing at all!" I laughed. "A disease is just a malfunction in the body, but changing genetics would mean going against Nature — an endeavour doomed to failure."

Polina sighed in disappointment.

"I will leave you alone now to think it all over carefully," I said as gently as I could. "If you decide to give yourself — *and me too*," I added to myself — "a chance, meet me here tomorrow morning. Otherwise, we'll have to say goodbye."

Without further argument, I disappeared from Polina's sight, and she remained sitting on the warm sand, hugging her knees, gazing at the almost perfectly smooth, murmuring sea, as if hoping to fish the right answer from its silvery waves. The poor girl's heart ached, torn between her thirst for knowledge and fear of loneliness. The latter is inseparable from the freedom of spirit in the world of homo sapiens — it is an ordeal too much even for most adults. One thing was clear: my indigo girl, though unconsciously, was already turning to her subtle essence for guidance. All I could do was hope that a piece of Lemuria would triumph over human imperfection and help Polina conquer her fears.

Invisible, I stayed near her until my heart grew tired of aching in unison with hers. Being unable to help my beloved felt unbearable. No matter where I went, I could still hear her thoughts. The only way to distance myself was to find something to do, so I headed to Veliky Novgorod to visit the Pilatovs. I didn't announce my presence but decided to simply observe how Uncle Pasha and the young lovers were getting on.

***

A month and a half had passed since Nina Vladimirovna's funeral. The radio played softly in the house of the retired KGB special agent. Lyuba Pilatova, for almost a week, busied herself in the spacious kitchen. Something simmered on the stove, yet the young woman kept freezing in place, arms crossed, staring blankly at the white birch trunk outside the window, lit by a ray of midday June sunlight.

Fleeing her parental home before her father's imminent arrest felt like an outright betrayal. Lyuba was tormenting herself, and although she had not the slightest doubt about the former SS officer's crimes or the justice of the punishment awaiting him, guilt gnawed at her, mercilessly eroding the joy and love for her husband that was blossoming day by day. It felt as if the vampire still fed off his rebellious daughter's energy, maintaining his grip on her even from afar. For days now, Lyuba had been restless, bitterly comparing herself to Pavlik Morozov*. It was drizzling grimly and foully in her soul, and that drizzle's drops kept spilling from her kind golden-brown eyes now and then.

She felt particularly wretched now, just after a very quiet wedding ceremony at one of Kiev's registry offices and receiving the university diploma in her new surname. After her graduation, Andrei had brought his new wife to this beautiful old house on the outskirts of Veliky Novgorod and journeyed to Moscow the next day to resign from the service, while Lyuba stayed back in the care of Colonel Pilatov.

She knew almost nothing about her husband's uncle, except that Pavel Andreevich, a highly respected man, had retired, allegedly due to a terminal illness. Yet she saw no sign of it. Uncle Pasha, perhaps even too energetic for his age, was kind to his niece-in-law, but his piercing eyes, one transparently blue and the other light brown, unnerved her almost as much as Vasyura's dark, menacing gaze. Andrei had mentioned the colonel only in passing, claiming there was no time for details yet, but it was clear he was deliberately keeping something secret.

Lyuba suspected her relation to a traitor of the Motherland was the reason for this mistrust, and she felt so small and wretched that she dared neither speak unnecessarily nor raise her eyes, instead losing herself in speculation. The involuntary comparison of the charismatic colonel to her father sent shivers down her spine every time Pavel Andreevich appeared. What terrified her most was the realisation that her current situation was indeed the best solution possible.

The retired KGB special forces colonel returned from the garden. Striding briskly into the kitchen, he instantly took in the gloomy atmosphere pervading the woman's domain. *"Time to build bridges,"* he thought, and addressed his young niece-in-law as cheerfully as he could. "Well, Lyubasha, settling in? It smells wonderful!"

Lyuba flinched, turned around, panicked, and replied in a near whisper. "Y-yes, Pavel Andreevich. Thank you…"

"By the way, my dear, you're not obliged to handle the housekeeping," the colonel continued gently. "The neighbour did a fine job before you came, and we're quite comfortable to continue this way, thank god."

"Oh, no, Pavel Andreevich, it's no trouble," Lyuba replied softly. *"What else can I offer in return for shelter?"* she thought mournfully, only to meet the old scout's perceptive gaze.

"This isn't a shelter. It's your husband's ancestral home," Pilatov said seriously, as though reading her thoughts. Lyuba was so startled she was speechless, but Uncle Pasha asked imperturbably, "Have you been crying?"

The girl shook her head.

He smiled wryly. "It's pointless lying to me! Turn off your stew and let's have a chat. The kettle's boiling too. Perfect timing!" Taking his frail new relative by her slender shoulders, Pilatov guided her to the sitting room and pointed to the light green sofa. "Take a seat."

Completely crushed and even more frightened, Lyuba obeyed. She sank into the corner of the sofa, picked up an old doll she'd brought from home, and began fidgeting with the yellowed lace of the once-luxurious dress of the toy princess, in which I recognised Jadwiga, Sonya Yaskievich's favourite toy.

While the terrifying Pilatov brewed tea, Lyuba's heart pounded in her temples, and tears again began to fall. Entering the sitting room, Pavel Andreevich reflected that only at such a young age could someone endure so much pain without lasting damage.

"What a beauty!" he praised, pointing at Jadwiga. "What's her name?"

"Oksana," sniffed the niece-in-law.

"She looks older than you."

"She is," Lyuba replied in a sad voice. "Father sent her to my sister as a war trophy… a gift, but my sister never liked her. And I… Oksana's like a friend to me.

"My only friend!" she finished silently, inhaling sharply and suppressing a sob.

She'd always felt Oksana was alive, mourning something and guarding some tragic secret. I too was curious how Jadwiga, now renamed Oksana, had ended up with Vasyura's daughters when Vasyura could hardly have set foot in the Yaskievich household in person.

"Listen, my dear," Pavel Andreevich finally began. "What kind of relationship do you have with your father?"

The young woman sighed heavily and shrugged, shivering at the memories Vasyura's name invoked.

"Got it," the colonel concluded. "And yet you feel guilty for leaving. As if you ran away."

"Another guilty one!" I thought irritably. *"It's worse than a disease with them!"*

"But I did run away!" Lyuba objected. "You see, it's killing me!" She clasped her hands in despair and gasped.

The old man, however, remained calm as he probed further. "What exactly do you think you're guilty of?"

"Betraying my father!"

The former KGB colonel nodded. He was a homo sapien and therefore understood Lyuba's feelings better than I ever could.

"I won't preach to you about how that man betrayed his country," he said quietly but firmly. "Let's leave that aside. He betrayed human nature itself."

"Spot on!" I thought, praising the old hypnotist.

Uncle Pasha repeated the question Lyuba had often asked herself.

"So, is that good or bad, betraying a traitor?"

Vasyura's daughter stared at him in confusion.

"I — I don't know... Maybe bad. Because that would make me a traitor too!" And her tears started afresh.

Pavel Andreevich sat beside Lyuba. He rested his strong, dry hand over her thin wrist.

"You feel ashamed of both yourself and your father, so your reasoning makes sense," he said. "Now, imagine if you'd stayed with Vasyura. You'd carry the stigma of being a Nazi's daughter your whole life — and would still change your surname eventually. You wouldn't have helped your father, nor would you have wanted to." Vasyura's younger daughter lowered her head, reluctantly accepting the colonel's argument. "As for whether betraying a traitor is right or wrong — there's no answer. Or rather, everyone has their own."

"Well played, Uncle Pasha! No pressure on the girl. Nicely done!" I thought.

"What should I do now?" Lyuba asked through quiet sobs.

"Just live!" Pavel Andreevich declared. "Don't think about atonement — think about restoring balance. You're a good girl. Just by existing, you counterbalance your father's sins. Live for others. Do as much good as Vasyura did evil. It's simple. You're a trained teacher now. We'll find you work at the local school.

Just make sure you learn to understand goodness properly. It can't be forced."

And so, the daughter of former SS executioner Grigory Vasyura and the retired KGB colonel became friends.

***

When I returned to our spot the next morning, Polina was already there waiting for me. If it hadn't been for her change of clothes, one might have thought she had spent the entire night here, gazing out at the sea in search of answers. My indigo girl not only wore a new dress — she seemed to have crossed an invisible boundary and stepped into a new dimension. The moment I brushed against her thoughts, I exhaled in relief. After weathering a powerful emotional storm through the night, Polina had ultimately embraced her true nature. The decision had been made. Now the girl's heart was beating steadily, and her mind was clear, as if the previous day's struggle had never occurred. Only by knowing her thoughts could I grasp the intense contradictions this young soul had managed to overcome in just one day.

I was in awe of her willpower. Polina no longer fled in haste at sunset. When old habits threatened to resurface, she used the technique of mental detachment I had taught her. That is, imagining herself as someone else and observing events that caused emotional discord as if from the outside in. Homo liberatus rarely use it. Devoid of fear, the source of a good half of complex human emotions, my kind consider strong feelings refreshing. Nevertheless, mental detachment has proven invaluable when dealing with humans. Without it, I might have killed Vasyura on the first day, and Polina might have lost her innocence already. And for her, the mental detachment had become as vital as air to achieve inner balance.

The energy centres of my young indigo were restoring themselves not by the day but by the hour. Liberating her lower chakras gradually paved the way for visible progress, and it wasn't long before results came. Polina almost immediately learned to move sand without touching it, though shifting heavier objects did not come as easily. She grew frustrated at her lack of progress — and this frustration only held her back. At least I thought so.

One warm July evening, the girl announced she wouldn't go home until the beach bag flew straight into her hands. Polina sat near the water's edge while the large bag lay under a bush ten steps away. After countless unsuccessful attempts, when it had nearly grown dark, I decided to step in.

"It's time to go home, remember?" It appeared we have swapped roles.

"Yes, yes, I know!" Polina waved me off in irritation, and suddenly a branch of the bush bent and gave the bag a good shove while my indigo girl drew the long-awaited item towards herself. I couldn't believe my eyes. Her ability to communicate with plants surpassed even mine, and her anger at her repeated failures had transformed into a driving force! That was remarkable! Not everything about indigoes worked the same way as it did for homo liberatus!

It was completely dark by then, and I had to teleport Polina home. Baba Olya greeted her with a barely noticeable tremor in her voice. "Why were you so late today, Pólya? Are you all right?"

The granddaughter wrapped her in a tight hug and sang out, "Sorry for being late, Granny, everything's just wonderful!" She planted a kiss on the wrinkled cheek and waltzed across the spacious veranda, adding, "I love you so much!" This was a new, stronger Polina.

The indigo girl didn't get along particularly well with the local children. When Polina was little, Baba Olya had tried to provide her with company, occasionally taking her to play with two rather dim-witted and noisy neighbour boys with whom

Olga's granddaughter had nothing in common. Polina rather preferred to sit with a book in the garden or build sandcastles on the beach, alone. Two years ago, when her granny finally deemed her old enough to explore their surroundings independently, the girl was over the moon. Of course, Krasnodar Krai was no Lemuria. A fourteen-year-old couldn't stop depending on others simply by making such a decision. I stayed invisible to the human eye almost the entire time I was near her. If the villagers saw Olga's granddaughter in the company of a strange adult male, Polina's freedom would likely end.

The neighbour boys had grown up too. Their parents worked at the collective grape farm and saw very little of their children during the busy summer season. The teenagers stayed around the house to help. When chores were done, village boys, dressed in long shorts, roamed the shore in small groups with fishing rods, craving adventure. Although Polina and I had chosen the most secluded corner of the beach, seemingly walled off for us by a natural barrier of rocky outcrops, the arrival of the ever-curious local youth was only a matter of time.

So, one day, about six boys spotted a female figure from the cliff overlooking the beach. Polina sat motionless in the lotus position on a strip of white sand. Those lads knew better than anyone how impossible it was to reach that spot from the shore, but seeing there a girl, whose face they could not recognise from afar, they couldn't resist issuing themselves a challenge. Slowly and stubbornly, and risking broken limbs, the boys began to make their way to our inaccessible beach across the slippery boulders. Polina and I usually teleported there, but seeing the unexpected visitors, I recalled her recent telekinetic success with the beach bag and decided not to intervene too soon this time. I picked up the notorious bag from the sand and vanished from sight.

As soon as the boys' voices echoed over the boulders, Polina called out without turning around, "Yan! Ya-an!" Talking to the intruders was the last thing she wanted. She would have to explain how a girl had managed to climb over sharp wet rocks alone and what she was doing there anyway. Besides, Baba Olya couldn't find out her granddaughter was taking such risks, and the neighbour boys wouldn't keep quiet. "Ya-an!" she called again, glancing around, but there was no answer and no sign of me.

Exposure loomed closer. Finally, the bare feet of the most agile boy landed on our side of the rocks, where he would see the girl's face and identify her. Yet the proud hero with a tanned torso saw only a couple of jellyfish washed up on the sand.

"Where's the girl?" he exclaimed.

"Maybe it was just a trick of the light?" guessed one of the others.

"What, for all of us at once?"

Proud of having successfully stormed this elusive spot, the group sprawled out on the beach, clearly planning to stay for a while. And Polina pressed herself against a large sheer rock, still not realising the breakthrough she had just made.

"Shhh..." I whispered, turning up behind her. "Look at your hands!"

Finally realising she had become invisible, my indigo girl clamped her transparent palm over her mouth, trying to stifle a cry of surprise and joy. I took her by the shoulders, and we teleported to the other side of the rocky wall.

Thus, I discovered that strong emotions and a sense of imminent danger could indeed push homo sapiens to the very edge of their potential. I had heard about it before, at Unity, but only with Polina did I see firsthand how human fear, both primary and secondary, could transform into strength. My kind had discarded this response mechanism hundreds of millennia ago, though it was likely fear that initially spurred the Lemurians' desire to master the art of vanishing from enemies' sight and teleporting to safety. For modern homo liberatus, adrenaline is more a companion to exciting adventures or a precursor to romantic escapades. I often felt its surge near Polina and didn't always resort to mental detachment, because never had I experienced such a thirst for life as I did during each day spent next to my indigo girl.

Our time was running out. I was glad that I had not been disturbed for these three moons, but I found it amusing that while Polina had learned to move objects over considerable distances and become invisible to the human eye, not to mention using mental detachment and anxiety-relieving meditation, the government could not simply arrange for Vasyura's arrest. The bureaucratic procedure was ridiculously long. According to Colonel Pilatov, this was completely unsurprising and nothing to worry about... So I did not.

Undoubtedly, I could be proud of my protégé's progress. She still couldn't read thoughts, but that didn't seem to trouble her much. However, her failures with teleportation deeply upset the girl, despite my repeated warnings about the difficulty and potential impossibility of mastering such an art. Polina felt perfectly fine "riding my coattails," but she couldn't manage to move through space on her own, and it was the ability to overcome great distance in mere seconds that she saw as the key to her freedom. Day after day, she exhausted herself with desperate attempts to teleport at least a couple of metres. My indigo girl worried that training time was running out, and she hated herself, pushing back her success precisely because she wanted to succeed so badly. The only way out of this vicious circle was becoming free from despair, the main stumbling block.

"You must understand," I tried to explain, "a truly free person is one, who isn't ruled by desires, anger, resentment, or fear of failure. These are the things that enslave homo sapiens far more than any physical limitations."

Her utterly hopeless gaze was the answer. How could a teenager raised in a consumer-driven society even begin to imagine a state of freedom from desire? And then her despair burst out in a flood of tears. I felt so sorry for the poor girl!

I must say that throughout our acquaintance, I had never touched Polina, except when necessary to hold her shoulders for teleportation. I avoided physical contact to keep myself in check because I wanted this humanly imperfect yet utterly enchanting being too much. I wanted someone whose soul was entirely unprepared for love…

But how could I not comfort a crying child? I lost my vigilance and embraced Polina, and she buried her sniffing nose into my bare shoulder, her warm, salty tears soaking my skin. My beloved shook with sobs in my arms, and a wave of heat rose within me. I held her, perhaps too tightly, because suddenly my indigo girl stopped crying, lifted her tear-streaked face, and, blinking her wet eyelashes, looked questioningly into my eyes. Her glistening bright crimson lips were right in front of mine, and I couldn't resist. I kissed her. Properly, as a man kisses a woman with whom he is passionately in love. In the blink of an eye, she was behind a nearby rock, twenty paces from where I had been holding her.

Polina had transformed into a beautiful young woman before my eyes over that summer, but she had thought of me as a friend until that moment. Once we started the mental practices, she had viewed me as a teacher, that is, someone entirely devoid of gender. She had no idea that the only reason a man devotes so much time and effort to a woman who crosses his path by chance is because he feels a powerful attraction to her…

Polina sat on the grass, bewildered, not just by the sudden first-ever kiss but also by her unexpected success with teleportation, on which she had given up hope only moments earlier. Even from a distance, I could feel the vibrations of her energy — not thoughts or desires, but actual vibrations.

The incident stunned me too. I had never heard that anyone of my kind used such methods to train indigoes! Something had to be done, because it certainly wasn't the time for a confession of love.

I began slowly closing the distance between us, sensing Polina's racing heartbeat. Mine wasn't any calmer, to be honest. I stopped behind the cliff. She couldn't see me but knew I was some two steps away.

"Did you get frightened?" I asked cautiously.

"I… I don't know," came the quiet — and honest — answer. "Why did you…?"

I was glad my indigo girl hadn't yet mastered telepathy. Once again, I used the homo-sapien trick — a lie.

"That was a last resort. To provoke an emotional reaction. Like when you wanted to hide from those boys, remember?" Despite her silence, I could tell my explanation had almost worked, so I promised her this: "I'm sorry. It won't happen again."

She sighed disappointedly, and her disappointment sent a wave of triumph through me. But it was important to seize the moment and consolidate the breakthrough. Besides, my natural curiosity as a homo liberatus took over once more. I have said before: in the Lemurians, abilities of soul and body develop through prolonged meditation, interaction with Nature, self-awareness, and mastery of energy flows — and certainly not through emotional upheavals! The way my indigo girl kept reaching new heights through adrenaline surges was a true revelation.

"Let's try to focus again on the sensations that led to the teleportation," I said, then indicated the spot. "Sit here. Close your eyes. Try to evoke the same feelings, starting from when you fell into despair and began to cry — and beyond. What was it? Surely something powerful." I admit I enjoyed revisiting her fresh memories. “Despair… Surprise?” I tried to sound detached, though I probably failed.

“Shock!” Polina said. That seemed to her the main cause of the “miracle” that had just occurred.

“Shock played a role, of course,” I agreed, “but not quite in the way you think. It stopped you from forming a judgment of whether what happened was good or bad, right or wrong. Now you’re already trying to fit the kiss into your value system. That’s what distracts you and blocks your energy again. Forget it. It’s completely unnecessary. Just try to relive the emotions, including the urge to be somewhere else.”

I fell silent, letting Polina sort out her mental space. She sat in the sand with her eyes closed, replaying the past few minutes, and suddenly the girl disappeared and reappeared again, this time sitting in the water, where the gentle waves lapped at the dark sand. She squealed and jumped to her feet, her thin, soaking through dress clinging to her legs. Polina burst out in happy laughter, and I laughed too.

“Good thing you didn’t end up in deep water!”

“So what? I’m a great swimmer!” she retorted cheerfully.

In truth, the risk of uncontrolled teleportation into the open sea was unlikely at this stage. The progress was still rather humble. Over the next few days, my indigo girl managed to stabilise her teleportation, though only by a few metres, and even that did not happen regularly. Still, as they say, a journey of a thousand miles begins with a single step.

Polina’s best skill remained invisibility. Who could say why? Perhaps because it didn’t require physical interaction with other objects, or perhaps the desire to become invisible had long been rooted in the soul of this introverted teenager.

Only three days remained before her departure back to Belorussia, and the Unity was about to begin on the New Lemuria.

Then Polina announced, "I don't want to go back. I want to go with you!" She used her most forbidden trick, looking into my eyes so that everything inside me turned upside down. "Pleeeeeease!"

I cast a regretful glance at her figure, shaped and matured over the summer, her two heavy braids, sun-bleached from straw-coloured to almost pure blond, and her long, tanned legs... I wished never to part with her more than anything in the world! Polina knew perfectly well that there was no place for her in Lemuria, yet she was still waiting for my answer with some crazy hope. She sensed my hesitation in the prolonged pause.

"How will I live among others now?" she whined, playing the victim.

I smirked. "The same way as before, unless you go boasting about your achievements."

"And what if I do?" she asked with a hint of provocation.

"Well... in that case, the intelligence service I encountered two months ago will probably pay you a visit, and that'll be the end of your childhood."

"Wow! They might recruit me as a spy?" Polina exclaimed, her eyes gleaming with vanity.

"Most likely," I sighed. "I imagine they'd be especially interested in your ability to turn invisible... And if that happens, you'll regret it soon enough."

"What's so bad about it?" my naive protegee asked.

"The problem is that any intelligence service, by definition, targets an enemy based on the assumption one exists — and thus creates and perpetuates hostility among members of your species, leading to self-destruction. Do you see?" Polina shook her head, so I explained further. "Any spy aims to prevent anticipated harm from others. The harm that, fundamentally, is unnecessary. That's why intelligence work is absurd, just like hostility itself. If all of you were telepathic, you'd understand that."

"I've never thought about it that way," Polina replied nonchalantly.

"You, homo sapiens, don't think much at all. And when you do, it's like walking through a dark tunnel," I said, frustrated. It had been foolish of me to expect a teenager to completely break free from the matrix in such a short time. "Wouldn't it be better to use your love of plants to heal people?"

Polina wrinkled her nose in disdain. To her, healing others couldn't compete with the legendary exploits of a scout, and the questionable morality of such exploits wasn't obvious to the schoolgirl at all. Meanwhile, I finally decided to make an offer.

"About your request… Do you want to see New Lemuria?"

"You'll take me with you? Really?!" Polina's eyes lit up and she immediately forgot all about espionage.

"Don't get too excited. I'm talking about a short visit, like a tour, and I'm not even sure I can bring you there. No one has ever invited homo sapiens to our new home, and it's unclear how teleportation to another planet and staying there might affect you. It's a huge risk. Are you scared?"

"Of course not!" Polina blurted out.

"Of course? That's just plain foolish! You're not afraid of something that genuinely threatens your life, but you were in a panic, imagining your mum or grandmother might have a heart attack because you were an hour late? I'll never understand that!"

Polina made a sour face and wrinkled her nose again. Unfortunately, her carelessness wasn't due to a lack of fear but to her poor idea of death. Well… I wanted to show her my world, and I was almost certain I could. And since I couldn't be afraid, "almost" didn't count.

"Tomorrow morning, then," I said seriously. "Be ready for an adventure."

---

*Pavlik Morozov was a boy from the Urals area, born into a troubled family, who in 1932 informed the communists about his father's plot against them. During the Soviet era, he was regarded as a pioneer hero

Chapter 22. Indigo in the New World

I had deliberately set our journey for the morning. I wanted to give Polina time to reflect on the dangers of teleporting through space and perhaps change her mind about the whole idea. When my indigo girl arrived at our meeting spot the next day, it was clear that she, indeed, had barely slept, but the potentially disastrous outcome of the journey troubled her the least. On the contrary, the stubborn teenager had fully convinced herself that she would regret it for the rest of her life if she passed up the opportunity to become the first homo sapien to visit another planet.

Polina was also carrying a plastic bag with a change of clothes, as I had advised. She wore a dress the color of muted emerald that made her green eyes, already gleaming with anticipation of an incredible adventure, appear even brighter. I ran my fingers over the fabric on her sleeve and suggested regretfully, "Change into the clothes from the bag and hide the dress under that rock over there." I pointed to the boulder furthest from the water.

"Why?" my indigo girl asked in surprise. "I thought, one was supposed to dress up when going as a guest!"

I tapped my forehead with my finger. "Have you completely forgotten how dishevelled I looked the day we met?"

"Oh yes, you were in rags! By the way, what happened to your clothes back then?" she finally thought to ask.

"During interplanetary teleportation, the physical body disintegrates into atoms, although only for a split second. Fabrics are too unstable. Their elements don't return to their original form," I explained, suddenly desperate for Polina to reconsider and abandon the trip. "And on arrival, the sensations are, to put it mildly, unpleasant. It feels as if your body is boiling and exploding from the inside. In a way, it does explode, being exposed to a vacuum. One must be able to hold their particles together, and I'll have to hold both mine and yours." I paused meaningfully, but my indigo girl still refused to be frightened. Instead she worried about something entirely different.

"So, what will we be wearing there? Nothing?" she asked, giggling nervously.

"We'll be greeted," I replied briefly. "So, are you sure? Aren't you scared? Have you really thought this through?"

"I'm sure! I want to go!" Polina waved me off, sinking her feet into the sand, and marched with her bag towards the rock I had pointed out. After taking a couple of steps, she stopped, glanced back at me, closed her eyes, and successfully teleported. Ending up exactly where she intended, the girl stuck out her tongue at me and ordered, "Turn around!"

She returned wearing an old tracksuit and handed me her warm dry palm, but I pulled her close, locking my fingers to ensure my love wouldn't scatter into particles in interplanetary space.

"Ready?" I asked. Flustered by our closeness, Polina nodded. "Then you'd better close your eyes for safety, so they don't burst," I said. Sensing her heartbeat quicken with rising panic, I added icily, "That was a joke. Almost…" And while she was still trying to figure out whether I was joking, we teleported.

Simon and Mina were already waiting to provide the first aid I needed almost as much as my companion. As soon as we materialised at the Falls of Hope, Simon enveloped me in an energy cocoon for a few seconds to stabilise all my internal organs and then shoved me into the unearthly pure water. Mina did the same with Polina, so we both ended up in the waterfall's flowing pool, completely naked. I recovered from the vacuum shock almost quickly, but my indigo girl, who had arrived in New Lemuria in a deep faint, had stayed in the water for half an hour before her nausea and dizziness stopped. My father and his girlfriend handed us identical green tunics, and only when Polina had dressed in the light fabric did Simon address her aloud.

"Welcome to New Lemuria!"

“Th-thank you,” my indigo girl replied quietly, looking around in awe.

“How wonderful that you didn’t explode!” Mina blurted out ingenuously. Her words sounded so casual that Polina winced.

“Don’t mind her, dear!” my father added reassuringly. “We rarely see death. You already know how long homo liberatus live, don’t you? We don’t fear our own death or anyone else’s because we’re incapable of fear, but…” And he squeezed my shoulder painfully. “… it was sheer recklessness to put your life at such risk. Dragging an unprepared body through the cosmic vacuum, all for the sake of a tour?”

“I love her, Dad, and I wanted to show her our world!” I retorted.

“And were you ready to lose her for that?” Simon shot back, before replying aloud, “We are free from fear because our loved ones are as strong as we are, and she…” He poked Polina's stomach with his finger. “… she isn’t one of us!” I had never seen my father so irritated.

“Oh come now!” Mina interrupted, touching his arm just above the elbow. “Everything turned out fine!”

Simon sighed and looked at his companion with the sadness of someone misunderstood. All these years, he had been haunted by the memory of the Khatyn massacre. Through our Unity, we had all felt his heart ache at the slightest reminder of that day. Still, aside from me, Simon was the only living homo liberatus who had personally experienced the tragedy of losing a loved one to an untimely death, and although that allowed my father to bring me here, he never stopped thinking that my mother could and should have been saved…

Homo liberatus under a hundred years old considered New Lemuria their home, as did I, despite having been born on Earth. I had arrived at an age when one lives in the moment and when relocation isn’t followed by nostalgia. For older Lemurians, however, the century spent on the new planet had been a time of both discoveries and challenges. Oddly enough, the greatest challenge was the carefree life compared to Earth. A life without homo sapiens.

Polina's first impressions reminded Simon of his memories of relocating to New Lemuria. Once she recovered from the intracellular storm caused by teleportation, she noticed how much easier it was to move around here than on Earth. She pushed off with her feet, jumped, and gently landed.

"Amazing! It's like floating rather than walking! How does this work?"

"New Lemuria is smaller than Earth, so the gravity here is weaker," Mina explained. "And all our wonders of Nature exist because of it. Look at the waterfall!"

Polina turned around and only then noticed that calling it a "fall" was perhaps an overstatement, for lack of a better word. As it left the sheer cliff, the water did not rush down as quickly as it would on Earth. Large droplets drifted through the air, gathering into a whimsical cloud that shimmered in the sunlight with hundreds of rainbows. Gradually, they reached the pool of water below and settled into the stone basin with a melodious splash. Our guest stopped to admire the extraordinary sight, but Mina tugged at her hand impatiently.

"Come on, we've got more to show you!"

Mina loved surprising people, especially since such opportunity was rare with Lemurians, who could see right through each other. That was why she took charge of my indigo girl and pulled her forward, leaving Simon and me behind. I revelled in the lightness of my steps and the company in which I could be myself once again.

My kin had travelled to many corners of the Universe before finding the only planet similar enough to Earth to be suitable for life thanks to its water and oxygen. The sky on New Lemuria was also blue, and the trees were green, but that was where the similarities with the old planet ended. Everything here was different. It was better, at least to me. There were more trees, and they were taller. The air was richer in oxygen, and the water purer. The elder settlers claimed Earth had been the same some five thousand years ago. Lemurians blame homo sapiens, with their industries and distorted ideas of cleanliness, for making it hard to breathe even far from cities, while Earth's unpolluted water reservoirs could be counted on one hand.

Our guest followed Mina along the quiet river, whose banks were lined with trees twice or even three times the height of full-grown oaks from the forest near Polina's home. She couldn't reach the leaves, but her love for flora made her eager to examine them. I wrapped my arms around her waist and lifted her off the ground so that my beloved could touch the round, flexible leaf of a kumakura, compatible in size to human' height.

"So soft! Like velvet!" the girl exclaimed.

"Just like your tunic, right?" Mina chimed in, catching up to us. My indigo girl touched her new outfit in confusion, and Mina confirmed her suspicion. "Yes, tunics are made from whole leaves! There's no need to do anything but cut holes for the arms and head."

"We were very pleased about it," added Simon, who had grown bored waiting alone below and joined us. Answering Polina's unspoken question, he said, "Because there are no humans here with their looms, and we don't produce machines, or anything really."

"Actually, we rarely wear clothes," Mina informed her, pulling a funny face.

The girl's eyes widened. "You mean you walk around naked? Aren't you embarrassed?"

We all burst into laughter.

"What is there to be embarrassed about?" I teased.

"Well..." Polina said, blushing so deeply that we almost felt sorry for her.

"Sweet child!" Simon answered for us all. "Some people here don't even know that word, 'embarrassed,' especially the younger ones who've never been to Earth or met homo sapiens with their so-called civilized shame."

"We don't get cold because we can regulate our body temperature," I added, building on my father's point. "And there's no reason to cover ourselves from other Lemurians' eyes."

"Why not?" Polina didn't understand.

"Because everyone can see right through everyone else, even through clothes!" Mina reminded with a mocking wink. "And anyway, when you grow up running around naked and see others doing the same, you stop noticing nudity altogether."

"Besides, all Lemurians have beautiful bodies, thanks to our vegetarian diet and ability to maintain energy balance," Simon added, "so there are no imperfections to hide."

"Then why are you all dressed?" the girl from Earth finally dared to ask.

My father and I exchanged glances, and Mina smiled as she replied, "For you, silly!"

We returned to the river and carried on our way. On both banks, behind a ridge of dense riverside vegetation, towering cliffs rose like giant walls, so high their peaks touched the occasional cloud. To Polina, these cliffs seemed menacing, but Mina reassured her. "Rocks hardly ever crumble here, and even if they do, they fall pretty slowly."

"Why?" Polina asked.

"Because the gravity is weaker than on Earth!"

"Yeah, falling there is fast and painful," I confirmed, recalling my first landing.

"Look, there's an arch up ahead," Simon said, pointing to a narrowing of the river, where above the water, a stone semicircle rose, streaked with emerald patches of grass and a couple of small shrubs. "No, it's not a bridge, it's the remnant of a weathered mountain… It doesn't fall because it's not heavy enough. Sure, you could use it as a bridge, but as you've probably guessed, we don't need to!" he said, answering our guest's questions before she managed to voice them.

In the meantime, a barely visible dot appeared in the clear sky and began to grow rapidly. Finally, Polina made out a white bird which, upon closer inspection, turned out not to be a bird at all but a female white kumma, probably the most elegant and proud predator of New Lemuria. Once directly above us, it hovered for a moment, shading the sun with its five-metre wings. None of those present showed any signs of alarm, so Polina decided there was no need to worry. Tilting her head back, the girl studied the creature's four slender, muscular legs equipped with sharp claws and its bluish-white down covering the belly.

Eventually, the kumma glided down towards the river, threw a long, thin tail out of the fold of skin on its back, and wrapped it around the arch, like a lasso, pulling its powerful body to land on the stone. Eventually, the animal swooped onto the narrow surface of the bridge. Like a giant cat, the white kumma squinted disdainfully and observed our group from afar with its yellow eyes, set close together on its elongated snout. For several seconds, it flicked the thick tufts at the tips of its pointed ears back and forth, then released its flexible sensors, which began to quiver in the air as though operating independently of the motionless figure merged with the rock. From one sensor emerged a sharp spike that, like a slender spear, pierced some invisible prey. Without changing its position, the predator bit off the head of the semitransparent creature it had caught, one that Polina only noticed when a sky-blue liquid began to drip from its remains.

"It caught a flounder," Mina commented matter-of-factly, examining the predator's snout, smeared with the pale blue blood of its victim.

"A flounder?" Polina asked. "A fish?"

At that moment, a human figure separated from the thick mane that ran along the kumma's spine. A short muscular young man with tanned skin jumped down from the creature's back. He raised his hand in greeting. Simon and Mina responded in kind.

"That's Don, my father's nephew," I told Polina, watching my cousin fuss with his giant pet.

"Can't he fly himself, like you?" the girl asked.

"Of course he can."

"They're just inseparable," Mina interjected, adding with thinly veiled disapproval, "I think Don loves this kumma more than he loves women. I can't even remember the last time I saw him with one of ours."

"Don't gossip!" Simon said playfully. "You know perfectly well..."

Polina didn't understand this fragmented conversation, so I filled in the gaps.

"Don is still quite young. He's thirty. He really does spend most of his time with animals, but he already has a daughter."

"Is his family here?" Polina asked.

"It's not a family. Lydia wanted to raise the child on her own, so Don doesn't see the girl."

"Wanted to?" my indigo questioned in disbelief.

"Does that sound strange to you?" Simon replied, unsurprised. "Of course, in the human world, women rarely choose to have children outside of a partnership. Caring for a child, protecting it, and providing for it with limited access to resources is difficult for a single person, whether woman or man. For homo sapiens, raising children truly requires two people. For us, however, food grows right above our heads, and a mother can create an energy dome or cocoon to shield her child from falls and attacks. She also doesn't have to guess her baby's needs because she can scan its body and emotions at a glance. Our infants have no need to even cry."

“So, women truly have a choice,” Mina said with dignity. “Besides, our children are born with mutual consent only. Homo liberatus learn to control every cell of their body by the age of ten, and either partner can refuse or prevent conception. If a woman doesn’t want to share the joy of motherhood with anybody, she can simply ask a man for a child. It happens quite often here.”

“What about love?” Polina asked with a hint of disappointment.

“Love...” Mina echoed softly. “Complete reciprocity. Harmony of astral, mental, and physical states — that’s the only condition we call love. It’s extremely rare. When any of the three components are lacking, fortunately or not, we know it too well...” She sighed and cast a wistful glance at my father.

“Love can’t be willed into existence,” Simon replied. “Not every homo liberatus experiences that happiness even once in our rather long lives, and if children were only born out of true love, our race would have gone extinct long ago, just like yours would have.”

“And yet many raise children in pairs, similarly to you,” I pointed out.

“Do you have more children?” Polina asked, surprised.

“Yan has an older brother,” my father's girlfriend answered proudly. “He’s ninety-three years old if measured by the Earth’s calendar.”

“And you’ve been together that long?” the girl exclaimed in amazement.

“Since we moved to this planet, except for the time I spent with his mother,” Simon replied, nodding towards me, and Polina noted Mina’s calm. “It’s been almost a hundred years now. Hardship brings not only homo sapiens closer together.”

By this time, Don had finally left his winged pet perched on the bend of the stone arch and approached us, his muscular body completely exposed.

"Hello, uncle, and everyone!" he greeted silently.

"We have a guest from Earth, my boy, the first in the history of the settlers. She doesn't have telepathy," my father explained to his nephew.

"Really? Wow!" the young man exclaimed, staring at Polina with interest. On top of everything else, he was intrigued by the stupor caused by his nudity. Simon's nephew had been born on New Lemuria and had never encountered homo sapiens. Don's amusement at our guest's discomfort began to annoy me.

"And could you put some clothes on?" Mina asked flirtatiously, feeling sorry for the stunned girl who was seeing a naked man for the first time in her life.

"Please!" I pressed, not hiding my irritation.

"Fine!" The nonchalant boy shrugged carelessly, extended his hand, and a fresh kumakura leaf appeared in his palm.

"Never used this before!" he laughed, awkwardly dressing himself in the velvety organic fabric.

"Thank you for agreeing to join us," my father said.

"Don is our chief expert and lover of the local fauna," Mina explained to the indigo girl. "He knows everything about the animals of New Lemuria."

"Well, not everything, of course," my cousin replied with false modesty. "But they are amazing! Wonderful!"

Polina finally dared to ask the newcomer a question. "How did the fish end up in the air?"

"Fish?" Don looked puzzled but then quickly read the Earthling's associations and laughed. "Oh no, in New Lemuria, a flounder isn't a fish." He extended his hand, and a flat, translucent creature gracefully descended onto his palm. It relaxed, letting its body's edges, which rippled gently in the air as it floated, droop.

"Do you want to pet it?"

"Like snot," Polina thought with a grimace, but still extended a finger timidly and touched the flounder's back, just behind its

round head that had a tiny proboscis instead of a nose. The creature's jelly-soft back quivered, and its thin, snakelike tail with a suction cup at the tip began to sway back and forth.

"It likes you!" Don beamed.

"Before we arrived," my father said, "there were no beings on this planet that used language as we understand it, so there was no one to name the animals and plants. We didn't have the time or need to invent new words, so we gave them names from Earth based on their resemblance… which sometimes is quite remote, to be honest," he finished with a smile.

"Let's feed it!" Don suggested to the girl. He moved his free hand through the air as if beckoning something, and Polina saw the blue tip of the creature's proboscis open like a flower and begin to suck in something invisible to her.

"What does it eat?" she asked.

"Organic particles and single-celled organisms that rise into the air due to weak gravity," I explained. "We can see them, but the human eye probably can't."

"Flounders are the planet's true orderlies. Without them, it would be difficult, or even impossible, to breathe," Don added lovingly, stroking the translucent creature along its back.

"And those… cats?" Polina pointed to the white kumma still sitting on the stone arch. "Won't they eat all the flounders?"

"Of course not!" Her question surprised Don. "It's the natural food chain!" He turned the trusting, well-fed flounder onto its back. "See these suction cups on its belly and tail? They let it cling to cliffs to sleep or hide from predators, and its tail is like a rudder. A healthy, strong flounder can dodge a kumma's spike, while weaker ones get caught. Natural selection. We hardly interfere."

"Don't you pity the poor creatures?" the girl pressed.

"What does 'pity' mean?" the true son of New Lemuria asked, and they stared at each other in bewilderment. I came to his rescue.

"We live by the laws of Nature, and for Nature, balance is paramount. Neither homo liberatus nor other inhabitants of this planet know violence for the sake of violence, and so, in a world without cruelty, pity has no place too."

"Don has never met Earthlings before, so he didn't understand you," my father told Polina.

She looked directly at the young man and suddenly, without apparent connection, asked accusingly, "So, you'll never see your daughter?"

The young Lemurian glanced at my father's girlfriend and smirked. "Have you been discussing my dodgy past?"

"Yeah, we used your example to explain the homo-liberatus lifestyle," Mina confirmed, and then, in a tour-guide tone, addressed Polina as if the subject of their conversation weren't present. "Lydia is three hundred years old, and Don is thirty. He's a child to her." Though she thought to herself, *"A child... but what a magnificent one! A true Apollo!"*

Don paid no attention to Mina's playfulness. Like most Lemurian women, she admired this muscular lad, so unlike the rest of our short and slender kindred men, who had preferred energy exercises to physical training for centuries. Don's muscles had developed because he spent most of his time with animals that didn't share our superpowers. He often ran alongside them, rode them, and carried their young in his arms. My cousin was used to such thoughts from women, but his heart remained untouched.

"When Lydia's daughter grows up and joins the Unity, we'll meet, of course," he told Polina, flashing a carefree smile. "After that, it depends on our wishes."

"Don only joined recently. About a year ago, right?" Mina defended him, still reading judgment in the girl's thoughts.

"Then why did Lydia want a child specifically from you?" Polina asked my cousin with even more pressure in her tone, but Mina interrupted before he could reply.

"Because the most gifted children are born from young men, and there aren't too many of them on Lemuria, given our longevity," she said, glancing at my father before adding, "Sorry, Simon, no offence..."

"Well, that's a trend, not a rule," he replied good-naturedly, giving my shoulder a meaningful pat. I thought of Cassandra and her persistence.

"We'll discuss that later," my father responded, then said, more to his nephew than to Polina, "Sadly, Don's soul has yet to be touched by love or even friendship with anyone other than our lesser brethren."

"By the way, has Malanya been seen here?" the young man asked, perking up. Right on cue, a long-haired head with a wide, slightly flattened jaw peeked out from the bushes.

"Ah, there she is! Come here, my beauty!" he called gently, beckoning with a finger. The creature blinked its long eyelashes that framed bulging yellow-orange eyes, then stepped out of the bushes and moved cautiously towards us on two legs, grinning widely and disarmingly with huge dark pink lips.

Polina, stunned and slack-jawed, watched the approaching wonder. *"Ew! Freak! A face like a frog's!"* she thought, and Mina elbowed her for that.

Despite the long silky light blonde hair — or fur, if you prefer — that almost completely covered Malanya's body, my indigo girl couldn't help but realise that the creature was female. The firm nipples of two large breasts, covered not with hair but with smooth pink skin, jutted noticeably forward. Her wide, smoothly swaying hips and slender waist looked as though they had come to life from illustrations of Arabian tales.

"Oh, you've already washed yourself for me! What a good girl!" Don said, running his hand along the fur on Malanya's lower back quite explicitly as she drew level with us. Malanya pressed herself impulsively against the young man, gazing at him with adoration and offering a tender smile that revealed large, even teeth with a greenish hue. "Be patient, my dear!" the young Lemurian said gently. "Come walk with us."

Everyone except Polina knew that Malanya, a female Lemurian hominid, was my cousin's favourite. Despite her complete lack of telepathy and a brain that was relatively small for her body, she somehow always managed to turn up wherever Don went. Lemurian hominids were native inhabitants. These friendly creatures were almost the first the homo liberatus encountered after landing on this planet. Most likely, Malanya's future kin will evolve into intelligent beings by human standards, but they are far from that point yet. They are omnivorous, live in small groups, and communicate through guttural sounds. Naturally, mutual understanding between us isn't a problem.

My people quickly noticed that the energy exchange system in these creatures is more complex than in other inhabitants of the planet, but it's simpler than in homo sapiens, hence the name "hominids." Lemurian hominids have only five chakras. With little to no imagination, they cannot form religion, which is precisely why we didn't become gods to them, even though homo liberatus immediately began helping these hospitable and peaceful beings. We saved them from wild beasts and healed their sick, but soon realised that overdoing it is unwise, as a saviour always becomes the centre of a hominid's life. That was how Malanya started following Don everywhere after he rescued her, still a juvenile at the time, from the jaws of a local predator.

Now the female hominid gladly joined Don's company, paying no attention to the curious gaze of the indigo girl, who, in Malanya's eyes, was no different from the rest of us. As we walked along the river, Don's pet frequently flicked out her long flared tongue, catching insects in midair and swallowing them on the go. This only heightened Polina's disguast. *"Like a frog indeed!"*

The weather was heavenly, as usual. The scorching rays of the daytime star, casually named the Sun by the settlers from

Earth, were softened by moisture droplets suspended in the air, turning into pleasant warmth. The tall grass reached human height, and tiny dragon-like creatures fluttered within it. Polina stopped and watched as a snakelike body, covered in blue-green feathers, dived into a flower cup, soon surrounded by blue petals the size of a human head. The tiny dragon wriggled inside, sucking up pollen with its long threadlike proboscis.

"A proboscis like a flounder's," Don answered our guest's unspoken question. "All the small creatures on this planet — and not only the small ones," he added, patting Malanya's plump lower back again, "feed on particles and organisms from the air that aren't heavy enough to stay down. This one does too and takes pollen for dessert."

Meanwhile, the bird-like wings and elongated snout of the nectar-feeder emerged from the flower. The creature looked at us with beady brown eyes fearlessly.

"Does it bite?" Polina asked cautiously.

"It doesn't even have teeth!" Don laughed. He placed his palm near the flower, and the nectar-feeder stepped onto his hand, clinging to his skin with its back legs, its clawed front fingers fidgeting expectantly. "Although if it feels endangered, it might scratch you badly."

"Like a cat," Polina concluded.

"Well, sort of!" Mina chimed in, playfully poking my cousin in the chest. "And yet he's never seen a live cat!"

"Really, Don," Simon said, "aren't you planning to visit Earth? At least to see its fauna?"

Don grimaced and stretched out his reply. "Maybe... someday..."

"I see you're not in a hurry for interplanetary teleportation," I remarked mockingly.

"Why should I be?" Don retorted. "I don't see you enjoying disintegrating into particles and trying to reassemble yourself!

And I'm quite happy at home." He waved his hand nonchalantly, releasing the nectar-feeder.

"At home…" Simon and Mina echoed wistfully.

Wanting to steer the conversation to something more pleasant, Don plucked a fluffy little creature with a blunt muzzle and large, round lilac eyes from the smooth trunk of a tree. He stroked its bluish-grey fur, which matched the colour of the tree bark, and showed it to Polina.

"Look, this is a fluffik!"

"Oh, what a cutie!" my indigo girl squealed. "It looks like a kitten!"

"If you say so!" Don laughed.

"But without claws!"

"This one bites a little, and even headbutts," my cousin warned, stroking the horny lashes on the creature's nose and between its ears. The creature opened its mouth, revealing numerous tiny, almost invisible teeth, and licked the hand holding it with a round, oversized tongue.

"Ah, this is so sweet!" Polina laughed.

"It's not about being sweet. It's just eaten," Don corrected, carefully taking the fluffik's paw with four tiny fingers and showing it to the girl. "See? It uses these suckers on its fingers to cling to rocks or tree trunks and lick insects and other small creatures off their surfaces. Pick it up, and it'll clean your hands too."

Polina extended her hand to pet, or perhaps feed, the fluffik, but it hissed and snarled, pulling a funny but quite unfriendly expression.

"I wouldn't recommend it!" Don laughed. "Those teeth are for defence. It'll bite anyone it doesn't trust." Polina quickly withdrew her hand, and my cousin returned the creature to the tree, where it instantly blended into the dark blue-brown bark. "Luckily for it and other small species, no one except us can inspire a sense of safety here."

We approached the delta of a river flowing into a vast, deep lake, and almost simultaneously, a small herd of trunkoids emerged from a grove between the rocks and the shore. From a distance, they looked like gigantic horses. Their tall, powerful legs carried their muscular bodies with ease and speed. Thick black, light, and reddish manes adorned their long necks and ran along their spines. Their slender tails ended in shaggy tufts.

As we drew closer, our guest was in for a surprise: the animals unfurled their long, flexible trunks, which had been neatly coiled under their lower jaws while they ran. They began to drink. These creatures, with completely bare, thick-skinned sides, sucked up the lake water through their slender, nozzle-like trunks and then sprayed it into their herbivorous mouths, which were perpetually chewing.

"Are they horses or elephants after all?" my indigo girl asked aloud as she wandered among the trunkoids, who paid us no attention whatsoever.

"If I were you, I'd stop trying to compare," Simon told her. "It's a pointless exercise. Any resemblance to Earth's animals is purely coincidental, or, more likely, an adaptation to similar living conditions."

Don announced in his usual calm voice, "We'd better get away from the water now."

There was no time to move on foot, so we quickly took ourselves and our non-teleporting companions about a hundred paces from the lake. A moment later, the placid surface rippled, swelling with powerful waves, and then seven enormous heads on long serpentine necks burst from the depths with a deafening roar. The master head, larger than the others, had round, closely set red-and-yellow eyes and commanded the six smaller, underdeveloped ones that were designed for hunting. Each of these six heads had a single barely visible but sharp eye and a far more prominent, foul-smelling, tooth-filled maw.

To feed their massive shared stomach, the hunting heads snaked along the shoreline, snapping their sharp teeth at any creature that lingered too long. This time, two trunkoids, too engrossed in siphoning water into their mouths, were not so lucky. Thirst had caused them to miss the brief window when they could have fled.

The monster was so enormous that, by fully extending its necks, it could easily have reached us. Yet not a single homo liberatus flinched, not only because we were incapable of feeling fear but also because, even before the beast emerged from the lake's depths, Don had implanted the idea in the alpha head's mind that we were not prey.

Polina instinctively hid behind me. She was speechless with terror, despite seeing the Lemurians calmly observing the monster's spectacle. The sight of the trunkoids being devoured alive shocked her even more than the appearance of the creature itself.

"W-w-what is that?" she whispered into my ear, trembling.

"That's Charybdis."

"Charybdis?" The girl sounded astonished. "Do they really exist?"

"You mean the Greek myth?" Simon interrupted in his usual matter-of-fact tone. "Of course not. We gave the name to this planet's most dangerous predator because of its striking resemblance to the description of the mythical beast. The one that, by the way, never existed on Earth and certainly couldn't have threatened humans by the time homo sapiens were sailing and fighting with iron swords."

Meanwhile, Don was distracted from his role as a guide by Malanya, who was trembling like a leaf. She too had taken cover behind her protector, clinging to his tanned shoulders with all eight of her long, sharp nails. A couple of years ago, Don had rescued her from the jaws of one such monster. Now, he began gently stroking Malanya between her legs as awakening an instinct opposite to fear really was the easiest way to calm her. After all, living beings only reproduce when they feel safe. Naturally, Don wasn't concerned with how this looked to Polina — he didn't even grasp that his actions might surprise or embarrass anyone present.

Charybdis, having swallowed a few more unfortunate creatures, retreated to its deepwater lair to digest the meal. By that time, Malanya was so aroused by Don's touch that she sank onto the grass, spread her legs, and released her "flower." That's what we call the display performed by many female species of New Lemuria.

The males here are almost the same as those on Earth, but the females' wombs emerge externally for mating. They open like a glistening red funnel resembling a flower that moves with suction-like motions. It's an unambiguous signal of consent or invitation.

Since Lemurian hominids are highly affectionate and sensual, some of my kin, naturally drawn to experimentation, couldn't resist the opportunity to try something new. The pleasure, in my opinion, is questionable at best, given both the hominid females' appearance and their unconventional method of mating. Neither is everyone's cup of tea. As for my cousin, who was born and raised on New Lemuria, he even preferred the simple and devoted Malanya to the women of his own species, especially since she couldn't hear his thoughts.

"I must take care of her!" Don said, looking anticipant at the pet eagerly offering herself to him.

"Just spare us from having to watch your idea of care," Simon replied with a grumble.

My cousin flashed a mischievous grin, enthusiastically scooped up Malanya, who was burning with desire, and teleported with her into the grove.

And Polina sat down on the grass and buried her head in her hands. She was shaken to the core. She felt like that girl from the book who fell through a rabbit hole into a world where no familiar rules applied. The homo-liberatus actions appeared utterly wrong to my indigo girl. Yet the way we weren't rushing to save the trunkoids from the charybdis, and my cousin's indifference to his own daughter, and his "shameless" interspecies relationship with a hominid female, somehow made sense here.

"This is how it should be," Simon said, trying to calm the poor Earthling. "Everything permitted by Nature can be understood, and we've learned to value it all." With a fatherly touch to the crown of Polina's head, he shared energy with her, restoring what she had lost from shock and fear. Thanks to my father, the indigo girl quickly regained her composure and began bombarding us with questions.

"What about male hominids? Don't they get jealous? Don't they attack you?" Polina was more stunned by Don and Malanya's affair than by any other wonder she had seen on New Lemuria, probably because homo sapiens feel disoriented without their social matrix.

"First of all, our ladies also take an interest in hominids' rather well-built males sometimes," Mina smirked. "And secondly, it's impossible to attack us. We don't live in groups or build cosy homes stuffed with things. We can simply disappear whenever we want. So even if someone wanted to fight, there'd be no one to fight with. Homo sapiens have never managed to harm us in all the millennia we've lived alongside them."

"Of course, a full act of love with a Lemurian hominid is out of the question. I mean the merging of auras, achieving harmony, and uniting on an astral level," my father clarified. "These interspecies relationships are more like what homo sapiens have with dogs: you give and receive unconditional love, but it can never replace love for one's own kind. Although some people do prefer the company of dogs… As for jealousy, have you ever seen a dog jealous of another dog over a human?"

“But humans don’t sleep with dogs!” Polina objected heatedly.

“The idea of mating with Lemurian hominids only arose because of their physical resemblance to humans. It’s a random development. Such closeness provides only primitive pleasure, and no children can be born from it.”

“Don prefers simplicity,” Mina added sarcastically.

“Don is an exception,” Simon said, defending his nephew. “The creatures of New Lemuria are his greatest love for now. He’s unique in that regard. He spends most of his time with the local animals, studying them and helping them when they’re in need. Malanya is part of his life. What he’ll move on to in the future is unknown, but as long as Don remains part of Unity, we know this ‘friendship’ with a hominid female doesn’t harm Nature, so there’s no reason to interfere.”

“Well, are these hominids intelligent or not?” Polina persisted.

“On New Lemuria, we don’t divide beings into intelligent and non-intelligent,” I finally spoke up. “Even on Earth, that classification is just a human invention. We pay attention to how many chakras a living being has, what kind, and how they interact with each other and the outside world. Of course, biologically this relates to the nervous system, which, like all living things in the Universe, evolves.”

“Besides, from my experience on Earth, most homo sapiens can’t even control their own energy and states. In that sense, they’re less ‘intelligent’ than some animals,” my father noted.

Mina nodded in agreement. “Technology has especially weakened them. Machines do too much and make humans lazy!”

At this, Polina recalled hearing the same thing from me.

We entered the grove and refreshed ourselves with one of the sweet fruits ripening on the sprawling branches like giant balls, exuding a sweet, almost intoxicating aroma. Polina, after biting into the soft, nourishing flesh, blurted out, "Tastes like a banana!"

"Really?" Simon asked with comical amazement. "Then you won't be surprised by its name."

"What is it?"

"Banana!"

We burst into laughter, and my indigo girl couldn't stop. She laughed until she cried, releasing all the tension of this crazy day.

"Actually, this banana has a pleasant side effect," Mina said with a conspiratorial tone and a mischievous wink.

"Does it make you laugh?" Polina guessed, catching her breath.

"Not exactly..." my father said unexpectedly seriously. "We'll all feel it in a few minutes. I think we should split up, so we don't shock you again." Then, turning to me with equal seriousness, he added, "I hope everything goes well for you, my boy. You may not get another chance for a very long time." With that, Simon gently took his girlfriend by the elbow and led her deeper into the grove. Before disappearing, he waved to our guest.

"Goodbye, my dear! Or rather, see you later. We'll meet again."

Once my father and Mina were out of sight, I pointed to the top of the cliff.

"Let's climb up there. I want to lay this world at your feet!" Having uttered such a lofty, romantic phrase, I surprised even myself. *"Ugh, how pretentious! I'd never say that in a normal state!"* But my indigo girl offered me such a soft, inviting gaze that I forgot about rhetoric at once. Yes, the magical banana was beginning to take effect, and not just on me.

Standing atop a ridge of sheer cliffs, Polina saw that their far side sloped gently down into a basin, overgrown with dense jungle. At the very bottom, there was a flat grey wasteland where nothing grew, but white jets of steam burst forth from cracks in the rocks, swirling like fluffy vapour. Droplets of mist hung in the air, and the cloudless sky above the basin was adorned with a dozen magnificently vivid rainbows. The sight was so beautiful that my Polina caught her breath.

"Wow!" Then, to my surprise and her own, Polina suddenly kissed me on the lips and immediately stepped back, flustered. "Sorry…"

I barely managed to resist returning the kiss. I would have poured all my pent-up passion into it, but instead I found myself trying to appear indifferent, like a lovestruck human boy unsure of his beloved's feelings. The truth was, I knew Polina hadn't fully grasped her desires yet, and I was willing to wait. Otherwise, our intimacy would feel too much like seduction and deceit. That single kiss, after which my indigo girl teleported for the first time in her life, held no deeper significance for her. An inexperienced being, constantly criticised by her mother and convinced of her own unattractiveness, had naively believed it was a "training necessity," and she tried not to think about it, although with mixed success.

By the laws of her country, Polina was underage, and although biologically she had been ready for the joys of love for about two years, she hadn't dared to entertain such thoughts. Only here, on a planet unshackled by the matrix and under the influence of wondrous bananas that awakened the desires of the flesh, did the first wave of heat stir in her young body and carry her into my arms. I didn't want to frighten her off, so I needed restraint now more than ever. The long wait for pleasure was unfamiliar here. It turned out to be maddening, plunging me into sharp, sweet torment, as if I were burning from within. Yet strangely, I enjoyed this human game. Instead of kissing her back, I simply smiled and said calmly, "Don't worry, my dear. It's just the bananas. I feel the same way…"

Absorbed by the rainbows above the basin earlier, Polina only now followed my gaze and noticed the others. About a hundred steps away, on the edge of a neighbouring cliff, a man and a woman sat facing each other. Their bodies were tightly pressed together, arms and legs entwined. They had been there for some time, completely absorbed in each other, and hadn't noticed their uninvited audience. After meeting Don and Malanya, the girl from Earth was no longer easily shocked, but this was different. I hadn't even dared to hope to share the sight of true love with Polina — a rarity even for the eyes of homo liberatus! Now, after our rigorous training, it was easy: I simply joined her energy field, and she saw how the lovers' auras, the young man's bright orange and the girl's sky blue, gradually merged, forming an ever-growing cocoon, rich with light and colour.

"How beautiful!" Polina whispered in awe. "What are they doing?"

"Meditating," I replied, struggling to keep my voice steady, "before making love."

The young Earthling blushed and tried to look away, but she couldn't. In her world, watching would have been shameful, forbidden even. Yet she didn't avert her eyes. The lovers sat on a rocky ledge.

"Like a play on a theatre stage!" Polina thought.

"A play for whom?" I countered. "There wasn't a soul around before we arrived! They simply found the most beautiful place to enjoy their intimacy in full. You call it romance, I believe. Perhaps humans prefer to love in darkness, behind closed doors, and in haste, as though, by joining their bodies, they're stealing something from each other… but it's different for us."

Polina narrowed her eyes to get a better look at the seemingly motionless couple, and then exclaimed, "They're younger than me!"

"In Earth years, she's thirteen and he's fifteen," I said. "So what? Even homo sapiens have legends about love stories at a very young age. Juliet, for instance, was thirteen. True love is a rare gift from Nature in any world."

"But it's..." Polina's mind buzzed with epithets to justify the words *forbidden, shameful, too early, dangerous*, and, of course, *scary*.

"Not for us, my dear," I said, wrapping an arm around her shoulders. "Homo liberatus are free to follow Nature's call as soon as mutual desire arises, and it's impossible to hide in the company of telepaths. Mutuality is the only condition. Otherwise, Nature's law would be violated."

"What about children?" Polina shook her head in disbelief. "What if such young ones have children?"

"Only if they wish to!" I laughed. "Remember what Mina said? Lemurians can control all their cells and even others' long before they're ready for reproduction."

"So, you can... for me? To make sure I don't..."

"Of course!"

By then, the lovers' auras had fully merged into a single sphere. Their lips met repeatedly, and their hands grew bolder, exploring and caressing. Each touch sent forth bursts of white sparks, and as their pleasure intensified, so did the brilliance of the light. Finally, their bodies united. I saw it clearly, while Polina, from our vantage point, could only observe the bright white glow within the orange-blue sphere. Of course, my indigo girl understood what was happening, as the entire area became saturated with the energy of love — unstoppable, all-consuming, and all-giving. Polina remained silent, but her mind and body sang, *"I want this too!"* She timidly touched my hand and looked into my eyes.

"We won't manage to be that beautiful," I responded. Suddenly, now that the love of my life was asking me for intimacy, I felt a wave of sadness.

"Why not?" Polina asked, startled.

"Because it takes true harmony. I've loved you since the moment we first met, but you..."

“And I love you!” my indigo girl whispered passionately. I embraced her and kissed, at last.

“If only it were so!”

“I don’t understand…” She pulled away and frowned, hurt. “Do you think I’m lying?”

“Of course not!” I drew her back into my arms, holding her even tighter. “It’s just… yes, your body has indeed awakened to love, and it’s beautiful, but your soul isn’t ready yet. And it’s impossible to predict when it will be.” More than anything, I longed to drown in those pulsating violet waves, even though they didn’t merge with mine but merely blended into an intricate mosaic — her indigo hues and my emerald-green. And there was nothing I could do about it!

Resigned, I whispered, “I promise to please you, my darling.” I kissed the high cheekbone near her flushed, delicate earlobe, slipped my hand under her tunic, and began to caress the sinuous groove from her long neck to her waist, savouring every shiver of bliss that rippled down her spine at my touch. I was just about to allow myself a bolder touch when my fingers froze on the threshold of the sanctuary. A sudden sobering thought forced me to pull back. “Listen, you need to know…”

Polina reached out to embrace me again, but I firmly held her wrists back. “Wait! This is important!” For several seconds we struggled, breathless. Finally, she realised I was serious, relented, and gazed at me with questioning eyes.

“After we return to Earth, we won’t see each other for a long time. I don’t want you to think that I tricked, then seduced and abandoned you. It’s not too late to stop and take you home right now.”

My voice sounded hollow, like someone else’s, but Polina only laughed and kissed the hand that gripped her wrist. She understood me well, but she also understood herself, and now she knew for sure that she no longer wanted to restrain her nature, which had slumbered until that day in the shackles of the matrix-prescribed innocence. The only thing that remained innocent in Polina after that night was the soul of a homo-liberatus heiress... And I had knowingly condemned myself to eternal torment because I understood: every moment of that night would haunt me for the rest of my life.

Anyone who has possessed a beloved woman, knowing for certain that his feelings were not entirely reciprocated, will understand the bitterness of the aftertaste, no matter what race he belongs to. With access to the experiences and emotions of most homo liberatus, I knew all too well what true love's harmony looked like. It turned out that a high level of initiation and the power of telepathy could cause pain too. For the first time in my life — if not in the history of my species — I felt envy towards homo sapiens, towards their ability to live in the comforting captivity of illusions. Perhaps I loved in a human way, for not only had I never met a Lemurian so deeply, so bitterly, so darkly consumed by unrequited feelings, but I had never even heard of such cases in our legends.

Meanwhile, Polina opened to my caresses like an untouched bud opening its petals to the warmth of the sun. My ability to read desires compensated for her inexperience, and my indigo girl reached the peak of pleasure several times — a peak a man strives to bring the one he truly loves — but her delight and gratitude for the sensual joy I gave her that night remained just that. *"For now!"* I thought hopefully...

A crystal-clear dawn of New Lemuria peeked into the valley of geysers. The effects of the miraculous bananas had long since faded from our exhausted bodies. I woke first and let my hand glide along the bare curve of Polina's back, brushing my lips against her shoulder. She opened her eyes, and I drowned in them, as if in the depths of a stormy sea, once again... I loved her without any bananas.

"It's time to take you home."

Polina stretched languidly on the silky grass we had so thoroughly crumpled during the night and murmured carelessly, "I've completely lost track of time… Is it morning there too?"

"I don't know," I admitted.

We had returned just in time. Darkness was just beginning to thicken over the Black Sea shores.

Chapter 23. Unified Consciousness

Pity the one who lashes me with a whip —
One must be mad to do so!
Rasul Gamzatov, "Song of Fools and Sages"

I arrived in New Lemuria utterly exhausted: three interplanetary teleportations in a row, mixed with a night of passion — all of it had taken its toll! Having lost track of time, I rocked on the lulling waves of the Sea of Decisions, gazing thoughtlessly into the lilac-blue expanse of the sky. The warm water filled the air with ions, gradually mending the energy fissures in my body, which had been battered by adventure. At first, I lacked the strength to even follow with my eyes the occasional translucent creatures gliding above the water. The air flounders ignored me too, but only until my energy was fully replenished by the ocean's power. Once the balance was restored, little limbs latched onto my shoulder, and a tiny proboscis began probing my skin for food. I did not interfere with my guest, although I knew the flounder would be disappointed, as microorganisms, naturally, perish during interplanetary travel. The blessed, serene cycle of Nature — a harmony so hard to achieve on Earth — had a calming effect on my heart, still aching from parting with Polina. This fissure was not so easily healed, and I did not want it to be. Of course, my challenging mission left no room for lovesickness, yet I would not have traded thoughts of my indigo girl for any treasure in the world.

Only one Lemurian day remained before the Unity. I was in no hurry to meet my kin ahead of time. My return the next day to the Unified Consciousness was the most significant event in the lives of the peaceful homo liberatus race, forced to escape the all-pervasive march of technological progress to this distant planet. My people awaited answers, and before sharing them, I needed to sort my thoughts out.

New Lemuria has only one continent, at least for now. The rest of the planet's surface is covered by an ocean whose floor is in constant flux: underwater volcanoes erupt and tectonic plates shift, pushing up islands or burying them in ocean depths. If my people wished to settle like humans, not even one generation would enjoy permanence. Fortunately, our understanding of peace and stability differs from that of homo sapiens.

The Sea of Decisions earned its name because it holds the Island of Unity, large enough to accommodate all adult Lemurians at once. Others gather on a neighbouring island, where adolescents are left entirely to their own devices, while toddlers are supervised by young adults, who wait for *the call.* The exact moment of their maturity is impossible to predict, but from time to time, a new homo liberatus arrives at the Unity from the Island of Wait.

The latter is also known as the Island of Joy. Independent yet carefree youths, not yet burdened with the duty of shaping the fate of their people or even with the desire to do so, spend their time here immersed in fun and games. Rowdy youngsters of Polina's age are perhaps the only ones among us who enjoy large gatherings — making noise, fooling around, competing in games, and plunging headlong into the euphoria of first love. Of course, they have access to all this during ordinary days too, but as we all know, there is something exhilarating about the absence of parental supervision, even when no one ever restricts you. During the Unity, adults withdraw from their selves, losing the ability for astral and telepathic communication with the outside world, including their children.

To prolong the fun, homo liberatus aged thirteen to thirty begin arriving on the Island of Joy a couple of days before the Unity begins. I stopped by briefly as well. I wanted to relive the time of my own youth when the mission had still felt more like a fantasy. Fully rejuvenated by the ocean waves, I strolled towards the rocky shore, the water caressing my bare feet with its cool, moist tongues of calm. Seeing a group of excited children running across the water's surface as if on land — the smoothest, most open space for playing tag — I smiled. Homo sapiens would have been quite surprised to witness this carefree crowd of their god's relatives, infinitely distant from calling themselves gods!

Having spent over thirty years awaiting the call of the Unity, I knew this place well, so I headed for its highest point. There, I spotted another group of teenagers noisily discussing the rules of a game. Within minutes, the first boy pushed off the cliff and soared upwards, legs together, arms spread wide. Imagining himself a bird, he opened his hug to the wind and sun. The kids decided to compete in flight duration, and I thought they would be waiting for this daredevil's return for a long time as, at fourteen, he was already performing aerial acrobatics more skillfully than the most agile flounder.

I climbed the cliff and decided to walk down the gentle, jungled slope to breathe in the invigorating forest ozone and have a snack. There too grew magical bananas, from which I kept my distance this time. Instead I treated myself to a feast of nuts and sweet, juicy, red-rimmed roole fruits. After lunch, I cheerfully continued to the opposite side of the island. Along the way, in numerous but scattered hollows on the gentle slope, I occasionally noticed meditating young adults and very young couples who had not shied away from the bananas — or perhaps had eaten them deliberately to heighten their sensations. These half children, half adults kissed, touched, caressed, and tickled one another, merging their bodies — none of it done silently, and none paid any attention to the chosen one who had wandered onto their Island of Joy. Passing a particularly sparkling pair, I paused for a few minutes. Their clumsy touches radiated youthful energy, yet love was nowhere near, and only raging hormones played instead. Strangely, this vibrant scene amused me and soothed my pain. After all, expecting deep, harmonious feelings from a girl as young as these immature teenagers was hardly sensible. From an indigo who had not yet figured out even her own essence! *"I will definitely return to you, Polina,"* I thought, *"but much later. Perhaps by then, you will be ready too."* And I set off for the Island of Unity with a lightened heart.

The Lemurians arrived gradually. Some wished to socialise before the meditation began. Homo liberatus are natural loners and often don't meet anyone between Unities. Many become so engrossed in their pursuits that they forget time entirely and appear only when the powerful call of the Unified Consciousness becomes impossible to ignore. Parents of young children also do not rush, leaving their offspring in the care of maturing youths for longer than necessary. A small handful of mothers arrive with infants not yet walking. Their way of merging with their babies and Unity at the same time is mysterious even to a man who can read women's thoughts. When everyone had already settled at an arm's length apart and the island became aglow with a golden-white energy dome, two young men and a girl appeared at the plateau's edge and sat down there in a lotus position. They had sensed the long-awaited call for the first time and joined in the mind of their people immediately, without any initiation, as quietly and naturally as a new bud blooming on a flowering tree.

Being a part of this mental whole, we are unaware of the passage of time throughout the entire Unity. Yet, on that day, even before the meditation began, everyone understood that it would take longer than usual. Sorting out our future relationship with the planet Earth felt vital to all. When not a single separate "I" remained among us, everything found and lost, everything studied and suffered, instantly merged into the Unified Consciousness. So did the fruits of my research, anticipated here with special reverence. Now it was time to carefully consider everything I had discovered and experienced and then decide how we should proceed. The decision was not easy. It caused the most serious contradictions in the last century, which was why homo liberatus stayed on the Island of Unity for almost two months. However, emotions are transient — they are not worth close attention. Thought is eternal — and I will limit myself to quoting it further.

***

"So, what do we know about vampires now?

"This pathology in homo sapiens can be either congenital or acquired. In the first case, the two-way exchange of energy with the surrounding world is disrupted due to a mutation, where the density of grey matter in the brain's orbitofrontal cortex and anterior insular lobe is significantly lower than in ordinary representatives of the species. Such a difference prevents vampires from feeling as normal people do. Thus, the natural exchange of energy through the full spectrum of emotions is inaccessible to them. Mutants are incapable of empathy, love, or self-sacrifice, and therefore lack any moral or ethical guidelines, nor are they susceptible to secondary, that is, social, fear. They may still be afraid of physical danger, but they can accurately assess its typically low probability even then. This is why mutants often act boldly and may appear even reckless.

"Unburdened by secondary fear, vampires do not lose their composure in difficult circumstances. They make tough decisions without hesitation, which is often mistaken for courage and earns admiration from normal homo sapiens. Furthermore, people regard fearlessness and a cold mind as leadership qualities, and so they readily allow vampires to govern society, thereby digging themselves a grave. Homo sapiens despise their fear so much that they are willing to entrust the fates of entire nations to those who do not display it, and often for this reason alone! They cannot read minds and do not know the true causes of the mutants' fearlessness. Yet, the essence of courage is overcoming fear, whereas there is no merit in defeating an emotion one does not experience in the first place.

"Mutants are intelligent, well versed in the rules of the matrix, and skilled at pretending to care about improving the existence of their kind. This deception is the greatest danger of vampires: in truth, they care for nothing but stealing energy, that is, for their own pleasure and benefit.

"And the source of pleasure for them is entirely different from that of normal homo sapiens. Vampires themselves rarely understand why the sight of others' pain excites them so much, but we know that a suffering living being loses energy the fastest. So, the more suffering there is, the more a vampire is able to indulge! Others' physical pain satiates mutants the most, and the brutal crimes, wars, and genocides are exclusively their doing.

"In peacetime, vampires inflict emotional torment since there are few laws against this, let alone the death penalty. The souls of most ordinary homo sapiens suffer from secondary social fear, which vampires evoke through skilled manipulation, mockery, accusations, criticism, and threats of future suffering. That is how they feed and rip resources from society.

"Does the lack of fear make vampires like homo liberatus? Of course not! Mutants' fearlessness helps them steal energy from Nature and violate the exchange that is of the utmost value to us. Homo liberatus are incapable of killing or causing any form of pain intentionally, whereas a vampire will trample over others, including relatives and those who love them, for the sake of personal gain, that being physical pleasure in the material world and energy influx at the subtle level. There is an abyss between us and them, and any similarity is superficial.

"In vampire mind, understanding good and evil revolves around rewards. Yet ironically, in pursuit of satisfying their thirst, mutants sometimes even serve society, from society's perspective. How? It is very simple. For example, a cold-minded lawyer may well save an innocent person from execution or imprisonment for an attractive fee, but they will also defend the

most brutal murderer without hesitation. Such a person fundamentally does not care whose side is truthful.

"And what has the truth become anyway? Under vampires' influence, homo sapiens change their values like gloves! We live long and know better than anyone how unstable their notions of good and evil are and how they drift away from Nature. For example, killing is considered a blessing if it involves destroying an "enemy," whoever that may be. Thus, Vasyura was well regarded by the Nazis precisely because he did not hesitate to execute and torture "hostile" old people, women, and children. In the eyes of German commanders, he was a fearless officer loyal to the Führer, although both Vasyura himself and his comrades from the 118th Battalion frankly did not care about the Führer. They were simply feeding on the energy of their victims' terror and pain.

"So, do mutants experience no emotions at all? Well, we certainly observed one emotion in them. That is, boredom. A vampire's boredom signifies energy thirst. It causes anger and signals the time to feed on death, fear, and suffering. When harming people is impossible, mutants revert to tormenting animals, but human energy is the most delicious for them.

"How did these vampires come into existence, anyway? There is no complete certainty about this, but one thing is certain: such mutation results from a disturbance in the natural balance. Our race is much older than homo sapiens. Moreover, we originated from the likes of them. Yet there are no vampires among us! Having learned to teleport, our ancestors began observing humans when they still lived in caves and warmed themselves with animal skins, when danger came to people only from the outside. While humans fought the wild predators, gathered fruit, and hunted, there were no vampires among them! Perhaps this is why that time is called the Golden Age...

"Most likely, mutants appeared when homo sapiens settled down to grow their food and decided to stop relying on Nature's

provision, thus breaking the balance. Farmers wanted to have more children to get help with the crops. They treated children as tools. They stopped valuing life. They lacked the energy to care for all their offspring properly, and many children simply died in infancy. The surviving ones, raised in fear of supply shortage, eventually began to fight each other for resources.

"When homo sapiens realised they were destroying themselves behind the plough, it was already too late. Returning to foraging frightened them. Then the smartest, though far from the most farsighted, came up with the idea of forcing their fellow humans to till the land, exploiting others' lives and appropriating their energy. This is what was probably the catalyst for vampirism! The imbalance grew broader and more profound, like a crack in the ground. Manipulating the fears of their kind, vampires invented power — the right to receive willingly surrendered energy in exchange for protection from... what? This is where the primary contradiction of homo sapiens lies!

"Possibly, people initially believed that their goods and money, handed over to leaders, would be used entirely for protection against external threats. That was the natural order, as all healthy living beings strive for natural exchange! So how and when did protecting people from external dangers — the harsh weather and predators — become less important than protecting them from each other? Who was that first homo sapien who decided to hoard what was given by their brethren instead of using it for the common good, then declared a resource shortage and sent their tribesmen to raid neighbours? We will never know the name of the first violator of the natural balance, but the whole history of humanity has turned into a story of vampires fighting for the feeding trough, feasting on the labour, pain, and suffering of coerced and deceived victims!

"And our ancestors? How could they remain idle?

"In those distant times, observing homo sapiens was seen more as fun. The Lemurians hoped that humans would someday learn everything and free themselves from fear like us. Then Old Lemuria sank, and homo liberatus were too busy relocating to the Bermuda colony. It seems that's when humanity slipped out of view... And when they returned, perhaps it was already too late. No matter how hard they tried to change something, no matter how many "prophets" and "sages" they sent, the primal fear dictated its terms. The mission of Jesus proved ultimately that overcoming the destructive influence of fear on humanity could not be achieved by simply teaching people to live in harmony with the Nature that they call God.

"In just two millennia, homo sapiens distorted Jesus's teachings to absurdity. They killed and enslaved their kind in the name of our messenger! They turned his precepts against both the Earth's Nature and, ultimately, their species. That's what happens to our knowledge when passed through the prism of human fear! After Jesus, the number of vampires among humans has only increased. This mutation spread so widely that it even received a name in their medicine — psychopathy, which means both "passion" and "disease" of the soul. Very apt. And now psychopaths rule the world and drive Earth's Nature to the brink of survival.

"While ordinary homo sapiens struggle with or succumb to fear, wrestle with moral questions and dilemmas, and make sacrifices in the name of love, vampires, unburdened by such things, waste no time. Incapable of feeling fear but adept at instilling it, they climb to the hierarchical peaks of the matrix, become its elite, and increasingly enslave humanity.

"And here's another trick of human hypocrisy: homo-sapien doctors do not consider psychopathy an illness! If vampirism were considered a disability, then, according to the matrix's laws, villains would have to be pitied for being born as villains. They would need to get treated rather than punished.

"Just imagine how half the prisoners would move from jails to psychiatric hospitals! Many of those in power would have to follow along with the criminals. Would they allow this to happen?

"So, does it turn out that normal homo sapiens are unable to resist vampires, and no one else but us can do it?

"Hold on, could Nature have created vampires for a reason? If vampirism is a disease, we can and obviously should intervene to bring the psychopaths' brains to the norm of other homo sapiens... But what if vampires exist by Nature's will? Perhaps we don't understand its designs? Can't see the full picture?

"On the other hand, parasites are also created by Nature, yet every living being strives to get rid of them, and if it can't, it weakens and dies...

"What if, by changing the brains of vampires, we disturb the natural balance and betray our core values? Isn't mutation a sign of an impending evolution?

"Let's presume so. If a new species — vampires — is indeed emerging on Earth, then someone must turn into their prey — energy donors or slaves. Could this be about the evolutionary polarisation of homo sapiens, splitting into two species — predator vampires and helpless donors? This idea was already suggested by a writer. Herbert Wells was his name. After all, that's how it is in the animal world— there are hunters and prey, and we don't interfere. So why should we now?

"Because there is another path! Among homo sapiens, there are very few who can resist vampires, such as Ruslan Batalov, for example — but they exist! Our ancestors were homo sapiens too, and each of us present is proof of an evolution leading to the irrelevance of both power and the fear that gave birth to it.

"Nature's law is energy exchange, and vampires undermine this foundation. Yes, vampirism is a mutation, and it arose as a reaction to environmental conditions. So, what are these conditions? Resource scarcity? That's not true though, because

humans have learned to take everything possible — and impossible — from Nature. Besides, the population of homo sapiens is growing rapidly, and this wouldn't happen naturally under resource scarcity, would it? Yet people still fear running out, and they are hoarding endlessly. The more they hoard, the more they fear losing it. And so, there's no peace for them because of this fear. Meanwhile, everything saved as a reserve is energy taken from Nature and not given back. An imbalance.

"Most homo sapiens dream of having more resources than they can use in a lifetime. They accepted a culture of vampirism that idealises wealth and encourages taking as much as possible and giving as little as possible. So, the spread of this mutation is indeed an adaptation to an environment — the one created by humans. It has nothing to do with Nature! Vampires must go.

"What about another form of vampirism, the product of this very culture? It's a soul's illness caused by prolonged anxiety and fear of resource shortages, especially in childhood. It's likely a transitional stage preceding actual mutation. Such vampires have normal homo-sapien brains. Like all people, they not only avoid but feel disgust at blood and violence. They are not devoid of moral values, yet stealing energy is the survival model they have learned from a difficult childhood. They simply don't know another way. After securing resources, the uninnate vampires feel peace and triumph — but only briefly. For them, stealing energy is an intoxication they crave repeatedly.

"Uninnate vampires are less dangerous than mutants, but they are harder to spot because the developed pathology only manifests when its carrier falls into anxiety. Sakhno, for example, reverted to a normal state during peaceful times, started working, and felt quite comfortable in a society based on exchange rather than accumulation — but as soon as the danger of his past sins' exposure arose, he killed an innocent person without hesitation.

"Can uninnate vampirism be cured? Since its cause is external, hypnosis would most likely help, requiring far less skill and energy than interfering with brain structures. On the other hand, there will always be a risk of relapse. Furthermore, tracking down this hidden type of vampire will be far more challenging than identifying mutants: it will require observation and an understanding of human relationships, which is a science in itself. Uninnate vampires might use only selected donors — more accessible victims — rather than anyone indiscriminately. They manifest in a much subtler and more variable way than the mutants do. For example, Polina's mother limits herself to the energy of her own family, while stronger ones, like Vasyura's accomplices, use a wider circle of donors. So, uninnate vampires could be even harder to restore to the natural balance than mutants since normalising the latter's brain would require just a single intervention, after which there should be no risk of them returning to old behaviours.

"Now, as the picture is clear, here's the question: why do we even need to deal with all this? Wouldn't it be better to simply leave Earth, permanently resettle on blessed New Lemuria, and live in peace?

"The idea is appealing, of course, but what about our indigo relatives? Are we really going to abandon them to the mercy of evolution? When the superpowers inherited from us combine with their fear, what will indigo become if the homo-sapien race truly splits into two species"?

Perhaps the inhabitants of Lemuria would have remained indifferent to humanity's fate if not for an extraordinary event: one of the oracles decided to reveal her vision to the others. Seers do this only when the survival of our entire species depends on the decision made in Unity. It would take the fingers of one hand to count the instances of this happening in almost a million years of homo-liberatus history! And here is what the Unified Consciousness envisioned.

"We have always believed that we were helping people out of pure altruism, that our kind was not in danger — but that is not the case at all! If homo liberatus completely withdraw from Earth, the polarisation of the remaining race into vampires and donors will indeed occur. This evolutionary path will be a dead end and fatal for homo sapiens. In a world ruled by vampires, only vampires will have a chance of survival. The mutation will solidify and spread, the birth of psychopathic children will become the norm — and there will not be enough love on Earth to stand against these monsters. Even indigoes will begin to be born as vampires and grow into the most dangerous carriers of this mutation. Permissiveness will make them truly insatiable. They will draw energy from all living and nonliving things and will not care about replenishing it. Within a couple of hundred years, or perhaps even sooner, vampires will exhaust and destroy not only the donor race but all of Earth's Nature and themselves with it!" the prophetess explained.

The pain of the depleted, weakening planet scorched the hearts of homo liberatus. The unified soul of my people became filled with the sorrow of Nature, which, like an aged crone who had outlived her time, had resigned herself helplessly to the inevitability of approaching death. Then we all felt Earth's agony, so unbearable it was as if we were trapped in a state of interplanetary teleportation, slowly and painfully disintegrating into atoms. The Unified Consciousness froze amid this torment as though Arctic cold had covered a stream with ice — the stream that had never stopped flowing for a single moment before. And this was not yet the end of the prophecy!

"Here, on New Lemuria," the oracle continued, *"the humanoids will ascend to a higher evolutionary stage in a few millennia, but, just like homo sapiens, they will not overcome fear. Lemurian hominids too will face the mutation of vampirism and create an even more brutal matrix than humans. Eventually, life will also become unbearable here, and our descendants will*

once again have to search for a new home. Beyond that, nothing more can be seen..."

The visions of a future untouched by our involvement shook the Unity to the core. The race that considered itself free because, so far, it had managed to leave threats behind without engaging with aggressors, the race that believed in the rightfulness of noninterference — the entire race of homo liberatus suddenly realised that it could no longer turn its back on the suffering of Nature's children!

"So, are we just going to keep running?

"No! That's enough! In the end, it always turns out that the problems of other species become our problems, and it may happen that there will simply be nowhere left to retreat. Searching the Universe for another Earth, like an insect in thick grass? In all our years of astral wandering, we were lucky to find only New Lemuria!

"We may be stronger and more advanced, but we need a habitat just as much as any other species. We need Nature, which is harmonious and healthy, not polluted and desecrated by machines — those sticks wielded by former apes!

"These machines give humans the power to move giant objects, communicate across vast distances, and travel anywhere on the planet — this is what they devote their lives and energy to! This is how humans achieve almost everything we can do and assert dominance over all living things. However, homo sapiens have no right to dominance because they are biologically stagnant!

"It is because of their vampiric machines that we find no peace on Earth! And Earth itself has no peace from them anymore!

"If we do not act, we will simply lose our place in the sun! In the two suns even...

"Maybe we should just destroy their technology? Throw humanity back into the Stone Age? Leave them to the mercy of natural selection?

"No, no, we mustn't give in to anger! As tempting as the idea of disabling all machines on Earth is, such a mission would demand enormous energy from us, the energy that would never return to Nature. And we ourselves would have to recover by drawing from Nature and thereby weakening it. We don't want to become like vampires!

"Besides, destruction is repugnant to homo liberatus. None of us would agree to such a course of action...

"Humans already have so many machines that even if we sent one homo liberatus to each of their factories, there wouldn't be enough of us to stop all production at once. Destroying machines gradually would be pointless, as humans would simply use working ones to repair the broken ones.

"Vampires have already become the strongest of homo sapiens and have invented so many ways of taking energy from Nature and freezing it. They are already ravaging the world! If we deprive homo sapiens of their usual energy supply, the starving vampires will become even more dangerous and will convert the best part of humanity into donors even sooner. By suddenly breaking the matrix, we would create a cataclysm and only hasten the final polarisation of the species. Then, the best genetic stock of homo sapiens — donors, creators, and volunteers for Nature, who give their energy to ensure its prosperity — would be enslaved and destroyed...

"What should we do then? If we stay idle, a bleak future awaits not only us...

"If the imbalance is the vampires' doing, then we must rid Nature of them before destroying their tools. Yan took the first step, but now this is our shared mission!

"What lies ahead? First, we need volunteers. We have no shortage of them after glimpsing the future, but most must stay

behind to continue settling New Lemuria, raising children, and helping the Lemurian hominids overcome fear, teaching them to use all the gifts Nature has bestowed upon them. Before it's too late. Only this way can we save this blessed place from losing its harmony.

"Those going to Earth must be able to bring real value to the mission. Yes, all members of Bermuda Lemuria and settlers born on the old planet are our main force. They know both Earth and human customs. And young volunteers must examine their motives before leaving this planet. If your zeal is driven only by a thirst for adventure, staying here is better! At the start of the mission, we will make mistakes, and hotheads will only get in the way.

"Those who have never been to Earth before will need training and adaptation. The Bermuda colony is well suited for this. From there, we will disperse across the planet. All volunteers understand that both hypnotic and physical influence over the vampires will be needed, but we must first find out what happens if a mutant's brain is restored to its original homo-sapien state. We will have to act blindly, as no one has ever done anything like this before. Homo sapiens would call it inhumane... and they'd be right! That's why we must spend time on additional observations and studies of the vampires before performing any intervention. Fortunately, our knowledge spreads at the speed of thought so that a single success will pave the way for the mission.

"As for uninnate vampires, they will require separate handling, and it's unclear how much time that will take. The number of volunteers is minuscule compared to the growing Earth's population.

"Then, why don't we involve the indigo people?

"Yes, that's a solution! There are significantly more of them than us, but it's not so simple either. Time is needed to locate and teach them. Besides, the indigoes' participation must be

completely voluntary, with a full understanding of the mission, not done by blind obedience.

"But if even half of them join in liberating Earth from vampires, indigoes would become an army!

"How long will it take to complete such a mission? A hundred years? Certainly no less!

"And under the current circumstances, it risks turning into a race against the vampires: either we neutralise them, or they completely exhaust and destroy Earth's Nature. One way or another, we must act after seeing the vision we've been shown.

"...By the way, why isn't Cassandra among us? Is she expecting a child? With Yan? Is that certain? Pregnancy might have prevented her from teleporting between planets, although skipping the Unity on New Lemuria to protect a child conceived on Earth hasn't happened in these hundred years. The strangest thing is that Cassandra completely disappeared after that trip to KGB. Moreover, the seer has shielded her mind and blocked us from hearing her! No one knows where she is now..."

Not once before had a Lemurian woman done anything like this! By leaving everyone in the dark about her fate, Cassandra was subjecting to trials not only herself but us too, as every oracle is our shared treasure. Still, homo liberatus trusted their seers as these women were endowed with absolute wisdom. No one doubted that Cassandra knew what she was doing and that she was doing it for the good of her people. I was the only one feeling uneasy...

Chapter 24. The Iron Cataclysm

The return of nearly a hundred Lemurians to Earth disturbed the ocean's calm near the Bermuda colony. We dived into greater depths for recovery at once, but within mere seconds, a powerful wave surged from the ocean. Slicing through the water with its conical head, an imposing metallic body filled with destructive energy charged toward us, rapidly closing the distance.

"Some welcome party!" one of the newcomers blurted out. "Don't you have the dome here?"

Barely managing to reassemble their atoms, all homo liberatus, who had just arrived from New Lemuria, teleported into the depths of the impenetrable jungle at the heart of the island.

"What was that?" my brethren wondered as they settled into the curves of tropical branches and the tangles of thick liana stems.

"Not what was, but what is," the elderly Peresvet stated grimly. *"That's a weapon, a human invention."*

"In the water?" Three young Lemurians, for whom the just-ended Unity was their first experience, had followed us despite warnings. Their enthusiasm and craving for adventure had led them here, but they had not expected this kind of adventure.

"Did you think humans only fight on land?"

"How did they find our island?" Mina asked the question that was on everyone's mind. *"And the energy dome is gone... Does that mean the colony is now visible to any ship or plane?"*

"I'm afraid the colony might be gone too," Simon presumed. He looked preoccupied.

We had spent about six Earth's weeks on New Lemuria, and since telepathy and astral travel were impossible during the Unity, no one had watched over the events in the colony or could explain what had happened here. The protective dome, which had shielded Bermuda Lemuria from humans, was formed from the Earth's energy. It had been intact for centuries, even in the absence of homo liberatus on the island. And yet, almost simultaneously, two of us had the same thought. *"Jim!"*

After interplanetary travel, the stay in the ocean's waters was too short this time, so hardly anyone had managed to recover fully. Everybody needed rest, but there was also no time to delay reconnaissance. Who knew if the human devices could detect us again? Leaving our companions in the tropical thicket, so dense it would take hours even for someone on foot to traverse it, my father, Indo, and I set off for the village of shipwrecked homo sapiens.

It had only about twenty houses, but now nearly every one of them had a military vehicle parked nearby. These vehicles, supported by four or six thick wheels, carried bulky, armoured, sand-coloured cabins with small window-like openings. From soldiers' thoughts during the war, my father had learned how unbearably cramped and stuffy it was for the young men inside these metal boxes, yet they rejoiced at the lack of windows because it gave an enemy less chance of killing them. The armoured vehicles, arriving and departing with deafening roars, reeked of burnt oil and other noxious substances, worse even than the smell in Polina's father's garage.

Among the huts, people in uniform matching the vehicles' colours bustled about. Judging by their scattered thoughts, almost all the island's settlers had been evacuated, and only two stragglers remained in a house on the village margin. Both Marcus, a middle-aged Spaniard, and Roger, an elderly American, had arrived at the Bermuda colony around the same time as Jim. However, unlike our would-be suicide, they had taken this change in their lives far more calmly, even somewhat positively.

Marcus had been almost a child and an orphan back then. A distant relative had decided to take him to the United States, but the ship carrying the boy fell under our dome, leaving Marcus stranded there. So now, he was in no hurry to leave the island, uncertain where to go if he returned to the mainland. His memories of life among humans consisted only of a bleak orphanage where no one cared about him. The colony had become not only his home but also a school of "magic," although in all his years on the island, he had mastered only telepathy and the basics of telekinesis.

Roger was the sailor who had been paid to ferry the boy to America. Marcus's cousin uncle was a garage owner and Roger's casual acquaintance. He had hired more than one relative from war-torn Europe believing this act of "charity" to justify the low wages he paid the immigrants. So, Roger was tasked with bringing yet another cheap worker but never reached the destination. The old sailor was now accustomed to the island's tranquillity and feared leaving until he knew how to survive on the mainland. The two men, thrown together by fate, had been inseparable since the shipwreck.

We decided it was best to observe them in disguise at first. They sat at an old makeshift table with food that bore no resemblance to the diet islanders followed under homo liberatus. Eighty-year-old Roger chewed on canned beans in tomato sauce with his remaining teeth while his younger companion hungrily scooped foul-smelling tinned stew from a metal can. Hunting animals had been forbidden in the colony under Lemurian rule, and while the settlers had grown accustomed to a vegetarian diet, not all embraced it with equal enthusiasm. Even these two, who had developed some "paranormal" abilities, still doubted the direct link between their achievements and abstaining from eating corpses.

"Human hedonism is contagious," Simon thought gloomily, seeing the two's feast.

"Contagious and harmful!" Indo agreed. *"Soon their skills will start to decline, so there's no harm in interrupting this dreary meal."*

At that point, Marcus stirred and cautiously asked the empty air, "Who's there?"

Indo, who was familiar to both men, seemed sufficient to clarify the situation. He revealed himself to the settlers while my father and I stayed invisible.

"It's me, don't be afraid," Indo said in a deliberately calm tone. He nodded toward the window. "What happened here?"

"Can't you see for yourself?" Roger grumbled. "They swarmed in like an iron locust plague!" He added silently, *"Won't even let one die in peace!"*

"Where are the rest of our… I mean, your people?"

"They crossed over to the mainland," Marcus explained, wiping his greasy lips with the sleeve of his new sand-coloured shirt.

"When?"

"Just yesterday…"

"And what are we supposed to do now?" the old man said grimly. "Noise and stench, orders and commotion. You've been gone so long this time! Missed it by just two days…"

"But how?" our companion pressed on.

"Take a look for yourself!" Marcus grabbed a rolled-up newspaper titled *Daily Motion* from the bench and handed it to the Lemurian. Indo read the headline aloud.

"'THIRTY-SEVEN YEARS AS HOSTAGES OF ALIENS! The Mystery of the Bermuda Triangle Finally Solved!'" He looked questioningly at his companions. "What aliens?"

"You of course!" Roger barked, as elderly people often do when faced with someone's incomprehension.

Indo raised an eyebrow ironically and continued reading. "'United States citizen Jim Moleskin has returned to his family after a thirty-seven-year absence. During this time, the former pilot of a commercial airline was presumed missing, along with all passengers of the *Tiger* aircraft, which vanished in the Bermuda Triangle on January 30th, 1948. Mr. Moleskin claims he was held hostage by aliens who set up a colony on one of the Bermuda Islands, disguising it from the American authorities.'" Indo paused and remarked calmly, "Jim knows full well we're not aliens."

"The reporters just find that more exciting!" Roger snapped back.

The Lemurian shrugged and continued with the newspaper.

"'The former pilot claims that not only his entire crew and passengers but also citizens of various countries who disappeared in the Bermuda Triangle over the decades are still on this invisible island. Mr. Moleskin reported that the aliens who rule there possess every imaginable superpower: they can read minds, move objects remotely, teleport, and cure all diseases. The poor man, who miraculously returned home, asserts that the aliens also trained their captives in these abilities, promising that anyone who mastered teleportation would be allowed to leave the island freely. However, according to Mr. Moleskin, this has never happened in all the time he spent there.'"

"Well, Jim told them everything about us quite accurately," Indo concluded, and Marcus laughed carelessly.

"Exactly! So what? Who's going to believe him?"

The homo liberatus responded in a professorial tone. "And most won't believe him precisely because Jim himself barely learned anything." Years spent in the settlers' company had clearly left their mark.

"He hated your lot. That's hardly a great motivator!" Marcus smirked, then, unable to hide his resentment, added, "Why did you make an exception for him anyway?"

"It was a deal, an important one for us," Indo replied with restraint. "But what reason did he have to hate us? He should have practiced and teleported himself home. In all the thousands of years the colony has existed, we've never once broken our promise!"

Sardonic laughter rang out in response, both men amused by my companion's supposed naivety. However, Indo was neither naive nor joking. He had been born in the Bermuda colony four hundred years ago and had seen several such returns of homo sapiens to the continent. True, all these events took place long before old Roger's time. Humans only believe what they see with their own eyes or what they think are facts, though they rarely have enough access to the latter to judge accurately.

"They say Jim ran straight to the police the very next day!" Marcus announced.

"And wasn't afraid they'd think he was crazy!" Roger chimed in.

"Wouldn't you have done the same?" Indo asked curiously.

"Who knows? If someone had been waiting for me back on the mainland, I'd have been there ages ago. No dome would've held me back. But as things stand..."

"That's unlikely," the Lemurian interrupted. "Still, how did all these soldiers and machines get in here?"

"How do you think? Looks like they broke through your barrier with a laser cannon or something like that," Roger explained, though without much certainty.

"I heard their thoughts," Marcus added. "Apparently, with even a vague idea of the island's existence, they could have found it long ago, but if you don't know something exists, you don't look for it."

"We're no experts on this sort of thing," Roger grumbled with a touch of challenge, "since we haven't followed technological progress for the past forty years, thanks to you." He sighed. "Now they won't leave us alone and probably won't allow us to stay here. When I get to the mainland, I'll just be an old fool who's out of touch with life."

"Or you'll be famous, like Jim!" Marcus teased.

"I don't deal with paparazzi, and I wouldn't recommend it to you either," the old man snapped, then, jabbing a finger toward

Indo, added, "Not that I have any complaints about Lemurians! It was good here, almost like the Garden of Eden."

"So, what are you going to do now?" Despite the trouble that had befallen us, Indo, who had spent most of his life in the Bermuda colony, continued to care about people. "Do you need help? We can carry you to any continent you choose."

"Thanks but no thanks!" The old man even snorted. "You help me now, and then I'll never get rid of the press, or, worse, the secret services!" He glanced at his companion. "Better for both of us to keep quiet about what they taught us here. It might cost us dearly!" Marcus nodded in agreement, and Roger turned to the Lemurian. "We'll sort it out ourselves. There are plenty of helpers around now!" He groaned as he stood and looked out the window. "The bigger question is, what will *you* do?"

"We'll have to think about it," Indo replied tersely.

Roger was right. By making a deal with Jim, we hadn't considered that his hatred could lead to such a disastrous outcome or that homo sapiens had advanced their technology even further since my people relocated to another planet.

"Which is exactly why we have relocated," Simon replied. *"This was inevitable. You shouldn't have let Jim go. You simply took the easy option in your chase for the hypnotist."*

Leaving the hut, Indo said to the settlers, "I wish you luck. I hope everything works out well for you. I have only one request: do not tell *them*" — and he nodded towards the window — "that you saw me."

Having received a promise from Marcus and Roger not to reveal the presence of the "aliens" on the island, we left their hut. It was true that the colony on Bermuda Lemuria, which had served as the home and refuge to homo liberatus for millennia, had come to an end. We were no longer responsible for the settlers, but we wanted to know whether they had kept secret the skills we had taught them and everything they knew about us.

So, returning to the jungle where our kin awaited news about the current situation was still premature.

There was steady yet unhurried activity between the houses and beyond the village boundaries. There were so many soldiers that the huts left vacant by the island's former "hostages" could not accommodate them all. As a result, the village became surrounded by spacious tents supported by deeply driven metal stakes and fastenings. Inside these tents was an abundance of equipment that soldiers might need but that could also be packed into rucksacks if necessary. The tents, soldiers' uniforms, and backpacks were made of sand-coloured fabrics. From a bird's-eye view, all this might have been hard to spot, but up close, everything gave off a strange, repellent smell, not of dirt or human sweat, but of military gear. It was difficult to pinpoint what exactly the soldiers' belongings smelled of. Simon's mind was instantly flooded with memories of all the human wars he had seen while wandering the world of men in search of my mother.

"A hundred years have passed, yet the stench of war is still the same!" he thought.

"This isn't a war, father," I objected. *"They are just staying here and hanging around."*

"War is not an action, son, it's a state of mind," he explained. *"A miserable human mind, twisted by fear and the hatred of it, in a desperate attempt to get rid of it, to defend oneself, or at least to imagine that there is a force against fear. And lacking a force of their own, homo sapiens use the power of machines and weapons."*

"So, is this the smell of machines and weapons?"

"Among other things, yes."

Several soldiers slept inside the tents, while others, awaiting an alarm, busied themselves with tasks whose purpose was unclear to us. We saw them servicing machines, checking weapons, and preparing for a possible — our possible — attack.

Of course, no one intended to attack them. Moreover, none of this equipment could defeat or capture a homo liberatus, so these healthy men were simply wasting the what precious time remained in their already short lives.

Duty filled the soldiers' mental space almost completely. The rest of their thoughts were occupied by their meagre human relationships with their comrades and families, if they had any, and with the belief in their righteousness as defenders of freedom and the national interests of the American people. Only a few of these men really wanted to kill. The rest suffered from the most perverse form of fear — the fear of making choices. These men were prepared to risk their own and others' lives just to enjoy the luxury of replying to any accusation with, "I'm a soldier. I followed orders."

"We need to find their commanders," Simon suggested.

The headquarters was in the largest hut. We carefully teleported inside, staying invisible, and only a five-second interference in the radio centre could have given away the presence of homo liberatus if anyone had suspected it. We quickly compressed our force fields to the minimum and froze, waiting.

The far wall of the room was almost entirely covered by a map of the Bermuda Islands. Our Lemuria was not printed on it, but someone had drawn the new island in red with remarkable accuracy. It now stood out, like a drop of blood on the light blue of the ocean. The room was cluttered with rows of awkward folding chairs, and between the map and a small window was a compact table with coloured markers, sharpened pencils, and several sheets of handwritten notes.

Half an hour later, two men entered. One was, as they say, a seasoned wolf and, judging by his appearance, the senior officer. He was a short, stocky blond man. This last detail could only be inferred from the barely grown stubble on his shaved head. The tanned, weathered face of the major was lined with fine wrinkles that spoke of a hardened character rather than age, as this excellent specimen of healthy homo sapiens was about ten years younger than me. Beneath the short sleeves of his military shirt, his impressive muscles flexed, and his trousers, evidently very practical, had numerous pockets filled with everything a constantly on-the-move field officer might need.

The second man, a lieutenant, was younger, leaner but also muscular, dressed in the same camouflage uniform. He seemed to look up at the major despite being taller. This one was an ambitious careerist and... an uninnate vampire. He had darting, drilling brown eyes, perpetually pale skin, and a thin mosquito-like nose. The lieutenant closed the door quietly and asked, "What do you think of all this, Commander? Where did those aliens go?"

"Aliens?" the major snapped. "Nonsense! Collective hallucinations of the poor survivors, driven mad by hopelessness."

"But someone kept them here and managed to hide an entire island from the authorities, didn't they?"

The infantry brigade commander had seen many places in his service, from Vietnam to Grenada. Having fought for the freedom of nations across planet Earth, even when the nations stupidly resisted their own freedom. He knew all too well how inventive enemies of law and democracy could be. A hardened pragmatist, the major had learned through experience that every miracle eventually had a ridiculously mundane explanation. So, his subordinate's words made him wince as if from a nagging toothache, and he replied, not entirely convincingly, "Pirates, I suppose."

His plan was fairly straightforward: wait for the pirates to return, deal with them, and then hand over the "cleared" island for yet another military base. It didn't matter to the major which agency would take possession of the territory.

"You'll be waiting a long time for nothing!" we laughed in unison.

"And how did the pirates manage to keep people here all these years? Hypnosis, perhaps?"

"Maybe. Who knows? Hypnosis is a perfectly real thing," the commander replied, flipping through the notes on his desk.

"Then why did they keep the captives alive?" the lieutenant pressed on.

"Well, not everyone is as bloodthirsty as you, mate!" the major smirked, wincing again.

"Alright, let's say they were kindhearted pirates," the lieutenant snorted, ignoring the commander's jab. "What about that defence system our ship breached? Were they conducting experiments right under the Pentagon's nose? What if it wasn't pirates but the Russians?"

The major shrugged and thought, *"Was there really a defence system?"* He wasn't interested in science fiction. *"Maybe it was the Russians. If that's the case, it's far worse than pirates!"* The major found this version quite plausible but didn't want to believe it, as prolonged, undetected Russian activity in the Bermuda Islands would bode nothing good.

"And the Russians have powerful hypnotists. They work without any medical drugs. I've read about it!" the young vampire insisted, enjoying the opportunity to irritate the commander. The major glanced impatiently at his water and shockproof personalised watch, the award for military merit he was very proud of. Looking at this watch always lifted his spirits. However, it was also showing that the third participant in their meeting was disgracefully late. Then they heard the roar of an approaching vehicle outside.

The final participant was the captain of the military ship that had been drifting where our protective dome used to end. When the ship detected water and air disturbances caused by the teleportation of the homo liberatus into the ocean, the torpedo had been fired from it. As soon as the third man entered the hut, we sighed in relief: although our plunge into the ocean had been detected, the ship devices hadn't identified what it was, and the torpedo was fired had been just in case. Still, the captain looked worried.

"A large number of organic bodies fell into the sea between the shore and my vessel," the captain blurted out as he stepped inside. "A torpedo was fired, but it hit no targets. The targets disappeared."

"Disappeared?" the major asked incredulously.

"That's just it, we know no more! There was a cluster of living beings, and then they were gone."

"Could they really have teleported?" the lieutenant exclaimed in awe.

"Don't talk nonsense!" the commander barked at him before turning to the captain. "Could they have been dolphins?"

"Maybe dolphins," the captain replied, twisting his lips. "But dolphins don't fall into the sea out of nowhere, and we would have tracked their movement..."

"I don't like this at all!" the major said with deliberate dryness. "And the radars? Could these objects have been dropped from a plane?"

"If it was air transport, it must have been cutting-edge technology because the radars showed nothing but calm seas and skies."

"Well then it must be the Russians!" the lieutenant almost shouted, sounding oddly excited.

"Looks that way," the infantry brigade commander muttered through gritted teeth. "Order a full assembly."

"Yes, sir!" And the young vampire, energised by the commander's frustration, rushed off to rally the troops. This was, of course, a complete waste of time and effort since, within a minute, we had already slipped back into the jungle to rejoin our own. And within seven minutes, all the mission participants had teleported to the other hemisphere, to an island in Halong Bay, where I had spent two weeks before it all began.

Suddenly, our now-shared task had become even more complicated. Spontaneously, we experienced a merging of consciousness to achieve unanimous agreement on what needed to be done next.

Our mission had not been compromised, not even now. On the contrary, the fall of Bermuda Lemuria only reaffirmed our determination to rid the planet of the vampires, whose strong presence, unsurprisingly, was noticed among the military. Still, finding a new colony was a must.

Homo liberatus had spent millennia hiding from humans, never seeking power, world domination, or even influence, as we had always found everything necessary for a happy life. All we had ever needed was one peaceful place on this planet where we could meditate and recover, connecting with the Earth's energy without the risk of being interrupted or attacked. Could we still find a corner of the world where, by the twentieth century, no human had ever set foot, and none would in the next hundred years? As beautiful as this island in Halong Bay was, it was far from suitable. Traces of a campfire were visible right nearby. Homo sapiens had already been here, and they were bound to return!

So where should we go? Scatter across the world and explore the most impenetrable regions? Perhaps we should inspect areas with harsh climates that are less appealing to homo sapiens?

The search for a new promised land was entrusted to the younger ones, who had teleported from New Lemuria for the first time. For them, this quest would be something of an educational expedition, a chance to study Earth's Nature and observe the behaviour of those who believed themselves to be its rulers. The rest decided to continue the mission and start with finding as many indigoes as possible. For the most experienced homo liberatus, the research and experiments aimed at neutralising the mutant vampires remained the focus. This was true for me as well, despite my youth. Vasyura still walked the Earth, and I felt it was my duty to walk him on his final journey in person.

We left the bay slowly and quietly. Like the other young Lemurians, I was disheartened. So abrupt ruination of our Bermuda colony felt like the loss a leaning point. During the group meditation, I clearly heard that few believed there was a place left on Earth where no homo sapiens had ever set foot. My father, however, viewed the destruction of the Bermuda colony differently.

"Disclosure of the island was only a matter of time," he explained philosophically. "Sooner or later, it was bound to happen. Bermuda Lemuria survived right under the Americans' noses for two centuries! The timing, however, is truly unfortunate."

"If it was expected, why didn't our colonists start relocating earlier?" I retorted, unable to hide my irritation.

"There was no reason to," Simon replied calmly. "None of the oracles raised the alarm. A hundred years ago, the seers insisted on searching for a new planet, but this time, they were silent. That means the fall of the Bermuda colony is part of events that cannot be avoided."

I struggled to accept his words. The oracles were impossible to understand. Their thoughts were almost always veiled, except in extremely rare cases. If they shared their visions more often, the temptation to change everything that seemed "wrong" would be too great. And who are we to distort the course of events? One change inevitably triggers a chain of others. Besides, time and the totality of everything that happens in the world, both joyful and tragic, are part of Nature's design, and we, who cannot see beyond our noses, have no right to challenge its mysterious ways. And so on…

I had heard it all since childhood, yet I couldn't shake the feeling that we had been betrayed. The prophetesses of New

Lemuria hadn't even joined the mission. Not even one of them! Cassandra too had not turned up. *"And that can't be a coincidence,"* everyone thought. Yet they still believed in her.

Chapter 25. Investigation

The end of the workday meant nothing to a KGB investigator of high-priority cases, though Yevgeny Dalatovich could have gone home that day. His wife Ira had probably already prepared something delicious, since she wasn't on a night shift. But Ira had long since grown accustomed to her husband's hectic, unlimited schedule. From the very beginning, she knew who she was marrying. Almost straight from their wedding ceremony, Yevgeny, then a junior lieutenant, had gone on an assignment, and his young wife went to assist in a complex surgical operation. No questions. No reproaches. No disappointment. Ira loved her job as much as he loved his. Her husband protected the Motherland, and she saved the lives of its youngest citizens. They were a perfect pair. Two dedicated souls. Having children of their own never seemed to fit into their lives, sometimes making them sad. It seemed they had both been born to serve others…

Twenty years later, Yevgeny had earned a reputation for investigating and exposing war crimes, while Irina had become the leading paediatric surgeon in Minsk. She has improved her cooking skills too.

His assignment to the Vasyura case did not surprise Dalatovich. Yet the investigation reached the authorities only six months after Ruslan's visit to the awards department at the Brovary military enlistment office. The arrest of the last Nazi collaborator was being prepared meticulously, and therefore, not without delays caused mainly by interdepartmental bureaucracy. If I hadn't been preoccupied, first with Polina, then with Unity and the aftermath of the Bermuda colony's collapse, I might have gone mad watching the human red tape unfold. When I at last returned to the Vasyura case and discovered that he still hadn't been arrested, I was shocked and began to regret leaving the vampire's punishment in the hands of homo sapiens, but Simon, ever wise about human nature, calmed me.

“What did you expect from the beings incapable of telepathy? If they could read the vampire’s mind as easily as you do, they, of course, wouldn’t need to chase the evidence of his crimes. And without telepathy, the cumbersome justice system of homo sapiens is a blessing.”

“How is it a blessing?” I fumed. “It gives criminals time to come up with defences or even escape! And in Vasyura’s case, the old man might die before the trial. No justice at all then!”

“That’s true when the accused is truly guilty,” Simon replied. I stared at my father, puzzled, as he exclaimed, “My god, Yan, you still have so much to learn! Imagine if a non-telepathic judge imprisoned an innocent person. Meanwhile, some cunning murderer who framed him would walk free!”

My father was right. I’d become too fixated on Vasyura. Besides, the investigation and trial once again offered me an excellent opportunity to better understand human ways, as flawed and dead-ended as homo sapiens themselves. So, while my kin explored Earth’s most inaccessible corners for a new colony, I followed every step of the investigation alongside its participants, blending in and staying silent.

Copies of documents handed over by Ruslan to Nikolai Seliverstov were, of course, insufficient to justify such serious accusations against a respected elderly man. These matters were no longer resolved quickly. During the document review, the case got nearly buried again. It survived only thanks to Uncle Pasha’s vigilance, who, as Colonel Pilatov, kept his finger on the pulse, pushing the case to the USSR’s general prosecutor, who overturned the findings of the earlier postwar investigation into Vasyura. Only then did the military board of the Supreme Court open new charges against my vampire. Finally, the papers accusing the Red Army officer of desertion and collaboration with the enemy were sent to the Military Tribunal, where a lead investigator was appointed, while Yevgeny’s task was limited to finding and delivering witnesses this time. He welcomed the role, as he already knew most of the witnesses and had interviewed them repeatedly during earlier processes.

Lieutenant Colonel Dalatovich wasn't heading home. Instead, he pored over documents that had been gathering dust in the archive for a decade. He kept rereading records of interrogation, many of which he had attended himself, and he agonised over them.

"How could it happen," the investigator wondered, *"that Vasyura escaped justice until now? How was he allowed to live among people who might still have photographs of relatives he killed? And now what? Vasyura's an old man. Even the death penalty can't take away the years he lived comfortably — a gift this monster never deserved. And worst of all, there's no one to blame. Maybe I missed something then. Maybe I didn't double-check at the time!"*

Yevgeny pressed his balding head between his hands. Almost every interrogation record of former policemen from the 118th Battalion mentioned their chief of staff, yet no matter how hard he tried, the investigator couldn't recall Vasyura, who had testified as a witness in the Meleshko case. Here were the traitor's written statements, which were very detailed and listed dozens of names, but they didn't hold a word about his own high-ranking position in the battalion. The phrase "I can't remember" emerged throughout the document instead.

Over the years, much had truly been forgotten, and now Yevgeny struggled to find the thread in his memory, which seemed to taunt him, always leading him back to the beginning.

...Forty-three years had passed since his first task as a partisan courier. The nine-year-old boy had fought the Nazis with the same zeal he had shown playing cops and robbers when he was seven, before the war turned that game into grim reality. Through secret forest paths unknown even to most villagers, Zhenya* carried underground messages to the partisan camp and returned to his home under the unsuspecting wing of his mother. Until one day, the partisan commander called the boy into his dugout after everyone else had left. The battle-hardened man placed a trembling hand on the boy's shoulder and said softly, "Listen, Zheka. You can't go back to Osovy today." Meeting the boy's questioning eyes, he added in a hollow voice, "Or ever. Osovy is no more."

Unwilling to comprehend the dreadful meaning of what had been said, Zhenya stubbornly asked, "What about Mum? Misha? Nastenyka?" Tears were already streaming down his cheeks.

"There's no one left, son." The commander forced those words out, and while he held the orphan, trembling with sobs in his arms, a single salty drop crawled down the face of the Red Army officer — that drop was worth an ocean of tears.

Zhenya stayed with the detachment until the Germans were driven out of Belarus. Then the commander wrote to the cousin aunt of Dalatovich, a teacher in Minsk, asking her to take in the former partisan messenger until the boy's father returned from the front. But the father never came back. He was killed in 1944, leaving the single, childless Yevdokiya Grigoryevna as the sole guardian of the teenager, who was mature beyond his age.

The seasoned teacher quickly noticed the boy's sharp mind as he excelled equally in both mathematics and the humanities.

"You must study!" the wise woman never tired of saying. "If you want to prevent such horrors from happening again, you must put yourself in a position where you can help stop them."

Forty years had passed since Victory Day, but the war refused to let go. Or perhaps Yevgeny could not let go of the war that had taken his family…

… Two young students from the statistics college worked part-time as loaders at the state archive in Minsk. Dozens of heavy boxes had arrived at the freight station. Documents marked *Classified* had been delivered from Czechoslovakia, Poland, Hungary, and Germany. Who knew what lay in those boxes? Perhaps the devil himself was sealed within them. There was something ominous about the Gothic script stamped on the German labels…

Later, unexpectedly appointed as archivist of the classified section in the Minsk archive, Zhenya peeked into some of the documents from those very boxes but could make little sense of them. His knowledge of languages was insufficient. He had completed law school but had never quite mastered foreign languages. He had always felt they were mere shells covering the real treasure — the content. And it was the content that fascinated the KGB academy student far more.

His assignment to the prosecutor's office in Pleshchenitsy led to work in various Belarussian cities. Dalatovich's career turned into a relentless hunt for former Nazis and collaborators who had hidden themselves after the war like cockroaches. The hardest part was distinguishing the guilty criminals and traitors from the innocently accused. There were too many of both, and Yevgeny relived the war with every investigation. Yet he bore his burden without complaint.

Thanks to Dalatovich, charges were dropped against a woman who had spent fifteen years in labour camps because her son had served in the German police. In the aftermath of the war, filtering out former Nazi collaborators had been chaotic, while public anger against them was fierce and sometimes blind. The investigators who had probed wartime collaboration were only human and members of that very public. They had overlooked the fact that the woman's second son had fought in a partisan unit and that, for three years of the Nazi occupation, the poor woman had endured a civil war within her household. The charges were overturned after a reinvestigation led by Dalatovich during his time in the Pleshchenitsy prosecutor's office. This earned the young professional the local community's trust and a reputation as a meticulous investigator with his superiors.

Despite his youth, Yevgeny saw himself as a cog in the justice machine rather than the one steering it. He harboured no illusions: though he had restored freedom to an unjustly accused woman, it was impossible to return the fifteen years of her life that had been stolen from her. Meanwhile, dozens of genuine traitors continued to enjoy the benefits of the rising nation that had defeated the Nazis. That thought alone drove Yevgeny to keep doing his work, no matter how painful the memories…

He returned to the archive later with a translator colleague. Together, the former classmates dug into those very trophy documents. Even Edik, a polyglot, struggled with the intricate Gothic script, but their efforts weren't wasted. One by one, they unpacked the boxes that Zhenya himself had once hauled off the train and onto those shelves. Soon they came across a folder labelled *Borisov District Commissariat* and special reports from the Pleshchenitsy gendarmerie for 1943 in it. One document read, *On 22 March 1943, the 118th punitive police battalion, under the command of Erich Kerner, carried out an operation against partisans and the population in the village of Khatyn.*

By then, a memorial had already been erected at the site of the burned village. Guides there avoided mentioning the atrocities committed by the 118th Ukrainian as though the traitor battalion had never existed. Instead, tourists shivering at the eerie tolling of bells were only told about the village burned by German occupiers.

It wasn't that Senior Investigator Dalatovich was unaware of police units composed entirely of traitors to the Motherland, but the KGB prosecutors had had very little precise information after the war. And now, he held it in his hands. For years, this very information had just sat there, gathering dust!

I even felt a twinge of envy for Dalatovich as he caught *his* vampire long before I found mine. Using documents from the trophy archive, he tracked down the first five former police officers of the 118th Battalion, including the platoon commander's assistant who had destroyed the village of Osovy, Grigory Lakusta. Witnesses, former comrades, testified that this butcher had been especially brutal, executing civilians in the village where Yevgeny's family had lived. Lakusta himself might have murdered Yevgeny's mother, brother, and little sister. After the war, he managed to hide in Donetsk, working as a miner among ordinary Soviet citizens and enjoying the same benefits as they did. If Lakusta was a vampire, he hadn't been born one. Or so it seemed from Dalatovich's recollections of their encounter. The ex-punisher's eyes were filled with terror when the investigator met him.

Asked whether he had ever been to Belarus, Lakusta exhaled. "I've been waiting for you!" In peacetime, the killer's conscience had somehow awakened.

... A Komsomol girl, the daughter of the traitor in disguise, hung upside down from the fifth-floor window, thrashing in hysteria after learning about her father's horrific and shameful past. Dalatovich managed to grab her by the ankles and prevent her from killing herself. He saved the life of his mother's murderer's child.

"Now that truly clears karma!" I thought.

Lakusta and the other four revealed many details in the hope of buying a pardon. Trains, planes, and blurred and broken roads across Russia, Ukraine, and Belarus. Nearly nine months of investigation. The massacres of Belarussians, in which the 118th Schutzmannschaft Battalion played the main role, were not limited to Khatyn or Osovy — the list of settlements destroyed by these executioners spanned over four hundred names. Lakusta failed to buy his life — there were simply too many witnesses to this vampire's bloodthirstiness. It was truly hard to imagine the future of the poor girl, the traitor's daughter. "The son is not responsible for the father," ** but still... the other four executioners were sentenced to ten and fifteen years. Could they be helpful now?

Later, the trial against Meleshko began...

"So many thoughts are flooding my mind!" The investigator snapped out of his memories, irritated. *"And none of them are useful! So how could I have missed Vasyura?"*

I realised that without my help, it would be hard for the lieutenant colonel to get out of this dead end, because guilt is a poor assistant when action is needed. I knew far more now thanks to attending the vampires' banquet. So, I induced a perfectly understandable end-of-the-workday drowsiness in Dalatovich.

The lieutenant colonel didn't remember Vasyura because he had never seen him. After meeting an old acquaintance in the corridor of the KGB building in Kiev in 1974, the former head of the Nazi headquarters never made it to Grodno and didn't personally attend the interrogation. His former protégé agent was now a somewhat important figure who knew all the ins and outs of the complex judicial system. Together, the two vampires fabricated written testimonies, after which Vasyura went to Brovary and, with the help of a friendly doctor — the other vampire from the banquet — easily obtained a fake medical certificate claiming he was gravely ill and therefore unable to appear for questioning in person. And then…

The investigator startled, lifting his face from the desk. The strap mark from a folder was glaringly red, like a scar, on his cheek. *"What a dream!"* he thought, rubbing his eyes. Yevgeny stood, paced back and forth in the office, poured water from a glass decanter into a large, faceted glass, and downed it in one gulp. He walked to the window and stared at the snowflakes drifting in the streetlamp's glow.

Suddenly, he thought with absolute clarity, *"It's entirely possible that's exactly what happened!"*

I mentally praised the former archivist for trusting his intuition. He abruptly turned, strode to the desk, and began frantically rifling through the numerous thick folders containing details of cases that had been closed more than ten years ago. Finally, he found a brown official envelope with a telex from the

Kiev branch of the KGB, stating: *The witness in the Meleshko case, Grigory Nikitiyevich Vasyura, is unable to attend for questioning due to serious illness. Written testimony and a medical certificate are enclosed.* In the same envelope lay a small slip of paper bearing a diagnosis: *lung cancer.*

"There was probably no cancer at all," Dalatovich guessed. *"And how dared the doctor write such a lie? She could have brought it onto herself!"*

It never occurred to the honest investigator, who dedicated himself wholly to people, that psychopaths were indifferent to superstitions and unafraid of divine punishment. Now everything fell into place. Finally! In the seventies, when dozens of witnesses were still alive, both among the Belarussian victims and their tormentors, and when the latter had to be hunted down across the country with minimal resources, the likelihood of overlooking an aging traitor supposedly dying of a terminal illness was quite high…

Yevgeny still couldn't recall how he had decided not to pursue Vasyura back then and had even failed to create a separate file on him. His memory was like a gaping white void that grew more prominent as he focused on it.

Dalatovich finally threw up his hands. *"This is some kind of devilry!"* The investigator straightened the documents on his desk and headed home, feeling relieved by the thought that, most likely, ten years ago, he hadn't simply overlooked a villain but had shown humanity.

***

And so, more than six months after Ruslan visited the military enlistment office, a black UAZ with no rear windows pulled up outside the village council of the Velykodymersky state farm. Three civilians stepped out of the vehicle, though their military bearing betrayed them. Leaving crisp chains of footprints in the fresh snow, the visitors entered the two-story white brick building, opened the sturdy door marked *Deputy Director of Economic Affairs* without knocking, and stepped inside. They were met by a pair of malevolent eyes, black as the abyss, so piercing that the state security officer who entered first felt a chill run down his spine.

"Who are you?" the vampire growled hoarsely.

"Vasyura Grigory Nikitiyevich?"

"Let's assume so," came the sarcastic response.

"You must come with us. You are under arrest on suspicion of committing a war crime."

"What?" the former Nazi officer barked. "What crime?" Rather than the hoarse tremor one might expect in the face of such a grave accusation, his voice rang with the cold edge of steel, a metal used for sharp daggers.

"You have the right to remain silent."

"Krotovsky, bastard!" the vampire raged. *"So, he didn't come through for me after all! Fine. If it's the gallows for me, then we'll go together!"* Out loud, however, his voice transformed, becoming overly friendly. "Listen, lads, this is all some kind of mistake! I'm a war veteran!"

The news that Vasyura had been taken to a detention centre spread through Velika Dymerka almost as quickly as if its residents could transmit thoughts over distances like Lemurians. Barely an hour later, Deputy Head Galina Grigoryevna demanded her employment record book from the school's personnel office. The document bore the surname of her late husband. In the evening, she boarded a train for the northern capital, carrying a suitcase and a large handbag, inside which, along with hastily gathered essentials, lay a passport under the same non-Vasyura surname. And thus, Galina vanished without a word to anyone, hoping to avoid being tracked on the banks of Neva.

***

Dalatovich was fortunate not to be in direct charge of Vasyura's case. It was led by Colonel Viktor Glazkov, chairman of the Military Tribunal, who also had experience with high-profile treason cases, albeit those involving officers. To the credit of both investigators, they felt more inclined to shoot the vampire than to flee in terror, unlike most homo sapiens who encountered Vasyura. Still, both agreed that few exposed traitors had ever displayed such slipperiness, such cold intelligence, paired with gambler-like excitement, and such brazen deceit. Viktor and Yevgeny felt like the suspect was one step ahead of them all the time. It didn't take long for this ability to be explained.

Dalatovich brought in the most useful — meaning talkative — witnesses, former punishers from the 118th Ukrainian Battalion, familiar from earlier cases. Yevgeny quickly found all twenty-six who were still alive. Those sentenced to prison were already serving their time, while seven or eight, released under amnesty in 1955, remained free, as their direct involvement in punitive operations had not been proven. Both groups had previously testified in cases from the 1970s.

Skrypko, who had served as a clerk at the 118th Battalion headquarters directly under Vasyura's command, was particularly helpful. He could hardly fail to recognise his former superior! Skrypko also revealed that Vasyura had enjoyed special favour with the Germans and had clearly attended not only their propaganda school but also their intelligence training program, which explained his mastery of interrogation techniques.

"Though he always preferred torture!" the former clerk added with a smirk. Glazkov and Dalatovich exchanged glances.

"Let's hear more about that," the military investigator demanded. "How did you know Vasyura was skilled in interrogation techniques?"

"Well… the chief of staff conducted training sessions for sergeants," Skrypko said before he coughed, trying to dislodge a lump in his throat. "Vasyura taught them how to behave during interrogation if they were captured by partisans. I was there at the time."

"Now it makes sense!" the officers thought in unison. *"That's why he's so adept at misleading responses."*

"Would you be able to confirm your testimony in court?" Glazkov asked the former clerk.

But Skrypko suddenly began trembling like a leaf and responded with a loud, convulsive sigh.

"Your former commander is now a seventy-year-old man under guard. You have nothing to fear," the investigator reminded him.

"You don't understand..." Skrypko stammered, shaking. "Vasyura is a devil!"

The officers exchanged another glance. Glazkov approached the witness, placed a reassuring hand on his shoulder, and said gently, "But surely helping to expose and punish a devil is a good deed." Looking into the former clerk's wide, terrified eyes, which were haunted by an inexplicable fear of the absent vampire, Glazkov added, "Perhaps it might even earn you favour in the next life."

Skrypko shuddered, then nodded. He was not the only one who had called Vasyura a devil. Nearly every former policeman said so, with only slight variations. The guards assigned as his escorts also shared this opinion, so I became curious and popped into the vampire's prison cell invisibly to directly extract the answers from his mind. And this is what I discovered.

Back during the war, Vasyura noticed that whenever he imagined himself gleefully strangling someone, that person's expression would change. They'd go pale or flush, become frightened, and often obey Vasyura's will without question. They'd give up what he desired or simply step out of his way. In peacetime, Vasyura tried to save up money "for old age," and making money depended on various people. So, he didn't abuse this ability frivolously. He even suppressed it, being too clever to bite the feeding hand, but under investigation, he began entertaining himself by using his dark talent on anyone who was forced to deal with him. It turned out to be even more fun than it had been during the war. Selectivity was no longer needed since there wasn't a single living soul at Volodarka*** who could be on his side, so the vampire honed his sinister skills. He marvelled at his progress and fumed at the thought that "because of bloody materialism," he'd ignored such power all his life. His anger only made him more dangerous. Naturally, Colonel Glazkov bore the brunt of it during the first interrogation.

"Where were you in the autumn and early winter of 1942?" the investigator began.

"I was in German captivity," the accused replied in an emotionless voice.

"You're lying. When you were captured, you immediately agreed to serve the fascists. In your testimony from 1974, you wrote about this, and that after completing German propaganda training, you were sent to Kiev in January '42 to serve in the 118th Schutzmannschaft Battalion."

"I don't remember. I was very ill when I gave that testimony."

"So, you were lying then?" The investigator stepped up behind Vasyura, an extremely careless move, and almost whispered into the vampire's ear, "People usually tell the truth on their deathbeds! Or are you lying now?"

Vasyura turned his head and gave Glazkov such a look that the poor man gasped and stepped back. The air in the interrogation room seemed to have thinned to the point of suffocation. An invisible vise clamped around the colonel's head, his breathing became laboured, and it felt like a lump of lead was stuck in his throat. Although Viktor desperately tried to suppress his sudden wave of panic, his adrenaline levels soared beyond control, bypassing the entirety of his willpower. Forcing himself not to crumble in front of the suspect, he sent Vasyura back to his cell without explanation and spent the rest of the day trying to recover.

That was when I decided the colonel wouldn't last long on his own. So, whenever Vasyura was brought in, I set up a protective mirrored block around Viktor.

"You mentioned many names in your written testimony," Glazkov continued at the next interrogation.

"I don't remember who I named. It was a long time ago," Vasyura retorted obstinately, wondering to himself why his suffocation technique no longer worked.

"But the document remains. Here it is, written in your hand and bearing your signature." The investigator held up the pages I had already read. "Several collaborators you named are still alive, and we managed to track them down. All of them identified you from photographs. The witness Skrypko, for example, claims that you initially served as a company sergeant but took over as chief of staff after your predecessor fled to join the partisans."

"I don't know any Skrypko!" the vampire snapped.

To this, the colonel replied, "But he knows you. He was the clerk of the 118th Battalion, and we learned his name from one of your old testimonies."

"It was a long time ago," Vasyura said again with feigned indifference, growing increasingly irritated by his failed attempts to unnerve the investigator. "I don't remember any Skrypko. Whoever he is, it's not true."

"So, is Skrypko lying?"

"He must be mistaken," the vampire explained in an even more emotionless tone.

During every interrogation, he responded with the exact same seemingly prepared words, becoming calmer with each repetition, which was an unmistakable sign of lying, as any experienced interrogator would recognise. Vasyura felt no fear and barely anything else except for the triumph of success and a surge of strength each time he managed to mislead the investigation. The vampire had long understood that this was the final game. Inwardly, he celebrated every moment stolen from life as a victory.

Vasyura's powers of suggestion were so great that most victims of his prison experiments succumbed to panic. Just like Colonel Glazkov during that first interrogation, anyone who met the gaze of the spiteful old man found their breath taken away, their heart pounding wildly and their energy rapidly drained, absorbed by the vampire. Only the young and healthy men who worked in the central prison, fortunately on a fixed schedule, could withstand the advances of this mutant. I even began to suspect he was related to the Lemurians, though I doubted any proof of that could be found. Regardless, had it not been for my constant unseen presence in the gloomy interrogation rooms, Vasyura would most likely have managed to escape his punishment yet again. After each conversation between him and Glazkov, I too had to leave the city to recover. It was clear, however, that the vampire grew angrier and weaker with every failed attempt to siphon energy from the investigators, so I knew I was doing the right thing.

Having decided to protect the colonel from Vasyura, I ignored my father's advice for the first time. Like the others, Simon was travelling to study vampires more closely and find indigo children, but he visited me often and always tried to convince me not to interfere.

"How can people judge a criminal correctly if they don't sense how dangerous he is? You must let them fight evil on their own," he kept repeating, but I couldn't stand by idly while a vampire drained energy from homo sapiens, who were my only hope. After all, this was *my* mission. The time for inaction had passed.

***

While I participated in the interrogations this way, the Lemurians searched Earth. Finding mutants proved not too difficult, as these monsters quickly revealed themselves through their cruelty and shamelessness. The descendants of homo liberatus, born with the mutation of vampirism, turned out to be the worst of vampires. They were a rare few, but the devastation they caused was equivalent to legions. The Unity pondered the grim news.

"...Psychopaths who embrace their power and seek knowledge are particularly dangerous. If Vasyura had been fully aware of his abilities during his entire life, this monster's crimes might have been global in scale...

"Having even a fraction of our powers, combined with unrestrained greed, underdeveloped fear, and a complete lack of compassion, how much can indigo vampires deplete Earth's Nature?

"They've been doing it for a long time already! History offers plenty of examples of the mystical reigns of evil. We believed that humans should evolve naturally, like other biological species, and that Nature itself would support balance. Yet these very mutants have already driven humanity to world wars and devised ways to harness uranium's power to keep humankind in fear. Look where it's led: hundreds of thousands dying from leukaemia, oceans shaken by test explosions turning them into dead zones, forests and fields contaminated with radioactive elements that should never be present on the Earth's surface! And nuclear power plants? Homo sapiens' greed for energy has already outweighed their fear of mortal danger, and the Chernobyl disaster, though shocking, was a predictable result. How long until this planet's Nature cannot restore its balance?

"And what have we done so far? Turned away from its suffering. Washed our hands of it. Nature won't forgive us if we fail to stand up for it now. The oracle's vision of vampires

developing in New Lemuria is no coincidence. Everything in the Universe is interconnected."

***

By the time the trial began, I was back on Earth, and Glazkov had returned from Germany, where he had travelled on assignment to visit Yakov Ruderman, who had changed his name to Arthur Lev after the war.

Both investigators, Viktor and Yevgeny, were troubled by contradictions in the reports about the attack on the German convoy, during which SS officer Velke had been killed. The burning of Khatyn was believed to have been Germans' retaliation for the death of this Olympic champion. According to documents and fragmented accounts from survivors, it appeared that by attacking the convoy, the partisans had set up innocent civilians. Yet the partisans themselves, interviewed by the War Tribunal investigator, insisted they had never planned to fire on the convoy, no orders had been given, and the incident had taken them completely by surprise. The old men weren't lying, but the weight of guilt had nevertheless hung heavily over these heroes for years, for no better explanation had been presented. Matvey Ivanovich, the Khatyn Memorial complex director, was just one of many. Even I, able to read witnesses' thoughts, couldn't determine what exactly had happened that day.

Glazkov and Dalatovich weren't driven purely by professional thoroughness in pursuing this strange inconsistency. Both had been born and raised in Belorussia and personally knew a few old partisans who were so unlikely to have knowingly brought death upon their neighbours and families! For years the question of who had really killed the Führer's favourite lingered in the air. Meanwhile, it turned out that completely unexpected third parties had been involved in the attack on the German convoy.

The Jewish theme emerged gradually. Yevgeny met a new, previously unexamined witness in one of the small villages, whose written testimony he presented to the investigation upon returning to Minsk.

"'In August 1943,'" reported Ivan Shakal, "'the partisans warned us that the punitive forces were preparing a blockade against them. The local residents were advised to hide in the nearby forests and swamps for the time being. I also hid in a marshy area about three kilometres from my village. Soon after, the punitive forces arrived to comb the forest. They were dressed in khaki uniforms and spoke Russian and Ukrainian. I concealed myself in the thickets, and although they passed very close by, they failed to spot me and moved on. Shortly thereafter, from the direction they had headed, I heard grenade explosions and gunfire. I waited until the shooting stopped and the punitive forces had left and ran in that direction to find out what had happened, assuming they had killed some of my fellow villagers. About seven to eight hundred metres away was a small island called Luchinsky Bor. When I arrived there, I saw the entrance to a camouflaged dugout destroyed by an explosion. I had known nothing about the existence of this shelter. Around the dugout lay bodies torn apart by grenade blasts — elderly, women, children, and men. There were quite a few of them, but I cannot say exactly how many. I could not count because some of the mutilated bodies were on the surface, while others were under the rubble of the dugout, and I did not go down into the shelter itself. All the people who had been killed were of Jewish nationality and resided in the village of Bakshty in the Ivye District.'"

After receiving the new information, Glazkov remembered reading a similar story from one of the former policemen, who was already deceased. The well-organised investigator easily located this testimony of Gavril Dulich, dated the 4th of May 1974.

"'At the end of July 1943, I and the entire 118th Battalion went on an operation in the Naliboki Forest. Vasyura and Meleshko were also there. In the forest, we came across a small mound resembling a hill. I don't remember which policeman from the First Company stepped into a hole with his foot, but we all gathered around the mound. The police began digging at the spot where his foot had sunk. Then, a shot rang out from the hole and wounded him. After the shot, we realised that it was some kind of hiding place and that there were people inside whom we assumed to be partisans. Meleshko then shouted for everyone inside to come out. However, no one did. Then one of the punishers threw a grenade. After the explosion, people began to appear from the hiding place. There were about twenty of them. It turned out they were Jews. Among them were four or five women, one child about three to four years old, and the rest were men. They brought out two or three rusty carbines. I don't remember who gave the order, but they were told to line up in a row. While this happened, four or five men and one woman tried to run towards the nearest swamp. Our police started shooting at the runners. I saw Ivankiv firing from a machine gun, Meleshko from a ten-round rifle, as well as Lakusta, Katryuk, and Kmit. I and some others did not shoot at the escaping Jews. As a result of the shooting, all those who tried to escape were killed. Then Meleshko told the remaining Jews to say where other Jews were hiding, promising that if they did, nothing would happen to them. One of the Jews stepped forward, saying he could show us the hiding place. Police Officer Kushnir and another, whose name I don't remember, went with him. This Jew led them to a large oak tree, said something in Yiddish, and two more Jews emerged from beneath the tree roots. Kushnir and the other police officer, following Meleshko's orders, took these two and the one who had revealed them to the battalion command. Kmit and his squad shot all the Jews who were lined up. Meleshko was present during this and later reported everything to the battalion command. German officer Muller ordered the execution of the remaining three Jews. Meleshko ordered me to shoot them, but I refused, saying I could not do it because I had no conscience for it. Meleshko shouted at me, saying I was not a soldier, and upon returning to Novogrudok, Smovsky sent me to a penal unit in Minsk for failing to follow orders. The aforementioned Jews were executed by Ivankiv with a machine gun in the bushes. Ivankiv did this on his own initiative, as no one had ordered him to kill those Jews. Thus, Jews we found in three different locations in the forest, about twenty people in total, were executed. Their bodies were left at the execution sites. Vasyura and other battalion commanders were present only during Ivankiv's execution of the three Jews.'"

Viktor and Yevgeny concluded that the two testimonies referred to the same incident as both stated that the timing of each of these events was approximately within the same period. Additionally, Dalatovich learned in the village that those dugouts were discovered by one of the search expeditions after the war. Based on the skeletons that remained in the holes for years, it was determined that twenty-eight people had died there. Later, Vasyura's presence at the killing of the unfortunate Jews in the dugout was confirmed by two more former collaborators. That might have been the end of it if not for Matvey Ivanovich, who came to Minsk to testify for the case. The old partisan had fought in the area mentioned in both accounts of the massacre.

"I know only rumours, unfortunately," said the museum director, "but generally speaking, Jews had it the worst. The ghettos and labour camps were already being destroyed by the Nazis, so only those Jews who hid in the forests managed to survive. There were quite a few of them wandering there, which is why the police constantly combed the area and often found partisan camps instead of Jewish hideouts… Yes… Civilians faced brutal death for harbouring Jews, and the villagers… well, they had their prejudices too. While there was no outright hatred for Jews, people weren't willing to risk their lives for them either. If Belorussians could be spared for loyalty to the Nazis sometimes, Jews were simply killed by default, and the Ukrainian nationalists hated them even more than the German Nazis did."

"Why do you think that?" Glazkov asked.

"I don't think it, I know it!" Matvey Ivanovich retorted. "From a policeman who defected to our unit at the time."

"Didn't the partisans help the Jews?" the investigator wondered.

The museum director sighed, looked at the colonel with sadness, and thought, *"If you had been there, you wouldn't be asking such silly questions!"* Aloud, he replied, "The partisans often didn't have enough food for themselves. We couldn't shelter all the women and children hiding in the forests. Once, nearly three hundred people joined the Vengeance partisan detachment. What were we supposed to do with them in enemy-controlled territory?"

"Wow! I'm sure there were fewer actual fighters in the unit!"

"Exactly!" Matvey Ivanovich chuckled. "The partisans tried to help, of course. They requested permission from headquarters to evacuate the Jews from Belorussia. A fighter from that same Vengeance detachment, Nikolai Kiselev, was tasked with leading those three hundred people across the front line. And he did it."

"Just like Moses!" Viktor said, recalling the biblical story, which was vaguely familiar to the Communist Party member.

"Except Moses saved the Jews from slavery, while our Russian partisan saved them from death," the old man remarked. "Kiselev knew the forest like the back of his hand, but even so, they couldn't avoid all the German ambushes. They walked for almost a month. Not everyone survived, of course, but Kiselev personally saved a little girl whom the Jews themselves wanted to drown. Can you imagine?" Seeing the investigator's puzzled look, the old man explained. “Because Berta started crying from exhaustion and put everyone at risk while crossing the front line. It’s like they say, everyone looks out for their own skin…”

“Hmm…” the colonel snorted disapprovingly.

“But Nikolai managed to pick up the girl and somehow calm her down. Berta is still alive. She lives in New York now. And Kiselev was listed in the book *The Righteous Among the Nations*!”

“Really? A Russian Nikolai is in the Jewish book of the righteous?” Viktor was astonished.

“Well, it’s called *Among the Nations*, right?” Matvey Ivanovich laughed. He grew visibly animated as he recalled this story. “You know, I’m a historian by profession, and after the war, I had the chance to meet Nikolai! Imagine this. Our people arrested him after he led that exodus across the front line. Thought he was a deserter. And then, it was the Jews’ turn to save Moses. They all pleaded for him — successfully.” The investigator wisely chose not to comment on the outrageous fact that a hero had been arrested. Matvey Ivanovich didn’t blame anyone but simply reflected aloud. “Yes… So, Berta is in America now. Hardly any of those Jews stayed in the country.”

“Maybe that’s why they’re mentioned so rarely?” Glazkov guessed.

“Or maybe it’s also because the number of Jews killed in Belorussia is just a drop in the ocean. One in three Belorussians died when the Nazis tried to turn this place into a dead zone.”

“Did Jews fight in the partisan units?”

The museum director smirked. “How should I put this? It’s not an easy question to answer. Their men didn’t just sit back — they resisted, that’s for sure, but, you know, ‘the chosen people’ always sing their own tune. They weren’t so much into the idea of defending the Motherland. They were simply protecting themselves and carrying out raids in small, independent groups. Communication with them was poor, and the coordination of actions suffered because of that… though some Jews were officially listed in partisan detachments."

Suddenly, Glazkov had a revelation. "So, they could have ambushed the Germans and then vanished without consulting anyone or reporting back?"

"Quite possible!" Matvey Ivanovich confirmed, not immediately grasping the colonel's point.

Untangling this web took considerable effort. Glazkov pored over the lists of partisan fighters from the archives, even though investigating the attack on the convoy wasn't directly related to Vasyura's case. The severity of his crimes couldn't reduce if the provocation had come from other than an official partisan detachment. So, Viktor's decision to spend time digging into this old story rather annoyed me. However, when he finally unearthed several names and prepared to visit one of the listed Jews in Düsseldorf, I was pleased. I made sure the timing of Glazkov's trip coincided with the period of the next Unity.

The investigator returned from Germany convinced that the Nazi Olympian had indeed been attacked by an independent group of seven Jews rather than an organised partisan unit. Another participant in the attack, Israel Shparberg, confirmed the same story when Viktor and Yakov called him together from Düsseldorf to the United States. Nevertheless, both refused to provide written testimonies. The former Ruderman explained that he was receiving a pension in Germany and didn't want his wartime past revealed to the German authorities. *"What an irony!"* the investigator thought bitterly.

It turned out that the trip could influence neither the court case nor historic records. Yet Viktor Glazkov didn't consider it a waste. Although the court and history wouldn't accept oral accounts as evidence, the red partisans, his childhood's role models, were vindicated in his own eyes.

***

In the military tribunal hall, all the furniture was wooden — more precisely, it was made of thin sheets of glued and lacquered wood shavings. The smell of glue and lacquer, which homo sapiens had long ceased to notice, along with the stark white walls, gave the room an air of hopelessness and artificiality. This perfectly matched the human judicial system. According to Simon, courtrooms in most "civilised" countries looked similar to this, further proving how little homo sapiens differed from one another.

The game rules were clear, even in an empty hall. Each participant's place was enclosed by a square rostrum, and it was obvious that fulfilling one's role required standing within the designated square. All the podiums were positioned to the left of the public entrance, while rows of wooden chairs, fastened together in groups of four, like those we never managed to get at the Velykodymerska school, lined the right side.

These rows began to fill long before the trial of the war criminal and traitor to the Motherland, Grigory Vasyura, commenced. People arrived in pairs or small groups. Elderly men, reeking of tobacco smoke, wore clean, pressed shirts and modest grey or brown jackets. Women, their faces deeply etched with wrinkles, were dressed in dark, straight skirts and thick, hand-knitted cardigans buttoned over simple light-coloured blouses. Most women kept woollen scarves or hats on their heads. I remembered Cassandra and her elegant suit, which would have looked out of place and even ridiculous here. Many people did not know each other, so I decided not to hide. There was one familiar face though: Ruslan, who, true to form, had arrived long before the event began.

"Good morning, Comrade Batalov!" I called from behind. He turned quickly, his face breaking into a genuine smile as he greeted me.

"Oh! Hello, Yan!" He was excited, anticipating justice that, as the journalist knew, might not happen without him. "Where have you been? You vanished after the recruitment office! I wanted to interview you…"

"Not worth it!" I grinned. "But you, if I'm not mistaken, deserve congratulations."

"Yes, yes, with your prayers!" Ruslan nodded, his smile growing even more expansive. "As soon as the case was launched, they whisked me off to Moscow. So, thank you and Andrei for my career!"

"And you're here as…?"

"The only accredited reporter!"

"That's only fair, mate!" I patted Batalov on the shoulder.

"Couldn't agree more!" laughed my red-haired companion. His laughter rang out too loudly in the solemn hall, where everyone else spoke in hushed tones. Ruslan quickly realised this, covered his mouth with his palm, and asked more quietly, "What about Andrei? Will he be here?"

I hesitated. It wouldn't do to tell a reporter that now-ex-captain Pilatov had married the daughter of today's defendant. The journalist seemed to sense a scoop.

"Why the silence?"

"Uh… I'm not entirely sure," I hedged. "The thing is, Andrei got married, and they're expecting a baby, so…"

"I see," Ruslan replied, clearly disappointed, but he quickly brightened up again. "Still, that's wonderful news!"

"There we go," I thought. *"No need to mention Lyuba. Maybe it won't be necessary."*

Andrei had managed to persuade his wife to skip the trial. Pregnant Lyuba wouldn't have been much use as a witness anyway, having been born after Vasyura's return under amnesty. Her inevitable distress and tears would only have harmed the baby. Instead, Pavel Andreevich had arrived and, before joining us, handed a rather large plastic bag to the secretary of the Military Tribunal.

"Ruslan, meet Colonel Pilatov, Andrei's uncle!" I said, introducing the hypnotist as he approached.

"Retired colonel," Uncle Pasha clarified with a smile, his piercing gaze unsettling the journalist.

"Pavel Andreevich, this is Ruslan Batalov, the sole representative of the press."

"Pleasure to meet you!" Ruslan enthusiastically shook Pilatov's hand, trying to dispel his discomfort while wondering what this strange man was doing here.

At the hypnotist's mental request, I tricked Ruslan out of the hall by asking, "Where's the restroom?"

"Uh, this way. The session's about to start… Oh fine, come on!" With mild annoyance, good-natured Batalov tugged me by the sleeve towards the exit…

A low hum filled the hall. Some witnesses, painstakingly gathered here by Lieutenant Colonel Dalatovich, had known each other since the war but met rarely, if at all. They had tried to move on with their lives, avoiding memories of what monsters like today's defendant had done to their loved ones. Some had already been questioned in earlier trials, where a hypnotist team helped these people recall details needed by the court and forget them again afterward. Today, Pavel Andreevich decided to handle everything in person, and now the victims were again forced to stir up terrible memories. It brought no joy to anyone, but staying silent about the war was impossible.

"God, when will they catch all these scum?"

"They'll never catch them all, but it doesn't matter. The scum will die off anyway."

"So will we…"

When Ruslan and I returned and sat closer to the back wall, he nudged me with his elbow and nodded towards a tall, lanky young man in a well-tailored suit and large round glasses who had approached the defence podium. The man sat down, spreading out papers on the built-in table.

"Look, that's the defence lawyer! Krotovsky," Ruslan whispered. "I wonder what it's like to defend such filth. He doesn't look enthusiastic."

The young lawyer was indeed visibly nervous. His thin, bony fingers trembled slightly, occasionally dropping a thick ballpoint pen.

"Do you know him?" I asked, already reading the answer in the journalist's mind.

"Not at all," Ruslan replied. "He's from Kiev. Though why be surprised?"

I feigned ignorance. "What do you mean?"

"Well, Vasyura must have connections..."

My perceptive acquaintance had no idea how right he was. The young lawyer, Sergey Krotovsky, was a nephew of Vasyura's crony Valerian Karpovich. The latter had avoided the trial, citing sudden illness after his old friend's arrest, and had pressured his nephew to take the case. Sergey, a quiet nerd who knew legal history and the criminal code inside out, typically felt uncomfortable in courts. However, unable to refuse his uncle, he had taken on the case. So, Vasyura's advocate pretended to help while inwardly despising both his client as well as himself.

"Rise! The court is in session!"

Three men in uniform entered through the doors opposite the public entrance, took their seats behind the long judges' table, and arranged the fourteen thick folders containing Vasyura's case. I marvelled once again at the sheer amount of human effort and time spent on something that had been clear to me from the moment I met the old psychopath.

"Bring in the accused!" commanded Colonel Glazkov.

At last, the doorway of the public entrance was filled by the all-too-familiar tall old man with short-cropped grey hair. He paused on the threshold, cast a piercing, appraising glance over the hall, narrowed his dark eyes, where a spark of contempt for the *"worthless rabble that had gathered here"* briefly flickered, then dropped his gaze to his feet. He moved them with exaggerated caution, as though he might stumble and crash to the floor at any moment. Vasyura shuffled towards the defendant's bench, holding his right hand over his chest. It must be said that his health was excellent, and these deliberately slow movements were purely for show. The vampire was well fed in every sense, while the guards escorting him, by contrast, looked tired.

A deathly silence fell over the hall. It was heavy and oppressive, like the calm before a storm. Within this silence, only the shuffling of the defendant's steps could be heard, ticking like a bomb. As Vasyura drew level with the children of Khatyn sitting in the middle row, whom, of course, he didn't recognise, he inexplicably turned his head and met the eyes of Sofia Yaskievich. At that very moment, from somewhere in the back row, a woman's voice burst out, full of hatred.

"Bastard!"

It wasn't the voice of the girl who had managed to escape a painful death in old Joseph's barn. Sofia stared at the vampire with wide, horrified eyes, as if paralysed. She hadn't known Vasyura's face either, but under his black stare, she again felt like the eight-year-old she had been, too afraid to even breathe for fear of revealing her hiding place in a pile of sprouted potatoes, exactly where she wanted to be once more. Naturally, the thread of her energy stretched towards the mutant.

The cry, however, belonged to an old woman who had recognised in the defendant the Nazi officer who, during the occupation, had lived in one of the best apartments in Pleshchenitsy. He was then a well-groomed man, clean-shaven, in a well-fitted uniform and polished boots. He had beaten a neighbour's teenage son to death with a ramrod. Until the start of the trial that woman hadn't known the name of the officer. All these years, she had thought he was German, but now…

Her outburst shattered the already tense silence like a cannon shot. As if on cue, most elderly men and women left their seats and surged forward. These people had no need for a trial — they could have strangled the vampire then and there for their lost loved ones, their destroyed homes, their orphaned childhoods. Young men in military uniforms blocked the crowd's path, stepping between them and Vasyura, who quickened his pace towards the safety of the defendant's bench. It took all the effort of the court officers to hold back the wave of human pain and hatred that had swept through the courtroom.

"Order in the court!" shouted Lieutenant Colonel Glazkov several times. When the crowd finally began to settle, he added firmly, though his voice carried a note of warmth, "There must be order in this courtroom. Next time, I will be forced to remove any troublemakers."

Vasyura, once safely behind the barrier, felt more secure and altogether much better. Naturally, the wave of hatred directed at him had been a burst of people's energy, which only served to strengthen the vampire. A mocking and even somewhat triumphant smile played at the corners of his lips. The defendant felt neither fear nor regret nor guilt. He was simply playing the game, determined to drag it out for as long as possible. Until the end.

---

*Zhenya is a short for Yevgeny (the Russian version of Eugene)
**"The son is not responsible for his father's deed" – a phrase attributed to Stalin about the families of those accused of treason. The phrase has remained famous thanks to A. Tvardovsky who used it in his poem *By the Right of Memory*.
***Volodarka (Pishchalauski Castle): the central prison of Belarus in Minsk built in 1825

Chapter 26. The Trial

It lasted for a month and a half. Proving Vasyura's leading role in the punitive operations in Belorussia was difficult to the point of absurdity, even though no one doubted the man's crimes. Colonel Glazkov, who was both the chief of the Military Tribunal and the leading investigator, had developed a plan for interviewing the witnesses, and according to this plan, each one was summoned to court on a designated day.

Witnesses were elderly villagers, often unable to make it to Minsk on their own. Dalatovich commissioned a UAZ, provided by the military district commander, and he shook within it as it rattled across the November roads of Belorussia to bring the witnesses from the villages scattered in the woods for the appointed time. Yevgeny had long since forgotten when he last spent the night at home, and people struggled to tear themselves away from their seemingly small but quite important daily concerns.

"How am I supposed to go, dear?" cried an old woman. "Manyka will calve soon! I can't abandon the animal!"

And Yevgeny slept on a guest mattress in a village hut, praying for Manyka's swift and safe delivery and for the chance to make it to the hearing on time and avoid a delay in the already protracted case. He travelled alone, as, despite the large scale of the process, little extra resources had been allocated to it. In fact, both investigators had the feeling that someone higher up was not particularly enthusiastic about the whole affair.

***

"Witness Elena Alekseyevna Butkevich, born in 1911, is called to testify."

A frail, village-dressed woman rose from the hall, her headscarf tied under her chin. Elena Alekseyevna was quiet, not used to being in the spotlight. Furthermore, she felt guilty towards the investigator for the delay in departure and towards

Manyka and her calf, both of whom had to be left in the neighbour's care so soon after the birth. She was still thinking about the cow as she approached the witness rostrum. Elena Alekseyevna glanced quite indifferently at the defendant and thought, *"Ugh, what a devil!"*

And yet, Vasyura's face stirred no recollections in her.

The chairman of the Military Tribunal began the interrogation with the standard procedure.

"What language would you like to answer the questions in?"

The old woman finally composed herself and replied in a complete sentence, as she had done at another trial eleven years ago.

"I will answer in Russian."

After the formalities, the prosecutor began the questioning.

"Where did you live during the Nazi occupation?"

"During the fascist occupation, I lived in the village of Zarechye, Logoisk district, Minsk region."

"Did you work anywhere?"

"Only in my household."

"Tell us what you know about the punitive action carried out by the Nazis in the village of Zarechye. When did it happen?"

"'Around mid-February 1943. The invaders attacked Kateli and Zarechye from the Pleshchenitsy side.'" *

"Where were you when the police went to the village of Zarechye?"

"'I was at home and heard the sounds of gunfire. Later, people said that partisans were in Kateli and had fought back, but the shooting didn't last long. The invaders burst into Kateli and Zarechye and set houses on fire immediately,'" Elena Alekseyevna said, trying to speak evenly. Moaning was uncommon among peasants, and she had long since shed all her tears — or so she thought. "'First, they set fire to the school and two houses on the edge, and then they started setting everything on fire. From the window of my house, I saw the invaders moving through the village in carts and setting houses on fire on their way.'"

'"What language did the invaders speak?'"

'"Mostly Ukrainian, but I think a few Russians and Germans were among them.'"

'"Did you stay at home the whole time?'"

'"No, only until they headed towards our yard. Before that, they had stormed the yard of my sister-in-law, Vera Butkevich. They shot her and her daughter Tanya on the spot and then set them on fire.'" The burning corpses of Vera and Tanya, under which the snow melted quickly in her brother's yard, appeared before the witness's inner eye, and a tear ran down her cheek.

The old woman took a deep breath, regained control, and continued in the same steady voice. '"They also set fire to the house, the barn, and the chicken coop. Then they killed and set fire to our neighbour, old Marushka, in her yard. After that, the invaders headed towards our yard. Seeing this, I rushed to the door and ran out into the yard, where one of the invaders struck me in the head with the butt of his rifle, and I fell unconscious onto the snow, where I lay for a long time. That's how I survived.'" Baba Lena understood perfectly well that the policeman who had hit her didn't care about her life. Still, when she woke up that evening after the police had left, and then, many years later, she blessed the man in the Nazi uniform for his indifference. For being too lazy to finish her off. The childless witness Butkevich had never confessed this to anyone, but the first feeling she had had when she regained consciousness was the joy of surviving.

'"Was there anyone else in your house?'" the prosecutor continued.

'"Yes. I ran out, but my mother stayed in the house… and got burned along with it…'" Elena Alekseyevna suddenly sobbed. '"Later, we found Mum's remains in the charred stove among the ashes of the house. The stove was made of raw clay, so she hid there, probably hoping the heat wouldn't reach her. Only her torso survived the fire. Her head and arms up to the shoulders were completely… completely burned.'" The witness's quiet, steady voice now sounded eerie. If not for the tears streaming down her cheeks — the tears she didn't wipe away because she didn't even notice them — those in the room might have thought this woman felt nothing. She indeed was down to earth and had immersed herself in her peasant concerns, like in a protective shell, after the war. Yet the image of her mother, crouched in that clay stove, writhing in pain and fear, suffocating and yet still hoping to endure and survive, until her consciousness drifted away with the murderous smoke, was the one thing Elena Butkevich had envisioned her whole life with tormenting clarity. *"If only I had taken my mother outside back then,"* Baba Lena always thought, *"she might have gotten away with a rifle butt strike, just like me."*

"'How many people in total were killed in the village of Zarechye?'" the prosecutor continued, trying to ignore the witness's quiet tears and the defendant's infuriatingly bored expression.

"'About eighteen people were killed, and all the houses were burned down, leaving only ashes.'"

"'Do you know why the punishers burned your village?'"

"'Yes. The day before the massacre in Kateli and Zarechye, the punishers had a battle with partisans near our villages. Witnesses said several punishers were killed, so they came to our villages for revenge.'"

"Did the punishers loot the houses before burning them?"

Baba Lena gasped. "'I don't remember whether they looted my neighbours' houses or mine. It was such horror, such savagery… The melted snow from the fire flowed through the village street… mixed with human blood.'" She was not exaggerating. When the young woman had miraculously survived after being struck with a rifle butt and had regained consciousness, her home was already collapsing into smouldering beams. She staggered out, barely aware of her surroundings, stepped over the broken fence, and wandered to where the main and only street of Zarechye had been. In a neighbour's yard, she stepped into a puddle of blood, which immediately soaked her soot-blackened felt boot…

"Do you recognise the defendant?"

The witness turned her pale blue, age-clouded eyes to the vampire.

"No, I don't remember this man," she quietly replied, slightly apologetically, "I hardly remember the faces of the punishers at all."

Glazkov turned to Vasyura.

"'Defendant, what was your role in destroying the village of Zarechye?'"

"'I was not in the village of Zarechye, and I cannot say what the police battalion did there,'" the former commander of the police headquarters replied without hesitation. He knew full well that Elena Alekseyevna was useless as a witness against him personally. Even in his youth, the vampire had been careful. With the clerk Sakhno under his direct command, Vasyura had deliberately kept his name out of German documents and reports. Then, he enjoyed a grey cardinal role as a game, and now this "humility" was paying off, allowing him to wriggle out of the trap that had been set for him and seize on every inconsistency.

***

The testifying victim Olga Ustin stepped up for questioning already highly agitated by the memories stirred up during the trial, so she spoke somewhat louder than necessary.

"'In May 1943, I don't remember the exact date, punishers burst into the village of Dalkovichi. They came from Pleshchenitsy and burned down the entire village. On the same day, the punishers killed my father, Gerasim Andreevich Kononovich.'"

"How did you survive?" the defence lawyer Krotovsky asked.

"'Before the punishers approached Dalkovichi, partisans warned the locals to flee into the forest.'"

"Was there a battle in the village?"

"'I didn't see a battle between the partisans and the punishers because we hid in the swamp in the forest beforehand, but we heard gunfire and explosions. I think the fight happened near the village.'"

"What did the village look like after that?"

"'When we returned to Dalkovichi that evening, we found my father's body in the yard. He had been shot in the heart… His heart even had burst out of his chest, and his body was completely burned.'"

The horror shattered the young woman's world that day. Later, it had turned into anger that would have killed her if it hadn't remained buried in the recesses of her memory for decades. And now, unleashed by Pavel Pilatov before the trial, it poured out at the defendant. The victim pointed her finger at Vasyura and shouted, "Monster! Are you a human at all?"

The vampire met her gaze with sharp, narrowed eyes and began to strangle his accuser mentally. Olga suddenly felt short of breath but, caught up in her testimony, ignored it. Meanwhile, the prosecutor continued his line of questioning.

"'When the punishers arrived, was anyone else still in the village besides your father?'"

"'Yes, my mother said some villagers didn't have time to escape to the forest and were killed by the punishers wherever the Nazis found them,'" the witness answered, her voice growing louder and higher and her face flushing deeply. "'All the others were tortured before death: Anna and Pelageya Kononovich were slashed with knives or bayonets, their intestines cut out and left in the gardens, their bellies slashed open. The bodies of old

man Arinich and blind Dorofei Kovshik were also mutilated.'"
Olga turned back to the man in the dock and screamed, "Why did you torture these people?! What did they do to you?!"

Vasyura remained silent, but his icy glare cut across her like a knife to the throat. Olga went pale, gasped for air, and began to slide down behind the witness stand. A bailiff caught her just in time and carryied her out of the courtroom. The hearing was interrupted until an ambulance took the victim, who had suffered from the vampire for the second time, to the hospital.

When Vasyura was brought back and asked if he had been in Dalkovichi on the day of the village's destruction and who had ordered the burning and torture of the civilians, he replied calmly and even cheerfully.

"'I don't know who tortured and mutilated people in Dalkovichi. I was there, but I didn't order my subordinates to burn the village or kill anyone.'"

The former police commander brazenly lied. Every detail of Olga Ustin's testimony played out in his mind in vivid, gruesome colour. Her story of mangled bodies didn't stir a shred of guilt — it rather entertained him. In fact, the vampire felt quite pleased with himself for putting the "shrew" in hospital, though of course, no one could prove it.

The prosecutor couldn't resist a sarcastic remark. "So, you quietly smoked on the sidelines while people were being tortured and killed?"

"I don't smoke," the psychopath retorted, ignoring the biting tone. He curled his thin lips into a smug grin and, paying no attention to the wave of angry murmurs in the hall, cynically added, "It's bad for your health."

It was as though the vampire had received an invitation to his final feast. Time and again, he imagined strangling the witnesses and victims stepping up to the stand, those whom the 118th Ukrainian Battalion had failed to eliminate in its time. These poor souls' pain from recollections of lost families and shattered homes became a source of inspiration for the mutant.

In turn, the tribunal members and court officials had to contend with the outcomes of his mental experiments. The mutual hatred between the former head of the punitive squad and the audience in the courtroom charged the air so heavily that breathing was becoming difficult at times. After Olga Ustin fainted by the rostrum, a doctor was stationed in the courtroom permanently.

***

The witness Nina Mikhailovna Skakun resembled a talking mummy, and I felt such pity for her that I hurried to shield the poor woman from the vampire's advances despite my agreement with Simon to intervene minimally.

"Where did you reside during the Great Patriotic War?" the prosecutor began.

"'I lived in my home village of Osovy,'" the woman murmured.

"Please describe what happened on the 27th of May 1943."

"'That day, I was at home with my three children. The punishers came to the village on the 26th of May, stayed overnight, and in the morning, they told me and other women from the village to dig up potatoes for them. The potato field was about half a kilometre away from the village.'"

The prosecutor turned to Vasyura. "Defendant, was this your order?"

"'I know nothing about punishers forcing local women to dig up potatoes for them. I gave no such order,'" he replied, drawing out his words.

"'What language did the punishers speak?'"

"'Mostly Ukrainian. Some spoke a mix of Russian and Ukrainian.' *Filthy traitors!*" Nina Mikhailovna finished silently, and she exhaled. '"Just before noon, the punishers loaded the wagons with potatoes and let us go home."'

'"What time did you return home?"'

'"Around twelve. As I was approaching my house, I heard screams and gunshots coming from the other end of the village."'

'"Was anyone home when you went inside?"'

'"No. None of my children were there."' Nina Mikhailovna began breathing heavily and unevenly but continued. '"I ran to my mother's, who lived nearby. She said that the punishers had come and taken all three of my children: Volodya, thirteen years old, Zina, seven years old, and Kolya, two years old,"' the witness sobbed, '"and drove them away somewhere."' She pulled a small handkerchief from the sleeve of her knitted cardigan, wiped her tears, and twisted the damp cloth in her hands as if trying to wring the strength to continue out of it. '"I ran after them and learned from others that the punishers had herded the partisans' families into a barn on the edge of the village, set it on fire, and shot everyone inside. My children were there! When I arrived, the execution was over, and the punishers had left the village."' The poor woman fell silent. Neither before nor after the war had there been a darker day in her life than that one. Her desperate screams, like the howl of a mother wolf that had lost her pups. Her frantic, helpless pacing around the smouldering ruins of the barn. The curses she hurled at God for not taking her instead of her children. None of it, even after forty-three years, could be erased. A mother's grief over outliving her children has no statute of limitations.

Yevgeny Dalatovich had heard about the destruction of his home village many times, yet each retelling burned painfully, like a hot iron pressed to his chest. He had known Nina Mikhailovna his entire life and had been childhood friends with her eldest son. When the Nazis came, the boys took turns carrying messages to the partisan detachment. It was his turn to run to the forest that day, and Volodya Skakun was not so lucky… Dalatovich could not bear seeing what grief had done to this once-plump and once-radiant beauty. Thanks to my mirroring, Vasyura couldn't draw any pleasure from the mother's sorrow, and his defiant, discontented expression made the KGB lieutenant colonel clench his fists.

Yevgeny rose from his front-row seat, approached the quietly weeping witness, still standing behind the rostrum, and put his arm around her shoulders. It was a breach of protocol, but the judges remained silent, all of them.

"Would you like to postpone your testimony, Aunt Olya?" Yevgeny whispered to the elderly woman, but she straightened up, dried her face with her soaked handkerchief, and replied, still quietly but now with steel in her voice.

"No. Now." She looked at Vasyura with hatred, took a deep breath to gather her strength, and finished. '"People said that my brother's wife, her three children, and several other families were forced to march ahead of the punishers to Nivki to clear the path of partisan mines. After reaching Nivki, the punishers burned them all alive.'"

It was the young Krotovsky's turn to ask questions. As he was a devoted son himself, he felt awkward. As he had listened to the witness's story, he imagined his own mother in her place. Now Sergei nervously stood up and, in a higher voice than he was planning on, asked, "Where was your husband during the war?"

'"My husband, his brother, and almost all the men from our village joined the partisan detachment, and the rest of the villagers helped them as much as they could.'"

The defence lawyer cleared his throat to clarify. '"So Osovy was a partisan village?'"

"Yes. Of course yes."

"How did the punishers find out about the partisan families?"

'"I don't know for sure who betrayed us. There were rumours that it was the praepostor Ivan Ostrovko, but the punishers burned him in the barn too because his son was fighting in the partisan unit.'"

The defence pointed to Vasyura. "Have you ever seen this man before?"

Nina Mikhailovna studied the face of the man in the defendant's seat, hesitating. "Perhaps… but he's old now. Back then, I saw an officer who stepped out of a car — a tall, young, and polished man. We thought he was German…" When the tearful witness was shown old photographs, she sighed regretfully and honestly admitted, "I can't say… I only saw that officer from behind and slightly to the side. He didn't speak then. And I tried not to linger near them."

"That's all," Sergei Krotovsky finished with relief. His questions could, at best, be construed as an attempt to defend his client, nothing more.

The line of defence was partially based on the fact that none of the burned villages' residents had seen the chief of staff of the punitive forces in person. First of all, this concerned the witnesses from Khatyn, who were children during the war. They had survived precisely because they hid from the eyes of the executioners, one way or another. That is, they did not see the Nazis at close range that day. Thus, although dozens of surviving victims of the 18th Battalion's crimes were present in court, none of them could accurately identify Vasyura so far. It seemed as if only former punishers, who had yet to be interrogated, could. More than two dozen living Schutzmänners had been brought to the court, and the vampire was already making plans to counter-accuse his former subordinates of slander out of envy or resentment for the fact that he was a strict commander and did not allow "these scum" to run wild. Vasyura did not expect Vitaly Sukhobokov to have survived. Strictly speaking, the vampire had not even remembered him until this witness testified.

A stocky man with short-cropped temples, silvered with grey, walked confidently to the rostrum. He looked at the skinny figure sitting on the dock, calmly met Vasyura's hateful gaze, and smiled. He repelled the vampire's advances quickly and completely independently! This man was an ordinary homo sapien, but a very strong one, of which I had met so few so far. He resembled Ruslan Batalov. For such people, exchanging energy with Nature is the same as breathing. They readily share and just as easily receive what is given voluntarily, and no civilization can interfere with this natural turnover. Vampires cannot access such individuals' energy, so this witness did not need my protection.

After completing the formalities, the prosecutor began the interrogation.

"'Citizen Sukhobokov, do you know the defendant?'"

The witness, again showing no anxiety, met the vampire's hostile glare. "'Yes, I know this man.'"

"Where, when, and under what circumstances did you meet?"

"I wouldn't exactly call it a meeting," Vitaliy said with a bitter smile. "'We were arrested around the 25th of April 1943, during the Easter holiday.'"

"Please describe in detail the circumstances that led to your encounter with the defendant."

"'On the premises of the starch factory near us, Agafya Korsakova lived. She worked at the factory and maintained contact with the partisans,'" Sukhobokov began. "'In 1942, the commissar of the partisan unit instructed us, through her, to collect ammunition and supplies for the partisans, which we did. At the end of 1942 or the beginning of 1943, a Ukrainian police battalion arrived in Pleshchenitsy and stationed themselves in the barracks of the former border detachment. Two policemen, Kozelko and Spivak, frequently visited the factory. They expressed an interest in contacting the partisans through Korsakova and eventually joining their unit.'"

'"Did these policemen later join the partisans?'"

'"No, they didn't. It's quite likely they were saying that as a provocation…'" Vitaliy said, recalling how cautiously everyone had spoken to the two men, afraid of both irritating them and giving away too much. That caution turned out to be justified. It had saved Vitaliy's life. '"In April 1943, one of the Ukrainians who visited the starch factory discovered two boxes of ammunition and five pistols at Korsakova's place. Korsakova herself managed to escape into the forest because someone warned her that arrests for partisan connections were being prepared at the headquarters of the Ukrainian 118th Battalion.'"

'"How do you know the battalion's number?'" the prosecutor asked.

'"From Kozelko and Spivak,'" the witness explained without hesitation. '"Korsakova fled into the forest with her two sons to join the partisans. The next day, fourteen residents of Pleshchenitsy, the local area of the starch factory, and the nearby village of Rudnya were arrested. The Ukrainian battalion's police officers drove around in a covered vehicle at four in the morning, rounding up the detainees. I remember that this man was among them when they came to our house.'" Sukhobokov nodded towards the defendant. '"He asked my mother which of the children was the eldest, and when she said that I was the oldest of five brothers, they arrested me.'"

'"Were there any other children or teenagers among those arrested?'"

'"No. I was the youngest among those detained that day on suspicion of partisan connections.'"

"Where were you held in custody?"

'"We were taken to the police battalion headquarters, where we were held, beaten, and interrogated for several days.'"

"What were you interrogated about?"

'"They asked whether I had delivered weapons to the partisans, where the weapons were hidden, how they were transported to the unit, and what information we had gathered for the partisans.'"

"How were you treated during the interrogations?"

"'The detainees were taken one by one for questioning, made to walk through two rows of police who beat us with rifle butts, sticks, metal rods, whatever they had on hand. This man'" — and Sukhobokov pointed directly at Vasyura, whose fantasies of strangling the "insolent fool" bounced off Vitaliy like a rubber ball — "'he came in and beat the prisoners first with a hefty stick, which seemed to be made of bamboo, and then kicked us. I didn't know his name then and saw him for the first time during the arrest.'"

"Apart from the defendant, who else was present when you were interrogated?"

"'Two Germans, Kozelko and Spivak, their battalion commander, and him.'" The witness pointed at Vasyura again, looking the vampire straight in the eye. "'This man questioned me personally, beat me with his stick and a metal rod, and said he would strip off my Bolshevik skin.'" He could not help adding with a slight smirk, "I don't think it had anything to do with Bolsheviks. He's just a sadist who enjoyed torturing people — anyone, really."

Most homo sapiens, once deeply frightened, remain fearful for their lives. Only a few become hardened by fear and learn to resist it, like the teenager Vitalik, who had passed through the gauntlet of tormentors and survived Vasyura's metal rod. It's what happens to one who, having lost hope of rescue and prepared for death, nevertheless survives.

"Do you have anything to add?" the prosecutor asked, ignoring the witness's opinion of the defendant's nature.

"Yes. 'Nikita Khodasevich was tortured especially brutally. They demanded he reveal where he had hidden grenades and ammunition left at his house by a Ukrainian police officer. After the interrogations, I saw that Khodasevich's fingers were blackened because his captors had crushed them between the doors. His body was covered in bruises from beatings with rods and sticks. Two or three days later, Khodasevich, Klimantovich, Shavenko, Tenenbaum, and I were transferred to the Pleshchenitsy police prison. For about ten days, we were also interrogated there in the presence of German gendarmes, the local police chief, and a translator. The gendarmes later took Tenenbaum Haim from the cell and executed him as a Jew. Nikita Khodasevich died from the torture too. Maria Perkhorovich also died.'"

"And what happened to you?"

"'I was accused of collaborating with the partisans through Agafya's son, Aleksandr Korsakov, but someone who had visited our house said it was Aleksandr who had shown them the ammunition boxes, not me. After that, I was sent to work in Germany, where I stayed until the end of the war.'"

"Why are you sure this is the man you saw during your arrest and interrogation?" the defence lawyer asked. "It's been over forty years."

The witness glanced at Krotovsky and smiled ironically, thinking, *"You'd remember too if someone had nearly killed you!"* He met and held Vasyura's searing gaze once more without flinching.

"It's true, many years have passed, but his eyes haven't changed. They're just as malicious as I remember. Back then, we called him the devil. He was about thirty years old and stockier."

"Can you identify the defendant in photographs from that time?" Colonel Glazkov asked, handing the witness two group pictures. Vitaliy picked one at once.

"'Yes, this is him,'" he said, pointing to Vasyura's visage in the photograph.

A faint growl escaped the defendant's lips. "Whelp! I should've finished you off when I had the chance!"

And thus, Vitaliy Sukhobokov, the only surviving witness who had come face-to-face with the chief of staff of the 118th Ukrainian Police Battalion during the war, ruined the vampire's defence.

***

And for the first time in his extensive investigative practice, Dalatovich was pleased that some Schutzmannschaft punishers had not been sentenced to death in the 1960s and 70s. The twenty-six former policemen brought to trial filled in all the gaps in the victims' testimonies.

When Ivan Kozychenko was called a witness, a very tall, gaunt man, slightly older than the defendant, stood up from the audience. He was dressed in a dark brown formal suit, adorned with medals for the Victory Anniversary and commemorative badges, including the ill-fated Order of the Patriotic War, particularly incriminating for Vasyura. At the sight of such audacity, a wave of indignation swept through the courtroom.

"How dare you wear these medals?" the prosecutor thundered with disgust, violating the protocol. Deep down, Kozychenko was trembling, but he answered with feigned dignity.

"I fought in the Red Army."

"And you betrayed it by siding with the fascists!"

"I have already paid for my mistakes," the man with medals replied in a dull voice, referring to the years he had spent in labour camps until the amnesty of 1955. He had been free since then, as no further evidence of his crimes against civilians had been found. Kozychenko had served as an armour technician in the Red Army for a year, then in captivity, after agreeing to work for the Germans, and finally in the 118th Ukrainian Battalion. Technically, he hadn't killed anyone himself — he had only prepared and repaired weapons for killing.

"A skilled specialist," this pathetic homo sapien sincerely believed, *"has the right to earn a living, no matter who he works*

for." Colonel Glazkov, greatly surprised by such a blatant oversight of the system, declared firmly, "As a result of this case, you will be stripped of all these awards. That, I promise you. So, you'd better take them off now."

"But I have the right to wear what my country awarded me! I fought for it for a whole year, risking my life!" Kozychenko continued to protest. He had donned the medals not so much to impress the judges as to influence the audience — and had miscalculated severely. This technician had buried his conscience and any connection to the spiritual world in pragmatism so profoundly that he had utterly lost the ability to judge people's feelings!

The hall was filled with angry hisses and cries.

"Shame on you!"

"You scoundrel!"

"Take off those medals, you fascist bastard!"

The commotion made it impossible to continue the questioning. Eventually, Kozychenko awkwardly took off his jacket and began to unpin the awards with visible frustration. This scene amused the defendant, who enjoyed the distraction immensely. With a smug and contemptuous grin, Vasyura quietly sneered at his former subordinate's foolishness and the prosecutor's anger.

Finally, having removed the medals and put on his now-drab jacket, the hapless mechanic stepped up to the rostrum.

"Witness Kozychenko, do you recognise the defendant?" the prosecutor began.

"Yes, I do. That's Vasyura Grigory Nikitovich."

"Under what circumstances did you meet Vasyura?"

"He was the chief of staff of the 118th Police Battalion, where I served as an armourer," Kozychenko replied. Catching the hostile glare of his former commander, whose lips moved soundlessly, as if a snake's forked tongue was about to come out of the defendant's mouth, the witness hastened to add, "But I didn't have much interaction with Vasyura."

"Why not?"

"Because of the difference in rank. He liked to have the best of everything, while we..." Kozychenko faltered, then rasped, "Your Honors, I request that my earlier written testimony be read out. I'm not feeling well. May I sit down?" He slumped into the chair swiftly provided by the bailiff. One of the three tribunal members picked up a sheet of paper covered in fine handwriting and began to read.

"'Testimony of I.I. Kozychenko, dated the 6th of August 1973, Grodno.

"'In early summer 1943, approximately in May, I took part in a punitive operation against partisans and civilians in the Begoml district of the Minsk region as part of the 118th Police Battalion. The operation lasted for about a month. Besides our battalion, other German punitive units also took part. The 118th Battalion left from the settlement of Pleshchenitsy. <...> During the operation, the police committed serious crimes, burning villages and executing captured partisans and civilians. <...>

"'When we were passing through the forest between the villages of Gornoye and Novaya Vileyka, two bursts of automatic fire were shot at our convoy from the left side of the forest. They injured one driver's horse. At the time, I didn't know who had fired at us. Some policemen from the third company returned fire into the forest, but no one fired back anymore, and we didn't encounter any partisans there. <...>

"'When we arrived in Makovye, the chief of staff, Vasyura, was there with the headquarters. I don't know where he had been earlier. I remember that in the village of Makovye, some policemen brought in two young men about seventeen to eighteen years old, suspected of having ties with the partisans. Vasyura and Interpreter Luckovich interrogated them in the headquarters. They beat and tortured them to make them confess and reveal information about the partisans. Vasyura and Luckovich then forced the young men to dig a grave for themselves behind the barn near the headquarters. Even after this, the boys said nothing. Then Vasyura and Luckovich took them to the grave and shot them at close range with pistols. I saw all this while at the battalion headquarters. <...>

"'After the operation, Vasily Filippov from the First Company told me that when our convoy was fired on in the forest near Gornoye, it wasn't by partisans but by Filippov himself. He staged the provocation to justify reprisals against civilians. Filippov had indeed been with the First Company, moving on the left flank from the headquarters and convoy. He was armed with an automatic rifle, and as far as I remember, two bursts were fired from that type of weapon at the convoy.'"

A murmur of indignation swept through the courtroom again, and Vasyura smirked. He remembered that scout Filippov, a resourceful thug with no hint of a conscience. Vasyura had loved working with such rogues and encouraged their "creativity," although this provocation was news to him. In truth, justice had never concerned the vampire, neither then nor now. His interest lay solely in opportunities for the sense of satisfaction, that is, for energy gain.

Meanwhile, the second member of the tribunal took another sheet of paper from the folder and announced, "We also have Kozychenko's testimony from the 4th of April 1974."

"Please read it out," Glazkov requested.

The tribunal member began.

"'At the end of the winter of 1943, three police officers from our battalion were executed by the Pleshchenitsy gendarmes. Presumably, they were shot for collaborating with the partisans. I do not know their names. Around April 1943, Vinogradov and another policeman, whose surname I cannot remember, were also executed. I personally witnessed Vasyura and Luckovich interrogating and beating Vinogradov and the other policeman at the Ukrainian headquarters.

"'I am not sure what they were executed for, but I assume it was for connections with the partisans. Some civilian man identified Vinogradov and his companion. The entire company were lined up in the courtyard. The civilian walked along the line, inspecting each man closely. After he pointed out at Vinogradov and the second one, they were arrested immediately.

"'The next day, Vasyura and Luckovich interrogated them in the presence of a German officer. I happened to enter the headquarters and saw with my own eyes how Vasyura and Luckovich, taking turns, beat Vinogradov and the second prisoner with a rubber hose. They called them obscene names and demanded confessions about something. The prisoners remained silent. I was not in the room where the interrogation took place for very long, but while I was around the headquarters, Vasyura and Luckovich continued to beat the prisoners with the hose…'"

Vasyura truly missed Luckovich after the war. The latter engaged in far more than mere translations. Educated and intelligent, much like the chief of staff himself, Luckovich was not just Vasyura's trusted assistant — at times, he seemed like the vampire's twin. Free from the burdens of command, this schemer invented such sophisticated methods of torture and abuse that Vasyura, who typically relied on sticks and ramrods, could never have conceived of. Yet, the two of them drooled at the prospect of putting Luckovich's methods into practice and together, they always found enough excuses to implement his macabre ideas.

"Ah, those were the days!" thought the defendant, sighing nostalgically.

The interpreter of the 118th Ukrainian Battalion had no family and no reason to return to the Soviet Union when the war ended. He gladly accepted the French authorities' offer to serve in the Foreign Legion, the only escape from repatriation available to former Schutzmänners. That marked the final separation of the two vampires. Vasyura never heard from his comrade again and knew nothing of what happened to him. Yet, occasionally, the vampire imagined the havoc they could have wreaked together if Luckovich had been a member of his Velykodymersky coven.

***

The case concerning the destruction of Khatyn held a special place in the trial, but Vasyura stubbornly denied his involvement, let alone commanding the punitive action, which was considered one of the most atrocious events of that war. Everyone, from members of the Military Tribunal to the bailiffs on duty, was puzzled: what was the point in denying it when, even without Khatyn, there was more than enough evidence of Vasyura's crimes to warrant a death sentence?

However, the vampire had calculated well. Some time back, he watched a television report about a group of elderly Germans who had travelled to Khatyn and walked several kilometres to the memorial despite their frailty and disabilities to atone for their sins. Knowing that the burning of this particular village had gained global attention, Vasyura realised that, in the eyes of the Soviet — and not only the Soviet — public, his case would also remain incomplete without proving his involvement in this particular crime. Until then, the inevitable death sentence would be delayed, and he would live.

As investigators strained every nerve to gather the necessary evidence, the vampire grew increasingly convinced that he was right and took delight in continuously leading the judges by the nose. The former police staff officer kept saying that he remembered nothing about Khatyn. When the village's destruction date was mentioned in court, his first response was that he had been on leave visiting his wife in the Baltics and had conceived their eldest daughter with her then.

"Could it be that the 118th Battalion destroyed Khatyn while I was on leave?" Vasyura asked defiantly, staring at the prosecutor.

"Call witness Galina Novikova," was announced in response.

Vasyura's elder daughter entered the courtroom. Dalatovich, using logic, and partly my suggestion, had managed to track her down in Leningrad, where Galina was already working at a school and had even begun climbing the career ladder. Galina's birth certificate stated, *13 February 1942*, but in attempt to evade responsibility for the Khatyn massacre, the vampire himself had confessed to having ordered his wife to change the year of Galina's birth from 1944 to 1942. This was to conceal from the NKVD the fact that he had met with his wife in the spring of 1943, as he was officially listed as missing in action from July of 1941. Many documents had been lost during the war, and a woman's request for a new birth certificate for her child would not have raised anyone's suspicion.

After Galina Novikova had answered all the formal questions, the secretary carefully handed a large plastic bag brought by Colonel Pilatov to the prosecutor. And the doll, dressed in lace that was yellowed with age yet still retained remnants of its former beauty, emerged from its disguise. An astonished female voice came from the hall.

"Jadwiga!" Sofia Yaskievich was struck as if by lightning at the miraculous resurrection of her childhood treasure.

"Citizen Novikova, do you recognise this item?" the prosecutor asked, ignoring the exclamation from the hall. "Please remember your responsibility for giving honest testimony."

"Yes," Galina replied, curling her lips in a cold smile and shrugging. She had never liked the dressed-up princess. "According to my mother, my father sent me this war trophy from the front as a present."

Vasyura scoffed to himself. "*What a circus this is!*" And out loud, he interfered. "What does the doll have to do with anything? It was given to me as a gift by someone else!"

"Do you remember who gave it to you?" the prosecutor asked Vasyura.

"No!" the vampire snapped.

"How many children do you have, defendant?"

"I have two daughters, Galina, born in 1944, and Lyubov, born in 1962."

"Thank you," the prosecutor said with pointed politeness. "Next, we call the witness Sofia Yaskievich. Citizen Yaskievich, do you recognise this item?" he asked the impatiently fidgeting telegraphist.

"Yes! It's mine! Or rather, it was… my favourite doll!" Sofia answered, wiping away tears of emotion. "Jadwiga… I was playing with her when the punishers came to our village. My mother sent me to my aunt's cellar, where I was saved, but the doll was left on my bed. I thought it had burned along with the house!"

Then, the former weapons technician Kozychenko was called again, and the prosecutor asked him the same question.

"Witness, do you recognise this item?"

"Y-yes," Kozychenko answered awkwardly. "I took this doll from the belongings of a mate who died in a shoot-out with partisans. I know that he had taken it from a house in Khatyn while herding the residents into the barn. I didn't have children then but thought it was too beautiful to throw away."

"Are you certain he said the doll was taken from Khatyn?"

"Yes, absolutely certain."

"And what did you do with the doll afterwards?"

"I put it under my bunk and almost forgot about it. I remembered it only when the chief of staff, Vasyura, received a letter about his daughter's birth. I gave it to him as a gift, hoping to curry favour… just in case."

"Idiot!" the defendant growled quietly.

"When exactly did you give the doll to the accused?"

"In early spring 1944," Kozychenko replied.

"Which month specifically?" the prosecutor clarified.

"March or April, I think. The snow had already melted. I can't say for sure."

"Could it have been earlier?"

"No, definitely not. Vasyura's daughter was born on the thirteenth of February. He bragged about it to Luckovich, who then told me. That's certain! I then thought, 'The devil's child born on the devil's dozen day!' And the letter only arrived in spring."

"Idiot!" Vasyura hissed again as the technician hurried to the courtroom's back row after being dismissed.

"Let us compare the dates," the prosecutor said. "It's easy to calculate that a child born in February 1944 could not have been conceived earlier than late April or early May 1943, which is over a month after the destruction of Khatyn." He turned to the tribunal. "Comrades, judges, this calculation contradicts the defendant's claim that he was on leave on the 22nd of March 1943. A wartime leave could not have lasted a month or more."

Vasyura was about to object and claim that Kozychenko was mistaken, and that Galina had been born on the thirteenth of January. However, for some reason, he changed his mind and told the truth.

"I remembered now that I did, in fact, go on leave in April, not March. And on the day you're asking about, I was unexpectedly kept at headquarters. During my lunch break, I went to get a haircut."

Everyone present in the courtroom thought it would have been hard to come up with a more ridiculous excuse than this. Yet, Vasyura still got what he wanted: the court adjourned until poor Dalatovich had travelled to Pleshchenitsy. To everyone's great surprise, the investigator returned with old Anna Ivanovna, who had worked in the only barber shop in the village during the war. She was brought in for the sole purpose of saying in front of the Military Tribunal:

"No one came in that day."

Still Vasyura continued to insist. "I don't remember Khatyn! I was off that day! I was seeing a woman in Pleshchenitsy and spent the night at her place."

And once again, the lieutenant colonel set off for Pleshchenitsy. During Vasyura's service in the punitive battalion, he had indeed had a lover, a widow with two children. Other witnesses mentioned her too. The vampire hoped that the woman was already dead, as she had been about five years older than him, but a week later, she was found too and testified, showing no sympathy for her former affair.

"I slept with that monster, of course, but what kind of love could there be? Everyone knew he was a beast. He set his sights on me, and I had no escape. I had children… He didn't come that day!" And to herself, she thought, *"Even if he had, I'd have said he didn't."*

The head of the punitive unit's headquarters never stayed the night at her place. He showed up in the evening, placed a loaf of bread on the table, and pointed a finger at the corner, curtained off with chintz, while looking at her eight-year-old twins, who invariably went mute at his presence. Without changing the impassive expression on his handsome stone-statue face, he would repeatedly do his business with the terrified twins' mother, whose Slavic beauty brought her nothing but misfortune. He always demanded cleanliness. Then he would leave for dinner in his comfortable, spacious apartment…

And so, using excuses that seemed laughable to the judges and audience alike, Vasyura managed to buy himself almost a whole extra month of life.

---

* The cited case materials are punctuated as "'"…"'" in both types of scenes when read out by a tribunal member and used in witnesses' replicas

Chapter 27. Crime and Punishment

During the war, most policemen from the 118th Ukrainian Battalion turned into vampires out of animal fear for their skins. Later, when brought to trial, they cooperated with the investigation with the same desperation to avoid the death penalty. However, by the time they were called to testify for Vasyura's case, the former Schutzmänners had either served their sentences already or were nearing the end of their prison term. So, the twenty-six traitors no longer needed to testify for survival, yet, in their simple and far-from-noble minds, I read a clear enthusiasm for participating in the process. Although it had long been said that Ukrainian Schutzmänners would sell even their mothers for the right price, their main reward this time was mere revenge. The former chief of staff had forced many to regret joining the Nazis because he used to punish his subordinates' misconduct almost as harshly as he punished enemies. Vasyura was a mutant vampire. He truly did not care who suffered.

The paradox of cowardice lies in hatred towards those who inspire fear. Former police officers testified unanimously that behind every act of genocide against Belorussian elderly, women, and children, alongside German officers, stood the Head of the Ukrainian headquarters Vasyura, and Regiment Commander Smovsky.

Stepan Sakhno was brought to the trial from the colony near Syktyvkar. He seemed almost invigorated by the news that the cruel chief of staff would finally face punishment. The old zek had summoned all his courage. He looked Vasyura in the eye and then turned to the tribunal.

"This man is a real monster. Fine, partisans, their families, and sympathisers, but why torment your own?"

"I protest!" Vasyura shouted from his seat. "I didn't torment anyone. I merely enforced military discipline."

"Oh really? And what about my friend Gritsko? Why did you knock out all his teeth?" Sakhno retorted passionately. "Your

Honours! Two of my comrades were on leave in the village and had a bit too much drink. Who wouldn't? We were all terrified. People tried to forget their fear. When they came back, they crossed paths with *him*" — he pointed directly at Vasyura — "and he beat them right there in the headquarters, knocking out all their teeth. Blood everywhere! Then he made the lads lick their own blood off the floor with their tongues! And all under the barrel of a gun! I've seen a lot in my life, but never anything as horrifying and humiliating as that!

Throughout this tirade, Vasyura glared at his former subordinate, absorbing the anger and horror of Sakhno's creepy memories, and the image of drunken blokes licking the floor brought a contemptuous smirk to the vampire's lips. He had thoroughly enjoyed himself back then. Now, he raised his hand.

"Your Honours! I protest! The police officers under my command were real bandits, the scum of society, cut throats and sadists. The only way to make them obey orders and maintain discipline was through their own methods — by keeping them in fear!"

Meanwhile, Sakhno had worked himself into such a frenzy that he could no longer stop. "Your Honours, don't listen to him! Vasyura is the main cut throat. He's a devil! He simply loved torturing and killing people. When our battalion was redeployed to Poland in '44, we had a long stopover one night. So, we stepped out of the train carriages for air, laid out our rations, and started having supper. And then *he* shows up…" Sakhno jabbed his finger towards the dock again. "*He* grabs a little boy, seven or eight years old, and lifts him into the air like a puppy. The lad had a piece of bread, stolen from our supplies, in his hand. He must have been starving to risk stealing from the police.

"We all stood speechless, watching. I had the words 'Let the boy go!' on the tip of my tongue, but I was too afraid. Afraid of ending up like the thief!" Sakhno paused, struggling to catch his breath. His face turned a deep purple, but he refused to hold back. This was his swan song.

"And what happened next?" asked the prosecutor.

"What next?" Sakhno replied in a hollow voice. '"He drew his revolver and shot the child." The witness closed his eyes, reliving the blood-chilling scene. Almost whispering, he added, "He shot the boy right there, point-blank, while holding him up in the air.'"

Sakhno no longer had the strength to describe how the commander had tossed the little body aside like a bag of junk, then turned on his heel silently and marched away, leaving the police officers paralysed with horror.

The courtroom fell into a deathly silence.

Vasyura rolled his eyes, thinking, "*God, such trivialities!*" Then he shifted in his seat, crossed one leg over the other, and broke the silence with a sharp voice. "He made it all up! They feared me — and that's exactly what I wanted. That's why they're spinning these tales."

"I protest!" the prosecutor interjected. "We have identical testimonies about the murder of the boy written by another witness, now deceased. The prosecution has already submitted them to the tribunal." And he pointed to the folders lying before the judges.

The witness was exhausted and barely made it through the rest of the questions. As he left the courtroom, he clutched his chest and collapsed. Sakhno was then examined by a doctor and sent to the prison hospital, where he died of a heart attack before nightfall.

Thus, it turned out that, while sitting in prison, the old vampire had learned how to not only torment people from a distance but even to kill, which seriously dampened the former punishers' satisfaction from taking revenge on their cruel commander. News of Sakhno's heart attack quickly spread both among those detained in Volodarka and beyond its walls, once again stirring a mystical fear of Vasyura.

***

"The prosecution calls Ivan Danilovich Petrychuk as a witness."

A short man, not yet old, was brought into the courtroom under guard. He was clean-shaven, with an angular skull and brown teeth. Petrychuk wore a dark grey baggy suit that looked almost new but had clearly been bought in much better times for its owner when his body was still in prime shape.

Upon seeing the elderly man in the dock, the witness recognised Vasyura and promptly informed the court about it. Then the prosecutor asked, "Did you take part in the punitive operation in the village of Khatyn on the 22nd of March 1943?"

"Y-yes," Petrychuk replied. Throwing a fearful glance at the elderly Belorussians seated in the courtroom, he hastily added, "'But… my unit was only on the perimeter.'"

"Tell us about the events of that day and what you know about Grigory Nikitiyevich Vasyura's involvement in them."

Petrychuk drew in as much air as he could and began, starting with Velke's death, but soon felt the hair on his head stand on end and falter. Under Vasyura's hateful glare, as he muttered curses at the witness's back, the former policeman began to tremble. He had heard about the heart attack that struck Stepan Sakhno after testifying in court and had no doubt that the *devil* had something to do with it.

Petrychuk, convicted in the 1970s for treason and crimes against civilians, expected to be released soon and planned to enjoy his remaining years in peace. He had no desire to risk his health out of revenge.

Turning to the presiding judge, he said, "I don't feel well. May I have my written testimony read out?"

The prosecutor had anticipated such a turn of events and had the testimony ready. He handed the document to the court, and one of the judges read out Petrychuk's statement.

"'As a squad commander, I did not remain in one place the entire time. I moved along the line, spoke with commanders of other units, and approached the barn where the villagers were being herded. At that time, I saw near the barn Battalion Commander Smovsky, Battalion Chief of Staff Vasyura, Germans Kerner and Herman, and Company Commanders Naryadko and Vinnitsky. Other police officers from our battalion were also there, along with SS soldiers.

"'When the residents of Khatyn were locked in the barn, the police began throwing grenades inside. The grenades exploded, and cries and wails could be heard from within. Then the barn was fired upon with rifles and machine guns. It was a horrifying sight.

"'At that time, I saw a child, about six or seven years old, running from the barn towards the forest. The child was shot and killed. I cannot say for certain whose bullet struck the child, but upon returning to Pleshchenitsy, there was talk in the battalion that the shot was fired either by Smovsky or someone else standing with him near the barn.

"'The barn was then set on fire. Soon, other buildings in Khatyn were also set ablaze. By the time we left, the entire village was burning.'"

"Citizen Petrychuk, do you confirm the testimony that was read out?" the prosecutor asked.

"I confirm everything," replied the witness, whose teeth chattered nervously. Only after he was finally led out of the courtroom did the former executioner breathe a sigh of relief and head towards the safety of his prison cell, hoping that he had seen Vasyura for the last time.

Now all the former police officers of the 118th Ukrainian Battalion, called as witnesses after Petrychuk, almost begged from the outset to have their testimonies read out instead of undergoing oral interrogation. Prison gossip about the oppressive atmosphere in the courtroom recreated the panic-inducing terror once instilled in the cowardly uninnate vampires by the chief of staff mutant. Moreover, they had not forgotten how Vasyura bent even German SS officers to his will. The former Schutzmänners were in no hurry to face the devil again, even though they could not explain their fear of an old man under guard. This fear was not diminished in the slightest by the defendant's unenviable position. As a result, Ostap Knap, who, too, had been brought from snowy Syktyvkar, preferred not to open his mouth at all and merely confirmed the accuracy of what he had written during pre-trial questioning.

"'In view of the punitive forces' evident numerical and firepower superiority, the partisans were forced to abandon the village and retreat into the forest. After this, the punitive forces entered Khatyn unopposed,'" one of the tribunal judges read out Knap's testimony. "'Two or three houses, presumably set alight during the firefight, were burning. Soon, our platoon was ordered to form a semicircular chain opposite the gates of a large wooden barn, to which the men from the first and third platoons of the First Company, together with SS men, began driving the villagers. Meanwhile, the Third Company surrounded Khatyn to prevent a possible partisan attack and to block anyone from escaping into the forest. Some SS men and punishers of the 118th Battalion, along with police and gendarmes from Pleshchenitsy, searched homes and outbuildings, looted villagers' property, and took livestock. The punitive actions were led by Kerner, Smovsky, and Vasyura. The police chain, including me, was positioned about thirty metres from the barn. Opposite the barn gates, a heavy machine gun manned by the police officer Leshchenko was set up in front of the chain. Once all the villagers had been herded into the barn, the police from the First and Third Platoons joined the chain in front of it. Kerner,

Smovsky, Vasyura, and the German SS officer commanded the punitive forces at the barn. I cannot judge who gave which specific orders, but being in close proximity to them, I clearly saw that all four of them were directing the punitive operation in Khatyn.

"'After all the villagers were locked in the barn, the interpreter Luckovich set fire to its straw roof. Those inside began to scream, cry, plead for mercy, and pound on the locked doors. At that moment, someone among the commanders, who had already moved away from the barn and taken positions at the flanks of the police chain, gave the order to fire at the barn. Everyone in the chain, including me, opened fire. Along with us, Vasyura fired at the barn with his submachine gun. I saw this clearly, as he was no more than ten to fifteen metres away from me. We continued shooting until the burning roof collapsed and the cries and moans of those inside fell silent…'"

***

Through the testimonies of the uninnate vampires, former punishers of the 118th Ukrainian Schutzmannschaft Battalion, the events around the extermination of my fellow villagers were reconstructed minute by minute, and the leading role of their Chief of Staff Grigory Vasyura in this punitive action was proven indisputably. The prosecutor could find no more compelling accusations than the eyewitness testimonies, which he merely paraphrased in his closing speech. The defence lawyer was brief. Seryozha Krotovsky understood the absurdity of his role and the futility of any attempts to prove Vasyura's innocence. The lawyer only asked the court to consider that his client had "redeemed his guilt through dedicated hard work for the good of the Motherland." At the mention of "dedicated hard work," someone from the audience, one of the Velyka Dymerka's residents who had attended the trial, shouted, "Yeah, he dedicatedly punched anyone who didn't do as he said!"

Although the chairman of the Military Tribunal reprimanded the disruptor, even the minor impression made by listing Vasyura's peacetime merits was completely obliterated. Then Colonel Glazkov addressed the defendant one last time.

"Citizen Vasyura, we have questioned twenty-six former police officers of the 118th Schutzmannschaft Battalion, whose service with you in the named unit you do not deny. All these witnesses have confirmed that you were not only present at the burning of the village of Khatyn but also played a leading role in committing this monstrous crime against humanity. Regardless of whether you confess or not, your guilt can be considered proven. Nevertheless, I am obliged to ask: do you now admit to organising the destruction of the village of Khatyn and its entire civilian population on the 22nd of March 1943, as well as to your direct participation in this punitive action?"

Vasyura did not hurry to respond. He savoured the unbearable silence that had fallen over the courtroom, the power he held over these "miserable insects," even if only for a few moments, even if for the last time, the illusion that, even from the defendant's bench, he instilled terror in these "worthless creatures..."

Still unwilling to accept defeat, the vampire cast a hateful glance at the prosecutor, then at each tribunal member in turn, and finally swept his cold, contemptuous eyes over the audience.

He spotted me in the back row.

I couldn't resist and waved at him cheerfully.

And all the ephemeral power of this psychopath over the people tormented by anxious anticipation crumbled to dust. Vasyura flew into a rage and spat out, "Yes, I burned your Khatyn!"

The hall exhaled a sigh of relief as though the vampire's confession truly changed something. The tribunal members remained silent for another minute, as if still under hypnosis. At last, the chairman came to his senses.

"The court will retire for deliberation. The verdict will be announced tomorrow at ten o'clock in the morning."

***

"'"In the name of the Union of Soviet Socialist Republics, on December 26th, 1986, the city of Minsk…"'"

The verdict delivered to Grigory Vasyura spanned twenty-five typed pages, listing his crimes, proven during the trial and amounting to the murder of at least three hundred and sixty civilians. Judging by the vampire's thoughts, which I had overheard, even this list was far from complete.

"'"… to sentence Grigory Nikitiyevich Vasyura to the highest measure of punishment — execution by firing squad. The verdict may be appealed and contested through the Military Collegium of the Supreme Court of the USSR via the Military Tribunal of the Belarussian Military District within seven days of its announcement…"'"

When it was all over, I met Ruslan Batalov in the corridor. He was fuming. The article he had prepared with such care and passion — a piece intended to take up an entire spread in *Izvestiya* — had been pulled from print even after it had already been sent to the printing house.

"Can you believe this?" the journalist raged. "They say the general secretaries of both republics 'expressed concern'! And that's it!" I sympathised with his indignation. Concealing Vasyura's story from the public was profoundly unjust. "How can they not tell people about this? And why stay silent, especially now, when everyone is shouting of Glasnost at every corner?!"

Out of nowhere, Colonel Pilatov approached us. Throughout the lengthy trial, he had managed to form a friendly rapport with Ruslan. He now shook Batalov's hand and looked him straight in the eye. "For the same reasons as before."

“Ah, I see,” the journalist replied with unexpectedly calm resignation, offering us a good-natured smile.

“It was a pleasure meeting you, Comrade Batalov,” the old hypnotist said amiably, gently steering the reporter towards the exit. “I sincerely wish you every success on your future assignments!”

With no further objections, Ruslan headed to the station to catch his train to Moscow.

“It’s a pity his work turned out to be useless,” I remarked to Colonel Pilatov, watching the journalist disappear through the double doors at the end of the corridor.

This, Pavel Andreevich countered. “It’s too early to judge its usefulness. I’m sure the time will come when those materials will be very much needed. I hope he keeps his drafts,” he added, fixing me with the inquisitive gaze of his peculiar eyes. “The more interesting question is what *you* plan to do now, Yan. You’ve cornered your vampire — what next?”

“Well, Vasyura hasn’t faced punishment yet,” I replied vaguely.

“True!” the colonel agreed. “I'm certain he’ll file an appeal if only to buy himself some time!” My companion too had read some of the vampire’s thoughts. “So, you'll need patience… What are your plans?”

For now, I had no clear plan other than participating in the broader mission. The time until the next Unity belonged entirely to me.

“I’ll probably head to New Lemuria… Get some rest… But first, I’d like to visit Andrei. After all, he’s expecting a new arrival. Will you invite me over?” I asked, winking at the elder Pilatov.

“Of course!” the colonel replied without hesitation. “The grandchild is due any day now — you should come and meet him!”

***

Everything happened just as Pavel Andreevich had predicted. Vasyura did indeed appeal the verdict. He requested that his execution be replaced with imprisonment, citing his age and postwar labour merits. Of course, his appeal was denied, but the process prolonged the vampire's life by nearly a whole year — and I wasn't the only one who saw it as a royal gift to the murderer!

In his prison cell, he languished from boredom. I only visited occasionally, ensuring not to be seen by the sentenced. Fortunately for others, Vasyura was kept in solitary confinement, which significantly weakened him. He seized every opportunity to drain energy from anyone he could — stealing from guards, escorts, or even other prisoners during walks. He often did this through imaginary strangulation, a method he had become even more adept at since it was the only way to extract enough energy in short bursts of time. Vasyura's reputation as a devil followed him everywhere, and after such "games," the vampire always felt invigorated and ready to continue fighting for survival.

Lyuba visited her father only once to tell him about the birth of his grandson. The news did not exactly bring joy but seemed to encourage the vampire temporarily. For some reason, he had always been concerned about the continuation of his lineage. As for me, I hurried to see whether the boy had inherited his grandfather's mutation. My visit to the Pilatov household turned out to be doubly pleasant: I saw that the couple were quite happy and content with each other despite their hasty marriage, and their baby was surrounded by a soft violet-blue glow, definitively confirming the origin of his grandfather's dark talents. Fortunately, Vasyura's grandson had a perfectly normal brain.

When the retired captain learned that he and the vampire's daughter had given birth to an indigo child, he was momentarily flustered and bombarded me with questions.

"What should we do now? You won't take him away from us, will you? And what do I tell my wife?"

"There's nothing you need to do," I replied, patting the worried father on the shoulder. "Let him grow up like other children. Just watch over your son and study his abilities and character. That will help him." And I added to myself, *"And help us too."*

"And Lyuba? What do I tell her? She doesn't know anything about homo liberatus or her connection to them. Why isn't she a psychic or something like that?"

"The homo liberatus gene is recessive," I explained to my friend. "The abilities don't appear in all our descendants. Don't tell your wife anything for now. No need to worry her unnecessarily. When the time comes, she might figure it out herself."

And I still couldn't find my own child. There was no news of Cassandra, but then, only I was inquisitive about this. The seer had spent most of her life on Earth and had become very skilled at hiding both her essence from humans and her thoughts from her kin. The Lemurians did not doubt that the oracle had a significant reason for her actions. No one could do anything about it but wait, and we looked ahead, cautious but calm.

Nevertheless, there was no doubt that Cassandra had given birth because something extraordinary happened at the end of January 1986, by Earth's calendar. I had a dream. This was for the first time since becoming part of Unity. Dreams are rare in homo liberatus, as meditation allows us to connect closely with our subconscious even while awake.

I dreamed of a tree, black as the coals of hell. At first, it was a small sapling, but it grew rapidly, spreading its crooked branches. The tree's crown hissed like a serpent and moved as if alive, expanding wider and wider until it resembled a dark, giant web. Greedy, indiscriminate, and relentless, its sinister branches-tentacles drained everything in their path, and a thriving forest turned into a cracked, lifeless desert before my eyes.

Suddenly I saw a large, radiant lake in the distance, on the horizon — and the insatiable crown, reaching for its life-giving waters, struck an invisible but impenetrable barrier. The black tree was not giving up. The tips of its branches transformed into huge, humanlike fists that pounded the air furiously, trying to break through the transparent shield and reach the source of light…

At this point, I woke up, confused and shaken — and saw Simon sitting next to me on the lush New Zealand grass where I had lain down to recover my strength. My father had been watching my dream too, and when I opened my eyes, he took my hand.

"You have a son," he announced.

The news brought me to my feet.

"How do you know?"

"When a boy is born to us, the father always dreams of a tree, no matter how far apart they are," Simon explained. "I remember when you were born, my dream showed a tree that was a place of power, a connection to Earth, like the apple tree in your friend's garden. And what you dreamed of… it takes energy. It doesn't give it."

"So, my son… It can't be!" The message about the dreadful nature of the child conceived in that dark execution cellar was more than clear, but I refused to believe in such an ominous sign.

"Let's not jump to conclusions," Simon said. "Although Cassandra's disappearance wasn't random, she must have insisted on conceiving this child for a reason." I nodded worriedly, feeling like a helpless pawn in the seer's secret game, and my father added thoughtfully, "And the lake — that's a girl. In your dream, it was far away… Perhaps she hasn't been born yet? Interesting… Is that even possible?" He looked at me questioningly.

"Of course not! No!" I exclaimed, jumping up again and pacing back and forth across the peaceful meadow, blissfully green and indifferent to the unsettling news that had just reached me. "I love Polina! Could I really have done this to her? I took every precaution!"

My father smirked and thought, *"Well, you know better what happened between you two."* After the day Polina visited New Lemuria, I had asked him to help me distance my mind from hers. This time, Simon agreed. It was a necessary, albeit temporary, measure to ensure that my burning desire to be near the indigo girl wouldn't distract me from the mission, which, as we all believed at the time, was at its most challenging stage. There were too many blank spots in our plans to neutralise vampires, and my role, as in the very beginning, was far from the last. I did not forget about Polina, but I could not hear her thoughts or meet with her to avoid letting this close connection, too close, take over and interfere with the matter conceived by Unity. Therefore, even after that strange dream, my father and I no longer returned to the conversation about my love.

When the sentence on the vampire was finally passed, I first visited the Pilatovs, and then, as I had planned, returned to New Lemuria to rest before the Unity. Simon and Mina went there before me, and they kept sending weird, mysteriously playful signals that irritated me slightly because, due to the huge distance, it was impossible to make out properly what they meant. The astral image of Mina, who adored surprises, appeared to me several times and practically danced with joyful impatience. It was clear that she was trying to tease me, so I decided to deliberately ignore everything until I got there, which slightly spoiled my stepmother's fun.

***

To plunge into the refreshing depths of the Lake of Hope after so many earthly tribulations was pure bliss! I wasn't in a hurry to return to dry land. I surfaced, let the waterfall splash against my face, snorted, and dived back under as if the entire world had paused its eternal cycle just for me. I thought I had earned it.

Finally, appearing before the group patiently waiting on the cliff, I saw eyes the colour of a stormy sea — her eyes! On the face of our infant — Polina's and mine.

It turned out Cassandra wasn't alone in her secrecy. Baba Olya, or should I rather say the Seer Olga, four hundred and eighty years old, had distanced herself from her people in her youth to have been forgotten by the time I was born. Now, she stood on the shore of the Lake of Hope alongside my father and Mina. In the arms of the oracle, who had hidden among humans for so long, babbled her great-granddaughter. This little girl with blond curly hair was a fearless homo liberatus, born by the will of Nature — the force none of us could confront. My daughter stretched out her tiny, soft, rosy hands toward me — and the world paused… But that's another story, for another time.

***

On the first of October 1987, I returned to Earth and materialised in the isolated cell of Grigory Vasyura — a vampire, a psychopath, a sadist, and the executioner of my mother and hundreds of other unfortunate homo sapiens. I realised this at once: neither before nor after his trial had he felt a moment of remorse for his crimes. The mutant didn't repent even as he faced execution the following morning.

For many centuries, Lemurians had refrained from experimenting on humans, but this time, my people were unanimous in assigning me an unusual and potentially even cruel task: restoring the vampire's brain to that of a normal human, which was supposed to correct his mutation. We had no prediction about an outcome. My task was to observe it on the spot.

My father had always tried to dissuade me from taking revenge on someone who, despite embodying evil, was ultimately just a product of the human matrix. I understood the futility of my desire to confront this evil face-to-face before eradicating it, and I hadn't intended to. I had planned to act invisibly and quickly, then leave. But once inside the cell, I read the prisoner's thoughts.

Since Vasyura could no longer inflict pain on living people in prison, he entertained himself with memories. And as luck would have it, at the very moment of my arrival, the vampire was imagining himself firing a machine gun at the villagers of Khatyn as they ran from the burning barn! His face bore the expression of someone gleefully crushing cockroaches in his kitchen. I simply couldn't resist!

Meeting my gaze, Vasyura quickly understood my presence in the cell wasn't a figment of his imagination.

"You? You again? It's all you!" the vampire managed to growl before I immobilised him for the operation. While I was restoring the mutant's brain to the natural homo-sapien proportions, he stayed fully conscious. His icy black eyes were wide open, and their expression softened and warmed gradually. The tightly pressed lips of the old murderer relaxed into a kind smile, unthinkable on a psychopath's face. Vasyura sighed deeply and happily, as if I had just exorcised a demon from his soul.

When I finished, and the old man regained movement, he looked at me for a few moments silently before falling to his knees.

"What have I done? Forgive me, boy! Please, forgive me for everything! I didn't..." The former commander of Nazi henchmen broke down in sobs, knowing full well there could be neither forgiveness nor justification for the evil he had committed. There is no amnesty for those locked up in mass graves.

“God will forgive,” I replied in a human manner, unable to overcome the disgust that still gripped me.

“Kill me, I beg you!” Vasyura moaned, drenched in tears. The ghosts of his tortured victims already crowded his mind, demanding answers, driving him mad, scorching his soul with hellish fire.

I shook my head in silent refusal and simply disappeared, leaving my old tormentor alone with his repentance — a burden that proved incompatible with life. That was the news I carried back to the Unity. As for Vasyura, he received both our mercy and my revenge: one more day was granted to the man who was no longer a vampire. A whole day alone with his agonising, awakened from lethargy conscience.

Epilogue

Cassia Koloss's mother-in-law, a professional designer, had dreamed of building a palace since her childhood. On a remote island, once purchased by her enamoured husband for their honeymoon, she was lucky enough to bring her obsession with glamor to life. Then, for the first time, she was not constrained by finances! A young wife who had risen from rags to riches by marrying one of the most powerful men in the world poured all her fantasies of unlimited luxury into this building and its furnishings. And, being of Slavic origin, she certainly had no shortage of imagination. All this extravagant splendour had now passed into the hands of a newly minted daughter-in-law, who had seemingly come out of nowhere, captured her son's heart, and become pregnant way too quickly.

"Let her live far away from decent society," the prudent mother-in-law decided. *"At least until we figure out what kind of bird she is..."*

Cassia, or rather, Cassandra, the wife of the heir to one of the richest multibillionaires on planet Earth, had finally managed to escape the senseless labyrinth of the palace's marble baths. At last, she had lost herself in the wild coastline! The pure white sand caressed her soles, which had been beginning to forget the feeling of walking barefoot. The tops of bright green palms leaned toward the surf, exchanging energy with the Pacific Ocean. Starved for communion with Nature, the Lemurian closed her eyes and melted into this harmony for a few minutes. Only in the tropical abundance of the deserted beach, so reminiscent of the lost Bermuda colony, could the seer, who had sentenced herself to voluntary imprisonment in a gilded cage, come back to life.

After restoring her balance, she watched with sadness as a black-eyed two-year-old vampire amused himself by killing helpless jellyfish, using the thorn of a tropical plant he had defeated the day before in place of a spear. As soon as this astonishingly beautiful child began to grasp his separateness from the surrounding world, he right away, though unconsciously, started inventing ways to extract psychobiological energy from everything that was not himself. He gave no rest to people or animals.

"Mum, look, I made jellyfish kebabs!" the precociously intelligent boy shouted proudly.

A tear rolled down Cassandra's cheek. Teaching her son love and kindness was as futile as appealing to his conscience or fear. Although to be fair, he did have a fear gene. It was simply repressed, as it was in all carriers of the mutation that Cassandra's Lemurian relatives had agreed to eradicate. It was from them that the seer was hiding her child, born of a messiah — the child with a violet-blue aura that was already starting to cloud and darken because the two-year-old indigo tormented small creatures way too often.

Had Cassandra not known the role her son was destined to play in the mission of homo liberatus, she would never have agreed to bring this little monster into the world. But this child had to remain just that. He was not meant to grow up into some rural sadist or even a conqueror of lands. The boy was to become the supreme leader of the vampires on this planet. And the seer was to sacrifice the third century of her life to little Alexander to stay by his side. Teach him to play human games. Play in the highest league. Play with mastery. The mother was destined to guide him in gathering a global coalition of evil. She was there to create the anti-messiah.

Printed in Dunstable, United Kingdom